Mortimer of the Maghreb

Mortimer of the Maghreb

STORIES

HENRY SHUKMAN

ALFRED A. KNOPF · NEW YORK · 2006

THIS IS A BORZOI BOOK
PUBLISHED BY ALFRED A. KNOPF

Knopf, Borzoi Books, and the colophon are registered trademarks of
Random House, Inc.

This collection includes the following previously published works:
"The Garden of God," originally published as Sandstorm, in its
entirety (Jonathan Cape, London, 2005), and the following stories
from Darien Dogs (Jonathan Cape, London, 2004): "Darien Dogs,"
"Castaway," "Old Providence," and "Mortimer of the Maghreb."

Library of Congress Cataloging-in-Publication Data

Shukman, Henry.
Mortimer of the Maghreb : stories /
Henry Shukman. — 1st ed.
p.   cm.
Contents: Mortimer of the Maghreb — Man with golden eagle — The
garden of God — Mystery of mysteries — Castaway — Old providence —
Darien dogs.
ISBN 1-4000-4325-5 (alk. paper)
I. Title.

PR6069.H74M67 2006
823'.92 — dc22   2005057862

Manufactured in the United States of America
First Edition

for Clare

Contents

PART I

Mortimer of the Maghreb   3

Man with Golden Eagle   41

The Garden of God   61

PART II

Castaway   271

Old Providence   293

Darien Dogs   335

Acknowledgments

Thanks to Arts Council England for a Writer's Award; to the Wordsworth Trust for a decisive year as poet-in-residence at Grasmere, Cumbria; to the Royal Literary Fund for a fellowship in Oxford; to Middlebury College, Vermont, for a Bread Loaf Scholarship; to the O. Henry Prize, for which "Mortimer of the Maghreb" was a finalist; and to Hawthornden Castle for a fellowship.

Thanks also to the Missouri Review, *the* Hudson Review, *the* New England Review, Prospect *magazine, and the* Arts Council Anthology, *in which some of this book first appeared. And to Robert Boswell, Don Kurtz, Alex Parsons, Eddie Lewis, Toni Nelson, Mc McIlvoy, Rob Wilder, Natalie Goldberg, David Cantor, Kathleen Lee, Tom Paine, Rebecca Abrams, Rory Carnegie, Hamish Robinson, Peter Cowdrey, Alex Cohane; to Carol Ann, Sonny, Leyla, Peter, and Robin; and most of all, for her staggering patience, thanks to Clare.*

PART I

Mortimer of the Maghreb

Charles Mortimer watched the rippled brown land wheel back to horizontal. He drained the last drops from the plastic glass of Johnnie Walker the air steward had given him, and decided: that's it, no more booze for a week. *Au boulot*. His former life, his real life, stitched together by the clackety-clack of the typewriter and the patter-patter of the laptop, and by the roar of jets, was coming back to him now. Once again he was baptised in the odour of jet fuel (which still made him sick), born again in the air, the medium of his real work.

They had been flying for two hours, deep into the desert. As the plane finished its turn for final approach, one of the MiGs stationed at the El Zouarte air base sliced through the desert sky like a steel meteor. His heart tightened. The old feeling came back, the feeling you almost smelled in your nose which told you this was the one, this was the right place to be, you would find what you needed here—the feeling that guided you to the front page. Enough of those blustering columns on page twelve. How good that he had returned Mohammed Ahmoud's telephone call and gone to meet him at the Wolf and Whistle, that he had got away from the little office with its blue carpet and oversize computer terminal and private fax machine—all the perks just for him, the grand old man come home to grow fat and die.

"Welcome, Mortimer of the Maghreb," a man in fatigues addressed him when he reached the bottom of the airplane steps. Mortimer squinted at the man, who was grinning broadly, by which Mortimer understood that he was to take the greeting as a joke. He chuckled back. Like his compatriot Mohammed Ahmoud back in London, the man looked like he would weigh very little. He introduced himself as Ibrahim. Mortimer noted a certain friendly roundness about his face, almost a clownishness. Men like that could be dangerous, Mortimer thought. They didn't care about anything.

"Welcome to SAR," the man said, speaking awkwardly, with excessive emphasis, as if it was difficult for him to utter each foreign letter of his spurious nation's name. He hissed on the S. The letters stood for "Saharan Arab Republic." A seriousness came over the clownish face as he pronounced them.

Mortimer followed the man towards a waiting Land Rover. As he moved across the tarmac, away from the airplane, the wind caught him unawares. It was an extraordinary wind. He had travelled a great deal—in the Pamirs, the Balkans, the Caucasus, in South Africa, the Middle East, in Sri Lanka, all the world's trouble spots over the last thirty years—but never, it seemed to him, had he known a wind like this. Strong and steady, and so hot he felt there must be some mistake, someone had left an engine running, or opened a furnace at the wrong time. It scalded his face, burnt his neck. It came from nowhere, from everywhere. Mortimer looked round. Beyond the airstrip with the one jetliner there was nothing but flat, open desert, beginning at the edge of the tarmac and stretching away for hundreds, thousands of miles.

What a place to live. It was an unfinished world, not ready for human habitation. What a place for a war. He remembered his wars being in beautiful landscapes, among valleys and mountains and rivers. You would wake up to see the dew glinting on a gun barrel and feel the sun warming your back.

You would eat your porridge overlooking a gorge. Or you would hike up a trail among fir trees. Or you might be staying in some dismal concrete city but from the hotel window you could see splendid dusty mountains. This was different. A construction site with no construction, an emptiness without end.

Mortimer had been here once before, over twenty years ago, but he remembered the terrain quite differently, as a glinting plain of gravel.

The Land Rover sped off down a paved road that soon became a washboard track and finally a set of tire tracks on packed earth. Beside the tracks ran an intermittent line of old oil drums, each painted with one white stripe. Finally the jeep passed several rows of canvas tents. The rows were very long. Mortimer couldn't see how long because far away the tents disappeared over a brow. This was the "canvas city," as Mortimer had dubbed it all those years ago, where the Rio Camello guerrillas and their people lived, the vast tent home of the "Nation-in-Exile," for whose homeland they had been fighting for more than two decades.

The jeep pulled into a compound of old buildings covered in peeling yellow stucco, some French desert post from long ago. Mortimer was left in a high room with a stack of foam mattresses and a pile of blankets in one corner. He understood that he was to arrange a bed for himself, a comedown after the way he had been treated so far, in Algiers and on the flight. He pulled the top mattress off the stack and began unfolding one of the thick, hairy blankets.

A soldier interrupted him. "*Venez, monsieur.*" Then, not sure if Mortimer had understood, he added, smiling: "*Vamonos. Yalah, yalah.*"

One thing about these men: they really knew how to smile

at you. Desert men were the ultimate brothers. Forget old-boy camaraderie. No men knew how to befriend one another like desert men. They held hands, they hugged, they sprawled by the fire with arms draped over one another's thighs like wild animals in repose.

He followed the man down a corridor, across the compound, and into a canteen. He took a seat at a long bench, along with some fifteen or so others, most of them local soldiers, but one a man in a pale blue shirt with a UNHCR badge over the breast pocket. A soldier brought Mortimer a plate of couscous with some red sauce and a lump of tough meat. A glass of a sweet pink drink followed.

Mortimer was halfway through the meal when the man called Ibrahim appeared beside him, squatting on his heels. "Are you ready?"

Mortimer was clearly still eating, but answered, with his mouth half full, "Whenever."

"Let's go," Ibrahim said, as if eating were merely a way of passing time.

Outside, another Land Rover, open-top, was waiting.

"Bring anything you need. We'll be gone four or five days."

Mortimer wasn't sure what he needed. He went into his room and pulled a toothbrush and a new notebook from his bag.

The men wrapped a headscarf round Mortimer's face, laughing, until he was left with only a slit to peer out of. The material smelled of plaster dust.

"You have to," Ibrahim explained. "We drive fast." A light chorus of laughter approved the remark. "The wind here, the dust. They can make you ill."

It was the most open a Land Rover could be: not even a windshield. Just the bare bottom half of the body, with two spare tyres and two giant jerrycans attached to the back. The whole thing was painted a dusty desert brown, and all bare metal had been coated in matte grey paint. Mortimer noticed there was no speedometer. No instruments at all. Just the pedals and the various gear sticks.

The Rio Camello fighters were good with their Land Rovers. They drove excellently and would long ago have had to give up their fight had they not. They likened the Land Rover to the old Bedouin's camel, to the corsair's sloop, to Britain's Spitfire.

Thus, so simply, before he was ready for it, Mortimer found himself finally embarked on another war story, another front line, back in business.

Charles Mortimer, chronicler of wars and plagues and ruptured governments, interviewer of popes and pashas, had had columns set aside for his use in papers the world over. He had smoked a Cohiba with Castro, dined on a Maine lobster with Reagan, and had drunk beer with the mad Billy Fuentes, beer baron of Bolivia, commanding chief of the death squads. He had been the toast of London and Washington. Mother Teresa and the Dalai Lama had agreed to a joint interview with him. Noriega in his heyday had bestowed the Order of the Silver Stork on him, and the queens of Norway and Tonga had awarded him honorary degrees. For twenty-five years Mortimer had ridden the biggest waves in the business. Embracer of causes, instigator of hunts, winner of media coups, Mortimer had redefined his profession.

He had done all these things, but he had done them five years ago, seven, ten, twenty years ago. Now was different. It surprised Mortimer, when he thought back, both how long and how short five years were. That so long a time could go by so swiftly, so emptily. Or not emptily, but filled with something so uncomfortable, so different from what had come before. Five years of doubt, drunkenness, regret. Regret, the great devourer, could swallow half a decade in one go. Regret was a terrible trap, people said. Stop it, don't think about it. You must look forwards, onwards.

Five and a half years ago Mortimer had risked everything on his biggest story. He had succeeded in gaining an interview with the Soviet president, and after exhaustive consultation of every source, he syndicated a story on the impregnable primacy of the Supreme Soviet. Contrary to all reports, he declared, the writing was not yet on the Kremlin wall. Everyone took the story—*Le Monde*, the *Zeitung*, the *Washington Post*, the *Times*. It was the coup of a lifetime. Except that just five weeks later the Berlin Wall came down, and six months later the Soviet Union was coming apart at the seams.

Mortimer had not just been spectacularly wrong, he had risked everything. It was as if every editor and source he had was implicated in his shame. A *Times* leader referred to him as a curiosity, an American paper alluded to his "disgrace," and the *Spectator* cancelled his retainer. Of course most people were too caught up in the excitement of the new events to think about him; but he wasn't. After such a debacle, a man needed a change of identity. He needed to start all over again. Which was out of the question at the age of fifty-six.

Saskia, his wife, had argued with him about it at the dinner table. She had told him again and again that he was wrong, and she took their differences personally. Which was unlike her. Also unlike her, after his great misjudgement she started minding about his peccadilloes—the publicity girl at the magazine where he was an honorary editor, the assistant at

the *Times* news desk. Their marriage had long been prag-
matic, accepting of human weakness, elastic enough to contain his work, his erratic urges, his sudden departures and
returns. But now Saskia talked to him only in public, at dinner. Otherwise, she slammed doors, left the house without
goodbyes, and forsook for the spare room the matrimonial bed
that he often forsook himself. Eventually, eighteen months
after his great embarrassment, she left him.

By then he was already caught in a swift stream of forget-
fulness. It wasn't that he stopped working—he dabbled with
foolish columns in the *Standard* and the *Mail*, long inches in
which he was free to scribble himself hoarse on any matter
that piqued him: waiters no longer wearing ties, wine lists in
which the Australian imports had squeezed the clarets into an
appendix; the new "Metro" taxicabs. The brash new world
springing up around his ankles was ripe for stomping on. At
three in the afternoon, with copy due for the evening editions,
it provided an inexhaustible supply of annoyances for a man
with a keyboard in his lap and a bottle of Pauillac in his belly,
a man who would much prefer to have remained before his
Camembert and gleaming glass than to have hailed a Metro
cab back to the grey-walled warehouse of an office where you
were no longer even supposed to smoke. At least they allowed
him that: a little box of a room all to himself, regarded, incredibly, as a privilege in that open-plan arena, where he was permitted to smoke up a fog as long as he kept the door shut.

Occasionally, in the office, Mortimer would look up from
his column—*Mortimer's Monday*; *Mortimer on the Movies*;
Metropolitan Mortimer—and sniff the air, test the ground: still
foul, still tilted. When life went wrong, why didn't it right itself
like everything else on God's earth? Five years on, the ground
was still skewed. And while you waited for it to recover, the

weeks turned into months, and once seven months had gone by, you saw that seventy-seven could do so, and before you knew it they nearly had.

The rushing chaos of these years could have gone on and on, he knew, until he found himself collapsed in a hospital ward with two weeks to live. Did you blame the drink? But he had drunk before, he had always drunk, except in Saudi or when he caught hepatitis. Was it Saskia's leaving? But he had never depended on her for his sanity or purpose. Things had gone wrong before she left, anyway. Was it really just his hideous error, then? But all men made errors. Editors knew that. They were willing to give him a second chance. He had only to indicate where he wanted to go, what war, what famine. Was it all these things combined? Why, every time he checked the weather, was it stuck on Stormy? All storms blew over. When, in short, would he no longer find himself churning out furious columns about newfangled menu items like arugula and pecorino ("What the devil is wrong with good old Parmesan?" he watched himself typing, like some foolish old colonel) and instead be back at work?

But it was a desperate not a hopeful question.

When Mohammed Ahmoud telephoned and reintroduced himself, they not having spoken for well over ten years, Mortimer had felt a stirring of old, good feelings—that simple enthusiasm, almost joy, of sensing that someone was about to do you a favour, and you would be able to return it, and together you would advance one another's causes. Over twenty years ago Mortimer had first brought Rio Camello's war to international attention, though since then the story had stagnated and dropped from the papers.

Chuckles of reacquaintance down the telephone line. It was morning, fortunately. Mortimer was more or less sober.

"Something important," Mohammed Ahmoud said. "Can we meet?"

Mortimer and Mohammed Ahmoud met in the Wolf and Whistle in Pimlico. That was something new—lunch in a pub, not at a white-cloth establishment. It felt good. It felt like things ought to feel.

"A major new offensive," Ahmoud said. "We cut through their defences in many places at once. We reduce the Moroccan army to nothing. They're just boys."

"When?"

They had to plan and arrange, Ahmoud said. Two or three weeks.

Mortimer watched the slight Arab facing him across the pub table, sipping his lemonade through a straw with his curiously big lips. Ahmoud moved slowly, with that desert economy born of unrelenting thirst. Mortimer liked that way of moving. It seemed more a way of being. Something in him loved a desert.

Sitting in the dingy Wolf and Whistle with the drizzle of Pimlico tapping against the window, Mortimer remembered how he used to feel in his heyday. It occurred to him that if he could still muster that feeling, then his heyday was not necessarily over.

"Can you get me to the front line?" he asked.

Mohammed Ahmoud put down his glass of lemonade and tilted his head to the side, trying to conceal a smile. He shrugged. "All things are possible," he said, in the way of desert men.

Before they left the camp, the guerrillas drove Mortimer between two rows of tents for mile after mile. They were big square tents, canvas, UN issue. Women sat in the doorways, some dressed in the traditional robes, a few in fatigues with a scarf over their head. The Rio Camello were proud of their particular brand of Islam, which did not subjugate women, many of whom held staff positions in the guerrilla force. Here and there children in tattered clothes stopped to watch the Land Rover pass. There was an air of slowness about the camp, as if everyone were living at half speed.

They drove past a huge old black Bedouin tent. Mortimer remembered such a tent from twenty years ago, when he had visited before. The guerrillas had held a kind of banquet in it for some delegates visiting the refugee camps. It had been like some bizarre folklore evening in a posh hotel, inexpertly rendered out here in the desert. They had slaughtered a baby camel, which sat, hump and all, on an ark of tinfoil, being slowly hacked to pieces as the evening progressed, while in the corner a band wailed on primitive oboes and thumped frenetically on goatskin drums.

He had enjoyed that evening, drinking endless glasses of tea and smoking pipes of rough tobacco. He had just published his first story on the guerrillas, his initial report on the Great Wall of Africa, as he called it, a phrase that had been used in the headline and became general currency. The Rio Camello's enemy, Morocco, had constructed a thousand-mile rampart of sand in the desert to keep the guerrillas out of the disputed territory. It wasn't really a wall, just a bulldozed dyke with military posts strung along it, but it was still a remarkable story, and Mortimer had broken it. He had been riding high then. Everything he touched came out right. Memos went round the news desk referring to him as "Mortimer of the Maghreb." He remembered dancing along to the crazy music, flirting wildly with a pretty Saharawi woman who was a guerrilla colonel. Celeste had been there too, though they hadn't met until later.

The Land Rover passed a well where a throng of people had gathered. Farther along, a water truck with a great green tank on the back crept past them, going the other way, dribbling on the dust.

Then they left the tents behind and accelerated on to the open desert. The day was cloudy now, and the desert stretched away as a sheet of grey sand, an endless beach without an ocean.

Ibrahim grinned at Mortimer and whispered, "I could pick them off with my Kalashnikov from here."

Mortimer believed him. He and Ibrahim lay side by side at the top of a mound, passing a pair of binoculars back and forth. Ahead of them, perhaps two hundred yards away, the top halves of three Moroccan soldiers showed as little figures above a long, low dune. This was the third time in one day that Mortimer had been asked to crawl up a stony bank to peer at Moroccan positions. He was tiring of it. He couldn't write a story about looking at soldiers. And it was uncomfortable. Little stones pricked his elbows and knees.

He nodded at Ibrahim and began to move down the slope. Ibrahim immediately started too, so that the initiative might seem his.

Back at the camp, Mortimer wrote: *The noisiest place on earth is not a pressing mill, not a rave, not an aircraft test hangar, but a war. War assaults not the ears but the bones.*

He closed his notebook. He was lying. This war was quiet. Now and then came the soft thud of a shell exploding far away, well off target, its sound absorbed by the endless desert.

The enemy had installed a radar artillery system at immense cost and to little effect.

Mortimer had forgotten the strange matter-of-factness of war, the way you could be in the heart of a war and not even know it. Nothing really happened. You just drove about in an empty landscape. You saw no one. Occasionally you heard a distant boom, but otherwise nothing told you a war was going on. Except for something in the men, perhaps, a calmness born of danger, as if you could tell they were saving themselves for something big, like opera singers or rock stars on the day of a show, who might laze by a pool, say, or just sit around in a way that would bore anyone else.

Several times on his first day Mortimer heard the distant thud-thud of the Moroccan artillery, followed a few seconds later by a pair of brief whines, two soft crashes. The guerrillas had long since learnt to dodge the radar. Ibrahim pointed out a faint stick on the horizon once, between two hills. "Radar antenna," he said.

Mortimer nodded and felt he ought to take a picture, but he was buckled up in his jacket and headscarf, and it seemed like too much trouble.

In the evening and all the second day they travelled on the terrain Mortimer remembered. It was an amazing land, a rolling plain of gravel — real gravel, as on a drive in Hampshire or Connecticut. It went on for hundreds of miles. In the morning it looked like a beaten sheet of silver. At noon it shimmered like overheated metal. In the late afternoon, golden light hovered above it, blinding like the ocean. And for ten minutes just after the sun slipped down, it wheeled itself through the entire spectrum, beginning with a fiery red, ending in luminous violet. Under the moon it glittered like sugar.

Day Two. Saskia, I have decided I must write to you. I don't know of course if I'll ever send this, but you are the one person I want to talk to. Being here makes me think of you, I don't know why. I feel that I have been a fool, an ass, someone despicable mostly for his obtuseness. But let's forget about that. I think you'd like it here.

They stop every five minutes. What? Hello? A puncture? Carburettor trouble? An ambush? No: tea every time. Tea after tea after tea. I had forgotten all about this. We all pile out, someone lights a fire, out come the tiny blue pot, the plastic bags of mint and sugar, the tin of fierce grey "chinois noir." Six shot glasses carefully twisted into the sand. No warming the pot. They just pour in the water, add a palmful of tea, and set the whole lot on the fire. When it fizzes they drop in a great lump of sugar and the interminable frothing begins: pot to glass and glass to pot, back and forth in the highest arc you can manage. The idea is to get up a good sweet froth. But the first glass is never sweet. The tea is too bitter. You can hardly get it down, it's so strong. Bitter like life, they say. They always have three rounds. The second is better: they add the mint, and more sugar. Strong like love. The third is easiest of all. Sweet like death. A sentiment peculiar to the desert?

Tea helps a man who has just come off the bottle, no question. My fingers are settling down at last. Yesterday I had such bad shakes I could hardly hold the blasted glass.

Amazing men. They lounge by the fire giving half

*their attention to the tea, keeping half on the alert.
You've never seen people so relaxed. And in the middle of
the Sahara, in the middle of a war. Tolstoy was right:
there's no laziness like a military life. You can spend
weeks doing bugger all and feel fine about it because
you're a soldier. You don't even get bored. Boredom is a
child of guilt, and there's no guilt here.*

*Have I done the right thing? Too early to say. Is there
a price? The thirst is intolerable. They ration water. I
drink five times as much as anyone else. They have this
way about them, like camels or snakes. They don't need to
take anything in. My asking for water has become a joke.
They call me L'eau. Yet I hardly mind the thirst. This is
one of the damn things about life. Do the one right thing
and everything else falls into place. But sit around doing
the wrong thing and you can't handle anything. What
makes you make the crucial move? That's the question.
Thank God I don't have to worry about that for now. Just
get on with the story. This must be the big one. The week
that changed the Sahara. I believe it still, though so far
we have done nothing but drink tea, and there's been no
sign of an offensive.*

Mortimer woke up disgusted with himself in the middle of
the night. He got up to pee. The men were still sleeping, and
as far as he could see no one was on watch. No sign of dawn
yet, but you could tell it was close. A kind of plain peace
hung in the air, a sense of ordinariness, which seemed to con-
note day.

His stream rustled on the dry ground. He was able to wonder why self-loathing had invaded his sleep. It was a strong,
sad feeling, but it was possible it made no sense. It was pos-

sible that in the early morning on the desert such a feeling might evaporate.

Nothing had happened yet. He mustn't forget that. He had come down to give their cause the limelight as he had done once before, just as the tide turned, just as they swept across that Moroccan barrier in a flood of mortars and grenades and Kalashnikovs, in a modern-day Bedouin swoop. And after two days of rambling and camping, and enjoying it, there was no question he was going soft on the story.

His hosts carried on in their leisurely desert way: twelve cups of tea a day, hours spent in repose, hours spent driving silently across the wastes in order to fire off two rockets at some lonely stretch of the Moroccan wall, then all the way back for a bowl of couscous.

Mortimer liked being with them. There was nothing brash or macho about them. When men were doing the most manly things—fighting wars, sailing ships—they appeared most womanly, doing the cooking and washing, taking care of themselves with a fastidiousness beyond the scope of suburban man. They were modest too. They went about their chores good-naturedly: the building of the fire, the opening of giant cans of soup and pasta, all mixed together in an aluminum cauldron, the tea ceremonies, the spreading of blankets as if for a picnic, the handing out of enamel bowls of couscous eaten with a mix of ease and dutifulness, without pleasure. For they were never hungry. They showed up the Western obsession with food and drink, the compulsion to fill the mouth. Nor did they ever tire, or sweat, or sneeze, or even cough. They were hard to pin down.

The truck had broken down once. Mortimer watched the man who fixed it. It seemed he had no idea what was wrong. He stared at the engine a long time, then reached in with a wrench—he didn't even have to find the right wrench—and turned a nut randomly, it seemed, vaguely, dreamily. The Land Rover started up at the next try.

Mortimer couldn't help admiring them. He felt himself become a little like them: perhaps that was what made a traveler. In Afghanistan, for example, he hadn't just laughed at the mujahideens' jokes, he had learnt to find them funny. In the jungle he had naturally squatted on his haunches and spat like the tribesmen. In logging camps he had drunk beer at eleven in the morning and enjoyed the feel of sweat spreading across an overtight T-shirt. In British country houses he developed a taste for port and cigars, for whisky before dinner. Now he remembered the taste and smell of other deserts, and began to recover a peculiar stillness of the mind which he had learnt from the Kalahari bushmen. A lizard mind: being still within the cave of your skull while looking out on the dazzling world. A useful way to be.

He felt better. Perhaps he was just a natural traveler, a man who couldn't live happily at home. Unless it was being with these men, who did not stand if they could squat, or squat if they could lie, who thought nothing of lounging by a tea fire for half the day, nor of rising at two in the morning for a difficult and dangerous ride without food or even tea until the afternoon. They did not respond to comfort the way other men did. Once, years ago, Mortimer had shared a hotel room with one of their diplomatic team in Geneva. The room had two big beds. The guerrilla unrolled his cape and slept on the floor. What was the point of a bed? What, when it came to it, was the point of a house? Tombs for the living, they called them. Only they could claim an unbroken line going back to the apes. They alone of men had never stooped to sow seeds. Their daily life mapped out the truth of human existence: that our home on the planet could only ever be a transitory camp.

❖

Day Three. The flies! You'd hate this. You've never seen anything like it. The absurd tea pouring attracts them. They settle all over everyone's fingers, first the pourer's then everyone else's. Once the glass is in your hand they line the rim completely, like margarita salt. Wave them away and they ignore you. Only if you touch them will they move, and even then you have to push. Reluctantly they step on to their neighbour then angrily buzz away. You lift the glass to your lips. Inches from your mouth, there they are still. Just as you think, Fuck it, I'm never going to be able to drink this, or else; Fuck it, I'm just going to have to swallow a couple of flies, they vanish. Lower the cup an inch and there they are again.

The desert is good for "fuck-it's." Who can be bothered in this heat?

A funny thing: how I like it here. How it suits me.

About the guns. Men want clarity and simplicity and that is what guns offer. Guns make life simple. They feel right. Let me explain: guns clarify life. They give you a buzz of direction. They make a man feel loved. They justify him.

On the fourth morning, Mortimer looked through his note-book and wondered: what was all this nonsense? This was hardly the first time he had been in a war. Perhaps he had soft-ened in the last few years; perhaps it was even a good thing. Saskia often said how hard he was, how he needed softening. He must surely be softened, if he thought softening good.

He wrote down: *Copy, you bastard. Enough bloody philosophy.*

They were lying in the lee of a dune, around ten o'clock. All trace of the morning cool had evaporated. Mortimer was having to resist the urge to pull away his headcloth, an action which they warned would make him thirstier. A trickle of sweat was making its way down his side. He remembered to lie still. The kettle gurgled as it heated. The man in charge of it opened the lid. He was a handsome man, the darkest of them all, dark as a Ugandan, with bottomless eyes and deep folds on his face.

"Ibrahim," Mortimer called.

Ibrahim was busy stuffing a pipe with the foul powdery black tobacco they smoked. He inverted the instrument and lit it with a twig from the fire. Exhaling a stream of smoke, smiling benignly, looking high, he raised his eyebrows at Mortimer.

"The paper is not going to be pleased," Mortimer said. "There are many other places they might have sent me."

Ibrahim rested his eyes on Mortimer in such a way that Mortimer felt easy about going on, in fact felt relaxed about his complaint, no longer especially wanting it acted on.

"I mean, at the very least I need an interview with Lamin Aziz."

Lamin Aziz was the "president," the guerrilla leader and head of the refugee camps—of the Nation-in-Exile. It was a toy town: toy government, toy politicians, even a toy govern-ment house, that giant tent of black wool, one of the original nomad tents. The intention was that one day all these toy institutions would be moved to a small dusty city in the disputed territory. It made one wonder about government and the machinery of state—it was all like a game at play school, not just here but everywhere.

Ibrahim shrugged and took another pull on his pipe. "*Vamos a ver*," he said, breathing out smoke.

We'll see. Mortimer shook his head. These people. So laid-back. They didn't mind that their war was going on and on. In fact it suited them. They could carry on living in tents and scampering around the desert in Land Rovers, just as they liked. What would they do with a country, if they ever got one?

All that day they stayed at the same camp, lying in the shade of the Land Rover. Three of the men dozed beneath it, crawling out only to drink tea. Mortimer's impatience grew, then dwindled, then grew again towards noon, as the strip of shadow he had been lying in became too narrow to cover him. He lay beside the hot brown iron of the vehicle, baking like a pizza, as hot as he had ever been, even in the baths of Siberia. Despair touched him: what was he doing here, wasting his time? If he was going to go somewhere, he could have gone to the oil spill in Greenland. The word "Greenland" felt like a rebuke. He thought of fjords and ice and turf. What a fool. Here he lay, pressed to the ground by an immense heat.

At four o'clock they returned the teapot to the back of the Land Rover, kicked over the ashes, and climbed aboard with their rifles in their laps.

Mortimer had slept. When he saw the sunlight glittering on the plain like water, he felt better. The day was nearly over.

He had survived. It felt like an achievement. They swayed and purred over the desert, then wrapped their faces for a long fast race across packed mud. At the far side the driver plugged the vehicle into four-wheel drive and picked his way between two gravel slopes, hidden from the world. When they stopped, Ibrahim took Mortimer's hand, which surprised Mortimer, and made him follow behind on his belly as they slithered up a rocky slope. At the top Mortimer slowly raised his head. Ahead of them, some fifty or sixty yards away, four black dots showed at the top of a sandbank: helmets, soldiers.

No one else had come with them. Ibrahim pressed a finger to his lips. They were evidently to wait for something. Mortimer had an idea he was about to be given a graphic display of guerrilla tactics. They were showing off to him.

Two cracks sounded. Ibrahim sank to the ground and pressed a hand into Mortimer's back. He lay with his cheek against a rock. A moment later he heard a whine, then another, each followed by a thud. They came from somewhere behind them. Mortimer eased his head round to look back down the slope. The Land Rover was gone.

Ibrahim kept his face to the ground and smiled. "They know we are here," he whispered. "But you see? They don't know where."

When they raised themselves on their elbows, the four little helmets had vanished. Mortimer felt uneasy. A clatter of gunfire broke out some way along the wall, accompanied by the whoosh of rocket grenades. Then there was silence, and another clattering of guns. Then some weapon made an odd noise, like a moan cut short. A little cloud of smoke rose up into the sky, faint and precious.

A few minutes later Ibrahim started crawling backwards down the hill. Mortimer followed. The Land Rover had returned. In it sat two new men, wearing faded navy blue caps. Mortimer could see at once that they were different from the others, though it was hard to say how. Perhaps they were a shade paler. All the guerrillas climbed in and they drove off in silence.

That evening they passed a group of nomads. Their black tent was startling on the empty land. The nomads were apparently friends, and greeted the rebels warmly. The rebels left a jerry-can with them, and drove off with a small goat. One of them, sitting on the side of the vehicle, held it clamped between his knees. At first the animal attempted to stay upright as the vehicle bumped along, then gave in, realising that it didn't need to, the man's legs would hold it steady.

They made a detour across a dry wadi and pulled up beside a knee-high shrub. One of the men dug around the plant with a machete and excavated a small log of root.

They camped in the middle of an open flatness. The driver simply switched off the engine and let the vehicle coast, and wherever it stopped was camp. Everyone spilled out.

The two newcomers with blue caps sat in the circle of men, drinking their tea slowly and thoughtfully, staring at the ground. Mortimer pulled out his notebook and began describing them: *Young men, moustaches (like all of them), heavy eyebrows, quite dark . . . in short almost identical to the others. Maybe not as lean.*

He nodded at one of them and asked where he was from, thinking he knew the answer.

The man glanced at Mortimer then looked away. He must have been astonished by the question.

Ibrahim stepped around behind the circle and sat beside Mortimer. "They're Moroccans," he said. "Fresh from the Wall. Prisoners. You want to talk to them?"

Mortimer asked them a few questions. Both were silent, unsure who this strange foreigner was, unsure whether they were being interrogated, suspecting perhaps that he might be a journalist and afraid of what might get back to their command. Mortimer left them in peace for the second and third rounds of tea.

He flipped through possible headlines. *Desert Rebels Stop for Tea. Tea on the Front Line. Desert Rebels Give Their Captives Tea.*

From a little way off, outside the fire circle, came a soft, anxious bleating, then the sickly liquid sounds of slaughter. One of the soldiers fed the tip of the big root into the fire, building up a blaze.

*Day Four. Barbecue tonight. First they flay the poor
beast (a goat), then spread out the skin, fleece down,
and use the slippery sheet as a butcher's block. They
dismantle the animal and store the various
components — legs, organs, skull, ribs — in piles at the
edge. The first fresh meat in almost a week, but I have
little appetite for it. Who cares? Eating is just something
to do.*

*I keep remembering years ago when I walked from
Timimoun to one of the little oases. While covering the
Malian famine. There was nothing but sand, dunes
forever as far as you could see. It was a windy day. After
half an hour Timimoun was lost from sight. We knew it
would be a few hours before we could see the first palm
gardens of the oasis. Just the compass to guide us across*

the ocean of sand, the Great Western Erg. What a place.
The wind blew away our tracks. Can you imagine that?
I can barely remember the sight now, but I remember
what it felt like. It was a lesson. No tracks. No past. It
was true not only of that journey but of everything, all
life. All of it blows away. I mean that not as a metaphor
but reality. We have no past. There is no going back.

They say the struggle for good and evil goes on in the
human mind. Nowhere is that clearer than in the desert.
This is the original tabula rasa, where whatever has been
is erased.

This is embarrassing but I keep seeing you in the
landscape, in the crevices between the hills, in the hill
on the horizon, which lies there just like you do, still, sure
of itself. I am beginning to realise how much I miss you.
Sometimes I see suddenly that none of this makes any
sense. I mean these last few years. Our situation. You
were always right. You understood in advance of me. It
has taken me a long time to see, to see myself, and you,
and us, and what remains to us. We must meet as soon
as I am back.

The last time he saw Saskia, ghastly time, he took her to dinner at L'Escargot. Why there, of all places? He should have
known better. The minute he held open the door and saw her
sitting on one of the stiff little sofas waiting for him, he knew
that it would not work. They had had to sit through an excruciating dinner. He should have had her over, if she would
have agreed to that, or else gone to a Chinese or an Indian,
even a pub. Somewhere informal. And why meet at night
even, like a pair of dating undergraduates?

She had looked beautiful. He didn't have the habit of

noticing her beauty. Seeing it that night, he felt excluded. The old sadness rolled over him. Her blond hair, pleasantly, outdoorsily grey at the roots, was pinned back the way he liked, sleeking her cheeks. She had lost a few pounds, she looked strong, lean. He recognised the beauty in her small frame. She seemed to have acquired shape. She sat very correct-looking, with her knees together, just showing beyond the hem of a black skirt. She had dressed up not for him but for the restaurant, he could see that.

What sharp intelligent eyes she had. She could look like some small, lean mammal, fiercely alert, sitting there hunched up and staring at you. Thank God, he thought to himself, that she had had a child. Imagine if she had come to him childless, and he had kept her that way, as he would have done. Only one thing, in the end, could redeem any life: progeny. Not for him, of course, but for her. She could survive whatever love threw at them, because she had her future assured. Children mitigated death, he thought, as if reproduction really were the one thing we were put on this earth to accomplish. He would go naked into death with nothing to diminish it but age.

Was Saskia the love of his life? His first answer would be no. That was Celeste, who he had worked with in the Sahara, and who had not come with him to Nicaragua. She had scarcely looked back. She was married by the time he returned, and she had made a good life for herself. Women were practical like that. But his second answer would be yes, of course Saskia was the love of his life, his actual life. The dream life might hang on, but in the end, he was sure, it would be the actual life that counted.

. . .

The prisoners were with them all the following day, silently doing whatever the party did—tea, drive, tea, eat, drive. They never looked at anyone, not even each other.

All wars were strange. You sat around a fire and chatted. The fact that your cousin or brother or friend was no longer at the fire with you made no difference. The fact that two of the enemy were, also made no difference. Still you sat and spat and smoked and drank tea and entertained the foreign journalist with little stunts. "Fighting" consisted of endless sitting around. Clipping nails, picking at dry skin, rubbing stubble, musing, composing letters in one's mind.

Just now they were all sitting on a caked white mudflat. They seemed to make their own little stage around the fire. They had to have their own reasons for all of this. The surroundings could supply none.

"Ibrahim, this is the end of the fifth day," Mortimer said. He had not showered since being down here and had lost all desire to. His skin and clothes had become one. "Is anything going to happen?"

Ibrahim chuckled deeply. At times he had an incredibly deep, rather beautiful voice. "No problem," he said. "Everything can happen."

"I'm only here another day and a half. I have to leave with something. It's the *Sunday Herald*. Why won't Lamin Aziz see me?"

"All things can happen," Ibrahim answered, with typical desert oracularity.

Day Five. We have taken two of the enemy. They seem nice enough. Life goes on. We all drink tea together. In

*the desert all men are brothers first, warriors second. It's a
little like those Christmas truces in the trenches. Another
tea, Maroc?*

Night fell. The huge planet wheeled its flatness across the
western sky, sending a band of deep blue shadow into the
pale east. The band deepened and spread. The orange west
became spangled with early stars. A sliver of a moon, a hair
caught on a camera lens, shone luminously on the glazed sky.

The two Moroccans and two of the guerrillas had vanished. They had slipped away somehow. Mortimer must have
been dozing. He got up to have a better look. All around, the
plain lay flat: no sign of anyone. Yet they could not have
gone far. The desert's apparent flatness contained hidden
gullies and ditches, even small canyons that you saw only
when you were almost in them, but still their disappearance
startled him.

He heard something. A faint crack. A whine, a high-
pitched groan. He stood still, staring into the silence of the
coming night. Nothing more. Just stillness. A hissing in the
ears. As he listened a wonderful feeling crept over him. His
legs felt warm and fluid, his heart seemed to tingle. Good
things would happen to him. They had before and they would
again. His fate was to clasp the globe in his fist. Never in
human history, perhaps, had there been a man of such wide
experience.

Another crack, a moan. Both sounds were very faint. Mortimer wasn't sure if it was his ears playing up. It could be a
desert fox, he thought. Or one of the birds. He had seen a bird
in the sky the previous day.

One of the guerrillas fiddled with the knobs on a big cloth-
covered military radio. He wore a pair of small hard-looking

headphones. He raised a speaker to his lips and spoke softly, then adjusted a dial.

Ibrahim approached Mortimer. "Get some sleep. We'll be up very early. Midnight."

"Where are the prisoners?"

Ibrahim smiled. "Sleep. The desert tires a foreigner."

Mortimer lay on his back. He could still feel the glow that had entered his body. The stars dropped from the sky and hung just above his face, so close he could stick out his tongue and lick them. They were coarse like sea salt.

Mortimer understood that he had been playing it too much their way. He must stay awake, but so they thought he was sleeping. He was a journalist, a reporter. He had got caught up in the romance of things. Back to basics: the difference between what they say and what I see equals the truth.

The soft human voices in the emptiness were soothing. The crackles of the fire died down to a low hiss. The voices became big and deep, superbly resonant out there on the flat land. Mortimer listened, imagining at times that they were talking in French or Spanish, and that he would understand what they were saying if only he listened harder. At some point the Land Rover left. When it came back there were a few hushed, concerned exchanges. He rolled onto his side and opened his lower eye. By the jeep's wheel, a cap lay on the ground. It belonged to one of the Moroccans. He decided to stand up and surprise them.

He did so. He yawned and shuffled off to pee, and saw what he needed: the two Moroccans bound back to back, lying on their sides in the back of the Land Rover, slack as a pair of socks. The face of the man nearer him was covered in dirt. The mouth of the other hung open.

Mortimer's stream made a pleasant sound in the wide

night. It drowned out the voices at the camp. He had a heavy feeling in his chest. He told himself: It's nothing to what you have seen, remember Eritrea, remember Cambodia, this is war, war is like this. But it didn't work. His stomach rose. He took a few steps forward, not as many as he had planned, bent over, and puked. Strings of phlegm swung from his mouth as his stomach hardened into a knot.

"Too much for you?" came Ibrahim's voice. "You've been to many wars, no?"

Mortimer didn't answer but walked with lowered head back to his sleeping roll.

The action that followed was hard to make sense of until it was over. In the middle of the night they dismantled the campsite and mounted the Land Rover. They drove for an hour, then parked at the foot of a low hill. Ibrahim clutched Mortimer's arm, guided him halfway up the hill, then pushed him flat on his belly. What Mortimer saw from the brow surprised him. The whole area between the hill and the Moroccan wall was covered in bodies, and the bodies were moving. It was an eerie sight: an infantry attack of the old school, the oldest school. This was how the pashas' caravans had been ambushed: a knife clenched between the teeth, elbows nudging forwards over the ground. There must have been fifty fighters.

Then: thud-thud, thud-thud, sounding far away. A moment later the screech-booms rang out. There was another attack going on a few hundred yards up the wall. Mortimer stared but could make nothing out.

The snaking figures had risen up in a silent wave and were sprinting up the bulldozed dune. Then they were out of sight. This was the strangeness of war: Mortimer and Ibrahim still just lay there on the ground, and unless one knew, unless one actually made the imaginary connections, it might seem that nothing unusual was going on.

A clatter of rifle fire sounded out. Then silence again. Figures came back over the dunes: more this time. Soldiers kept on coming, more and more. Most of them held their hands clasped on their heads. Everyone was jogging, jogging and stumbling down the dune, across the open space, and up the hill, the nearest within thirty feet of Mortimer. It all happened in silence.

Mortimer slithered back down the hill. He watched the new prisoners being loaded into a waiting Unimog. He wondered how they would all fit in. Somehow they did.

The Rio Camello fighters dispersed. Mortimer found himself back at the Land Rover with exactly the original band of six. Everything was as it had been before. It had been a good operation: slick, quick, and left no traces. Like a dream, the attack might never have happened. How would you know it had?

The two dispensed Moroccans were gone.

Day Six. Perhaps things are getting better not when the bad times are over, but when you stop thinking of them as bad times. When you can see good even in them. Heigh-ho.

For example? For example the locusts. Saskia, you have never seen anything like this. It changes you. I'm serious.

They passed the locusts on the way back to the camp. *Young locusts: lime green, wingless, the juveniles draw up in marching columns hundreds of miles long.*

They showed as a black line, some geological feature remarkable only for being long and straight. The Land Rover rode over it. Then Ibrahim called to the driver to stop and tapped Mortimer's knee.

The two men climbed out and knelt close. The insects were unaware of them. Ibrahim said the vanguard would already be in Mauritania, two hundred miles away. Every bit of them was bright green, the bent thighs, the heads and bodies, even the antennae, as if they had been dipped entire in green paint. They were at once horrific and magnificent. A thousand miles' marching lay ahead of them. Incalculable distance, incalculable number. You could just hear the rustle they made. Where were they going? What made them go? What made them that brilliant colour? They stopped neither to eat nor sleep. They belonged to a destiny vaster than man's.

Things of this magnitude, Mortimer wrote down, *require the whole sky in which to resonate.*

He put his pen back in his breast pocket and closed the notebook. His heart was racing. Had he been a fool? Had he failed to realise something perfectly simple? He thought all the trouble was to do with his work, but maybe it was quite different. Maybe he had nearly been doing the *right* thing these last few years, without knowing it. Perhaps he no longer wanted what he thought he did.

He looked at the locusts, and again his mind rang with a song to their magnitude. He didn't think: famine in Mali, 120,000 refugees within the year, logistical nightmare, UNHCR, etc. He thought: the world is so big. That was all. His head hummed.

Then he wondered: all those years in which he had flitted from atrocity to atrocity and horror to horror, perhaps an overarching question had governed his ceaseless motion. He had been looking for a reason not to have faith. And he understood now that he had failed.

He must stop and rest. That was the injunction of the plains of gravel: rest, traveler, rest.

On his last day Mortimer had still not seen the president.

He understood what had happened. The Rio Camello fighters had tried to impress him with their first small capture, and failed. They had tortured their captives for information, and carried out the bigger raid. It would benefit them anyway, of course, but more so since Mortimer was there to report that Morocco's defences were at least partially ineffective.

But it was nothing like the promised offensive. Mortimer had been had. Or something had gone wrong.

War wasn't the way the papers reported it. It was all an act. Those Moroccan soldiers didn't want to be killed. They were recruits who had just left school. Of course they would do what they were told if the enemy had them at the end of a gun barrel. A war was a show, a movie. Algeria produced, Rio Camello performed. Meanwhile, Britain, France, and the US bankrolled Morocco's side, pouring huge sums into the friendly autocrat's thousand-mile defence without any hope of return. What was in the disputed territory? A few thousand nomads, a barren seaport clinging to the Atlantic coast with a few streets of crumbling concrete, some phosphate mines long ago abandoned because of the war, and a thousand miles of nothing.

Meanwhile, Rio Camello lived in tents, drove Land Rovers, camped on the desert, just as they liked. They had a mission in life.

Mortimer was waiting in the same long, high room to which he had been delivered on first arriving. It might once have been a Legionnaires' barracks, he thought, though it had the air of a schoolroom. He had to wait until some time in the afternoon. The guerrillas had dropped him off that morning, and driven away with the minimum of goodbyes. Four of the foam beds had been made up. There were other visitors now. The same stack of blankets stood in the corner, shorter than before. Otherwise the room was empty except for Mortimer's bag, which sat open beside a pile of papers and books, his. He couldn't understand why he had brought them all.

He sat with his back against the wall. He was good at waiting now. In his lap was an open notebook, in his hand a pencil, but he was staring at the opposite wall where, just below the room's one window, a large section of yellow plaster had fallen away, exposing dusty brickwork. Something stirred in his mind and caused him to look up at the three big beams supporting the ceiling. It was a vacuum of a room.

He had been here three hours. He was covered in desert dust, but his appetite for what might have been a pleasure— washing off six days' dirt—had vanished.

Day Seven. I'm not sure how I'm going to leave here. I wish you could come and meet me at the airport like in the old days. I can see no reason to go back other than to see you. They killed our two prisoners. I was sick. Then they captured another batch. They want me to see that they can.

I leave this afternoon. There's no respite in this life. Not even in the desert.

A young reporter in Kabul once told me we were the

*reason people fought wars. Look at Lawrence of Arabia,
he said. You know Lawrence was made by that American
newspaper man. I thought he was crazy, but now I have
to wonder if he wasn't right. I do.*

Half an hour before he was due to leave, when his bag was
packed and he was still sitting alone in the barrack room, Mortimer heard footsteps advancing down the hall. Ibrahim
entered.

"*Yalah.* Let's go."

Mortimer was surprised to see him. He smiled. "I thought
you'd be back at the front by now." He zipped up the bag and
lifted it to his shoulders.

"No, no," Ibrahim said. "No bag."

Mortimer looked at him. "The airport?"

Ibrahim shook his head. "Important meeting."

"The president?"

"Important meeting," Ibrahim repeated, without trace of a
smile.

Outside, another Land Rover, dark green, hardtop, waited.
They drove Mortimer around the camp and away. At the side
of a hill a set of unlikely steel doors appeared. They opened
from within, and a guard spoke to Ibrahim through the car
window. The Land Rover entered a long ramp lit by intermittent bulbs. They drove downwards a long way, curving
always to the left. As far as Mortimer could see, the ramp
might continue endlessly downwards on its slow spiral beneath the desert. They stopped outside a grey metal door.

Ibrahim nodded. Mortimer climbed out and pushed open
the heavy door. A guard within led him along a dark corridor
into an enormous ambassadorial suite, full of huge armchairs

and ashtrays. You could feel at once that it was a room large and comfortable enough to absorb fierce differences, and probably had done so.

President Lamin Aziz looked like a young man. He had a moustache and bright eyes and wore combat fatigues. He shook Mortimer's hand and pulled a pack of Marlboros from his breast pocket, along with a gold lighter, and offered one to Mortimer. His English, French, and Spanish were fluent, Mortimer knew. He was an intelligent man. You could see it in his eyes. As the lighter flared at the tip of his cigarette a sparkle showed in them.

He lay back in an armchair, draping one leg over the chair's arm.

"Eventually he has to stop this insanity," he said, of the king of Morocco. "We won't stop. We are in the right."

Mortimer took notes and fired off his questions just as in the old days, yet the more he wrote down the less he felt he had. As his pad filled, his hands emptied. Why was there a war? Sitting in armchairs and discussing diplomatic initiatives made no sense. Once you heard someone talk about it, war became absurd. What made sense was streaking across the desert in a Land Rover, camping round a fire, sucking harsh smoke from a copper pipe, and baking bread in the sand. That was what humans were made for.

"I know we can count on you to understand our cause," the president said, blowing his smoke up towards the high ceiling. "You know the injustice of the Moroccan position. You know he has violated the UN resolutions repeatedly. You know this must not go on. You also know how we can deal with two prisoners if it helps our struggle. You know how we can deal with eighty-seven prisoners also." He paused, took a big draw on his cigarette, blew the smoke up again, following it with his eye.

"Eighty-seven?" Mortimer asked. He watched the president's face. It was rough, pockmarked, and shone with a contained excitement.

"From the other night." The president didn't look at Mortimer for a long time.

Another man let himself into the room, also dressed in combat fatigues.

"Ah, Mohammed," the president said expansively, waving his cigarette hand.

Mortimer nodded at the newcomer, who walked in smiling, took a seat, then asked Mortimer, "So how was your stay?"

Only then did Mortimer realise it was Mohammed Ahmoud, the London man.

"What the devil are you doing here?"

He felt the floor move, as if beneath the ground one might actually feel the flat desert wheeling through space.

Mohammed Ahmoud could plainly see Mortimer's surprise. He smiled. "I'm here to make sure everything goes well."

"We need to know we can count on you," the president continued. "You are a respected man."

Mortimer waited. The desert had taught him to wait.

"We know you support our cause," the president said. "Why does Britain still support Morocco? We must do everything to isolate them."

"I'm a journalist," Mortimer began.

"The struggle makes demands of us all," the president interjected. "I am a soldier by nature, not a politician. Look at

Mohammed Ahmoud. He is a teacher by training, yet he must work as a diplomat now."

Mohammed Ahmoud nodded gravely.

The president stubbed out his cigarette in one of the giant marble ashtrays. "Think of those prisoners."

"We can't trust anyone," Mohammed Ahmoud added. "We have been treated badly. By certain people."

The president shrugged, smiling vaguely. "You know our position is just. We do not like to mistreat our prisoners. It would be a pity if we were forced to."

Mortimer saw that the glint in the president's eye was not humour or intelligence but zeal. He was a dangerous man. It seemed obvious now that something like this would be said. Mortimer had no doubt whatsoever that he would do what they asked. He would print whatever they wanted.

As Mortimer was driven towards the airport, out of the refugee city, a terrible nostalgia seized him. Everything seemed sad. The huge red desert, the two men who had died horribly and unnecessarily, the atrocities committed under cover of vegetation, and the brown rivers of ugliness and waste threading through the world, all were sadness incarnate. So too the gleaming airliners that ferried you back and forth between these places. He felt flat as the desert, and the flatness stretched on forever. As he stood on the tarmac waiting to board, hearing the steel roar of the jet engines, his nostrils touched by the nauseous odour of jet fuel, he was surprised by the sudden knowledge that this was the last story he would ever do. He had crossed the wilderness now, the chariot had come to take him home, and he was going home. He would pay the warriors off once and for all.

Man with Golden Eagle

The windowpane sprang into the hotel room with a life of its own, showering like water over the carpet and one corner of the bed. Only after it shattered did Mortimer hear the machine-gun fire. Instinctively he dived to the floor.

Harry, the television producer, who was in the middle of lifting a typewriter from an aluminum travel case, dropped it back in its box and buckled stiffly to the carpet. He was older than Mortimer but his age was hard to determine. He had a face ravaged by sun and drink, a face of ghastly redness, flayed-looking, its folds and wrinkles seized into the appearance of a smile. He resembled nothing so much as a gargoyle, and looked permanently startled. Mortimer wondered if it was wars that had made him look that way, with their endless capacity for surprise. Above the face the burnt-out wisps of his hair trailed up like smoke, but whether he was thirty-five or fifty-five you couldn't say.

From where Mortimer lay, he could see the big bald patch on top of Harry's head, which had taken a lot of sun over the years and showed like a circle of coloured paper. Mortimer lifted his chin and grinned. "Here's the story all right. Bang on cue."

Harry grunted.

More gunfire sounded in the street, then everything went quiet except for an engine idling nearby. It was a big engine, and echoed among the buildings. Mortimer wondered what it was—a truck, an armoured car, a tank—and was surprised he had not heard it coming. But that was war for you: everything normal one minute, everything shattered, never to be normal again, the next.

Mortimer was happy. He was a young man in Central Asia on his first television assignment: twenty-nine, plucked by the BBC off the *Tribune*'s foreign page, signed as a roving war correspondent. He knew he was happy by certain symptoms. He missed his wife, Saskia, for example, in a peculiarly enjoyable way. When he thought of her, it was with a sense of capability, a spurt of warmth, anything but the usual suppressed unease. Normally it made him uncomfortable to be away from the woman he loved and to like it. He would feel he had to pretend even to himself that he would rather have been with her than in the middle of some unfolding disaster. But now he felt no such constraint; it was wonderful to be apart yet linked by a palpable bond; its glue was that warmth in his chest. Sometimes he had misgivings about going away on longer assignments. Not this one. Of course you must go, she said. I'll be cheering you every step of the way, it's your screen debut. She didn't always say things like that.

"One hell of a story, eh?" Mortimer said to Harry, who still lay flat on his face on the hotel floor.

Mortimer noticed now that the carpet, thin and scratchy against his cheek, reeked of dust, stale milk, feet. For a moment Mortimer was alarmed that Harry hadn't moved. Then without lifting his head Harry growled, "We should be in the basement, if they have one in this jerry-built building. They've got MLRS's up on that hill, you know." Harry had mentioned the multirocket launchers before.

Just then, lying on the floor of a third-world hotel room beside a pool of broken glass with a war starting up outside, his hunch to come here borne out, there was nowhere on earth Mortimer would rather have been. Through barefaced chutzpah he had persuaded the BBC to take him on, and right away it was paying off. Truly, boldness had genius in it.

Jimmy the cameraman burst into the room with his camera under his arm, grinning and breathless. "I thought they had me," he declared.

Harry looked up. "What do you mean, *had* you?"

"The tank. Pointed the barrel straight at me. I was sitting on the toilet." He started to do up his belt. "I hear the noise, I stick my head out the window, then I grab the dickens."

"Has everyone gone mad round here?" asked Harry.

Jimmy shrugged. "Just doing my job." Mortimer had already noticed that Jimmy liked to talk in stock phrases, phrases whose currency could not be questioned. He was pleased to see that he wasn't the only one excited by the turn of events. Jimmy's face beamed.

That tank filmed by Jimmy would turn out to be only Mortimer's first stroke of luck.

"May as well try and use what the madman got," Harry snapped. "It's three o'clock already, we'll have to jump to it."

If a report was to arrive in London in time for the following day's bulletin, they had to get the tapes into the French diplomatic bag on the Paris flight that evening. Harry hurriedly resumed the unpacking of his equipment, setting it up on the spare bed.

"What were you doing in the toilet with your camera anyway?" Harry let out a dry chuckle.

Jimmy was busy writing out a label with a marker pen. "You know me, married to the old bird."

As Mortimer grabbed a towel and began attempting to sweep the shattered glass off the floor—which wasn't easy, with the shining crumbs sticking in the weave—he could hardly remember ever feeling so flushed with confidence, so sure that he was in the middle of doing the right thing. Four years he had been working in print journalism, and had yet to make a name for himself. That windowpane showering into the room was the first intimation of success breaking into his life, and he was exhilarated to feel it. He glanced at the saw-toothed hole where the window had been. It seemed to hang on the wall like a gaping breach knocked through to another realm. Outside, the world beyond was strangely quiet now, as if arrested in time.

As far as Mortimer could see, success was much the same as luck.

Saskia had been waiting for him in a pub on Charlotte Street right after his final interview with the BBC.

"Well?" He could tell by the smile in her eyes that she had guessed things had turned out well.

"I did it," he had said.

"You got the job?" she asked.

"I handed in my notice at the paper."

"But do you know you're getting the job? Did they tell you?"

He took a long pull on his pint and nodded.

"What clinched it was Tajikistan. The fact they'd read my stuff, and I can get a crew in."

"Will you still know me when you're famous?" she had said, hugging him.

Half an hour after the window exploded, up on the hotel roof, Harry held the boom under Mortimer's chin and muttered, "I'll need your voice-over half an hour ago but let's get on with this piece to camera."

Mortimer was good. He wore a tie and they filmed him

with the city behind, and behind the city the dry mountains of the Tien Shan.

"Do I do the voice?" Mortimer asked.

"What voice?" said Harry.

"The BBC reporter's singsong. The funny stresses, the ups and downs."

Harry shrugged. "Do what you like, mate. What's he on about, Jimmy?"

While they were filming the piece to camera, the second stroke of luck came hurtling over the dry slopes to the east: a MiG screaming across the little city. With its sharp beak and short ungainly wings the plane rolled onto its side, pulled a turn, then tipped up and shot into the sky as if running up glass rails. As it went the cockpit winked at them. It was a wonderful sight. When he saw it Mortimer thought: if we can make machines like that there are no bounds to human achievement. His heart ached with awe.

As the MiG climbed, a bright point of phosphorescence went chasing up after it, wobbling slightly as it raced through the sky.

"Bloody hell," said Jimmy, swinging the camera upwards.

The ball of effervescent light gained on the plane and then found it. For a moment nothing happened. Then white streaks fanned across the sky and where the plane had been, a black ball of smoke hung absolutely still. The streaks shot out and down like fireworks, leaving trails that gradually dissolved into the blue. The spectacle was tragic, no doubt, but mostly it was impressive. Mortimer couldn't take his eyes off it.

Jimmy kept filming until the last smoke trail had disappeared. When he pulled the camera off his shoulder his face was bright red, beaming, his eyes glistening, a smile fixed on his lips. He looked a little like Harry, in fact.

"You ever seen that before?"

Mortimer shook his head.

"That's a SAM for you," Harry said. "Ground-to-air."

"That's news, is what that is," said Jimmy. "Beats *Grand-stand*. I wonder if anyone else got it."

"There's no one else here *to* get it," said Harry. "The man's a genius." He meant Mortimer.

The next day Mortimer had special reports on the six and nine o'clock news. He didn't see them until weeks later, but they included footage of a sniper filmed from the hotel toilet. The man, a Muslim freedom fighter, put down his rifle and sent the camera a V-sign. The camera zoomed in quickly, quick enough to catch the man's stubble-bound grin. Then a tank rolled onto the screen, its turret swivelling about. Suddenly, without provocation, it let loose a hail of bullets from a perforated barrel beneath the cannon. Puffs of smoke rose from the concrete buildings on the street. Then the turret turned all the way round and eyeballed the camera for several anxious seconds.

The morning after that a telegram arrived for Mortimer. *Can't you do something badly? Love, Es.*

"Es," he guessed, meant S. Saskia. He could hear her asking the question. She'd put a lot of emphasis on the "something." His heart rose into his throat, he felt slighly nervous, dizzy.

As he sat at the breakfast table holding the slip of paper, reality began to seep back in: he had made his television debut the previous night. A smile woke up in him. This was a laugh, TV was a breeze. Scribble out two hundred words of *Daily Mail* copy, stick your mug in front of the lens, and you're on your way. No *Give us five hundred words on the diplomatic efforts.* No *Rewrite the first paragraph or lose the job.* Here it was: get the pictures. The pictures, if they're good, tell the story.

Suddenly, holding the thin paper of the telegram in his fingers, he longed for her, her arms, her slender shoulders, the little pool of shadow in the dip of her neck cast by the bedside lamp: he missed all of it, even their bedroom and their house. Sometimes when he was actually in the house he would suffer from claustrophobia. He would come in from the *Tribune's* news desk at night, and his first instinct would be to turn around and leave. It wasn't her; it was the house: to be boxed up in a dark container of brick in the no-man's-land between the city centre and the suburbs, the transitional zone of endless terraces with a row of local shops at the end of the street, marking this as a district unto itself; and all the families clicking shut their doors each night on the world, sealing themselves in their own chambers: it seemed a frightening way to pass one's life. But after half an hour with his feet propped on an afghan cushion, sprawled on the spread of kelims, a glass or two of wine inside him, he'd begin to feel, amid the ethnic clutter of the household—which was all her doing—a sense of calm again, of his life making sense, and of this home making sense. Sometimes he could almost call the house a haven, a place of retreat. At least, he could understand how others might. He didn't think that he himself was a man who needed a retreat.

The living together had started early: he was away virtually half the time, although not on any regular schedule, so whenever he was back for a handful of days it made sense that he stay with her. She had a house and a settled life, both substantial enough to accommodate him; whereas he had a small, untidy Bayswater studio, not much more than a place to lay his head between assignments. Six months on, he had given it up and transferred the money for his rent to her mortgage. Because they were rarely together more than two or three weeks, a certain distance persisted between them, and gave their relationship staying power. Later, Mortimer would see that in fact they never got close enough. And later still, decades later, he would again reflect that perhaps they had had the right degree of distance and separation after all.

It had been Saskia who suggested he try the BBC. He had seen on the wire that rebel fighters in Kyrghyzstan had staged an ambush on a Soviet patrol. No one else seemed to have noticed the report.

Now, seated at the breakfast table of the Hotel Mir with the telegram in his fingers, he couldn't help smiling. She was truly on his side. She could see the noble side of his work, which one way or another consisted of bringing injustice to light. He didn't see it that way himself: he was a hack getting stories. But there was more to it if one wanted there to be, and it was good to be reminded of it. Twenty-nine, on the brink of fame, as in love as he would ever be with his wife, who was cheering in the wings: what more could a man ask? He picked up a crispy strip of bacon and crunched it in his teeth, grimacing as he washed it down with foul, strong coffee.

The city had changed overnight. Torched cars stood diagonally in the road; trash had appeared from nowhere, lots of it; here and there a shop front was gone, collapsed into rubble.

Mustafa, their guide and fixer, seemed undeterred by any of this, as if he saw it all the time. He swerved the car between the obstacles, accelerating whenever he could, until he reached the main boulevard, where a few other cars cautiously picked their way, as if their drivers were unable to believe it was really still possible to drive about the stricken city. Otherwise the streets were deserted.

Mustafa was one of those locals whose actual job, whose real station in life, was impossible to pin down but who seemed to know everybody in the country. He had fixed up the car, a Rover of all things, and found petrol for it when all the garages were closed. And he had a friend at every ministry.

They reached the suburbs, long walls of concrete and mud with ruinous houses behind them, then the highway for Kok-Yungak. On the drive south Mustafa said nothing. He kept his eyes on the road, dodging the potholes, moving rapidly down the highway. Twice they were stopped at liberation army checkpoints, where Mustafa wound down his window, and the fighters saluted him. Both times they told Mustafa something that caused him to frown.

It was one of those long empty roads peculiar to desert countries, a thread of black strung from town to town. Fifty miles it might go on without a single sign of humanity except for itself, a pencil line ruled across the plain. It came as a surprise when Mustafa flicked the gear stick into neutral and let the car coast. Perhaps he was conserving fuel, or wanted to stop for a pee or a drink of water. But he turned off the highway onto a dust track, which he had evidently known would be there, and headed into the hills. A cloak of golden dust followed the car.

Soon a white metal sign, a forlorn beacon of modernity, announced, "Osh," in three scripts. Mustafa drove fast up a narrow dirt street between dwellings of golden mud. Many of them stood roofless. A few wide-eyed children stared from doorways, and three old women at a street corner broke off their talk to watch the vehicle pass. Then a man sprang out from a side street and flagged them down. The tyres gave a light cough as the car skidded to a stop. They had to park there and walk, the man said.

"Why?" Mortimer wanted to know.

"The noise," Mustafa said, leading them up the hill.

"The noise?"

Mustafa waved him to silence. They all jogged along behind Mustafa, Mortimer carrying Jimmy's spare battery. He wondered what they were running towards, whether it was something dangerous, whether at a certain point Mustafa would make them drop to their bellies and crawl. It wouldn't have been the first time a guide had required that of him. There was no sound in the town except for the shuffle of their feet. They skipped over rubble, past houses missing their front walls, with tables inside on which cups and plates stood amid fallen masonry, all coated in red dust, then turned a corner into the main square.

This was where all the town's men had gathered. Jimmy muttered, "Showtime." Mortimer looked at him, but he was already lifting the camera to his eye.

A heap of crumbled masonry filled one side of the square, over which a number of men dressed in the region's baggy trousers and tunics clambered silently, picking their way like goats. The sight of them, and their silence, unsettled Mortimer. The rest of the men stood about watching.

The sun shone. The sky was steel blue. A yellow bird hopped from stone to stone, some brave little bird unafraid of the men. Mustafa whispered: "That bird was a man's pet, his friend. You understand?"

Then one of the men raised his voice and beckoned, without lifting his eyes from the stones at his feet. He began to pull them away one by one, carefully. Others moved swiftly to join him. Mortimer understood. These people had no dogs, had nothing but their own ears to guide them.

In a while a piece of dusty red cloth appeared where the men were digging. There followed a long, high, almost restrained wail, then a clatter of rock on rock as the men accelerated the excavation. Finally they tugged out a long shawl, nothing more.

"The mosque, you see," Mustafa said. "The Russians bombed the mosque."

A woman came running down the street, calling out, her cries turning into a single high-pitched whine. She flung herself at Mustafa, her legs gave way, and she sagged half to the ground, clinging to his shoulders. Mustafa wrapped his arms round her and held her as she shuddered against him, then lifted his head and let out a curious hoarse moan.

The camera did not once leave Jimmy's shoulder. All of it, the whole sequence, made an extended report in the bulletins two days later. Harry made Mortimer use Mustafa as the hook. At first he didn't think he could. It seemed wrong to intrude on the man's tragedy like that, with a camera. So Harry himself asked Mustafa the questions, and Mortimer had to stand in close with the handheld mike to receive the answers.

This secret war has already brought tragedy to the region. In a bizarre quirk of fate our guide took us to this town, Osh, only to find that, unkown to him, he had suffered a personal loss, when his grandfather died in Soviet bombing.

"I'm sorry," he told Mustafa when the camera stopped, and he meant it as much for the intrusion as for Mustafa's loss. He put out a hand and touched his shoulder, and Mustafa turned to him with a kind of smile, his thick eyebrows raised above glistening eyes, and said, "We're lucky you're here."

When Mortimer did his piece to camera, Harry had him sweep his arm round, leading the camera across the devastation at the heart of the town, reduced to that plaza of broken bricks where the mosque had been. Mortimer opened with the phrase, "This is the story the Soviets didn't want the world to know."

It was true: the Soviets had evidently thought they would be able to slip in their bombardment of modest Osh unnoticed. But Mustafa was the muse planted by the gods to grant the story. And here Mortimer and his team were, first on the scene, first on screen.

At the side of the square the men had collected a few pieces of shrapnel, some shattered bomb casings, and Jimmy filmed those too.

The Soviet bombers apparently timed their raid to coincide with the dawn prayers that are such an integral part of life for these devout people. Rescue workers hold out little hope . . .

It was a report that would win Mortimer his first television award. It wasn't that television loved suffering. It loved story, narrative, a plane flying through the air one minute, blown to pieces the next; a pile of rubble meant nothing until you had a figure weeping over it, picking at the stones. But Mortimer felt uncomfortable: his role was so slight, superficial, yet intrusive.

He told himself to get used to it.

Back in the capital, at the hotel bar, Mortimer lifted his glass and said, "Here's to the story."

Jimmy raised his eyebrows and shrugged.

Mortimer took a long swig on his lager, wiped his mouth with his hand, and said, "Good thing we're here."

Jimmy shook his head. "Let's hope so." He looked down the bar, past Mortimer to where Harry was sitting. "That hug the woman gave Mustafa. Something about it."

"Strain of the moment," Harry said. "It was his grandmother."

"How do we know that? Where is he now, anyway?"

"Mourning, I suppose," Harry growled. A friend of Mustafa's had driven them back to the city.

"Or keeping his head down."

As Mortimer sat in the middle of this exchange, listening to it, his head began to swim. Eventually, during a pause, he said, "What are you getting at?"

Jimmy shrugged again. "There was that earthquake here last month."

"So?"

Harry glanced at Jimmy.

"All we know is there was a pile of rubble. Why wasn't there more dust in the air, if it was only bombed last night?"

There was another pause. Mortimer said, "But we saw the bombed-out houses."

Jimmy replied: "What about those bomb casings? I'd swear I saw rust on them."

"Rusting or charring." Harry grunted. "It's hard to tell sometimes."

"All I'm saying is they might have wanted it to look worse than it was."

Mortimer looked at the two men on either side of him, neither of whom returned his glance. "So what do we do?"

Harry turned to him with a grin that was more like a grimace. "You should have been in Berkeley in sixty-seven. No one would do a thing until the cameras got there, then all hell broke loose." He pulled on his drink. "The cans are well on their sweet way, should be in London by ten a.m."

"We can call Bush House and tell them."

"We're not supposed to even be here, remember? They'll be listening to every phone call. We should be thinking about getting out the same way we came in. Anyway, can you imagine how long we'd have to stay here to be a hundred percent sure of anything? Jimmy's probably just being oversuspicious as usual."

"But surely we have to try and find out," Mortimer said.

Harry chuckled and shook his head. "It's a terrific story."

Another telegram came from Saskia the following evening. *That poor man. Can't decide if use or abuse of him despicable or admirable. Your abhorring, adoring wife, S.*

He turned the telegram over and over in his hand. Perhaps she was right that they had abused Mustafa. On the other hand, perhaps he had abused them. But Mortimer was surely neither adorable nor abhorrable. He was just a punter doing his job.

At least he'd like to think so. In his room he pondered a reply, and plucked a sheet of hotel stationery out of the desk drawer—the thinnest paper he could remember seeing, a mere shaving off the onion—and wrote: *I feel like a man who has spent so long beating against the door that he does not realize the door has already opened, he has stepped outside and is standing in sunshine. The work now is not to force the door but to take advantage of the open air.*

But he didn't feel like writing a letter. Nor did he feel like he was standing in open air. *This is a war,* he forced himself to go on, *and our job is to report it.* Which felt like a lie. *Don't you think it's right to let people know what is happening, however you do it? Which means: how people's lives are affected? That's the real story, after all.*

But as he wrote these words he could hear Saskia's voice uttering them. This was what she would say; that news, the real news, was not of armies and strategies and politicians, but of people.

Who uses who? he added. *It's impossible to say.*

As he wrote, he longed for the self-sufficiency of print, where there was no need to provide conclusions, where all manner of contradictory information could be bundled into a story, as long as there was one salient ingredient to make the headline. But the doubt he felt, which was almost a fear, was balanced by a quiet thrill at bringing his reports into half the mother country's living rooms. It was as if you couldn't know luck without paying some price. And he only had to remind himself that Saskia was right behind his television venture for his worries to dwindle. If Saskia thought it a good thing, it probably was.

On the journey southeast to Issyk-Kul, on a broad plain that sloped like a ramp towards snowcapped mountains, they stopped for a pee at the roadside. The land was desert tufted with straw and a dry sagelike bush. Dust blew across the empty road, swirling over the surface like brown paint, like a liquid. Mortimer watched it as he peed, and the thought came to him: where does that dust come from? It was the dust of centuries, the dust of ages, the castoff of time's passage. It was also the dust of wars, a dust that came from nowhere and went nowhere, like war which had no beginning and no end. Perhaps you could say the same of love, which in its draperies of pain and need still presented itself, again and again, as a simple thing—an orphan at the roadside who opened his shirt and pulled out an orange, a gift for you.

Mortimer the bloody poet, he said to himself, and shook his penis dry. It was nice to pee outside, especially in a dry land. You felt you must be doing some sort of good. Or if you weren't, at least your traces would be gone in minutes. Perhaps that was the beauty of a desert: a man could pass without trace.

Mustafa had switched off the engine. The car ticked. When Mortimer turned his head the wind hummed in his ear. Far off he could hear an airplane droning; nearby the wind whistled in the grass. Everything was all right, he told himself. He was on his way to more scenes of devastation, but it was all right. Except there was some kind of dread deep in his chest. Perhaps it had been there a long time and this war had merely unpeeled it, but already he imagined arriving back in London with a load of profound dissatisfaction, almost a nausea. He didn't know why, yet he felt implicated in the suffering of this country. Almost as if he was helping to bring it on.

Saskia had once told him, "It's strange, you've seen a lot of suffering yet I'm not sure you know what it is." And he had been lost for words.

The sun would continue to shine and the wind to blow and Mortimer to participate in the unfolding of his life. But just then, zipping himself up on the wide plain at a roadside in Western Asia, he caught a glimpse of his dry future and saw that nothing could prevent his going into it.

Harry banged the roof of the car. A strange sound in the quiet desert. "No dawdling."

As Mortimer turned to go the wind brought another sound to his ears, a faint concatenation of human voices. "Listen," he told Harry.

They climbed a scree slope into the next gully, towards the voices, and found a group of nomads gathered there, all talking at once, raising a clatter of consonants in the desert stillness.

One of them had lost his eagle. It had dived after a hare and taken off over the hills, but the man was convinced some rival had lured it away.

While Mortimer and Harry waited to see what, if anything, might happen, and while the nomads joked about the Soviets in front of the camera, the bird came back. It floated over a brow and hung above, as if checking that it still wanted to descend to its owner's arm. It seemed the largest bird Mortimer had ever seen, a monster.

The men fell silent. The owner's mysterious call rose up, an ululating plea to the heavens, whose winged representative came down in a series of drops, as if descending a giant flight of stairs. With one tremendous flap of its wings it took its place on the man's forearm. The air whistled, dust skittered across the ground. The man talked to the beast beside his cheek, then opened his jaws wide and took the bird's head, beak and all, right in his mouth, and gently shook his head. When he released the eagle and resumed talking to it, the bird flicked its neck like a wet dog drying off.

Mortimer watched and felt he knew how that man must feel. He even knew how the bird felt, if a bird could be said to feel. To have the mountains at one's disposal and settle for this tiny shoulder of bone and flesh; and equally, to own such a frail arm and have it be the home and resting place of a beast of the highest peaks. Mortimer realized he too knew the taste of such a transcendence. To a man who had known it, it could surely never be lost.

When they climbed back in the car, Mortimer watched the road of black riven across the desert of Asia feed under him, pulling him into years of triumph and disaster ahead.

The Garden of God

1996

At six o'clock the bar on the east side of Seventh Avenue had just been found by the late sun. Mortimer watched as the smooth frosted panes of its four windows were suffused with a dense gold glow. They lit up like sheets of light: a hazy rich light as of a harvest sunset in the fields back home and long ago in the England of his childhood, which no longer existed; or as of the desert in the late afternoon when the torture of daytime was over, when at last the sun granted a reprieve and for half an hour, while it rested above the horizon, all things settled into themselves, bathed in light like a charm. Mortimer remembered how at that hour in the desert it was as if you had been asleep all day, your consciousness beaten into a dark corner, and now at last it woke up, came out of its cave, and found the whole world waiting. He remembered how loose and fluid his limbs would feel, how happy he'd be to be standing on the dust in scuffed boots with nothing but the flat earth in all directions, every last foot of it empty of humanity, of vegetation, of clutter. It was a marvellous thing to be in the desert at the end of day. It was one of earth's prizes.

He thought of it now and was filled with emotion. Tears threatened to come to his eye. Terrible, he told himself, you're a terrible, sentimental old soak.

He lifted his glass and drained it, then set it down beside a three-day-old London *Times* which lay folded into a cudgel on the bar top. He glanced at it, then twirled his finger at the barman. "Another Ballantine's."

The barman nodded at the newspaper. "Any news?"

"News?" Mortimer picked up the newspaper and shook his head.

But there was news, and he couldn't resist another look at it. They had taken to having snapshot obituaries in a column down the side of the main page these days. He had stumbled across it by chance, while browsing through the foreign pages, and he had been carrying it around with him ever since.

French photographer Celeste Dumas, 53, died last Wednesday at her home in Pau, south-western France, of bone cancer. Once celebrated for her adventurous work as a war photographer in the Sahara Desert, in collaboration with controversial British journalist Charles Mortimer, she was best known for her portraits of provincial and rural France, in particular of the Languedoc peasantry. Last year the Centre Pompidou held a retrospective of her work. She is survived by a husband and two daughters.

He might even have shown it to the barman—as if it might mean anything at all to him—but reading that epithet about himself again, decided he had better not. Over here, not even the editor at the magazine where he sometimes worked seemed to have any idea how badly things had gone for him; or else they'd all forgotten. But back in London they still hadn't, apparently.

He had a swig of his fresh drink and wondered: how befuddled, how silted up and muddy-headed had he let himself become that for so many years now he hadn't even thought of

Celeste? He couldn't bear to, presumably. More than twenty years ago: he had been a young man, still starting out. And now, as an overweight, supernumerary hack who had lost his best contacts, been hounded out of London; now, when he was down and vulnerable, with a bad heart, with no dependable work, no plane tickets in his back pocket waiting to ferry him to far-off disasters that had nothing to do with him personally—now that he was defenceless, there she was again, and it was far too late.

For a moment he couldn't move. There was that desert light before him, on the windows. Briefly he could see Celeste's face again, the colour of desert sand, her eyes streaked with shards of sunlight on rock. A hot breeze touched his cheek, and he could smell the wonderful dry aroma of dust, something like fresh plaster except it spoke of openness not of walls; of freedom not cramped and cramping houses— freedom from clouds, from cities, from people, from beasts, trees, from everything: freedom to go into the garden of God with a light heart.

1976

1

Mortimer gave copy the final word and hung up.

He pulled a Jazira cigarette from the paper pack on the table, drew the heavy glass ashtray closer, and gazed out over the rooftops of Algiers. The impression was of a pale blue quilt, the square top of each house shining after a recent shower, reflecting the colour of the sky. It was a city of rooftops. In the distance he could see the sea looking like a sheet of zinc, calm under the departing rain clouds. The scene had the loveliness of any hot, dry country after it has been rinsed with rain.

It was good to be in a foreign city. He could have sat there gazing over the rooftops for hours. He had the sensation that he was surveying his own territory—own not in the sense of owning but belonging. This was his true home: a hotel room with a big ashtray, a solid desk, and a splendid window overlooking an impoverished sprawl of humanity. And not just his home but his proper life, his modus vivendi. The city below was like a ploughed field busy germinating the fruits it would soon yield.

It was good too, to be alone. For the first time he felt liberated from Saskia, his ex-wife, and sure it was right that they had separated. With a continent and a sea between them, he could cease worrying. He hadn't acted badly, it wasn't a failing on his part to have left rather than continue in a commitment that had scared him more and more.

Mortimer felt he ought to be picking up the telephone and making a call but he had forgotten to whom, and why. Then it came back to him: room service, that was all. The week's work over, all copy filed, at least for the moment: time for a little reward, a glass of the sweet pink milk known as a *frappé*. He smiled inwardly when he remembered: nothing more onerous than that. It was good to have work under his own control: a cigarette, a notebook, and a pink milk shake — all he needed.

The phone rang and he picked up the heavy black receiver, relic of an earlier decade.

"Nice. Very nice." It was Kepple, the *Tribune*'s foreign editor, calling from London.

"How on earth do you know already?" Mortimer asked. He had finished giving his copy to London only minutes before.

"I read it as Mildred took it down," Kepple replied.

"Well, don't start thinking such zeal gives you any special editorial rights," Mortimer said.

"The 'Great Wall of Africa,'" Kepple chuckled. "Excellent. That'll be the headline. You'll have to give us a few more on the region."

"Of course," Mortimer blurted without thinking.

Just the day before, Mortimer had returned to Algiers from the Western Sahara, where the Rio Camello guerrillas were fighting Morocco for a disputed territory. The war had been going on a year with barely a mention in the press. But recently the Moroccans had built a thousand-mile wall of sand across the desert in an attempt to keep out the guerrillas. It wasn't much more than a bulldozed dyke the height of a man, with military posts strung along it, but it was still a remarkable story.

Mortimer hadn't got as far as thinking where he might try to go next, but pleasure welled at the story's having gone down well. It was his first print story for some time. It would be excellent to stay in the region for now.

"I'll be taking it straight up to the boss," Kepple went on. "Bloody good stuff. The reportage too."

Mortimer had scribbled a lot of notes about the guerrillas themselves while with them, and cobbled them together into a small feature.

Kepple cleared his throat. "I'll see if I can get the Sunday supplement interested in something too. We think you should go into the Atlas Mountains, then down south. I'll fill you in later."

Even after six years in the trade—Mortimer would be celebrating his thirty-first birthday in two months' time—you couldn't be invited to contribute a series to the *Tribune* and not feel excited. Especially when this was his first story since his sojourn in television—a sojourn that now, already, he could see had been a hiatus in his real life. He'd always been a print man, always would be.

He'd been trying to get more foreign assignments for years. Mortimer had always longed to be a roving reporter. It was obvious to him: the thing to do with one's life was to travel. One had been given a number of decades in this sunny, tragic world—what else to do but explore and report back on what you saw? He couldn't imagine a greater freedom, and purpose with it. You had your notebook, your biro, your passport: you went where the wars were, and the earthquakes and famines.

His first few years in the papers had been nothing like that. He'd had the odd assignment abroad, and would come back bursting with a triumph of news making, only to find the editor hadn't yet run it, and see it shunted day after day until it was out of date.

Most of the time was spent regurgitating information one had been given, and meanwhile dropping cigarette ends in half-drunk cups of coffee that had gone cold on the desk, or banging out paragraphs for other people's pieces where the editor wanted a change in angle, or driving through rain in small cars with overweight men from the paper who didn't bathe enough, eating Indian meals with them, sitting at pub tables crowded with glasses. All of which might represent a measure of his having arrived, or at least having got started — and also, he reflected occasionally, when in good spirits, that he was in the midst of an apprenticeship, was learning his trade on the job — but it was a far cry from the global scope, the dusty suit, scuffed notebook, and leaky local biro in a hot country that he had once imagined.

Mortimer reflected how odd it was that he had had to move to television in order to be wanted, rather than tolerated, by a newspaper. There was no end to the respect television commanded. His year in it had been only a modest success, yet it had totally changed his status with the papers.

A month back he'd had a drink with Kepple, the *Tribune*'s foreign editor, in a bleak pub on the Gray's Inn Road.

"Why are we meeting here?" he'd asked.

"Scoping the new watering holes. In case we move." The paper had been talking about moving from its Fleet Street premises for some time. "So things didn't pan out on the small screen?" Kepple asked. "Can't imagine why you'd want to leave it."

"It wasn't my cup of tea."

"I thought everyone wanted to be on the box."

Mortimer shrugged. "Not me."

"Well, Bill told me to work something out"—Bill being the paper's proprietor. "Says you were one of the good ones to watch. I've got just the ticket if you want it. Desert nomads turn guerrilla fighters. Starting up a righteous war all their own in the Sahara."

"I'll need decent money," he'd said.

"Bill is constitutionally disinclined towards new salaries this month, so he says," Kepple had replied. "He likes retainers better. Perfect for you. A decent retainer, and fees per story."

"And expenses?"

"Expenses too, of course."

Mortimer had gratefully taken on the job. It was just what he had been hoping for.

The Saharan assignment had also been just what he needed when it came to Saskia. With things being over with her, and his therefore being free to go, free as never before. And his needing to. Saskia had delivered a string of ultimatums on which he had failed to deliver, and at last she had meant it, and packed his bags for him. He had moved into the spare room of a friend, a lawyer with a young family. Mortimer's presence in that already fraught domesticity was too much: it had been an untenable situation. And on top of that, the English winter had been drawing on interminably. March already, and hardly a sign of the sun since Christmas.

I'm like a mariner, Mortimer told his friends, I'm away too much. And when I'm not away I'm looking to go away. I never know when I'll be off next. It's no life for a partner. Saskia's done the right thing.

Or sometimes he said: *we*'ve done the right thing. Because it was mutual, more or less. True, it was he who had become ever more remote, ever less able to settle into home life, but it was she who had called their mutual bluff. And once they had started talking openly, it became clear they felt equally equivocal.

At least that was what they told themselves. He sometimes wondered if the real problem hadn't been different. He would think of their last formal talk about calling it all off. Formal was the word. They'd sat in her sitting room talking about the need to set one another free for something better. Mostly she had talked. He had listened, and in some way none of what they were saying had seemed true, or even important. He'd had the sense that they were putting up words like so much smoke, and the real story had nothing to do with what they said. They were wasting their breath. The truth, the real course of events, would come along regardless of their words. He'd felt an urgency to get away, as if only away from her, and away from their home, would he be able to order his thoughts and reconnect with the truth of the situation, and then be able to say the right things.

That had never happened. He had simply left.

He told himself it was the perfect arrangement: he had tried marriage, given it enough of a shot to know it wasn't for him, had cured himself of the dumb couple-hunger that afflicted so many of his generation, and would no longer hanker after the dull solace of domesticity.

Then along came a Saharan war on a plate, and an offer from a newspaper: there had been no decision.

2

Instead of calling room service, he decided to go down in person. He'd have his pink milk shake in the lobby lounge.

The Al Asra was Algiers's most distinguished hotel, a colonial legacy built like a municipal edifice of provincial France, which it more or less had been, with thick masonry, shutters on every window, and a mansard roof tall and steep enough to have two tiers of dormer windows, one of which was his.

The lounge, an area of low marquetry tables, stiff silk settees, and ornate trelliswork, spread around the lobby, up and down changes in floor level. It all looked mock Arabic, rather than what it was, Arabic, and was all but deserted just now: a table of men drinking glasses of tea, and a blond woman over in a far corner.

Mortimer stumbled as he took a step. The woman looked up from her book, and he recognised her as a French photographer who had been down in the desert the previous week, in the Rio Camello camps. He had hardly spoken to her then. There had been a pack of journalists covering a congress the guerrillas were holding, and he had seen her only once, and had noticed her because she was pretty.

When his glass of sweet milk arrived on its saucer he picked it up on impulse and walked towards her, threading through the tables and chairs of the dark interior, inspired to approach her by a feeling of bonhomie towards other journalists, kindled by his coup at the foreign desk. But as he made his way over, his mood changed to something nearer alarm. An acute shyness seized him. He couldn't now imagine spontaneously beginning an easy conversation with her, he would quickly have to prepare an opening line.

He wished he hadn't already got up and committed himself to speaking to her, or had waved or nodded first, done something to pave the way. Why was he nervous? He had been married, he wasn't some teenage ingénue, he made adequate money, he'd held down decent jobs: there was no need for this unease. He had already thought of a good first line, back when he had been sitting down and not worrying. He racked his brains for it now, and when he did miraculously find it, it no longer seemed a good line at all. But he was already upon her, he had to use it.

"Makes a change from the desert, doesn't it?" he said with an inward groan.

She looked up from the book in her lap, then down again, and snapped it shut. "The desert?"

"We met, remember? With the Rio Camello." He felt aggrieved: surely she couldn't have forgotten meeting him. True, they had done no more than shake hands, but there hadn't been that many foreigners down there. And he himself might be an unknown but his paper at least was famous. Another reason he'd noted her was that someone had told him she was working for *Le Monde*.

Perhaps she felt she needed to be discreet about having been there, Rio Camello being a sensitive issue locally. He felt himself blush.

"Well, do you want to sit down?" She smiled. "What is your drink, by the way?"

He tried to make a joke: "My drink? Scotch and soda." There was an uneasy pause. "That's my drink. What's yours?"

"At this time of day? Water." She frowned at his glass of pink milk. "You're telling me that's a scotch?"

He laughed, out of nervousness. "This is some strange

milk shake. They dye it pink and load it up with sugar. I rather like it." He nearly got back on firm ground then, but when she again invited him to sit down, and he did, there followed an impossibly awkward conversation. She seemed to miss everything he said, and yet at the same time to be two steps ahead of him. He imagined a pair of good dancers unfamiliar with one another might feel this way, able to see the sense in one another's moves yet unable to get in step.

Mortimer again wondered why he felt so nervous. She was beautiful, for one thing. He noticed it first in her eyebrows. They had a movement and shape that tripped one's heart up. She was blond, more or less, but the eyebrows were a thatchy brown, curving up towards the middle, where they ended in serifs tucked towards the bridge of the nose. The nose was very good, strong and fine with a slight bump in the middle, as if once broken. Altogether she had an air of anything but preciousness, as if she didn't treat herself like the beautiful woman she was, but lived a rough-and-ready outdoor life. Which she probably did, being a photojournalist.

Or perhaps it was that she was a little older than he was, and had a successful life as a foreign news photographer. She'd be one of the lucky ones, with steady work that kept her overseas.

There was something familiar about her voice. When she spoke it was as if he could sense the deep part of her from which its timbre arose. It arrived loaded with intimacy. He couldn't explain it. When she laughed it was as if she gave herself up to laughter completely. At one point in that first conversation he was convinced he knew her well from somewhere, and a bewildering excitement ran through him.

They arranged to meet later and he went back to his room

both delighted and scared, though he couldn't have said why. He flopped on the bed, exhaled as if out of relief, or from exhaustion, and discovered that really it was out of happiness. An Orthodox monk he had once met in Serbia had told him: the heart wants to soar up to God like a balloon. Why did he feel so good all of a sudden? He couldn't remember ever feeling so free, so lighthearted. He knew now what that monk had been talking about. He was full of a weightless joy. He saw a lake in mountains. He was living beside it, had all he needed just there. Beside the lake was a house, and in the house his one perfect companion. No need to go anywhere ever again. The lake had a name: joy.

Which wasn't her name. She was called Celeste: French, of course, but she had a dash of Spanish too in her blood, he later discovered. He couldn't remember meeting anyone with her forthrightness before. When they later found their birthdays were only days apart, give or take a few years, he was unsurprised.

It all seemed to happen by itself, as things did when one lived right: the Atlas to cover, then the Tuareg of the deep south; and a photographer planted by fate under his hotel roof.

That night at dinner in the medina he told Celeste his plans.

She listened, looking at him across the plastic-covered table. Her pale green eyes seemed to see into the pit of his belly, where her gaze touched a warm pool he hadn't known was there. Her irises were predominantly green, but streaked with gold, blood brown, and sky blue. He fell silent. He could see her pupils flinch, then swell slightly. They looked at each other longer than was necessary, long enough that he began to feel uncomfortable, to worry about how to end the stare, until he found he didn't want to.

Celeste had spent a month in the Maghreb already, she told him. She said that after the Far East, where she had been working for *Le Monde* and a Lyons paper for nine months, to be here felt like coming home. "All the French names, the French buildings, and everyone speaks French. And Marseilles is just across the water," she said with a smile that roused two sleeping dimples. "I just finished a photo essay for *Der Spiegel*, and I was thinking of going home. But I already feel I am."

Later, in a crowded bus heading back to the hotel, Celeste whispered in his ear, "You should take me with you."

His heart bounced, and he found it hard to swallow.

In the morning, lying in his bed, he was filled with a strange numbness. He was waiting until it was nine o'clock in London. He was able to lie absolutely still. Already his limbs were anticipating being back in the desert. He loved the desert.

When it was almost nine he reached for the phone and called Kepple. "I might want to bring a photographer along. You mentioned the Sunday magazine. Any chance of hooking up with them for some spreads?"

Did he have that kind of leverage? It was a mad idea. It was premature, in every way, madly so, but she was right here, in the same hotel. And there was something about her. It wasn't just that he liked the way she looked; somehow he felt she might be part of the auspices blessing his return to print. And he felt a tingle of excitement in his bones, presage of a scoop, the kind that surprises even its subjects, coming so early they themselves hardly recognise the news they represent, yet which changes the landscape for a long time. He had to act on it at once. There would be untold advantages to having a photographer along; in fact now he could not imagine proceeding without one.

Kepple hesitated.

"Listen, if you're right about the Atlas Mountains," Mortimer urged, "if Monsieur Taillot is right"—Taillot was a contact the paper had given him, whom in fact he had yet to call—"then this will be big and we'll need pictures. It'll be too late to send someone later."

Where this new boldness came from he didn't know.

Kepple grunted. "Well, there's not just the Atlas. You should go south too, down into the desert. There's the drought in Mali, for a start. And the Tuareg. Bill seems keen on you. He just dropped me another note saying he wants more. He even cracked a joke, called you Mortimer of the Maghreb."

Kepple let out a groan of reluctant assent. "Leave it to me."

3

From the café window, across the square, Mortimer could see a ship leaving port. Its stern seemed to swivel across the water without the vessel making any headway. To the side of it a faint brown stain hung against the milky sky. Meanwhile, in the street, all the *petits taxis* and *grands taxis* put up their aroma of exhaust, with here and there a grey plume hanging above the traffic. And in the café, on the square, on the street corners, wherever you looked all the men were smoking. This was a city whose life, if you wanted in any way to join it, you did first by smoking.

Mortimer sat smoking himself in the big café on the Place

Al-Ghazi, a bare, canteen-style establishment full of plastic chairs and faux-marble tables. There were no women in it at all, just a throng of black-haired men. They served coffee and mint tea in small or large glasses, and local sodas coloured bright orange and lawn green.

When Monsieur Taillot arrived, both of them immediately lit up. They would chain-smoke for the half hour they were there.

Taillot was indeterminately Mediterranean. Even his accent was hard to place: American-educated, perhaps, over a gravelly base that Mortimer thought might have been Corsican.

The conversation started to grow serious.

"Look," Taillot said, sipping from his little, gold-enamelled glass of tea, "this is dangerous stuff, believe me. If you don't watch yourself you'll get in trouble. The Atlas, they used to be like the Alps. Not anymore. It's turning into the Wild West. Nobody knows what to do, except to keep beefing up the arsenal. Everybody's doing it, Brits, Americans, French, and the Russians too. The arms contracts keep coming in. The last thing anybody wants is another civil war here in the heart of the Maghreb."

Taillot was an international observer, but in whose pay Mortimer had no idea.

"But who is the enemy?" Mortimer asked.

"That's Algeria's problem. They don't exactly know. But presumably it's village chieftains and such. The mountain villages have leaders who are also imams, or mullahs, religious men. But the Algerians have a history of invisible soldiering, as we all know."

Taillot was clearly alluding to Algeria's struggle for independence.

"The real problem for the West is that the current president has been a pleasant chap, helping out with Iran and Iraq and so on, always ready to talk. His neutrality is extremely useful. He has leverage not only with Arab states but the Eastern bloc. The West would hate to lose him." He cleared his throat. "But there's more."

Taillot drew out a Marlboro and twirled it in his fingers. Mortimer held out his lighter, and sensed by a slight hesitation that Taillot didn't want the cigarette lit so soon. He had planned to toy with it a little longer. Probably he wanted to tease Mortimer too, force him to draw out the clincher, beg for it: what more was there? Please tell.

Mortimer looked around for a waiter and leaned back in his chair. "More tea?" he asked Taillot when the boy arrived.

A moment later, each with a lit cigarette in hand and a refilled glass of tea, Taillot said: "Yes, there's much more. The Blue Menace." He squinted at Mortimer as he drew on his cigarette.

Mortimer racked his brains. This was either a clue or something he ought to know. Whoever this Taillot was, Mortimer had been getting the impression increasingly that he was a significant player, requiring deference. Mortimer needed to show he was worthy of his confidences. He succeeded in disguising the inward "Ah" he felt when he understood. "You're talking about the Tuareg, *les hommes bleus*. They're a problem?"

Taillot nodded.

"But they simply roam the desert, they go where they please."

"And where they please now is their own state. They have declared a nationhood, written a constitution. In Tamashek. Their language, as you know."

Mortimer didn't know. He nodded. There was a pause.

"What does Kepple know of all this?" Mortimer asked.

Taillot squinted at him again, then shrugged.

Mortimer left it. It wasn't important. It crossed his mind that Taillot might even not know who Kepple was, or who Mortimer was for that matter: it was a dizzying thought, however implausible.

"The government is anxious to keep a lid on things. That is why you would be even more careful, if you decided to go to the deep south. The place you start is Tamanrasset. Over the mountains, down in the middle of the desert. That's where the Tuareg are moving in. Coming down from the Hoggar Hills and the Southern Erg, we hear."

"The Southern Erg?" Mortimer asked.

"The sand sea, the ocean of dunes. A natural home to the Tuareg only." Taillot smiled. "A formidable place."

Taillot had a stippling of pockmarks on his left cheek: only the one cheek, Mortimer noticed. "Is all this new?" Mortimer asked.

"There have been rumblings. Even in the last century, under the French, some Tuareg wrote a declaration of independence. But it never meant anything. It's a huge area of sand, unpoliceable. To be perfectly frank, Algeria would have half a mind to let them have what they want, if the government had not been investing so heavily in the Sahara. The desert is the president's golden dream, a huge untapped resource. Algeria's Amazon, he calls it."

"A resource for the construction sites of the world?"

Taillot tutted. "There's much more than sand. Minerals of all kinds. And water too; it just happens to be a hundred metres below ground. And other things. But a Tuareg state with a bite of Mali, a chunk of Niger, Mauritania, and a whole lot of Algeria would be more than viable. And how do you stop them? They are completely nomadic. If their intentions get to be widely known, it could have an effect in the mountains, with the imams of the Atlas, who might start thinking: this unholy state of Algeria is crumbling, Allah's time has come."

Taillot took a long draw on his cigarette. Mortimer was enjoying himself, and had an equally deep puff on his own. "Not only that," Taillot continued, "but Westerners *like* the Tuareg. If Algeria declares war on them, not only will it most likely fail to defeat them, the enemy being consummately elusive, it would bring a lot of ill feeling. The West has a romantic attachment to the nomads. They're one of Algeria's assets."

Who was this man? Mortimer wondered. And why was he happy to brief him?

"So far, of course, nothing has actually happened. Or so one is led to believe. But I've heard rumours of Tuareg skirmishes in the deep south."

"With who?"

"The police, of course. The gendarmerie. Technically, you could call it civil war."

4

They jumped on a train the next morning. It was Celeste's idea. They needed to get moving right away, she said. They could neither afford nor bear to wait for the Wednesday flight into the mountains. It was reckless to travel overland, and Mortimer couldn't exactly have explained how it came about, but effectively he found himself hitchhiking across the Sahara over the coming weeks, with a beautiful French photographer at his side. Instead of reaching Tamanrasset in a couple of hops, and in one day, it would take them weeks. Or it would have done had they ever reached it.

In the morning, on the train, in the soft, dusty sunshine, Mortimer was filled with an inordinate sense of well-being. The guards had not closed the doors, and while Celeste sat at one of the tables, Mortimer stood on the steps clutching the bars and watching the suburbs pass by. There was such a pleasure to being one's own boss. The paper had put their trust in him. Whatever happened, whatever stories he came up with, it was all up to him. It wasn't that the warm breeze on his face with its smell of diesel smoke exhilarated him, so much as it filled his legs with a tingling warmth.

A strip of wasteland ran along the tracks. Beyond was a dirty white wall with scrap metal heaped on the far side. Then they crossed a little river, its banks strewn with rubbish. A boy sat on a rock beside four sheep that picked at the dirt. These ragged sights on the edge of the city seemed quiet, harmonious—as if away from the city's bustling heart peacefulness reigned over these scrappy, uncared-for things.

A hillside ahead was covered in a mosaic of little houses, some red, some pinkish, some white, and altogether resembled an intricately woven, pleasingly faded carpet.

He had an urge to grab Celeste and point these things out to her. It was good to know she was sitting just a few yards away, also traveling in the rattling iron beast that would take them far across this land, into the mountains and beyond, to the sand.

The train rode up the coastal plain into the foothills of the Atlas. It was a spring day, the hills sparkling, draped with gauzes of mist. Mortimer hardly knew what he was on his way to. They passed through rolling country where here and there men with pairs of small oxen ploughed little fields, long switches in hand. On some plots they had no oxen and three or four men would be stooped over hoes, ploughing by hand. Mortimer reflected what backbreaking work that must be, and what a household disaster a bad back could be. It was pleasant to witness all the small-scale husbandry.

Then the train slowed, the bends became longer and more frequent, the bridges and tunnels too, as they began to climb into the mountains.

Once, while he was standing to get a book from his bag on the overhead rack, as the train clackety-clacked over a girder bridge across a small ravine, nudging from side to side as it went, the carriage jolted and he swung against Celeste. She was warm and he didn't seem so much to fall against her as pour into her. It was a strange sensation. He pulled himself up and apologised but his heart was in his mouth. He glanced at her, and she was looking at him, her eyes bright, her lips open. In a flash he saw himself bending down and kissing her there and then.

But he didn't. He laughed lightly in response to her look, and said, *"Excusez-moi,"* as he sat down again.

The track flanked the side of a mountain now, and out the window a great view opened up through fir trees of the coastal plain already far below. What had seized him? How come everything had happened so fast? Here he was on a train heading towards a series of stories for the *Tribune* with a woman who already caused him sensations he had not known before. He could feel fate pressing in, trammelling and accelerating his life.

They got talking to a young man in black-rimmed glasses, a schoolteacher returning home from Algiers to spend the holidays with his family, who lived in the mountain town of Setif.

They were getting off there too, and he insisted they come for lunch at his parents' house.

"But your mother," Celeste said, "what will she say?"

"She'll be happy. *Très heureuse.*"

Celeste raised her eyebrows at Mortimer as they stood just outside the antique station building, beneath its fringe of elaborate wrought ironwork, and he could think of no reason not to accept. They'd need lunch anyway.

The young man embraced a girl of eleven or twelve wearing a white housecoat over a pair of trousers, and a white scarf on her head, and introduced her as his sister, who had come to meet him, then led them off through the quiet, broad streets of the little mountain city. As he had promised, the family home was not more than ten minutes away.

The mother, a small round woman in a blue dress and white scarf like her daughter, her face a shiny pale brown, embraced all of them warmly, even the newcomers, and even her daughter, who had probably not been gone more than twenty minutes, so overcome was she at her son's return. She bundled some notes into the daughter's hand and sent her off with a few words of soft Arabic.

The young man smiled. "Very nice lunch. Just wait a little while. Come. Sit."

He led them into a garden at the back, where they sat on homemade wooden benches. Small lemon and orange trees grew out of rusty tins. A border along the house was bushy with mint. Farther down, a washing line criss-crossed the yard, hung with recently washed clothes that had dripped dark lines onto the cement beneath them. Fat drops bulged from the hems of the skirts and shirts, awaiting their turn to fall.

Mortimer saw all these things and was inordinately delighted. This seemed somehow the perfect house for a family, the ideal yard where its various chores and functions could be carried out.

The mother came out with a tray of glasses and a jug of freshly made lemonade. The glasses were wet, just rinsed, and the drink was tepid but delicious. She apologised for having no ice, but the electricity had been down two days. They all heard the front door, and the mother went back inside.

An hour later they settled round the table to a large casserole of tripe stew. At the smell of it, Mortimer, a lifelong disliker of offal, felt his heart sink in exactly the way it had when he had been a schoolboy, and lunch in its aluminum serving dish turned out to be liver or kidney. He glanced at Celeste, who happened to catch his eye across the table. She frowned at him, muttered, "*Ça va?*" then shaking her head mouthed, "*Pas?*"

He sent her a quick look of dismay. She smiled.

"*Madame,*" she began. "*Excusez-nous. Moi, j'aime bien,* but he is not accustomed to eating *les tripes.* They don't do it in England. *Nous nous excusons.*"

The woman needed no more prompting. She apologised profusely, Mortimer did the same, and she instructed the son to serve everybody else while she went back to the kitchen to make Mortimer an omelette, in spite of his protestations.

Mortimer was embarrassed but Celeste seemed to find the little incident endearing, and after lunch as they walked into town to a *place* where they could hire a taxi, she linked her arm in his and leaned against him. His heart jumped, and he spontaneously put his other hand on her forearm and squeezed her wrist, feeling her slender bone through its sleeve of muscle.

"Thank you," he said, and she turned to smile at him. He almost lost his footing, seeing her face from so close, feeling the warmth of her skin, the heat of her breath. He could not help himself, and the next thing he knew he was standing in the sunshine of the street, hearing the quiet sounds of a city all but free of traffic, holding her face in his hands like a chalice, and kissing her. He could feel her cheeks smiling as she kissed him back, then they went slack, then slightly concave.

The kiss surprised both of them, awkward, clumsy, hungry, and not long. She pulled back, caught her breath, wiped her mouth, and said, "Not here." And gave him another peck on the lips and hugged him. "We must wait." She leaned her forehead against his. "Even if it's hard."

It was hard. Mortimer was left yearning for more, but also with a keen sense of the impropriety of kissing in public, a sense of shame even, which both shadowed and amplified the dizziness of his hunger to kiss her again. In the end it was six days before they could be alone together. Mortimer felt he had never waited so long for anything.

5

They hired a Toyota to take them to Batna, where the paper had given Mortimer a contact, and they could get to work. The prospect of work offered a welcome shelter from the intense awkwardness he was experiencing. He couldn't account for it: she was hardly the first woman he'd been with. Yet it felt as if she was.

They were quickly drawn into a company of Berber farmers and part-time mystics, quiet men with Sufi leanings, with whom Mortimer fell into profound conversations about the nature of life while strolling through apricot orchards. One, a farmer called Ahmed, took him up into the hills above his farm, on a long walk through a eucalyptus forest to a waterfall. All Ahmed wanted, he said, was to live as God intended. He described Mortimer's journalism as the footprints he left behind him as he walked through life. It seemed a pleasing idea.

In the evenings they sat about the earthen floors of huts, among circles of men chewing dates and sucking sheep's milk from a shared cup. They allowed Celeste to join in because she was not only a journalist too, but also his wife (there could be no question about that).

"The best way to eat dates, the best way to drink milk," Ahmed said of the date-and-milk combination. It was delicious, and made a good evening's indulgence. Alcohol didn't cross Mortimer's mind. He began to feel a bit holy himself, in such simple and trusting company. He even found himself wishing he really was married to Celeste, and did not have to lie about it. Yet he was glad too, somehow, that they had yet to consummate things. He felt like a child again, as if they were both children, side by side. In some still vaguer way he began to feel that they already were effectively married. He had never known one before, but in spite of spending so little time with her, he already felt he understood for the first time what a soul mate was. Deep down, a similarity of composition bound them, as if they were made of the same substance—which wasn't a figure of speech but an experience. When he was with her, he became aware of a bedrock within, and felt how it matched the equivalent in her: two tectonic plates meeting. It made him inexplicably at peace. When apart, he carried with him a sensation of this substratum: it had been brought to his attention by virtue of having met its twin. He would have talked about it with her had he been able to find a way. Sometimes he felt there was nothing to say on the subject that she didn't already know.

One late afternoon they found themselves alone on the packed dirt of the farm compound. They strolled out under olive trees and sat on a low mud wall. Before them the valleyside fell away in silvery green foliage, and the far side shone like a sleek horse's flank.

"How's the story?" she asked.

Her face was flushed, her eyes sparkled, and her pale lips parted, revealing the white tips of her teeth. There was something about her face, so open and full of intention. It made him dizzy.

He swallowed. "I should get two, I think."

She raised her eyebrows almost apologetically. "Good idea to come."

"Don't thank me," he anticipated. "It's good for me to have you."

He looked ahead but could feel her presence at his side so strongly, such a warmth beside him, that he hardly saw what his eyes were looking at.

The local imam was becoming a cause célèbre. Wild-looking men with rifles slung over their shoulders arrived in the town and danced in circles, shooting their guns into the sky. Celeste photographed them. Mortimer wasn't sure how they'd take to the sight of a camera, but it had an invigorating effect on them, he could feel it. The celebrations became more intense, louder, with more firing off of the guns. It was almost as if the festivities had now discovered their real point, once the lens was on the scene. Then the men all went off to pray with the imam.

He sat on his dais for hours on end, preaching and chanting. Mortimer tried to get an interview with him but could find no one willing to interpret. Celeste photographed a whole field of men bowing in prayer, with the little old man far away, alone on his makeshift stage.

The paper took the image, and another of the riflemen dancing and letting off their guns, a cloud of gunsmoke drifting over their heads. They ran a story: *Islamist militants finding a focus in the Atlas Mountains.* Two weeks later the imam was killed, an event which triggered a sequence of reprisals against the state authorities, and threatened to bring down a general disaster on the province, though in fact that wouldn't arrive for a few years yet.

Mortimer slept on the floor of one hut, Celeste on a cot in another, along with three women and several children.

When they finally came down out of the mountains in the back of a Peugeot estate car, winding past springs tucked into the nook of hairpin bends, through olive and orange groves, down hillsides of vine, and across meadows of tough, scrawny-looking flowers, they had hardly had a minute alone together since the train ride six days earlier. Sitting in the car, he felt so close to her she burned against his side. He knew, he was sure, that she wanted to be alone with him as much as he did with her.

They came round a bend of rock to see below them, where there ought to have been land, a broad, gold cloud stretching away like a sea. Only once they descended into the cloud did dark lines begin to show, marking where irrigation dykes ran across a plain, then faintly the outlines of shrubs appeared, and rows of young crops, and finally the red earth itself. By then they were on the outskirts of Touggourt.

Touggourt was a small city, and clung to the foot of the Anti-Atlas. It had a heart of palms, red mosques, and labyrinthine alleys. The streets were aromatic with stores selling grilled chicken and couscous. At night they filled with the smoke of vendors grilling brochettes over charcoal, and with the dust the crowds kicked up from the dirt streets. All the palms and eucalyptus—the hardy trees that survived on little water—were coated in dust too, and seemed to hover amid the clouds of drifting smoke. It was as if the purpose of a settlement were nothing other than for humanity to put up all this smoke and bustle and noise, its one big smoke signal.

They checked into the best hotel. It was their first night alone together, in a double bed, in a room whose door they could lock, with their own bathroom. Mortimer found he had developed a sense of sanctity towards his own body, and towards Celeste. As soon as the bellhop, a man in a dusty brown djellaba, closed the door, another cataclysmic shyness seized him, the worst yet. The room seemed quiet, too small. Just a few faint Arab-city sounds reached them through the blinds: someone calling, mopeds going by, someone hammering on metal a few streets away. He went to unzip his bag, and the sound of the zip seemed to fill the room, and also to cry out: this is the action of a nervous man. He hadn't realised how much shelter those holy men in the mountains had been offering. Suddenly there was no escape, no refuge. For a moment, crouching at his bag, he felt that he would not be able to rise to his feet, so enormous was the feeling running through him: a nameless feeling, one that made it impossible to pluck up one single word, let alone string two together. Then he did stand up and immediately thought he would have to drop into a crouch again. He turned and saw she had gone, then realised he could hear the fan humming in the bathroom. A moment's relief. He lay on the bed. But there was no relief. They were the worst ten minutes he could remember. He was trapped in a plain room in a desert town in the presence of something that had the power to swallow him whole.

Everything felt preordained: her half-drunk bottle of Sidi Ali water on the black bedside table. His having filed a third story on the mountains, being on his way to something bigger. His unzipped but still packed bag. The clothes he was wearing—jeans, faded blue shirt with salt lines faintly showing, stiff with dust, boots whitened by road dust. His six days' stubble, his hair thick with dust. The quiet thunder of the shower running in the bathroom. And his own rapturous terror. He had surely experienced all these things before, or had known all along that he would one day. He was transfixed. He ought to take a shower too but he couldn't move. Behind the bathroom door the water roared quietly. The sense of the moment's inevitability pressed in on his ears. For a moment his vision seemed bleached by desert dust, desert sun, and by this dust storm of emotion. Fate, he thought, was a lion that tore a life to pieces. It picked you up in its jaws and shook you. Whatever you thought, you were helpless really. You could do nothing but submit to what happened to you. That Saskia had finally and irrevocably left him at Christmas, that he no longer had to worry about that particular compromise, that he was staying on in the Maghreb, in the desert, had come down here in the first place—all these things were subsumed by inevitability, by a fate in which part of him too conspired. The current that carried him also had its unseen source in him.

Just before she opened the door he had time to reflect that

perhaps the experience he was undergoing had nothing to do with her. The idea brought relief. But the moment she emerged wrapped in a towel all the dread welled up again, and he knew it had everything to do with her. She went straight to her case on the floor by the window. She squatted down, legs held together by the towel, and lifted the lid. Then she stood and pulled the faded red curtain across the window. She rummaged in her case, found something, and blew her nose twice lightly. Then she stood and came to the bed.

He was sure she came intending to give him a hug. Perhaps they'd have a snooze in one another's arms. But as soon as he felt the bed give under the weight of her knee he knew what would happen. It could hardly have been a surprise, he reflected later, yet it felt like one. She said, *"Enfin,"* and loosened her towel. He opened his arms and burrowed, eyes closed, towards her face. He felt the curtain of damp hair against his temple, her breath hot on his shoulder, and she gave a little hum, then made a movement after which the towel had come away. Her skin was warm, damp. They were immediately into a deep kiss. When he interrupted things to untie his bootlaces he felt faint.

She was acrobatic, her stomach had internal engines of its own, a miniature sluice station he learned to manipulate so it pumped against his fingers. The deeper she let him conduct her into her own pleasure, the further he went into his own. He had never known anything like it.

"This sex is actually interesting," he said later. He meant: it's not just something we do because we know we should, which had essentially been Saskia's position; his position too with most of his one-offs: it was necessary, surely, to satisfy one's desire. But this was a different matter: here was a new land asking to be explored.

"Just for the record," he said, "just in case there's any doubt, I have strong feelings." He couldn't remember ever feeling so unequivocal.

Her body was evidently not that young. There were even faint lines, ghosts of lines, on her breasts. But he loved their shape and weight; and her prominent nipples, almost without aureolas, seemed to state something about who she was. Her body was her instrument and she used it. They spent two days in the room, breaking off now and then to eat kebabs in the hotel restaurant, priming themselves for more. They ordered wine but hardly touched it. Once he guzzled a bottle of beer straight down. Gauzy twilights, dusty dawns came and went. Going to sleep was like walking along the edge of a cliff. He felt queasy, excited, fearful all at once. And woke to find the same feeling still there.

When eventually they ventured into the town its raucous din was delightful.

6

Touggourt.

Essence, *the man puts on my boots. Petrol. That's ingenuity for you. Petrol, and a sharp little knife with which, after scraping it back and forth on the pavement by way of sharpening, he actually manages to restore my boots to a semblance of their original suede.*

A pleasant scene. Morning sunshine. A range of hills just visible in the distance, not yet eaten up by haze. And here under the umbrellas set in wheel hubs a number of men industriously scrubbing one another's shoes, and a far greater number sitting about watching. Shadows flit across the sunlit paving as the bustle of the morning goes by. I give him twice the accepted Nizara price. I too am a Nizara, apparently, a Nazarene, a white.

But I am avoiding the issue. To wit, la fille, la jolie blonde. Jolie yes, blonde yes, but hardly a fille. I'd say thirty-five, on balance. A touch older than I, travel-cured. There's a worldliness to her that betokens the crossing of life's watershed (i.e. three-o). Strange, considering the last three days, that I don't know her age. Will make enquiries.

Why do I feel so chirpy? What a question! Three days of bedroom acrobatics, mon brave! (I was about to say: because I'm away from rainy England and all its [my] problems. And truly if someone asked me now: you're never going to see the white cliffs again, how do you feel? my answer would be: relieved, there's a few issues I no longer need worry about.)

She is something else. This is something else. Not sure I want to defile it, or her, with ink.

Dust and smoke and noise and bustle. Smells of exhaust fumes, of swept-up dust, of cooking, wine, rotting fruit—these are what cities properly consist of, this is what the South does properly, in a way the North cannot match. Out in the road a boy twirls a length of thread round and round his head, making twine, right in the midst of gurgling mopeds streaming past. Meanwhile, a donkey cart is negotiating him and his string, and a minibus is overtaking the cart, as well as all the mopeds. The principle of traffic here is not to stop. If no one ever stops then all can predict oncoming trajectories and preempt likely collisions.

What an effect the simple press of humanity has in a

desert town. The buses and little Peugeots, and people
everywhere, so many of them: a marvellous thing, at
once exciting and reassuring. They create a sensation
unknown in the West. The dust of multitudes drifting up
as a haze into the unencumbered sky. The knowledge of
the desert, the emptiness, all around. The desert forces a
graphic understanding of the true human presence on
the planet: a something, in a void.

Celeste's Frenchness: he was in love with it. He loved the way
she had emerged from the bathroom that first time. "*Voilà,*
ça y est, enfin," and she slipped the towel's knot and let it fall,
and for the first time he saw those small breasts, firm nipples.
The buds themselves were large, the size of the little incense
cones people burned in braziers throughout the country. During lovemaking they became perpendicular. They were one
simple thing he appreciated about her. He tried to draw up a
kind of chart to get some perspective, but a nagging anxiety
that she might discover it held him back. He wanted to title it
"Pro and Con," assuming that there would be cons. Then
changed it to "Things I Like." Then crossed out "Like" and
wrote "Love" in smaller cursive.

It was hard to know how to categorise. Sexual and non-
sexual? But where did each begin and end? Her hair, for example. There was no question he found it sexy. It was partly
the colour, an ash blond with brown, grey, and rust all in there
too, along with the shining sun-cured blondness. It was a good
length, long enough to do things with, like pull into a ponytail, or have hang down either cheek, but also short enough to
leave serviceably all to itself. It seemed to him the perfect hair.
Which was precisely why he had to sit down and write about
it, along with everything else about her, to try and stick at least

the tip of his nib of rationality into the crack, which must surely still exist, between himself and his feelings; between him and her.

She had a basically though not perfectly flat stomach, and Mortimer had noticed sometimes when she walked a hint of flare at the top of her thighs. There was something about her Frenchness that encouraged him to notice how she looked. It was hard to define, but she put time and thought into her appearance: she had an agreeable workaday vanity, and it would have been a negligence on his part not to appreciate it.

She was a working woman who kept her eye on her job, yet at the same time was feminine, able to think about her attractiveness to men. Part and parcel of this was her body: lithe, supple, strong, and incidentally lovely. She was even capable of doing herself up for lovemaking—showering, shaving here and there, pulling on decorative underwear—in the same workmanlike spirit, which did not make it any the less sexy. If anything, more so. But then she was anything but workmanlike once they got down to it. She didn't hesitate to request, explain, insist. She was quite unlike the repressed Englishwomen he had known, whose lovemaking was blind and sudden. And she was good about getting to know his specifics too. All in all, in bed it was good in a way that was not lavish and extravagant, likely to be soon exhausted, but honest and candid. Mortimer had never enjoyed a relationship so much, even in the earliest days.

Gratitude at her having elected to come with him welled up again and again.

"I love doing this with you," he said. "Of course I always like it but this is different. I could go on and on. It almost doesn't feel like sex."

"What does it feel like?" She was lying very still on the pillow, eyes glazed, in a moment of calm when her whole body's peace seemed to exude through her irises.

For just a second he thought of an answer among words such as "exploration," "investigation," "discovery."

He kissed her soft lips that were resting and restoring, and couldn't bring himself to pull his mouth away. Without breaking the kiss, he said, "You know what it feels like."

Above and around him the room filled with thick darkness. They lay still, mouth to mouth, forehead to forehead.

At other moments—tidying up their blankets, straightening the sheets while she was in the shower—he felt sick, as if truly ill and suffering. His midriff almost hurt, so sharp was the talon sunk in it. At any time—as he brushed out a hair from their undersheet, as he poured her a glass of mineral water from the bottle beside the bed—that claw could give a tug, or even just a tweak, and release a spasm of yearning.

He and Celeste talked a lot those first days, yet when he looked back on it later, it was as if all their lovers' talk had just been background music, the sound track to unfolding love, and they had hardly talked at all. So many intimacies exchanged, yet they were strangely forgettable, as if every precious word of self-revelation was just a crayon stroke in a brass rubbing, its purpose being to reveal a truer image beneath the words; which in some sense he already knew. Those days passed in a dream, or as if he were on drugs, caught in a process over which he had no control, and to that extent were perhaps nowhere near as self-revelatory as they seemed. Yet in the few short weeks they had together, he gained a sense of who she was, and of who he himself was, that he carried with him the rest of his life.

7

There was a knock on the door. A voice called, "*Venez, monsieur, venez. Téléphone.*" Mortimer stepped into his shoes.

A telephone receiver lay on the reception counter in the lobby. "*Oui?*"

It was Taillot. Kepple must have told him where Mortimer was.

"You can't go south," Taillot said. "It's out of the question."

Mortimer waited for more. None came. So he asked: "*Pourquoi?*"

"It would be suicide."

He waited again. "Is that a threat? I assume it isn't."

"Don't be a fool. Of course not. It's out of control down there."

What did he mean by "it"? He clearly hoped Mortimer would accept it as "the situation." Why then had Mortimer seen an expedition of backpacking students cheerfully trundling off in their Unimog the previous day, on their way to the Hoggar Hills near Tamanrasset, in the deep south? Why had two German trainee doctors gurgled out of the hotel yard that very morning in their VW van, heading south? Was Taillot trying to scare him off the story? If so, why? Somehow he felt it might be a good sign.

An ambiguous answer was the answer. He said: "I'm always careful. Thank you."

"There's also the sandstorms," Taillot went on. "It's the season for them, you know, the worst time to be in the desert."

"Of course," he muttered. "Thanks again."

Taillot's information-giving back in Algiers must have

been far from disingenuous. Whoever had been telling Taillot what to feed the press had perhaps changed their mind. But who was it?

He told Celeste about the sandstorm part of the conversation, and was about to mention the rest of it, but something made him hold back.

The fat man had decided it would take him only two hours to drive Mortimer and Celeste to El Menia, the next town to the south, just as he had promised, come what may, no matter if conditions made it impossible, if landslides had blocked the road, or if, as was the case, a savage khamsin was blowing. It was the darkest storm Mortimer had ever seen, and blew up just as they left Touggourt: first a thunderous darkness visible through the windscreen ahead, then a roaring black wind that enveloped the Peugeot.

They had met the fat man in a chicken restaurant, one of many cafés along the main street. He owned this particular one, as he had rapidly informed them in fluent, accented French. He wore slacks and a shirt open to the navel, and picked at a plate of greasy chicken wings as he asked them questions. Where were they going? What were they doing? He'd take them to El Menia next day. Yes, he was going there himself. And when they arrived they could stay with his friend Ben Youssef, who owned the largest store in El Menia. He wiped his hands on a towel.

For the excursion the fat man had looked up his favourite concubine, a chubby girl with problem skin inexpertly disguised with pancake makeup. She twisted round in the Peugeot's front seat, beaming at the foreigners, trying to engage them in conversation, heedless that her pasha was screaming down a dirt track at 120 kilometres per hour straight into a blanket of driving fog. Except it was worse than fog, it was like thick smoke, and poured across the road, sending rivulets of dust sifting over the tarmac. Mortimer couldn't see how the man could make out the way ahead at all. Every so often he would jab the brakes, swerve, then accelerate again. Several times he had to really slam the brakes, and a pair of red lights would appear inches from the front bumper. Once, when the man stopped to pee and he stepped away from the car, he was instantly lost to view. Mortimer was surprised he could even find his way back to his door.

"Who is this maniac?" Celeste wanted to know. "Tell him to slow down. *Dieu*."

Mortimer tried, but the man only grinned back at him, resting a hand on his girlfriend's thigh, and offered some pleasantry that elicited gales of laughter from her, after which he tipped back his head and let out a long, delighted sigh.

Worse was to come. It turned out that the friend who owned the largest store in El Menia was actually an uncle, though he looked the same age, and he too had a concubine. They arrived around one o'clock, by which time the khamsin had blown itself out, leaving behind a day of consummate drabness. The red town brooded beneath a heavy sky of thick, dark cloud, dark such as presaged a thunderstorm, though there was little hope of that. A market was going on. It was the bleakest market Mortimer had ever seen: a few wrinkled tomatoes and limp white radishes. One trader had a sack of rice, half empty, the neck rolled down. Someone else was selling withered coriander. Mortimer made a halfhearted attempt to get away, find a hotel, or a lift on farther south, but the day was too depressing, he couldn't muster the necessary persistence. Both Ben Youssef and his nephew the driver would have none

of it. It was to be lunch with them, then the night. The following morning they would set up Mortimer and Celeste with a
driver for Tamanrasset, their proper goal, still three long days
away.

They ate lunch in a concrete room on a straw mat amid
piles of boxes and crates. One wall was stacked high with
large cans without labels. Mortimer wondered what they contained. Oil? Fruit? Meat? It was evidently a storeroom, but
among all the stock, space had been cleared for cushions and
rugs, and for the low table at which they sat. A local boy
brought in a basket of dates. The two merchants reclined on
their elbows, reaching out for the fruit. Then beers came (a
bad sign here, Mortimer thought, after his pure days in the
mountains: if they broke the alcohol precept, who knew what
others might follow), then dishes of stewed vegetables, fricas-
seed mutton, couscous, olives, fried potatoes. It was a spread.
The concubines were thrilled, and fell upon the food vigorously. Which galvanised their men into sitting up, stuffing
their thick thighs into cross-legged positions, and commencing to gorge too. It was a lively scene: greasy fingers, greasy
cheeks, and much slurping and belching. At first Mortimer
was slightly appalled, and yearned to be alone with Celeste. In
a way, he hated even to expose their love to the scene before
them; or perhaps to be reminded that other kinds of love
existed. The gluttony was so flagrant. But this was mid-desert,
the land of paucity: no wonder they would fall on a feast.
There was something almost biblical about it, the merchants
feasting like Old Testament kings in a land of nomads, dancing girls at their sides.

And Celeste didn't seem to mind; she ate and drank
gratefully.

"So what brings you to the desert?" asked Ben Youssef, wiping his face with a towel.

Mortimer hesitated. It didn't seem right to arrive in a town and announce that he was a journalist. Before he knew it he might end up at the police station being asked to show his credentials and explain his presence. Algeria was nominally a free country, but muzzled by religion on the one hand and socialism on the other. Foreign journalists would hardly be regular visitors down here. He shrugged and said, "Tourism." The word sounded unconvincing even to his own ears.

Youssef leaned to one side and brushed the opposite knee, smoothing his robe. "Your friend has nice cameras. Must be worth a lot of money." He eyed Celeste appraisingly.

"She likes to take photographs," Mortimer said.

Celeste frowned at him.

The man hadn't shaved in a while. His cheeks were smooth and round, but speckled with sparse little bristles. He asked, "What is your particular interest? The ancient sites of the desert?"

Mortimer nodded. He knew there were rock carvings in the hills near Tamanrasset which tourists visited. He added, "And the Tuareg, of course."

He felt uneasy. He would much prefer to have been open. Ben Youssef was a fine example of the Arab merchant, well fed, legs almost too chubby to cross, living amid his multifarious stock. He was a proper man of the world. Mortimer imagined he might strike up an easy rapport with a man like that, who would know the value of publicity.

Youssef said something to his nephew, and both men laughed. Then, addressing one of his knees, he announced: "But if you're interested in the Tuareg, you should go to

Timimoun. Perhaps you'll be able to tell us what the Tuareg are doing there. They don't belong round here, as you know."

"Timimoun?"

"Two hundred kilometres west of here. But surely you have a map?"

In fact, he didn't have a map. Within Algeria there were no maps of Algeria, except for the featureless colour mosaics on schoolroom walls.

"Of course," Mortimer said: anything not to arouse suspicion. "But I don't understand, are Tuareg settling in Timimoun?"

"Tuareg settle nowhere. They are gathering there, so one hears. Or near there. They don't like to come into a town. Anyway." Ben Youssef clapped, like some old sheikh. "Time for cognac."

It crossed Mortimer's mind that this might be a lead worth pursuing, but when the story about the Tuareg, if there was one, was anyway so amorphous, and when the heart of Tuareg territory was unquestionably Tamanrasset, right in the middle of the desert, still three days away, and when moreover travel in these parts was hardly easy—either finding a lift, or the state of the pistes, could potentially turn a twenty-mile journey into a matter of many hours—the idea of going to Timimoun registered only a flicker of a possibility in his mind. They'd do better to sit tight, let these two local bigwigs show off to them some more, then get sent on their way south with, hopefully, a reliable driver. At least this was a country where if a man could, he looked after a stranger. The local hospitality seemed so natural, in fact, that it struck Mortimer as odd that in the West such an ancient human practice, celebrated by Homer, long-established by biblical times, should have been so thoroughly lost.

As it turned out, chance was on their side. Just as the boy arrived to answer Ben Youssef's clap for the brandy, there came a rapping on another door. It opened to reveal a young man with his head wrapped in a scarf. He was one of Ben Youssef's shop assistants, and needed a German speaker to interpret for him. He apparently knew his boss was entertaining foreigners, and had come to see if one of them could help. Mortimer offered, even though he had only a smattering of German, and was led down a dark corridor into another storeroom, and from the far end of that into the back of a shop. The two German medics he'd seen in Touggourt were standing at the counter.

"We are trying to buy two jerrycans," they told him. "We arc thinking better to have more water and gasoline."

"*Jerry*," Mortimer explained to the shop assistant. "*Deux*." And to the Germans: "No chance of a lift out of here, I suppose? Two people, two bags? Well, three bags." The third being Celeste's camera bag.

Then it was a matter of setting the refrain going and sticking to it: "We are leaving with our friends. We have found our friends. *Nous partons avec nos amis*."

As Mortimer had anticipated, the two merchants were none too happy about losing their afternoon's entertainment. "But you must let us organise everything," they insisted. At least they still had their concubines to amuse them.

Then once Mortimer and Celeste had settled themselves and their bags in the VW van, the Germans decided it was too late in the day to set off. Instead, they parked up in the town's desolate "*Camping*," an empty lot enclosed by a red perimeter wall, that must have been installed back in the sixties, when the great southern highway was built, the highway that already, a decade on, was so potholed and heat-shattered that traffic preferred to meander along the old pistes that still ran beside it.

The Germans went off for a walk round town, leaving Mortimer and Celeste alone in the van.

They shut the orange curtains around the windows and folded down the benches to make up the small double bed, then spread out two thick blankets. All at once in the red-hued interior it was as if they were once again quite alone, and the world had retreated.

As they lay together she told him more about her family. When she was sixteen, her father had taught her to sail at their holiday home north of Bordeaux. She'd had her own dinghy for scuttling around the harbour. Her father was dead now. Her mother, now in her sixties, lived in Pau, in the foothills of the Pyrenees, kept busy by her younger sister, who though only twenty-seven already had four children. She was married to a baker who owned three *boulangeries* in the area. "They both drive new Citroëns." She shrugged and smiled. "And what about you?"

"Tell me more," he said. "Your brother, your uncles and aunts, grandparents, nephews, nieces."

She was pleased, enjoying herself, and lay propped on an elbow as she went through her family album. He found it fascinating to hear about them, as if he was being introduced to the cast of a film he knew he was about to enjoy.

Her younger brother was troubled. He was bright, but had dropped out of the Sorbonne and now no one was sure what he was doing in Paris.

She closed her eyes and kissed him. Mortimer told her he had never expected to have an experience like this.

"I expected it," she said. "But it never exactly happened so I stopped expecting it."

Then she frowned and rolled off him. "Maybe this is the Eden from which one must be thrown out."

He didn't know what to say. He felt he wouldn't mind even if it turned out to be true, as long as she was with him.

She asked about Saskia.

When he thought about Saskia now, there seemed nothing fearful or doom-laden about the two and a half years he'd been with her, nor even about the wrench of breaking it off. He no longer felt guilty, it already seemed part of his history that could not have happened differently.

Celeste was interested in her: how had they met, where had they lived, where did she work, what was she like.

"She's serious," he said.

"Like you too," Celeste said with a smile. "You're a serious man."

"Am I?"

She screwed up her face in a smile. "I like that."

He thought for a moment. "Saskia's a moral person. I mean, she was more political than me. I remember once telling her she was too moral for me. And she said: 'I'm too moral for you? You ought to think about that.'"

At the time he'd experienced a plunge of guilt. But now he thought that even if Saskia had been right to upbraid him, still there had been no cause for alarm. All things were possible. If he needed to adjust his attitudes, he could do that.

"I was engaged once," Celeste told him. "Sort of. We never actually told anyone."

"Who was he?"

"A psychiatrist. He worked at the hospital."

"What happened?"

"I wasn't ready to be tied down."

"Was that all?"

An answer caught in her throat. Then she said, "It's always more complicated. The timing was wrong. Some things were good, and right, but it wasn't going to work then, and it didn't. I didn't want it as much as I thought. You have to really *want* it. You know?"

Mortimer was silent. "What was he called?"

"What does it matter?" she said. Then thought better of it, and said, "Eric," pronouncing it the French way, and shrugged. "*Eric*," she repeated with a sigh.

It was different in different languages: *je t'aime* produced a flurry of feeling like an adolescent crush. *I love you* released a serious, grown-up sensation, full of importance. *Ich liebe dich* was exciting, with its wartime associations, the sense of being engaged with an alien power. *Ya tebya lyublyu* with its comic bundle of labials could be counted on to raise a laugh, and more often than not led to sex. But then in the throes of lovemaking, if they said it again it was deadly serious, and changed the way you felt about death. As she spread her knees under his arms, and he laid his forearms along the inside of her calves and closed his hands around the chamoislike soles of her feet, he would say it once more, only this time he would no longer be sure which was his own language.

Celeste and Mortimer wandered around a development on the edge of the town, a broad new avenue of red cement houses without roofs or windows, with curbs for imaginary pavements and rows of bare poles that would one day be streetlamps. It was a brand new ghost town. Yet already it looked down-at-heel, tatty, neglected. Other than one sheet of dusty plastic crackling in the breeze there were none of the usual signs of an active building site, no parked diggers or cement mixers, no wheelbarrows or shovels even, no stacks of bricks and blocks. It was as if the scheme had run out of money, or of will. Whorls of red dust skittered over the empty road.

This must all have been part of the government's Saharan initiative. Mortimer had heard that they had started building new towns along the southern highway. Algeria had for a long time been looking for a way to yoke the Sahara into its economy. Seismologists had been working to establish the most viable mines, natural gas they had already found, and a plan had been drawn up for a pipeline that would run north to the coastal city of Oran. There was a rumour of oil reserves. They had apparently decided they must go ahead regardless, and take advantage of the space the desert offered. New towns, new roads, persuasive incentives for people to move: if they could only get a critical mass of population down into the desert, they'd start reaping the rewards. The Sahara was their Wyoming, their territory west of the Mississippi: it was just a matter of inducing the prospectors, the entrepreneurs and homesteaders to make the leap.

It was strange to see a boy come down the empty street on a donkey, under the bare posts. But quickly it was the boy on the donkey who seemed ordinary, and the hollow shells of the cement houses extraordinary.

Mortimer and Celeste passed an uncomfortable night curled up in the camper van.

Mortimer loved it. This was how he loved life: an endless relay of new people, himself the baton passed from hand to hand. It seemed the ideal way to live.

·

❖

When Mortimer awoke the next morning he could hear a discussion in German going on outside. He parted the mini-van's thin curtains. A smoky desert dawn, the hiss of a camping stove. Mortimer sat up and rubbed his face, pushed the blanket off his legs reluctantly: he had grown cold in the night. The door of the van whined as he slid it back on its runners.

The Germans had spent the night in their large orange tent. They were standing now in sandals looking away towards the red wall of the campsite. They finally concluded their discussions and delivered the bombshell. It was a small bombshell: after all, they were not going south but west. They had decided to visit a clinic staffed by some Egyptian doctors they'd met at a conference the year before.

"Where exactly?" Mortimer asked.

"Timimoun."

Theirs was the only vehicle in the campsite. Mortimer bowed to fate. He climbed back into the van with the news.

Celeste was lying on her side propped on an arm. She brushed a lock from her face. "I heard." She frowned. She had a way of frowning before summoning something from deep within. What she summoned now was optimism. She said: "But that's great. We can go to Timimoun."

She opened her school map of the country over her legs. He settled beside her. Her body was warm. He could feel that she was happy. He was happy too: to be free and traveling, with a potentially terrific story ahead of him to which he need not hurry, there being no one else likely to be on its trail—the world cared little about the Sahara at the best of times—to be in this easy mobile state with a woman it suited equally well seemed a triumph, a fulfilment.

"What's so good about that?" he asked.

"It's perfect," she said. "We can check out these Tuareg who are supposedly gathering at Timimoun. Why not? And there are ksars around there, big mud forts. Library wanted me to get some pictures of them."

What it meant, in a nutshell, was that instead of going where Mortimer needed to go, the Germans were going where Celeste wanted to go. It was true, undeniably, that she could work in many places. You never knew where the classic shot might be taken. But she had pencilled Timimoun into her itinerary, apparently. And Mortimer felt good about it, a warmth kindled in his midriff: he could wish good for her without it costing him a thing. Quite the reverse, it gave him something in return.

Five straight hours down a decent track, a late instalment of the Saharan investment, and they were at Timimoun. Mortimer would never have guessed then that they were heading to the heart of the story.

8

The Egyptian doctors in Timimoun were not happy men. When they had signed up for their eighteen-month stints down here, they hadn't realised that the sizeable salaries they would receive in return for bringing the light of modern medicine into the darkest, blindingest Sahara would be paid in Algerian dinars, a nonexchangeable currency. They would leave the country with nothing. And there was nothing to spend their dinars on in Timimoun.

They represented a last ghost of a link to the modern world. There were five of them, and they lived in two new houses, the bleakest Mortimer had yet seen. Like the doctors themselves, the houses were part of the Saharan initiative. The government had constructed a compound of concrete homes outside Timimoun's old town walls, with plumbing, electricity, gas cookers, and baths. But the town seldom had electricity, its water often failed to arrive for days, and it had never had gas, so whoever lived in these houses did so in squalor far beneath the humblest Saharan home. So far only the Egyptians' two houses were occupied. The Germans were put up in one, Mortimer and Celeste in the other. The kitchen was impenetrably clogged with filthy pans. The doctors had given up going into it, preferring to cook on a fire outside. The bathroom stank. In the bathtub a large blue barrel stood under the tap, half filled with brown water. The tap was left permanently on: they had to catch the water whenever it happened to arrive.

The doctors gratefully changed money with Mortimer at an inflated rate, which neither side was supposed to do. Celeste felt sorry for them, in spite of the dark, lascivious glances they couldn't help casting her way, and changed more money than she would ever be able to get rid of.

One of them, a Copt called Mansour, was content. He dressed in a white kaftan and had a bushy moustache in his otherwise clean-shaven, shiny, bronze face. He might have been fifty, was a good size, well fed, and moved in a sleek and graceful manner.

"It's a special experience," Mansour told Mortimer, "to live in the heart of the largest desert."

He couldn't understand why his colleagues refused to resign themselves to it. He went for walks beside the town's red walls in the evening, when the heat was bearable, and played a lot of chess, gathering up his white robe and settling on a cushion with a sigh of satisfaction before a fresh board. He was good at it. Mortimer played several games with him and lost them all.

The desert light was sharp and clear around Timimoun. You'd see the sheet of land glinting away to distant hills, tinged blue in the morning, mauve and suave in the evening. The hills were smooth as porcelain on the skyline. Why did it always seem a time of healing just to be in a desert? Mortimer wondered. What was it in one that seemed to recover, find its feet again? He could already feel the desert working its magic on him.

Each time Mortimer attempted to get inside the walls of the old town, he was conducted to the same bare mud room with a hole in its roof, where he was left alone until sooner or later a man could be found to sit with the guest. There'd be a glass of tea, a munch of dates, and a lot of silence; then he'd be dismissed, escorted back to the gates. There was no question of a guided tour. The town was in the middle of some protracted festivity that forbade visitors.

The town gate itself consisted of a Moorish arch thirty feet tall built into the mud walls, and within it two tall wooden doors, each made of a patchwork of boards, elaborately carved and patterned, stained near-black by centuries of sun and dust. Some were set with designs of iron studs. It was as if wood had been made to resemble a local patchwork of rugs.

At night drums played behind the old walls. Mortimer longed to know why, to witness whatever ceremony was in progress, but it was Celeste who got to see it. The event was women-only, some rite of passage for the town nubiles. She came back late one night with her eyes glazed with excitement and her hair done up in a network of plaits. The women had made her up with henna and oil that made her face glisten, then taught her their hip-rolling dance. She couldn't believe how sexual the dance was. "Those women have a fine old time behind closed doors," she said. They'd let her take photographs too.

Mortimer felt pleased. Her evening inside the town gates underlined that this trip was good for her too. If anything, there was a pique that she had successfully penetrated the old town, and he hadn't. Except that feeling quickly transmuted into a satisfaction on her behalf, as if anything she gained was also a gain for him.

They spent three days here nominally achieving nothing; yet Mortimer didn't mind. He was a free agent, just as he had always wanted. Hiatuses were inevitable. They were good, they allowed a little mental digestion to take place. They had a barometric value. He told himself that when once more he ventured in pursuit of the elusive quarry he would have an extra layer of awareness.

When the drums stopped late at night Mortimer could hear camels bellowing and rumbling. Once he saw a Tuareg, unmistakably, a tall man in black wearing a high black headpiece, wandering off to the west on a camel with two asses in his wake.

Mansour confirmed that now and then Tuareg did pass through, and there had been a number in the town lately. But they had all headed into the sands to the west, probably to trade in the chain of oases a few hours' walk away. Mortimer and Celeste decided that since they were here, they would go at least to the nearest of these oases, where Celeste could photograph one of the mud forts: all the villages in the region had ksars. And they might possibly find some Tuareg to interview too.

Mansour introduced them to an ancient, wiry guide called Brahim, and arranged the first leg of their journey: four hours to the oasis of Tessalit.

On their last evening Mansour cooked them a chickpea stew, and they drank numerous small pots of tea.

"The desert is good for a man because there he meets God face to face," Mansour averred. "God loves the desert. It is the one place he left empty, just for himself. But you must be careful. Go nowhere without the guide. Even a village one hour away, it is easy to miss. And if you miss it—" He shrugged, opened his palms.

There was presumably always the consolation that even if one did lose one's way, one would already be in the arms of God, the desert being his private garden.

There was a kind of half avenue along the town wall, one single row of royal palms, splendidly tall, their crowns tossing like flags in the breeze, their trunks painted white to head height, which gave them a tame, French aspect. Mortimer and Celeste had a strange moment along this avenue the night before they left.

A crescent moon was up: it was not long after sunset. By now Mortimer felt the desert truly inside him: a powdery taste to his saliva, a wonderful chalky feeling in his limbs.

Lately he had been asking himself why he always exaggerated things. Love, for example: either it was the one terminal love for which he had been made and destined since birth, or else, as with Saskia, a thorough and deplorable compromise. Why couldn't it be a simple matter of caring and enjoyment?

Under those half-painted, half-moonlit palms, with the desert silence stretching off into ineffability, he had felt compelled to force the issue with Celeste. He had thought he wanted to be sure it really was the same for her, that she also had never felt like this before, and so on; but perhaps he had merely been trying to pass the load onto her: she could carry the great love for a while.

Just then he'd have been better off not asking. Before asking, it was clear she felt as he did. After, less so. Perhaps she indeed felt that this might be the love of her life, until that very moment of weakness, when he tried to check. At which point, a faint question mark was pencilled in the margin by his name. That was how he would think of it much later, though at the time he soon brushed the thought aside: it was a mistake to ponder things too deeply.

He had expected her to answer his question with a smile, a hug, a kiss. Instead, she kept staring out over the flat plain, and said: "What matters, all that matters, is deciding what you want. That is everything."

9

They set out before dawn. Brahim, the guide, was waiting by the town gates with a ruffled little donkey. They walked along the road awhile in the morning chill. Mortimer was pleased when they branched off onto a white path through rubble—perhaps a former house, or midden—and it led them into sunlight. Immediately the warmth felt good on his legs, the coldest part of him. The very first rays of the sun were peering over the lip of the flat earth.

The plain was a sheet of perfectly smooth plaster. Traces of salt showed here and there as white blemishes, and occasional coruscations of diminutive rubble had been glazed into the surface. The ground might once have been mud, Mortimer thought, perhaps part of the ocean bed the Sahara had been. It was a marvellous pavement for walking on. It was remarkable how natural things could look so man-made. At that hour, with the sun just up and warming the traveler's night-chilled limbs, it was a wonderful thing to be walking on such a surface.

It wasn't long before Mortimer had removed his sweater and draped it over his shoulders. Then that seemed too warm and he tied it round his waist. He was glad he had a hat. Then it began to be seriously hot. He undid the buttons of his shirt, reluctant to take it off in case his arms burned.

Celeste's face shone, with sweat, with heat, with the brightness of the day, and with what looked like happy surprise. But actually she wasn't happy. She hadn't slept well and her period had arrived in the night. There was some relief it had arrived at all, but mostly it was despicably inconvenient, as she said. How was she to go about dealing with it mid-march?

Early in the hike Mortimer said, thinking aloud: "I've never been on a job that felt so good. The Amazon Indians have one word that means both work and play. This is it." He turned to grin at her. That was when she told him about the sanitary problem.

After a moment, she said, "You know, I've been doing photojournalism for nine years already. One starts thinking about not becoming a lonely, leathery woman who is at home nowhere."

"Or at home everywhere. That's the best, surely."

"No. It's more or less the same anyway."

"What about the Tuareg? They live nowhere."

"They know where they belong. They have somewhere they belong. We all do."

He fell silent, listened to their footfalls on the smooth clay, a pleasant light sound in the warmth of dawn and the fresh new light. He couldn't quite believe what she was saying, that she really thought it. Maybe one day it would be right to settle. But when there was the whole world waiting?

They were halfway across the plain before Mortimer realised the far hills he had been seeing from Timimoun were not hills at all, but sand dunes. From a distance they had taken on the usual colours of hills—brown, blue, even green—but now, a mile or so off, they were a uniform orange. They formed part of the world's biggest ocean of sand, the Grand Erg, every schoolboy's vision of the desert, Saint-Exupéry's trial by fire, Père Foucauld's house of God, his burning bush. This was where they were going.

They hadn't even reached the sand when it became clear that Brahim was getting on Celeste's nerves. His donkey carried two large sacks, one of onions, one of oranges, on top of which sat Mortimer's and her bags. A rope was looped over the animal's rump, and Brahim decided that Celeste should hold it. She didn't want to. Brahim was insistent. Again and again he took her hand and placed it on the rope, only to have her let go a few steps later.

"Why does he want me to hold this stupid strap?" she eventually blurted out. Then: "*Non!*" directed at Brahim.

Part of the problem was their lack of Arabic, Brahim's of

French. But also there was something undeniably chattel-like about the position he wanted Celeste to adopt. Mortimer could understand her reluctance to be attached physically to their little caravan, quite apart from its interfering with her stride. Mortimer could imagine that had he himself not been there, Brahim would have got out a rope and tied her to the animal. Mortimer shrugged at Brahim noncommittally, meaning either *Ah well, what can you do?* or else *What is the purpose of your desire to have her hold on?* He felt he ought to intervene before any serious ill feeling developed. This wiry old man would soon be their only lifeline.

By way of reply Brahim made a fist and jabbed it forwards. Mortimer took it to mean that she wasn't walking fast enough. He hadn't noticed, nor could he imagine how Brahim had, for they hadn't been walking long, and Celeste hadn't been falling behind. But Brahim turned out to have been prophetic.

The dunes never seemed to get any closer.

By the time they arrived at the foot of the first slope, Mortimer had more or less forgotten that the dunes were their initial goal. He was just a man walking across a plain under the sun, his mind blank. Two hours had passed. Mortimer was hot now, though not sweaty. It was supposed to take four hours in all to the village of Tessalit, and he tried to ask Brahim if it was two hours more from here. *"Encore deux heures?"* he said a few times, holding up two fingers.

Brahim cracked a smile and said something in Arabic. His face was not so much lined as folded into deep wrinkles that became even deeper when he smiled. Then he said, *"Quat' heures."* The same four-hour story. It was disconcerting. It was possible he had understood Mortimer's question, and they still had four hours to go. People might consider the four-hour trek to begin once you reached the dunes, the plain being just a preamble.

Celeste was having a hard time now. *"Excusez-moi,"* she said, stumbling up the sand and disappearing over the nearest brow.

It was very quiet: just a rustling from where Celeste had gone. The donkey flicked its ears. Mortimer had a vague idea that he should try and appreciate the stillness, the silence, the expanse, but one couldn't do something like that while walking in the desert: it was too hot, the sun was too strong. It beat down on one's head, giving no respite for contemplation. The important thing was to keep moving, to get across.

There was something drab about the sand. There it stood in an enormous heap. A few trails of dust led off onto the pan of the plain. It was like a building site: the cement beneath one's feet, the heap of sand waiting to find a use.

Brahim kept looking up the dune Celeste had climbed. Mortimer assumed it was a reflex of prurience, until he started muttering, *"Yalah, yalah,"* under his breath: Let's go.

The rustling stopped. Silence. Then Celeste appeared at the top of the slope, and waded down towards them.

Brahim gave up on his bid to have her hold on to the donkey. They settled on a compromise: she agreed to allow the donkey to carry her camera bag, but only once it had been tied on to her satisfaction.

They had brought six litres of Sidi Ali, surely enough water for a four-hour walk. But four litres were already gone.

Brahim went barefoot. Mortimer could see why. It was hard enough wading up a sand dune, but doing it in a pair of heavy boots was gruelling. Brahim walked lightly, he seemed to skip over the sand, hardly sinking in. That was clearly the way to do it, but Mortimer didn't see how one could in a pair of boots. After they had scaled the second dune he took his boots off. Which was fine on the shady side of a dune, but alarming on the sunny, until he learned to accept the fierce tingle of the scalding sand. It wasn't exactly pain, and it made one walk faster, energised the limbs.

At the fourth dune things began to change. This one was three or four hundred feet tall, a monster. Brahim led them up diagonally, doubtless a good idea, but Mortimer found himself longing for just one level pace. It went on too long, having to plod with the right leg always plunging down, throwing the stride off kilter. Celeste was conspicuously lagging by the time they reached the crest. She paused when she was still thirty yards below them: a few minutes' worth of slogging. She stopped because they stopped.

The scene that greeted Mortimer from that first high ridge was of hundreds of still more enormous dunes folding away into the distance, a mountain range of sand. But the biggest surprise was when he looked back: the plain of Timimoun had vanished. All he could see was dunes, in every direction. *"Mais où est Timimoun?"* he asked.

Brahim looked up from feeding the donkey an orange.

"Timimoun?" Mortimer repeated.

Brahim pointed out a short dark line just showing between the brows of two dunes. What was it? The top of the town wall? Part of the plain?

Brahim cut another orange and gave half to Mortimer. He gestured towards Celeste with the other half. But she wasn't moving. She had sat down. Brahim called out. She was too tired even to look up. Reluctantly, Mortimer stumbled down towards her.

She had her head in her hands. She shook her head when he came close. "I'm all right," she said. "Just a bit dizzy. *C'est rien*. It'll pass."

Brahim called down again, gesturing that Mortimer should get her to her feet. He put a hand under her shoulder. "He thinks you should stand up."

She shook her head again, but eventually accepted the need to carry on, and stumbled up the slope.

Brahim gave Celeste the half orange. She didn't want it. He insisted, making a mime of eating. She obliged, frowning. The frown went away at the first bite. Juice ran over her fingers, down her chin. Mortimer felt pleased that she was now enjoying the same experience he had a moment ago. He had never known an orange to taste so good. She turned the skin inside out and gnawed it, then Brahim took it off her and fed it to the donkey.

A fly buzzed into Mortimer's hair. He brushed it away reflexively, then thought: Where did that fly come from? Either it somehow managed to live amid these piles of sand, or it came along for the ride with the donkey. In which case it had better not lose them. He imagined it buzzing over the dunes in search of its human ferry across the emptiness. It was the only living thing they encountered that day.

Brahim rearranged the donkey's load, and created a two-foot end of rope extending from beneath the pack. He insisted that Celeste hold it, and more than hold. He wound it round her wrist and put the end in her palm, so as she gripped it, it gripped her.

As he stood waiting for Brahim to fasten Celeste to the beast Mortimer was overcome by a wave not of fatigue but sleepiness. His body was primed and pumped for exertion, yet he could have nodded off standing up. It was disconcerting.

Twice Celeste untied herself and Brahim did her up again. Mortimer didn't try to intervene.

After yearning to stop, to rest, for the walk to be over, Mortimer fell into a kind of trance. There was nothing for it but to forget the painful necessity of putting one foot in front of the other, one step always higher or lower than the next, always slipping in the sand, and just keep doing it, until the mind lost all but the remotest awareness of what the body was doing. Up, down, up, down, shush-shush. The donkey was good to have along, not only because it carried things, but as a pace-setter. You couldn't get it to go slower or faster, and you stopped it at your peril. After the long halt for oranges Brahim had quite a time slapping and exhorting it to set off again. And then it was exemplary. It simply bowed its head and kept going. It was clear one must do the same, and the beast showed how.

Except the mind didn't exactly become unaware of the body. In a way it grew more aware. It was as if Mortimer slipped through the desire to stop, and arrived in a land where all things were clearer and more illuminated, but there was no desire here, one accepted everything as it was.

Celeste was silent. When Mortimer looked at her she seemed to have given up all will. Her right arm extended towards the animal's rump, and she shuffled along behind it, oblivious. Mortimer wondered if she too was learning from the donkey. Not to think, not to notice, just to keep on with no thought for where one was going.

The soles of Mortimer's feet began to itch. Every step became a way of scratching them. It felt good to sink one's feet grindingly into the grains. He wondered if perhaps he ought to stop and investigate, but he didn't want to risk either breaking his semitrance or finding that all was not well with his feet.

He could imagine the skin utterly dried out, cracking under the pressure of the dry particles.

The deep troughs between the dunes became gulfs of darkness. It was odd that they should be so dark. As the sun climbed it ought to have illuminated them more. Mortimer looked for the sun. It wasn't where it ought to have been: not high overhead but quite low. Its light was rich, orange, palpable.

Celeste was now manifestly being dragged by the donkey. She stumbled along behind it, her arm outstretched. She was wearing a pair of Mortimer's shorts on her head, from beneath which her hair hung lank. Her face was pink, shining.

When she tried to drink, Brahim took the bottle away and gave her another orange. Once, they stopped high on a crest. Tremendous mountains rose ahead of them, carved by the sun into slopes and gulfs of shadow. They were a magnificent sight, a range of gold. It seemed a sight not intended for human eyes.

The sand under his feet turned to gold, and it seemed that the whole landscape was made of gold, suffused with gold light. It was like catching a glimpse of a heaven, of one of the realms notated in the margins of the Koran. Like walking a land above the earth. They had in fact been steadily climbing. Behind, Mortimer thought he could make out a hazy patch that might have been the plain of Timimoun, visible once again because they were high enough. Brahim indicated with a downward gesture that they would soon be traveling down-hill. It seemed that they communicated more easily now, as if they had broken into a world where they could recognise and understand one another. Mortimer felt like he was onstage, under the gaze of people above.

He experienced intense waves of love towards Celeste. He thought of putting an arm round her, giving her a kiss. It was unnecessary. She was there too, standing on the same orange stage. The waves of feeling detached themselves from any object. They came by themselves. Just to be standing here was a pleasure, a wonder. He was no longer afraid of having to carry on. He could stop, start, climb, descend, look around, with every movement somehow abundantly simple, as if he'd been liberated from a heavy load.

Now he couldn't think of their destination. There was no destination; it had evaporated like a mirage. There was just the walking, and the world of sand all around. There was nowhere to be but right here where they were. The gold and rust brown slopes seemed to infiltrate his body, as if he were not looking out at the world, but somehow had entered the world, or the world had entered him. Every time he recognised that their destination had been snuffed out, more waves of warm feeling washed through him. Wakefulness, which was a kind of love, burned in him like a watchfire.

The donkey snorted, blew through its lips. They all ate another orange, which tasted miraculous to Mortimer, sweet and rich, then they gave the animal the husks, which it ate noisily, not minding when one of them fell, acquiring a coating of sand: he plucked it up, ate it anyway.

It might have been in another hour or two, as the sun was getting close to the horizon, that they saw land again. First a smoky red cliff, then a long dark line among the dunes. Brahim said the line was a palm garden. Then a tremendous red fortress appeared, perched halfway up the red cliff: a castle out of fable, missable at first, so closely did its colour match the clay around it, of which it was made. It looked so old and legendary that it could only have been a ruin. Then they were on the last slope of sand, could actually see a track below, pale in the gathering dark. It crossed Mortimer's mind that he should put his boots on. But he couldn't remember where they were, and anyway night was falling, they were walking through blue air now, and already a lone palm stood ahead, and beyond it he could see a dark geometry of more palms, an orchard, a forest of trees, and a dog was barking somewhere. The donkey bellowed as it walked, its head stooped, ears folded right back, then it swivelled its ears forwards. Far away a wheezing started that worked itself into a bray and came echoing back at them. Then they were walking beside a little earthen dyke, and they were under palms now, in a dark avenue of still trees. The fronds glistened overhead. The track ran in two parallel paths, pale in the darkness, just as if vehicles used it, which plainly they couldn't do. No vehicle could cross those dunes. The dust was pleasantly packed, smooth underfoot. There was no need for boots. It would have been centuries of bare feet and hoofs that made it that way. Faint stripes lay across it: moon shadows of the palms. Once Mortimer felt a prick in his right foot but it didn't come back, and soon they were approaching the goal. Mortimer didn't know what it was at first. He thought there was a tiled patio up ahead, implausibly laid out among the trees. But the donkey recognised it, and plodded straight towards it, lowering its neck. Even when it touched its lip to the dark surface and sent a ring of light traveling over it, Mortimer still didn't immediately recognise what it was. Once he did, instead of relief he felt a strange disappointment, unease, a mild nausea.

10

Mortimer woke to find himself lying in a room of bare earth with sand for a floor. It was cool sand, fine and clean. In the roof was a square hole, and through that a sky too bright to look at. A rectangle of white sunlight lay on the floor like a rug, one corner of it folding up on to the wall. It was a marvellous room, one felt safe in it. Why didn't everyone build like this?

Someone had thrown a blanket over him, and his head rested on a cushion. He sat up and realised a fly was sitting on his nose. Another person lay nearby. At first, oddly, he thought: Saskia. Then the tousled blond hair reminded him. He put his hand on Celeste's hip, let it rest there. No response. She was fast asleep. He could feel her slow breaths.

What time must it be? His legs ached. When he attempted to stand, pain stabbed the soles of his feet. He slumped to the floor gasping. When the shock had subsided, he pulled off a sock and inspected the sole. It was an awful sight. A maze of red crevasses crisscrossed the skin, some of them quarter of an inch deep. It was ghastly to look at, though the pain had already subsided. After the deep sleep he had been in, he was too dreamy to feel anything other than curiosity: what would happen now that his feet were unwalkable? He had a few Band-Aids, a tub of Vaseline somewhere, and an old tube of Savlon knocking around in a side pocket of his bag, but they weren't up to this.

He put the sock back on, introducing it gently to the skin. The gashes didn't hurt. The material tickled, that was all. He sat back against the rough wall, relieved that at least he wouldn't be walking anywhere soon: he wouldn't be able to.

The air in the room felt thick with desert light, with peace, with sanctity. Why didn't people back home decorate their rooms like this? All you needed was earth, sand, and a rug of sunlight, half of it spread on the floor, the rest hanging on the wall. He felt he had stumbled into a sanctuary from the troubled, corrupted world, the world that did not have the heart to cross thousands of miles of desert.

Celeste's hair lay over her face. The sunlight picked out a few strands and turned them into a tangle of gold filaments. The morning sun, the quiet room made of earth, the beauty asleep with her hair just touched by the sun, her warm body wrapped in a blanket of rough black wool: a flush of feeling swept into him: they had made it. Yesterday had been an ordeal. So much so that he had even forgotten their arrival at this village, wherever it was. Then he remembered: Tessalit, first oasis out of Timimoun, in the Great Western Erg. And he vaguely recollected the first sight of the ksar, a tower of clay among the palms, which he'd taken to be some outcrop of rock until he saw the dark doorway at the foot of it. That must be where they were now, somewhere deep inside it.

He began to feel wonderfully clearheaded, and rummaged in his bag for his notebook. When he stood up again his legs trembled and threatened to crumple, and he quickly settled on the cool sand floor.

Tessalit

What the hell am I doing? I love this. A whisker of purpose, and otherwise I'm tossing myself on the waves. Waves of sand, presumably. I mean, there's going to be a story somewhere, for sure, but in a little oasis in the middle of nowhere? On the other hand, we are digressively on our way south. In other words, towards:

1. *Tamanrasset, where I'll try and find Señor El Kebir, the Mr. Big, the Tuareg leader. Assuming there is one, and I can get myself pointed to him.* 2. *The Malian border villages, where the drought is said to be worst: the edge of the Sahel. Once the Sahel, now just more Sahara. Two surefire stories. (What the hell does Sahara mean anyway?) But that can all wait. For now it's too much just to be here in this medieval keep made of mud in the middle of the desert. With Celeste.*

He clipped his pen in the breast pocket of his shirt and steered himself across the floor on his knees. What a good floor sand made: you could lie or sit with equal comfort, and it even smelled good.

He planted a long kiss on Celeste's cheek. She drew in a slow breath, stretched an arm, then hummed, *"C'est bien, c'est bien."* A shudder ran through her and she fell asleep again.

His belly tightened. This was the woman for him: the idea arrived as a discovered certainty. It seemed obvious that all along he had been destined to end up with a gutsy Continental photographer from the Pyrenees, with golden skin and a couple of SLRs and her own agenda, from which nothing would deflect her, certainly not him. This was a real relationship, not the dark tomb in which most couples agreed to bury themselves. I'll go in if you go in, oh all right then, now let's close the door and wait till we die. What kind of life was that? The biggest notions in life were the biggest lies. To shut yourself up with the same person in some half-asleep life: it was how most people ended up wasting their precious days. Love was the biggest device known to mankind to speed the passage of decades, to rip the heart out of a life.

But this was something else: love like gasoline, that fuelled you in your own life, didn't demand you make impossible choices.

But he did need to get to where the action was, and before too long. A couple of days out here, she taking her snaps, then back on the road to Tamanrasset, to the Tuareg resistance. It wouldn't do to miss out on anything when he was so close. But he had a strange confidence that nothing would happen until he got there, as if he himself might be the catalyst the situation awaited. Whatever the situation was; if only he knew more.

Mortimer touched Celeste's hip and again she shuddered alarmingly. It was as if her body sensed the touch but didn't recognise him, and jolted in shock. Then she lay still, breathing silently. He felt her side rise, fill, then fall. At least she was warm to the touch. Decidedly warm, in fact. He put his hand on her forehead, scooping up the hair that lay over it. It was like a branding iron. He could hardly believe a human head could get so hot. He pulled the blanket down to her waist. She must have been running a fever. He didn't know what to do: get some water inside her, some aspirin, dampen her face? Perhaps it was best to let her sleep. Yet he couldn't quite convince himself that those dramatic flinches, her excessive temperature, weren't just strange symptoms of sleep that would vanish upon waking.

He knelt over her and kissed her ear. The cavity was hot. She stirred again. One arm stiffened, she seemed about to stretch, but all that happened was her body gave another jolt, and a stream of vomit jumped out of her mouth. It formed a yellow pool on the sand in front of her face, then soon drained away, leaving a residue of flecks on wet sand.

At that moment the door opened. It was a small, low board

of battered wood studded with bolt heads, which might once have been part of a grander door, and whistled over the sand. A man in sky blue robes stooped into the room. He put a hand against his chest and coughed resonantly, then stood to his full height, a tall man, and said: "*Salaam aleikum.*" He dropped to the floor with his legs crossed.

Mortimer returned the greeting, then gestured at Celeste. "*Pas bon. Mal,*" he said. He pointed out the vomit on the floor, and added, "*Excusez-moi,*" then wiped her mouth with his sleeve, and went to his bag in search of something with which to mop the floor.

The man came forward and without hesitation scooped up the wet sand in his palm and left the room.

A water jar stood bedded into the sand in one corner. Mortimer had yet to drink from it. A moment ago he had lifted the lid, seen the glistening surface within, and postponed deciding if it was safe to drink. Now the only thing that mattered was to get some of it inside Celeste. But it wasn't easy. The jar was too heavy to lift, so he had to tip it over, which its round shape ought to have made easy, except that its bed in the sand held it firm. He had to use both hands. Which meant gauging where to put the cup on the floor, and he gauged wrong twice. Finally, he knelt beside Celeste with the cup half filled and attempted to raise her by the shoulders. She was heavy as a corpse, still fast asleep. Another tremor shook her. He put down the cup and brushed the hair off her cheek, wet with sweat. She twisted away and kicked, as a hoarse rattle escaped her, along with a thread of silver mucus.

Mortimer wiped it away. "It's OK, it's OK." He held the water to her lips, and it spilled over her chin. He couldn't tell if she swallowed any.

He had the idea of feeding her a pill. He had two he

thought might be relevant: aspirin and Diocalm Plus. He didn't know if she had diarrhoea, but the pack claimed it would settle an upset stomach. Hence the "Plus," he supposed.

He succeeded in getting her to swallow the two pills. Not a minute later she vomited again, a gush of clear water that darkened the sand in front of her face. On it lay the two pills, completely intact.

The tall man returned, followed by a woman bundled up in robes and veil. Only by her shiny, wrinkled hands could Mortimer tell she was an elderly woman. It occurred to him that hands played a large part in local dancing because they were the one visible part of a woman's body.

"Do you speak French?" he tried.

The man glanced at him but said nothing. The woman took no notice at all, bowing over Celeste. Then she disappeared, returning soon with a second woman. Together the two of them lifted Celeste into a sitting position, talking to her quietly. Her head lolled on to her chest. They struggled to get her to her feet. The blankets slipped off, revealing bloodstains on her trousers. Mortimer's heart jumped in alarm. When he remembered that it was her period he was dismayed for her. The women put Celeste's arms round their necks and stood up. She let out a long, low sob, almost a bellow, and they shuffled out of the room with her between them.

The situation was hopeless until Mortimer found someone who could speak a word of French.

The tall man disappeared again, but soon came back, this time with two other men in tow. They all put their hands against their chests, then offered them to Mortimer. He shook, and one by one they patted their chests again. *"Bismillah,"* they said, dropping to the floor. Mortimer did the same. A boy came in and set a basket of dates on the sand. Mortimer didn't feel hungry, but once he bit into the sweet pulp he realised with a flush that he was starving. A clay jug arrived, and a metal beaker, and they passed around what he guessed must be sheep's milk, each taking a few sips of the thick, sweet liquid with its faintly rancid smell. Then in came a wooden bowl of couscous, and a pan of red sauce, which one of the men tipped over the cereal. He fished out four spoons from somewhere in his robe and jammed them handle down in the sand. "*Bismillah*," the men declared resonantly once more, and reached for the spoons.

Mortimer soon got the hang of the procedure, which was to excavate one's own eating cavity in the couscous against the nearest side of the bowl. When these pits were well established, another basket was brought in containing a plump organ, complete with the stumps of its severed arteries. One of the men growled approval, another grinned absentmindedly, chewing as he watched the third tear the organ apart with his fingers and drop pieces of it in each eating hole.

Am I hungry enough to enjoy even this offal? wondered Mortimer. He probably had no choice anyway, if he wanted to keep on the right side of his hosts, and bit into the first chunk of the innard enthusiastically. But he wasn't hungry enough: it tasted of cement, of putrefaction, of dung, just like the dry, tough liver he had been forced to swallow at school. Sweat broke out on his brow and his gorge pumped. He fought it down, and meanwhile the man put another morsel in his crater. Mortimer smiled and nodded. The man looked back questioningly. "*Shokran*," Mortimer added: Thank you.

The second piece he chewed hurriedly with head bowed, packing in couscous around it. The third he swallowed without chewing at all, pretended to chew once it had gone down.

The distributor of the food watched him. He had brown eyes, not the usual black, and a short grey beard, revealed when he first rolled down his headscarf to eat.

The meal ended with rumbling belches, each one concluded with, "*Alhamdulillah.*" The brown-eyed man managed to get his belch to coincide with the uttering of thanks to God, so the word came out with a long, emphatic third syllable. How did they all have such deep voices? Perhaps some deformity of cosseted modern man squeezed his voice into his throat, where it didn't belong, whereas these laconic self-paced desert men spoke from the pit of the belly.

The men entered a discussion in the course of which a teapot emerged from the same man's robe who had had the spoons, along with two small tins. A charcoal brazier and four shot glasses arrived with the boy who came to clear away the meal.

Mortimer couldn't remember ever feeling so helpless. What was he supposed to do? He had never been anywhere where neither his French, Spanish, nor English served him. And meanwhile Celeste was in the grip of fever and he couldn't even ask what they were doing with her. Perhaps they'd have traditional remedies, would know how to nurse her back to health with desert roots and minerals; presumably there weren't too many herbs out here. But where had they taken her? Did they know what was wrong with her?

And on top of all that, this wasn't news he was engaged in, but travel, the sort of thing that led to solemn literature about ennui in the desert. It irked him. In fact it panicked him. How was he going to get back to his job, get off this red herring? The last phrase made him think of his battered feet, and his mood plunged further. And he needed to pee, and even that he couldn't see how to communicate. Eventually he stood and stepped towards the door, which he now found was so low he would have to stoop to get out. He almost yelped with pain at the first few steps, and hobbled along, putting his weight on the sides of his feet.

All the men sprang up. They were less tall than he'd reckoned. He found his heart racing, and his face hot.

"*Excusez-moi. Toilette,*" he said.

They stared at him, their eyes bright, not happy. "*Toilette,*" he repeated. "*Salle de bain.*"

The bearded man with the brown eyes grunted something, and the smallest of them, a man with bulging eyes and a stubbled jaw, came forward to open the door. He led Mortimer down a passage so dark Mortimer could make out nothing except a fringe of rusty light at the far end. But the floor was sand and he trusted that there would be no obstacles. He stumbled along with one hand on the earth wall beside him, endeavouring to walk on the sides of his feet. The soles crunched with every step, burning and sparking. But that was better than setting them directly on the ground. The man turned down a staircase in pitch blackness, then along a short corridor, and finally down more stairs into an alley with daylight framed in a doorway at the end. The place was a regular labyrinth. As soon as Mortimer saw the daylight his feet began to hurt viciously. He limped along, and stopped to catch his breath.

They emerged into the splintered shade of a palm garden. The light was ferocious, even under the trees. Mortimer glanced up at the wall of the edifice from which he had emerged: fifty feet of solid mud. Last night, in the murky moments of their arrival, he had not taken it in. But the building was a single block of mud, with the warren of stairs and chambers burrowed out inside it. It was a massive defence against the sun.

The man led him along a raised path between two dry reservoirs, their caked beds stained white, and through a patch of small plants like young lettuces. Mortimer screwed up his eyes at the pain of his soles, and followed as fast as he could, each step seeming to blaze through his whole body. Finally, the man waved Mortimer towards a broken-down wall that might have been a ruined house. Beyond it rose a slope of sand flecked with dirt and stones. It was evidently the village refuse heap and lavatory, though it didn't smell bad.

Mortimer's urine sounded disconcertingly loud as it frothed on the sand.

On the walk back he saw camels grazing among the palms. He could hear their groaning and rumbling, as of rusty machines; the sound of camels at rest. A saddlepack sat on the ground under a tree with a water jar beside it. If they ever got out of here, that would be the way, he thought, what with his feet and Celeste's health. The prospect reassured him. If camels came, they could also leave.

Back in the room two new men had joined the others. These two were different, wore copious black headpieces shaped like drums, like Orthodox mitres. They held black veils over their faces with fine fingers, and glanced at Mortimer with flashing eyes. Two Tuareg. He had never actually set eyes on one close up before. They didn't return his greeting. None of the men did. Something wasn't right. Mortimer felt his chest constrict. The two visitors had muskets resting across their laps. There was no other word for their antiquated broad-barrelled weaponry, which most likely had been brought along as part of a man's formal attire, Mortimer guessed, rather than for imminent use. But they were still alarming to see in this small, earthen shelter. Alarming, then somehow satisfying.

No war without its correspondent, the thought came to Mortimer. Wars that had no reporter had no existence. There had never been a war without its chronicler, from Homer onwards.

Still no one greeted him. The man who had conducted him to the midden sat down again, so Mortimer did the same, with his back to the door but near it, slightly apart from the loose circle the men made, as if he didn't want to presume or intrude, but equally didn't want to appear aloof, still less timid. Something made this a delicate situation, he could sense it.

No one said anything for what seemed an interminable time. Then the door scraped open and another local came in, followed by three more Tuareg. It seemed that only Mortimer turned to look and nod. The newcomers sat down. More silence. At first Mortimer took it to be an uncomfortable silence, until it occurred to him that perhaps the men might be happy to sit quietly. Probably for visitors and hosts alike, this was an unusually busy day as it was. In the desert one could go years without visitors. Mortimer began to feel comfortable too, and realised that he too could sit waiting without a thought in his mind. In his own small way he too had had his baptism in the desert, he knew something of the danger of being out on the sand, and of the inner calm surviving it instilled.

His and Celeste's bags stood in a far corner of the room. He began to wish they were elsewhere. They seemed a graphic representation of his intrusion.

The door opened again, allowing in another local man

dressed in sky blue robes. He came in talking to himself, and unwrapped his scarf to reveal a scalp of silver stubble, a sunburnt glistening face, and fleshy protuberant lips. It was a moment before Mortimer realised the man was speaking a heavily accented French directed at him. He was saying, "*Vite, vite*, I came quick as I could, as soon as they found me. The monsieur speaks no Saharawi, they said, so it is my pleasure to speak French. We must leave these gentlemen, we will leave now. *Venez vite, monsieur.*"

None of the others made any sign of having noticed the new arrival.

"These are the bags?" the man went on, crossing over to them. He had spectacular buckteeth, such that he couldn't close his lips.

A husky, deep voice said something, and the man stopped.

"*Venez, monsieur*," he repeated, returning to the door without the bags, and sending Mortimer a toothy grin.

Mortimer said, "Will you please tell these men that I am honoured to be in their presence, and thank them for their hospitality?"

No reply came to the translated message, except for one deep belch. For a moment Mortimer was torn: whether to push it, to attempt right now, from the start, to be present; or to leave. He quickly concluded the moment was too sensitive, and he must go. He wouldn't be going far anyway, with Celeste in the state she was in. He pulled on his boots as gently as he could, laced them halfway, and let the heels drag as they left the room. The small man reached back to pull the door to. Mortimer heard an utterance beyond it, and a reply. The talk beginning? Had they been waiting for him to leave?

"*Les bagages?*" he asked as they filed down the passage.

"Later," the man said.

Mortimer's feet were burning. For a moment the pain seemed so livid and intense he felt he had no choice but to give in to it entirely. His eyes moistened in the dark. He blinked and tried to steady his breath.

They had to press against the rough wall to allow a pair of boys to pass, who went scurrying on, leaving an aroma of rose water behind them.

"*Et ma femme?*" Mortimer asked.

The man glanced at him. Mortimer could just make out his eyes gleaming in the dark. "*Oui, oui,*" he said.

Outside, the man paused to introduce himself as Hamed, shaking Mortimer's hand and giving him another display of his teeth. Mortimer had not noticed that Hamed had a bayonet thrust in his belt. He led Mortimer along the wall of the ksar, this time the other way. Mortimer traipsed along behind him, every step a step of fire. He wanted to weep: what a helpless state he was in; he couldn't speak to anyone, and he couldn't even walk.

Then they turned the corner, and a host of camels came into view, some seated on the ground under the palms with their front feet tucked neatly under their chests like cats, others standing on open ground beyond, ropes hanging from their chins. The impression was of light but immensely tall beasts. A few men robed in black stood among the camels, others sat in small groups, here and there a wisp of smoke rose.

A spurt of delirious excitement ran through him. Here he was, just what they needed, right in their midst. They didn't yet know their incredible good fortune, and he was just discovering his. *No war without its chronicler.* They shared in the same stroke of brilliant luck, he and they. He had judged right in giving himself to chance, and now it would—it could—pay off spectacularly for all of them. If only they could be made to realise it. The question of the bags and their contents—press cards, notebooks, cameras—had been troubling him, but now he knew beyond doubt that he had no choice but to be open with these people. They would surely go through the bags. He wanted them to know as soon as possible that he was here, the man who could champion them, raise their cause from obscurity.

Then a horrible misgiving hit. Suppose they simply rejected the edict of fate, and sent him on his way?

"*Ma femme,*" he said again. "Where is she?"

Hamed was leading him down a long path under palms. Mortimer could see no house ahead, but he couldn't imagine they would have taken Celeste far.

And it would be a great stroke of luck for her too, once she was better. She was in the midst of a treasure trove of classic shots. If this story turned out the way it might, and if the two of them did everything they might with it, they could become an impregnable team.

"*Oui, oui,*" Hamed repeated, as if he knew all about Celeste's whereabouts. Mortimer felt a twinge of doubt that he might know nothing at all, hadn't even understood his question.

"*Et Brahim?*" Mortimer tried as he hobbled along. The question had been bothering him.

"Brahim?" Hamed asked.

"The man with the donkey." He waited a moment to see if that would help. "The man who brought us here."

Hamed shrugged. "He has gone."

Mortimer asked, "Where?" as if it could possibly matter. Perhaps he hoped to find out if there was still the shadow of a possibility of leaving the way they had come. He felt alarmed that Brahim could have left without them.

"*Il est parti*," Hamed said again. "He has a long way to go."

The desert was a mystery: an empty land in which people appeared beside one along the way, then vanished. One had to pursue one's own business. But he wished he had a proper contact. He was so unprepared. It was exasperating. If he could only find one person in the leadership—assuming they had one—who had had some broader experience, who had been to Algiers, knew a minister, a colonel, who had heard of *Le Monde*, who knew there was a world churning and clanging along beyond the desert. Whether or not this person might care for that world was another matter, but perhaps if he didn't, Mortimer could persuade him to, at least enough to let that world know what was going on down here. Assuming that he himself could establish what was going on.

They passed into a straggle of old earth homes, ordinary desert houses that the man identified as the *vieux ksar*. By comparison, the main ksar seemed like a new apartment block to which the well-to-do had fled from this chain of ruinous slums. The farthest houses of the two rows were half buried in sand. Mortimer could see a set of palm fronds halfway up one dune, sprouted there with no trunk at all, like a plant strange to these parts. Another palm had a trunk only a few feet tall. One red wall ran straight into the sand. It was clear what was happening: the dunes were swamping these houses, and this would sooner or later be a sunken village.

Hamed stopped and opened a door. As soon as Mortimer entered, a woman left with a rustling of robes, so promptly he hardly got a look at her.

He saw Celeste lying on her side against a far wall on a kind of shelf, covered in a grey blanket. He knelt over her. Her throat rattled softly with each breath. Even in the gloom he could see her face was red with sunburn.

The room seemed cooler than in the other ksar, and there was something comforting about being in an ordinary dishevelled house. It seemed a better place for her to be. A transistor radio had been attached to a wall with wire, various plastic bags hung from nails, on a bench against the farthest darkest wall lay a heap of rumpled linen.

He put his hand under Celeste's blanket. She was hot like a furnace, and damp. Perhaps that was good, she was sweating out the fever. And she was still sleeping, which could only be a good thing.

Hamed left. Alone, Mortimer tried to gather his thoughts. But it was impossible that he sit tight here with Celeste as she slept while a troop of nomads with muskets held war councils not a quarter of a mile away. On the other hand, it was exhilarating beyond measure to be in the right spot. Assuming, again, that the accounts were true that the Tuareg were none too happy about Algeria's plans for the Sahara, and that there was indeed a resistance brewing.

Mortimer put his head out the door. A quiet sunlit morning in a village. A cock crowed somewhere, a hen crooned, and he could hear a goat bleating. It was a scene of remote, immemorial peace.

Over the brow of a dune at the end of the row of houses a black shape appeared. The shape swayed, grew, rising from behind the sand, and became the top half of a man. He floated along the brow for a while, swaying backwards and forwards, then rose higher, and the head of a camel appeared, bobbing back and forth. The rest of the beast gradually rose from the sand. The man must have been sixty yards away. Up on the animal, he looked huge. He crossed the brow and began to descend the village side, towards the ksar. Already another rider was bobbing up from behind the dune, and behind him another. From the saddle of each of them a stick pointed diagonally to the sky. Mortimer stood watching as more and more riders glided out of the sand.

If Kepple could see me now, he thought, and grinned. Something was getting up, and no mistake. But who was paying for it?

Hamed came running down the track. "*Si, si,*" he called, grinning from exertion. He held a small brazier in one hand and a plastic bag in the other. "*Du thé,*" he said, holding up the tea things.

They sat on the floor of the house while Hamed brewed up. Celeste inhaled sharply once, and let out a long moan. Mortimer thought she was waking but she slept on. Is she going to get a surprise when she pulls through, he thought to himself.

11

It was not a good day. Mortimer tried to get out of the house numerous times, but Hamed was adamant that they stay where they were. Later on a boy arrived with Celeste's two bags, walking stiffly under their weight, and left without a word. Ten minutes later he came back with Mortimer's bag.

Women came and went. They would put their head in the door, say something to Hamed, and disappear again. Sometimes they studied Celeste, stroked her head, tucked her up, and left.

Later, Celeste rubbed her face, said, "Strange sleep," and began to sit up, then groaned and lay back down. Mortimer squeezed himself on to the bench beside her. She was hot still, but less so, more like the ordinary warmth of someone rousing from a long sleep. Hamed was sitting on the ground outside at the time.

"I was worried about you," Mortimer said, stroking her hair.

She shuddered, turned to the wall, and was sick again. He fished a dirty shirt out of his bag and wiped away the dribble she had produced. She sat with her hands round her knees, and shivered. "I'm so cold."

He laid her back down and covered her with the blanket, then pulled out his jacket and draped it over her. He unfolded a sheet off the pile against the far wall and laid that on her too. In spite of all this, and even though it was warm and stuffy in the room, her teeth chattered. He lay down beside her, felt her jolt in his arms and her jaw shudder as he held her. Eventually she became still.

Hamed said, *"C'est le soleil."* But it seemed impossible that the sun alone could do this.

Hamed came by later with an old-looking rectangular battery with long brass electrodes, a kind of battery Mortimer had used in his bicycle headlamp as a boy. Hamed hooked it up to wires dangling from the base of the radio on the wall, flicked a switch, leaving the battery hanging there, and produced a whistle and crackle of static. He commenced searching for a station. A raucous Arabic voice with jangling music in the background shouted for a moment. Then a woman's voice, so fuzzed by static even Hamed could probably not understand it. Finally he hit on a military band playing a sprightly march, and stopped there. In a moment an old-fashioned English voice, the voice of another era, was declaring that this was the World Service.

It was extraordinary to hear, not so much because of the impossibly remote and timeless setting in which Mortimer was listening to it, but because of the world from which the clipped male voice seemed to come: a world of old-fashioned prewar cars and buses, of steamships and Morse code, a world of radar and propeller planes. What had happened while he had been gone?

In the afternoon he took an aspirin to ease the pain in his feet, and shuffled off to where the camels were resting under the palms. There must have been fifty or more, and as many riders. Here and there men had spread reed mats on the sand, and frayed strips of rug on which to perform their prayers.

"*Salaam aleikum,*" people called out, and invited him to join them. They'd roll down their headscarves from dark faces and sit up, accept a cigarette from him with lean, brown fingers that emerged from their copious robes, and Mortimer would settle on the ground to drink tea with them.

The room, the little house, began to feel wonderful once the afternoon drew into evening. Mortimer sensed that the crisis was past, and there was nowhere like a sickroom when the worst was over. It stirred memories of the comfort of being tended in his room when sick as a child, at an hour when he should have been at school.

Two women arrived with a clay bowl of water. Hamed and Mortimer left the room. Outside the sky was luminous, a sheet of electric lilac. Against it, the walls of the houses were dark, and glimmered like velvet. Palm fronds glistened, stirred by a light breeze. A gentle roar reached Mortimer's ears from somewhere in the distance, like a fleet of motors idling. It was the camels. Then a voice rang out, calling men to prayer, rising like a siren, holding a long note that mutated, moving through different vowels, and falling away. It rose and fell again, the herald of night.

Hamed fetched a kerosene lamp, dazzling to look at, yet casting a weak watery light around the room. The rafters, the walls, all were plunged into blackness, as if the little hissing light merely threw objects back into greater darkness.

The worst was not over. Celeste was feverish most of the night. Her teeth started chattering again, her lips vibrated as she inhaled, stuttering as if she was on the point of a seizure. A white line of spume formed on her lip. "So cold," she muttered, shivering. Mortimer piled all his clothes on her, then wrapped another sheet over them, making a great bundle out of her bed. He lay on the floor beside her.

He was woken by a cry in the middle of the night, and found himself lying under a heap of his own clothes. Celeste was on the bench above, writhing and groaning. He tried to get her to drink some water, wiped back the hair stuck to her cheek, but she recoiled at his touch. "Non, non, non."

He felt useless, hopelessly ill-equipped to nurse her.

At one point Mortimer crept past Hamed, who was slumped against the wall by the door, and went out into a night lit by a high quarter-moon. By the time he got to the end of the row of houses and caught a glimpse of the field of black shapes camped out under the stars, someone was at his elbow. It gave him a shock. He hadn't heard Hamed following.

He must learn to wait, that was all. That would be the desert's first lesson: patience. In such a beautiful scene—the silky land shimmering under the moon, the palms glazed and motionless, and all the desert men dozing by their beasts—it was easy to be a willing pupil.

12

He woke to find Hamed shaking him by the arm. A tall Tuareg made taller still by his headpiece was standing in the room. He loomed as a single piece of perfect blackness in the dark. Mortimer glanced at his watch: three-thirty in the morning. *"Bon soir,"* he said, and stood up.

The Tuareg put a hand to his own chest.

Hamed knelt to pump the kerosene lamp. It took a lot of pumping, and fiddling with the valves, but eventually spurted into flame, settling into a loud hiss as the bulb sparked and incandesced.

"Monsieur Mortimer, vous êtes bienvenu," the tall Tuareg said in perfect French, in what seemed the deepest voice Mortimer had yet heard.

At last, Mortimer thought: the interpreter he had been waiting for. He went to his bag and rummaged through a side pocket. Hamed appeared at his elbow, watching. Mortimer frowned at him. When he turned back into the room with his press card, the Tuareg had stepped back and was watching intently.

Mortimer held out the card. "I'm a journalist, from the *Tribune*."

"We know who you are," the man said in his good French, gesturing that they should seat themselves on the floor. "What we do not know is how you come to be here."

Mortimer was about to answer: by pure chance, *par hazard*, but he felt it to be an inadequate explanation.

"I was coming down to report on the Sahelian drought," he said. "Then I heard about things going on with the Tuareg, and we happened to be passing through Timimoun."

"Things going on with the Tuareg? What had you heard?"

"That the Tuareg were unhappy with the president's Saharan initiative."

"The government can do what they like, as long as they leave us alone. But who suggested you come here?"

"My editor at the *Tribune*."

"We must have a name."

"He's called Kepple."

The Tuareg shook his head.

"Is the *Tribune* not enough of a name?"

He shook his head again. "Not enough."

The lamp hissed. They sat for a moment saying nothing. Mortimer waited, and realised that the man would wait too. It was up to him, Mortimer, to make a move. He would have to do it. He shrugged. "I have a friend in Algiers."

The inevitable question came: "Who?"

There was nothing for it, he would have to use Taillot's name, and just hope that it would do no harm. It was appalling to be so hopelessly unvouched-for.

He mentioned Taillot, realising as he did so that he didn't even know his first name, let alone what he really did, or who he was. He was just one of Kepple's tricks, conjured from the demimonde of international advisers and observers. But he was evidently something in Algiers, and Mortimer had a hunch that he just might be known of down here. Why else would he first have suggested Mortimer come, then tried to scare him off?

In the fierce light of the kerosene stove the man's eyes shone hazel, translucent. He said nothing, but pulled down his shesh, his scarf, revealing a smooth face coloured an even nut brown. There was a mournful slant to his eyes, and his eyebrows rose a little in the middle, above the bridge of his nose. He looked slightly sad, and friendly. There were dimples round his mouth. His age was hard to judge but surely not less than forty. He was clean-shaven, but Mortimer guessed he was a man who would not have to shave often.

He said something to Hamed in Arabic. Hamed left.

The visitor treated the late-night hour like any other. One was awake: what did the hour matter? He showed no sign of fatigue at all, other than the general weightiness of his bearing. The thought crossed Mortimer's mind: this was a man on the eve of battle.

"And Rio Camello?" the Tuareg asked.

Mortimer shrugged and looked away.

"You were down there, no?"

Mortimer racked his brains for how the man could possibly know. There were only two ways: either he did know Taillot, and Taillot had told him; or else he read the newspapers and had seen Mortimer's reports from the Rio Camello territory. He nodded. "A few weeks ago, yes."

"So now you have a chance to see things from the other side," the Tuareg said.

It was a comment that puzzled Mortimer. Surely the Rio Camello could in no way be construed as the Tuareg's foe. He asked: "*Vous êtes Marocain?*"

The man tutted and shook his head. "*Je suis Tuareg.*"

Perhaps he simply meant that the Tuareg were struggling against the state that supported Rio Camello, namely Algeria.

The man asked: "Do you think you know why we are here?"

Mortimer demurred with something general. "For a long time the Tuareg have wanted their autonomy."

"For a long time the Tuareg have had their autonomy. Even the French never brought us under their law. We have our own law. We are like a river: anyone who tries to stop us, we flow another way. We are the only people to whom the desert is a true home." He gestured around the room. "That is why we have no need of houses. For us, a house is a tomb. We live on the sand, under the stars. We have always lived this way, we are the oldest people on earth, our ancestry reaches back to before the Flood. We alone of men never stooped to sow seeds. Our problem is just beginning with this government. They want to build a road to Niger, no problem. We simply walk our camels across the highway when we need to. They build some more houses in Tamanrasset or In Salah, no problem. Our problem is the oil. This is our land. We want nothing from anybody, only to be left alone, not to be like your Indians in America, shipped off our native land and moved where you will. We will never allow that. But in order to protect ourselves we need money. That is the only persuasion those people understand. Why should they suck the money out of our ancestral land? Why should we allow them to let the Americans suck it away? Once they come in, everything will change. We are not fools, we know what has happened in other places, in Arabia and the Emirates. Where are the Bedou's tents now?"

The man hummed, then went on: "We have friends. We have people who will help us. But we need more. We can do much with a camel and a rifle, but it is doubtful we can do enough. If Monsieur Taillot directed you here he would have a reason, *n'est-ce pas?*"

Mortimer ran his fingers over the sand between his knees. "If you think I can help," he said. All the more fortunate, he thought, that he had not heeded Taillot's warning to stay away.

The man glanced at the sleeping form on the bunk. "And her?"

"She is a photographer. Celeste Dumas."

"It is a difficult situation. We are not alone."

"Shall we go outside?" Mortimer asked.

But apparently that wasn't what he meant. He tutted, then got up, bowed, gave his name as Jean Baptiste, and left.

Hamed came back inside. He and Mortimer sat in silence listening to the rustle of the kerosene lamp. After a while Mortimer lay down. He didn't sleep. As he lay on the earth floor he saw himself as a tiny figure pinned to the great flat world. He could feel gravity holding him down, his limbs splayed against the ground. The flat plate of the world slowly turned, carrying him with it. In a while he would be no more. Before then all he could do was scurry about with great industry, caught in a frantic round of activity, achieving nothing, or at best very little. But he didn't mind. It felt like a glorious privilege.

The lamp hissed. The walls were black. A lone cicada chirruped. Meanwhile, outside, the sleeping nomads floated on the earth beside their resting barks.

Mortimer reflected that Jean Baptiste had given his name only at the very end, as if he'd been reluctant to do so earlier.

He wondered about that. Was there some kind of Tuareg belief, analogous to the Amerindian taste for silence before commencing a conversation, or the primitive fear of a camera, that held a name a talisman? Either way it seemed promising that Jean Baptiste had shared his name, and had already known Mortimer's. Perhaps that would give the Tuareg a reassuring sense of having a hold over him; if a few hundred guns didn't do that already.

Jean Baptiste returned in a while. He evidently had no plans for sleeping that night. He offered the chest-patting greeting perfunctorily, as if the gesture were merely a salute, and announced, slightly out of breath, that an important person was on his way.

Mortimer scrambled to his feet, which blazed with pain once more. He bent double, groaning, and slumped to the ground apologising, then pulled on his boots carefully. He really had to do something about his feet. Jean Baptiste merely looked at him and told him to cover the woman's head.

Two local men appeared in the doorway, whispering, "*Bismillah.*" They stepped inside with heads bowed. After them came an old man dressed in white robes and carrying a stick. He too uttered the name of God, in a reedy, piercing tenor.

Mortimer at once felt uneasy. The old man had a thin mouth, the top lip drawn up, revealing yellow stumps of teeth, and his eyes were puffy and bloodshot, full of mistrust. He stared at Mortimer with a sneer. Mortimer would have to tread carefully. He almost felt betrayed by this old man already: he could sense that the man had the power to block him from the role he was meant to play. It was unfair. Bitter old men should not have the right to come between a man and his work. He could feel the man's sneer as a sensation in his own belly, a twist of scorn.

The man gave a sermon, interpreted by Jean Baptiste. Did Mortimer realise a man could be pulverised into a thousand thousand pieces—Jean Baptiste made a point of repeating the number, as the old man presumably did somewhere in the thick of his Koranic invective—and every single one of those pieces would spend a thousand eternities in each of thirty-three hells, if he so much as thought of impeding a jihad? Mortimer did not have to answer the question, because the man's voice kept rolling on in its reedy twang, his lips turned out as if the words were sour in his mouth. He clutched his stick tightly, sometimes tapping it on the sand, sometimes jabbing it in Mortimer's direction. Throughout the oration he stared at a point on the wall to Mortimer's left. Eventually he fell silent, and settled his gaze on Mortimer's face. Mortimer bowed his head in what he imagined to be an attitude of reverence. He wasn't sure if a reply was expected, or if the man were merely probing his soul with those merciless eyes. Mortimer hedged his bets and said, *"Merci."*

One of the men accompanying the holy man was chubby, with a long Pancho Villa moustache. He sat motionless, fat fingers entwined, elbows on knees. It was he who broke the silence, in a rough, guttural French. "You see that stick he is holding." He pointed at the mullah's staff. His eyes slid over Mortimer in a way he could physically sense in his skin. "If he wanted to, he could point that stick at you and you would no longer be there." The man stared at Mortimer to see that the point had been made. "Or he could throw it on the ground at your feet and it would become a serpent and bite you."

A magic wand, Mortimer thought. He bowed again solemnly. His heart was thumping.

The old man began a high, insistent chant which suited his reedy voice. He had the voice of a shawm, full of dextrous inflection. The others joined in, in thick basses. They stared at Mortimer as they held their notes, their necks twitching and pulsing. Then Jean Baptiste sang too, in a softer voice, humming along compliantly. Mortimer wondered, under all their gazes, if he was expected to join in.

The old man's vocal line became higher and more intricate, an exotic descant borne along above the obbligato of bass, which then ceased, leaving his line high up on its own, his tune fluttering, dipping and swooping like a bird. It was something of a feat, and Mortimer assumed they were all to pay it special attention. But the man with the Mexican moustache addressed Mortimer right across it, with the half-pious, half-authoritarian smile of a pastor before a roomful of Sunday school kids. "You must say this," he said, and launched into a prayer.

Mortimer had no choice, he repeated each line as requested. *"Lah ilaha ulallah."* Meanwhile, the high voice buzzed and fluted on its own ecstatic trajectory.

Perhaps they felt it wouldn't matter much either way. Perhaps they reflected that Allah had seen fit to set Mortimer among them. Perhaps he was now one of the saved, having pronounced the necessary formulas. Either way, he was on board. They took him along.

13

The day began with a long camel ride.

As soon as the mullah finished his ceremonials a boy entered the room with a plastic bowl and a brass jug. He went round the men in turn, pouring out a stream of rose-scented water in which they washed their hands. The mullah's lustrations extended to his feet too. After pouring, the youth would flip a thin towel off his shoulder.

Outside, there was no shouting of commands, no apparent staff. Camels were brought to their knees, groaning and grunting, while others were levering themselves to their full height with the dark bundle of a rider on their backs, and some were already walking through the dark, as if they were the true leaders and instigators.

Jean Baptiste got Mortimer on his mount. For a moment he seemed inexperienced with the animal. When he tugged on its halter to get it to kneel, he succeeded only in making it circle round them. He swore quietly, clucked at it, held his stick to its neck. With great reluctance, with a shuffling of its hoofs and lifting of the high neck, and a whinnying grunt, the animal dropped laboriously to its knees.

The saddle consisted of a lot of blankets, with somewhere among them a layer of sheepskin showing a woolly edge. There was a wooden pommel, which Mortimer gripped before straddling the animal horseback-style. Jean Baptiste made him dismount and reboard sidesaddle, with the pommel tucked into the crook of a knee. It seemed a precarious position, but like jump-starting a motorbike it was easier to balance than it looked.

Far ahead Mortimer could see riders filing up a dune, a procession of dark shapes flowing up the pallor beyond the palms. He had not ridden a camel before, and was alarmed at first by the height, then exhilarated, seeming to soar through the high air of dawn. But he hated to leave Celeste behind, and in the state she was in. He didn't know what else to do, though. They had given him no time. And he had no choice, he had to go with them.

There was a faint smell of sour milk about his animal. He

passed other riders who had not yet mounted, one or two even still lying on the ground, their mounts resting like boulders beside them. He was relieved not to have to tell his animal where to go, or give it any kind of instruction. It knew where to go, caught in the general flow, which seemed no single person's decision. Riders streamed out of the palms like a fleet of boats on a current. To Mortimer, riding high on a level with all the others, it was as if the beasts had coalesced into a single transport for the field.

Already the sky was fading from its intense black. A last star burned ahead.

As if to underline the singularity of the body of motion, the sound of the camels' hoofs was a single hiss, like the sound of skis in snow. Mortimer listened, and could not distinguish the footfalls of his own mount from the general sibilance. Behind, he could hear a series of grunts emanating from some obstreperous beast, then a tremendous bellowing, which sustained itself a moment and died away. Someone was clicking his tongue. Someone else exhorted his ride in a rhythmic incantation: *ha-ta, ha-ta, ha-ta*. Beneath all these sounds, the single susurrus of the camels' feet continued. A moment later another rider pronounced the same exhortation closer by. *Ha-ta!*

No man could resist the allure of publicity, Mortimer reflected. It amplified and liberated a cause to know that it was going to be written about, would achieve fame. Fame, and through that a chance at immortality: it elevated what was a skirmish, a brawl, a half-baked and shoddy-looking enterprise, into a moment of history with a place in the annals.

He was sure he could detect a change in the rebels. They seemed to have not so much renewed conviction as liberation from conviction: as if it was no longer necessary to convince themselves of their cause, now that the action would be launched on a broader stage, would be widely known. It was as if the training wheels had been taken off a bicycle.

This was how it struck Mortimer as they rode through the chalky dawn. It could have been, though, that the sense of a new and higher motivation in the men derived from their having at last commenced an operation. Their gathering had been given the momentum it wanted.

A series of light thumpings became audible: someone moving up from behind in a canter. The muffled drumming of the hoofs became insistent to Mortimer's ear, growing louder. Then it ceased, receded into the general sound, and Jean Baptiste was at Mortimer's side, rocking gently.

Mortimer didn't recognise him at first, with only his eyes showing through his scarf. He unwrapped the cloth and handed it to Mortimer, mimed wrapping it round his own head, by which Mortimer understood that he was to wear it himself. He smiled at the way the two of them could have conversed had they wanted to, rocking along at the same height, ignoring their mounts, like two people in a chairlift. Jean Baptiste seemed to have nothing in particular to say, he merely wanted Mortimer to wear the shesh. He fell in as an escort, something Mortimer was happy to have.

Getting the shesh in place was a two-handed operation, and meant letting go of the saddle's pommel. The cloth was long, ten feet or more, and he had to wrap it round numerous times before he felt enough was enough and tucked a copious tail end in one of the folds. He felt hot and slightly sick. The cloth smelled of fresh paint. Was it really necessary to add to one's clothing like this? The sun wasn't even up.

But it soon would be. The world was light now. They rose over a shoulder of sand and down into a long defile of gravel, and what looked like shattered concrete. Mortimer wondered if it was the same gully that Brahim had brought them down on their way into the village. After a while he saw a great buttress of red cliff ahead, and recognised the ruined fort clinging to the spine of the ridge. That was where the sun first struck: a filament of bright yellow showed at the top. It was a marvellous sight: the body of smoky crimson rock edged by a fine line, a crust of light, like a skin on cream, or a hunk of cheese with that hard bright rind to it.

Jean Baptiste reached out to Mortimer with a handful of sticky crystallised date pulp, a staple of the desert. It could last for years before going stale, he had heard. Several times he was given a tin cup of water as he rode, never enough. He'd down it before he knew what he had done, and be surprised at the sight of the yellowed bottom with no more in it. At one point he found himself horribly bored, bobbing along like this up and down shallow dunes of yellow sand that stretched on forever. The dunes here seemed paler than the deep orange-gold of three days before. Then he'd remember what was going on — the posse of riders about him, the warmongering caravan spiked with gun barrels — and feel acutely fearful. What had he got himself into? This wasn't his war. He had no war. What an idiotic thing it would be to get killed, or even hurt. He seriously considered turning back. But would he find his way? The desert killed you if you got lost. And would they let him go anyway? Now as he thought back he realised he had never actually stated that he wished to ride with them. Perhaps they thought the boot was on the other foot, and they were taking him with them whether he wanted to come or not. And anyway, how on earth would he broach the subject of turning back? It was unthinkable. The march was on, it was happening, and he was part of it.

But it would make one hell of a story. He could already imagine himself seizing a hotel telephone to call through his copy. Of course, he'd have to have written something first.

Then a different fear would seize him: what if all this led to nothing, to an insignificant skirmish, a quick pacifying gesture by the authorities to keep the rebels happy? And they'd all go back to their flocks and Mortimer would have a travel piece on his hands.

Were they perhaps heading for Timimoun? he wondered. He thought they might be traveling east, in the town's direction, but the sun was already too high for him to be sure. And he wasn't sure that Timimoun was to the east anyway. If only one could get hold of a decent map. He had a vague idea that a road continued southwest beyond Timimoun, but he couldn't think why any route would do that. He had no recollection of there being any settlement in that direction before the Western Sahara and Mauritania.

Flies had settled on his hands. He gave up trying to send them away. Whatever he did, they only came back. They seemed to favour the cuticles. Several jostled one another in a line across his fingers. Knuckle dusters, he thought, and waved his hand in the air. They clung on doggedly, he really had to shake to get them off, and they immediately came back when he stopped.

Then another fear arose, a cloying anxiety about Celeste. Something might happen to her while he was gone; she might be alarmed to find herself alone; she might even recover and up sticks, slip out of his life before he could get back, believing that was what he had done. He couldn't bear the thought of her suffering in his absence, of not being there to comfort her. He might be the one living solace to her and he had abandoned her, sick, in an oasis a thousand miles from anywhere.

What did it say about him that so carelessly, so blithely he could walk away from something he had never known before, an unassailable, unasked-for intimacy with another person? He knew the value of work but not love? Was he already becoming the kind of pseudo–tough guy who lied to himself that he didn't care about things he did? Journalism was full of men like that. You could recognise them before they even opened their mouths. They weren't any fun to look in the eye.

But Celeste would understand the need to get after the story. Even when they were delivered to you on a plate, stories still had to be followed through, constructed, given substance. He was determined to get himself into the foreign print game, to make it to the front, and rightly or wrongly he had put work first, and if he had done so without a second thought at least he was having second thoughts now. If it turned out to be a mistake, then that was the way life went—but a trapdoor gave way as he reached the end of that thought: if he lost her, he wouldn't forgive himself.

He couldn't keep himself from the thought that in every life there came a turning point, one crucial moment when all that person's strength was summoned for a trial, not exactly between right and wrong, but between integrity and cowardice, gratitude and cynicism, courage and self-deceit. He couldn't just clop away from her over the dunes like this, without at least letting her know.

Just before leaving, he had knelt over her, meaning to shake her awake and tell her he was going. But she had been sleeping so deeply, the breaths rustling in and out of her divine, once-broken nose, her face calm, that he couldn't bring himself to. So he had written a brief note: *They're off, and they're taking me with them. I'm sorry*, he added. *You're sick, you must rest, forgive me. Will be back as soon as possible.*

Then came the decision, which absurdly he found excruciating, how to sign off. *I love you?* He hadn't yet written that to her. Would it seem flippant, coming at the end of such a brief note, which for all he knew she might see as a professional betrayal? Then he had the idea: no note. The message of that would be: they have whisked me off. Just as he was deliberating, Jean Baptiste had swung open the door and said, "*On y va.*" Mortimer had crumpled the paper and stuffed it in his trouser pocket and slipped out into the night.

He had been feeling that ball of paper against his thigh as he rode. Now that they had been on the hoof three or four hours, his sweat and body warmth, the kneading under the stretched cloth of his trousers as the camel walked, had softened the paper to the point where he could no longer feel it.

Mortimer looked round for Jean Baptiste, but he had moved off.

"*Ça va?*" asked a deep voice behind him. He twisted in his saddle. Sure enough Jean Baptiste was right there, just behind.

Mortimer's heart beat hard, and he felt the blood in his face as he said: "I have been thinking. I must go back."

Jean Baptiste made no response. Before he could, two camel riders who had found enough reserves of strength within their beasts to come trotting up through the field passed by, then pulled on their reins and slowed up ahead. One had to pull harder and longer than the other, and jogged about in the saddle as he did so, in a way that seemed less comfortable than for the rest of the riders. The first rider spoke to Jean Baptiste and they both laughed. His face was covered with a scarf, as was Baptiste's, yet they both knew right away who the other was.

The second rider urged his camel on, holding the reins

unusually high, slipping precariously in the saddle and failing to regain his seat as the animal skipped about, snorting. He attempted to steer it in front of Baptiste, then towards Mortimer, but only succeeded in cantering across the general flow of riders.

Mortimer caught up with the camel.

The rider turned round in the saddle and pulled away the scarf. It was Celeste. She wiped her red and glistening face. "They didn't give me any choice. These two men just about dragged me from bed. *Le monsieur n'a pas la machine. Pas machine. Madame a la machine.*

"*Machine?* 'The monsieur doesn't have the camera. No camera. Madame has the camera.' They shoved my camera bag round my neck and threw me on a camel. Here I am. At least the ride seems to have done me some good. I feel human again."

"You're fantastic," he called, and laughed, urging his camel closer. It seemed near miraculous that she had come, and just when he had decided to go back to her.

"Thank God you're better. I was terrified. I hated leaving you. I'm sorry. I should have just woken you and brought you. But you were sleeping so deeply. And you were so ill."

She smiled, jogging about in her saddle. "The women told me it was the sun. Can you believe it? I've never been so cold in my life. I feel like I've risen from the dead." She blew him a kiss.

The rest of the morning he felt like someone who had received news of a deserved but unexpected prize. Relief at her recovery, the good fortune of having a photographer along after all, and this extraordinary troop that was surely a hundred years out of date—everything was falling into place. Not only that, but here he was with a woman he loved for whom the whole expedition was every bit as good as it was for him: he didn't feel in the least held back. It was as if he no longer needed to strive to avoid anything; there was nothing to avoid.

14

The operation was a simple one. It occurred in the early afternoon. Up ahead, riders had begun to dismount. Everyone pulled up, and there was more talking now as people walked about between the camels. The scene reminded Mortimer of a livestock market he had once seen while on assignment with the BBC in the Yemen: the men conversing rapidly, smoking, chewing qat, and the animals standing about chewing the cud, emitting a bellow now and then. Some of the camels decided to sit, others stood waiting to see what would happen. One group of men got a fire going, and blue enamel teapots appeared on the sand, along with dusty plastic bags of tea. Jean Baptiste seized Mortimer's camel by its neck rope. As it bent down Mortimer slipped and found himself hanging by one leg. Baptiste hurried round and disengaged him. He landed heavily on his side, with a strong set of bony fingers digging into his armpit. Savage pins and needles sparked up his legs, and his feet were completely dead, but he was unharmed.

Celeste flipped herself off her mount.

After a glass of tea, Jean Baptiste led them up a dune. Mortimer walked easily for the first time in days: his feet had begun to heal. From the crest of the dune the sand dropped away in furrows, down to a plain that stretched to the horizon.

The one visible feature of the plain was a faint white line drawn right across it. Baptiste gestured to the left, and Mortimer picked out a wisp of dust many miles off. He stared and saw that the little dust cloud was moving: a blue funnel of smoke, as if something were burrowing just under the surface along that white line, throwing up a blue exhaust cloud.

"They will have to be quick," Jean Baptiste muttered. Mortimer assumed he was referring to whatever vehicle was barrelling down that distant track.

Elsewhere something small fluttered on the plain: a piece of plastic catching the sun, perhaps.

Jean Baptiste fumbled in his robe and pulled out a large pair of binoculars. He made a brief attempt to disentangle the strap from his shesh, but it was too much trouble. Mortimer leaned close, catching a sweet, thick animal whiff of the man, as he brought the lenses against his eyes and tried to find the image, then to steady it. In the midst of a grey circle was the little thing that fluttered. Then it vanished. Then he saw it again.

"*La police*," Jean Baptiste said.

Mortimer saw that it was a flag at the end of a pole.

"*La frontière*," Jean Baptiste told him.

"The border?" He made out a low building with a steel roof, and a second building, all but indistinguishable from the land.

"It's the last post. Then in six hours, Mauritania."

Mortimer swept the binoculars to the left, till he found the traveling object: there was the trail of blue dust, and at the head of it, gleaming like a beetle, a small black thing trembling as it moved.

"They go for supplies once a week," Jean Baptiste said. "We should have moved out earlier."

Mortimer was about to hand back the binoculars when he saw something else: two tiny black figures just below the edifices, then three more, then a little cluster of them—a platoon of diminutive black stick figures, ants on the plain. He tried to hold the heavy binoculars steady for long enough to get a proper look, then handed them back, and used his naked eye. He could just make them out, a little group of black riders, a vanguard. At this distance, on such a vast plain, it was impossible to tell how far they might be from the police buildings: half a mile or less, or perhaps as much as two miles. The land was so flat, so broad and empty, you just couldn't tell.

But it wasn't long before a crackle reached Mortimer's ears. It sounded like someone stepping on dry twigs. Then it came again: another footfall.

A few other Tuareg had joined Baptiste at the brow to survey the proceedings. The black figures below disappeared. The little burrowing animal on the plain had ceased to burrow. Mortimer could see no sign of it at all, as if it had never been there, or had taken itself underground. The ghost of dust had vanished.

In a while the black figures emerged again from wherever they had been. They stood motionless a long time. Then Mortimer perceived that they had spread along the white line on the plain. In another moment they had detached themselves from the line, dropped below it. Then they vanished again.

"*C'est bien,*" Jean Baptiste said.

"What is the police post called?" Mortimer asked. "How many people man it?"

These were the details he ought to be getting. What had he been thinking lately? Where had he been? He knew nothing: how many were in their own column; was there in fact a leader, and who was he; who was the mullah who had visited in the night; where did he come from; who were the riders with them that weren't Tuareg—among all the black-robed men rode quite a few who wore blue and white robes. He reflected how much information one could ordinarily count on being given as a journalist. Often you did little more than relay information you had yourself received in a succinct summary.

This story was as raw as it got. He had been given virtually nothing except a bit of background.

They shuffled back down to the resting camels. Jean Baptiste arranged more tea for them.

"*Voilà*," he said. "It has begun."

Mortimer kept glancing up at the brow of the dunes but missed the return of the warriors.

Later, Jean Baptiste adjusted his robes and conducted Mortimer to a group among which sat three men in green Algerian police uniforms. Two of them sat chatting with the rebels, drinking glasses of tea, smoking cigarettes, and seemed agitated but not unfriendly, nor uneasy. The third lay on the sand nearby with his arm over his face.

When they all set off Mortimer saw that each of these policemen rode on his own camel. The troop must have brought spares. Yet he hadn't noticed any earlier. Nor, apart from the fact that their three camels were roped together, was there any visible means to detain the captives. He guessed it was unnecessary in the desert.

One of them had a dark stain down one whole side of his khaki shirt. Mortimer noticed his head bowing as he rode, and he slumped forwards as if barely awake. Then he fell off. His fall made two clear thuds over the sibilance of the walking hoofs. He grunted, then lay there silently. After that, a fighter rode pillion behind him, holding him.

The sun hung low: a bronze coin just above the skyline of smooth orange hills, burnished. Time of day meant nothing to these men. Celeste rode beside Mortimer, the late sun shining on her face, turning her skin the colour of the enflamed sand. She smiled at him. In her white robes and headscarf she looked like some heroine from the pages of a Victorian romance. He could sense the bones in her arms, their strength and dryness. Out here, all creatures seemed dry, set free of the need for moisture, released into an existence where no water weighed them down. It was as if here the human body was drained of all excess, and found its true home among the minerals.

There was more talking now than there had been on the way out, as they rode back through a moonlit night. The sand kicked up around the camels' hoofs, pale in the dark like spray round the ankles of a barefoot walker in a beach's shallows. The day's work was done. Mortimer realised he had not eaten since dawn, and hunger had not troubled him at all. Peace tingled in his limbs. He could not remember ever feeling so good. The desert spread out in all directions. They rode its waves like a fleet of war canoes at leisure beneath the cool tent of night.

15

For three days they had the house to themselves. Twice a day a woman brought a bowl of couscous with vegetable stew. The first time she came Mortimer gave her a bundle of dinars; she accepted them without comment and put them inside her robe. The next time she came, she set the same notes down on the sand beside the new bowl of food. There was to be no

payment, evidently. But whether that was by force of hospitality or because Mortimer and Celeste were thought to be offering them a service, he never knew.

Other than that woman, they saw few people. Each dawn
and dusk Celeste would go out with her camera and Mortimer would either doze, if it was morning and she had left a
warm strip for him to roll into in their narrow bed, or else
catch up on his notes. He wrote out rough drafts of three stories: an account of what he had seen happen, with a little
background; a piece on the history of the Tuareg such as he
had gleaned it, and how their way of life was the only one truly
suited to the desert; and some fragmentary speculation on the
potential involvement of other parties interested either in dis-
comfiting Algeria or in exploiting the Sahara. If he could nail
any of that down, it could amplify the story enormously.

Mortimer found a house at the end of the row opposite
theirs where a woman would give him a trowelful of hot coals
and a pot of tea first thing. He hated to start the day without
tea. He copied the locals, alternately letting the pot heat on
the embers, and working up a froth by pouring back and forth
into a glass, with a hunk of sugar dissolving in it. He'd sit on
the edge of their bed sipping from the hot glass, and get to
work on his notes. In the ideal world he'd be able to file three
stories in one go, as soon as they reached a phone, though in
reality he'd most likely have to make a lot of changes. The
hardest part was not being able to interview anyone. He saw
Jean Baptiste only once in those three days, and he assured
Mortimer that he would let him know of any developments.
He also said he'd think about who Mortimer might interview,
though he never came up with anyone but himself.

Mortimer and Celeste spontaneously occupied the little
house as if it were their own. To be contained within their

own four walls of mud, to be left alone there, to have this temporary home that was nominally theirs, and see their things scattered about it—Mortimer loved the way they so readily made a home, occupied the house together. To be alone in it, working, knowing Celeste would be back soon but meanwhile was busy at her own work, bolstering his endeavours with hers, felt like a blessing. When she returned he'd pass her a glass of tea, fill the pot, and heat up more. There wouldn't be any food till midmorning. Sometimes they grappled with one another before it arrived. They'd cover themselves with a sheet of beige cotton and make quiet, intoxicating love. He'd smother her cries with his mouth. The heat of her body first thing, the sun outside, the sandy floor, the earth walls, the taste of her lips—all these things seemed to belong together.

For hours at a stretch he'd forget altogether about the newspaper. Once he said to her: "All day I have hardly thought about work. About the news, television, radio, what we think we are doing here." He could have asked Hamed to bring back his battery so they could switch on the radio again, but he had no desire to.

She smiled. "This is real life. The journalist is always looking for meanings, reading between the lines, interpreting, mistrusting. What happens if for a moment you take things at face value? Look at this place. Yes, things are going on back in Algiers or wherever that could affect it, but these people are just living. Not the fighters but the villagers. They're not thinking about what goes on behind the scenes, they're thinking about the scene in front of their eyes. Will there be enough flour for the children's birthday treat. Can I get home from the gardens an hour early. Will the lettuces come up. Will the rice arrive in time. All the normal day to day bullshit. Except it's not bullshit. We're so busy trying to figure out the story behind things. What if there is no story? Do you ever think about that?"

He had to admit he didn't. "But everyone's like us," he said. "Everyone is busy thinking about the next move."

"I met a Tibetan lama once. He wasn't. You should have seen just the way he drank a cup of tea. There was nothing else in the whole world but that cup of tea. It's marvellous to watch. It makes you feel—that life is simple. That whatever makes you happy is right. That there's nothing else worth striving for. And then you go outside, and for a little while it stays with you, that feeling. I remember looking around at the trees, the cars with the sun glinting on them, the mountains above Pau shining with snow, and thinking: Wow, this beauty—I really felt it for once. And I thought, This beauty is here all the time. Not just now because I happen to have had tea with a Tibetan wise man who is visiting Europe, but all the time. One could always feel this good. And I think those lamas do. They make it their life's work to feel good. Can you beat that?"

He stirred his fingertips through the sand of the floor. "We want to interpret, understand."

"But what if there is nothing to understand? I mean—" She leaned forwards and picked up her glass of tea, cooling in the sand, blew steam off the surface. "Not the way we think. One day, I want to stop all this, do something real. Stop moving all the time."

He couldn't help frowning. "This isn't real?" Then he managed a smile. "Family portraits in a small town in southwest France?"

"There's nothing wrong with that. We all belong among our own people."

He was going to say something but hesitated.

She smiled and touched his hand. "Your own people are

who you make them. Whoever you love, you should be with them. But in a community, that's what I mean. Working with others, I don't know, to make life good. Better. Trying to do something. Not just watching, observing, seeing others make all the mistakes. One should make mistakes of one's own."

"We don't do that?"

She thought a moment. "Not really. Travelers never really get their hands dirty."

"But we're not just travelers."

"Observers then. We watch, and comment, and judge. It's easy to when you're not part of anything."

"I try not to judge," he said.

Her face creased in a smile. "I know you do." She leaned towards him and kissed his forehead. "But still, what does it all actually consist of, day by day, hour by hour? Traveling. Being in foreign places. Getting on planes, walking around cities we don't know, crossing country we don't know. We think it's all about covering important events, but that's just our pretext."

Mortimer was silent a moment. "Maybe you're right. But I don't care, this is the life I want. Especially with you."

He glanced at her, and for the first time saw a remoteness in her face, as if she were looking at him from a distance. She let out a little laugh, and moved closer to hug him.

He frowned. "Anyway, how can all this violence keep our hands so clean?"

"We don't compromise. Sure, sometimes in work an editor wants this or that changed a way we don't like. But not really, not in our hearts."

He knew that right now it was true: there was no compromise in his heart. He was functioning like a well-oiled machine, doing exactly what he had been designed to: roam the lands reporting on the upheavals seizing them, and to be in

love. A rush of elation, but tinged with anxiety, or with anticipation, ran through him. Love without hesitation or reservation, love without doubt—he knew that it must be a privilege
to feel it, but right now it felt like a birthright.

One night, very late, just before dawn, he went out into the
dark village, needing to pee. A late moon hung above the
dunes at the end of the little row of houses.

Far away a man started to sing the early prayers, making
his voice resonate like a megaphone. He reached the peak of a
scale and held his note, then dropped it; and again began low
down, working his way upwards. He was singing the name of
God. Seeing the band of shadow at the side of the moon, you
could almost feel the globe hanging out there in space, not
too far from this globe; and also sense the ball of fire that hung
in space a long way away, whose light illuminated most of that
bright ball. To hear God's name then, uttered by the throat of
one of his creatures, seemed entirely appropriate. Whatever
balancing act this machine of his was, with its many self-
suspended spheres, what could be more natural than to sing
its praise? In that one word the human chest could encompass
the scale of creation.

Mortimer asked himself why it was special with Celeste, and
how he knew. He had no good answers. It was almost a physical pain, still, a cramp in the belly. He could never get enough
of her physical proximity. He wanted to be next to her, or else
talking to her, all the time. This feeling that was both a yearning and a satisfaction, a hunger and a happiness, filled his
limbs. He had not known a person could get this way. It was as

if his cranium filled with sunlight, as if he could already feel the scope of his future with her. It might well get worse, there would no doubt be troubles, but he wanted to go through them, ride whatever ups and downs being with her brought. He was ready to pledge himself, something that he had never wanted to do with Saskia, even though he had once.

But everything had been different with Saskia. Not just her version of femininity, which seemed to hold attractiveness almost something of which to be ashamed; not just her rushed, heated, but ultimately separate lovemaking, always conducted with the eyes closed. Even her version of morality was nothing like Celeste's. Celeste seemed to act if anything out of a desire to help people; whereas with Saskia it had seemed more a desire to bring down the bad people, and the doing of good was a duty. Her moral valour didn't fill him with aspiration but weighed on him, made him feel not up to the mark. It had got him down more and more.

Hamed had not come on the expedition and ever since, his behaviour towards Mortimer had changed. Instead of humouring him with overuse of the word *monsieur*, he spoke less now, and looked at Mortimer as if hoping to find some answer in his face.

One evening Hamed invited them to his garden. It lay a quarter of a mile away through palm groves, a square of raked earth the size of a suburban swimming pool. There wasn't a weed in sight among rows of young plants. Up above stood the palms, with clusters of dates like bunches of grapes forming under their crowns. The water that enabled the palms to grow, and the shade the trees offered, were the two conditions of the garden. A diminutive canal six inches wide and bone dry ran alongside, with neat little parapets of clay, as straight as if marked out with a ruler. From it an even smaller channel no wider than a cigarette pack ran to the pool in the centre of Hamed's plot. At either end of the pool was a hole with a piece of board set in it: the sluice gates. Tiny clay walls divided the garden into sections. The whole thing was a miniature flood-plain, with dykes a couple of inches high, like a model. The miracle of it, other than the fact of its existence here in the middle of the sand dunes, was the perfect horizontal it must have required. Any dip, any slope, would cause the channels to back up and overflow. Mortimer had never seen thrift like it. It was immaculate.

He was about to ask where the water came from when Hamed bunched his robes, tucked them in his belt, and with his mouth open in a grin presented himself to a palm tree. He placed one foot then the other at knee height on the trunk, and commenced to climb in a froglike action, jumping from one rib of the trunk to the next, rapidly, until he reached the crown, where he pulled the fronds out of his way and with a thrashing of greenery climbed through them. Once on top, he perched there motionless for a moment. Then he opened his mouth and began to sing, sending his voice high into the falsetto range, singing with an urgency, a desperation.

Mortimer clapped and called, "Encore."

Another voice could be heard singing far away. Then a third voice answered, not so far away, and after it the distant man sang back. Then Hamed sang again. It went on for fif-teen or twenty minutes, the three men singing to one another, perched like birds in the trees above their gardens.

All around lay the dusty land with nothing on it, just the crust of planet stretching away to the horizon. The men's voices seemed to rise out of the very sand and clay of the empty land. It was as if they were singing about the desert, desperate to spread the news not that God was in the desert, but that the desert itself was God.

For a moment it seemed to Mortimer that mankind's existence was the loneliest thing imaginable, a solitary perpendicularity stalking the flat earth with no possible notion as to why it was there. Yet in his sadness there was also a sense of being on the brink of an inner homecoming, one which he recognised probably would not take place, even as he sensed its possibility.

"Come down," he called softly into the treetop. Celeste's light fingers found his. Her face was deep bronze in the last light. A scarf of weak yellow lay across the west, and beneath it a band of mauve was already spreading up the sky.

16

An airplane came the next morning. The tactics were like a giant game of chess. The guerrillas made a move. They went in and collected a pawn off one square. The scale was enormous: squares hundreds of miles broad, and each move might take thirty-six hours or even weeks to effect. Next, the other side sent down a little speck that buzzed in the sky. This winged knight circled over the castle, rolled its wings in friendly fashion, as if giving a wave, then settled on the plain. The home side understood. They sent forth a posse to meet the challenge: a rook perhaps, or a bishop. The two faced each other down. It was a close thing. They brought the knight to the castle for negotiations. Perhaps they could effect a trade of some kind: two pawns for the knight, say.

But it was hard to get to grips when no one would tell him

anything, when he had to bob and crane over the shoulders of the two teams crowded round the board to catch a glimpse of the state of play.

Apparently there was not much to see. The party of delegates returned to their plane amid the same escort of camels that had ridden out to meet them. They had landed on the plain of Timimoun. Later, the plane could be heard roaring away through the afternoon. This time it did not buzz the village but pursued a straight course a thousand feet up, droning as it climbed. But something had evidently been achieved. In the middle of the night Mortimer woke to the gurgle of an engine. His first thought was that it must be a generator, though he had seen none in the village. He pulled on his boots.

Lights blazed under the palm trees. He could see the hulk of a vehicle, a Unimog with a canvas top, and beside it a man holding a machine gun. Mortimer was amazed that it could have driven here.

Then Hamed was at Mortimer's side. Before he had a chance to say anything Mortimer put a finger to his lips. Just then a man in an army cap, short sleeves, and fatigues, with a military bearing, came walking through the trees, chuckling, followed by two aides. The Unimog had a double-size cab, and they all climbed into it. The great vehicle performed a turn in reverse, then chugged away through the trees, its rear lights picking out the dust in its wake.

Hamed brought food, and they ate in the light of the kerosene lamp. Then he left, and they lay on Celeste's bunk.

"It's actually happening," Mortimer said. "A war is starting and we're here to witness it."

He heard an engine again at dawn, and shook her awake. She drank a quick bowl of water and they went out into the chalky air. At first he thought a thin cloud had settled over the oasis, but it was just the pale dawn sky.

The Unimog was back, standing in the same place. This time it was flanked by several camel riders holding up guns. Celeste circled out through the trees with her camera, squinting through it as she went. He heard the rapid, soft clicks, the whining of the automatic wind-on. She was quick about her business.

The camel riders didn't move. Three men climbed down from the vehicle and walked towards the ksar. It wasn't long before they strode back with their heads down, clambered up into the cab, and drove away. One or two of the riders turned their mounts to watch them go.

A tussle was evidently going on, without an outcome as yet.

Jean Baptiste came by later with Hamed, who prepared the tea. The situation was that the hostages from the police post, all three of them, were staying.

"It is all we can do for now," Jean Baptiste said. "We must make them understand that we are serious. We do not keep our heads in the sand, we know how the world is out there. Why should we not control our piece of it? Why should we not benefit from it? We have told them we might play ball, as you say, but they don't understand. Now we are telling them something else: unless we play ball, there will be no game. But things will become harder now."

Jean Baptiste blew on his little glass of tea, making the steaming froth lap over the side and onto his fingertips.

The rebels' plan was to perform similar operations in a number of places. It was better to capture than to kill, Jean

Baptiste said, not only because desert men preferred not to kill if they didn't have to. Even now in the deep south other bands were executing comparable raids. There had been some fighting, few casualties.

How did he know?

"Radio, of course," he said, with slight consternation.

So was this headquarters?

He wouldn't answer. He sipped the froth off his tea glass and mimed smoking. Mortimer offered him a cigarette. He smoked it in silence. Halfway through he said, "Much has yet to be decided. You ask the same questions we are asking ourselves."

A certain feeling had been dogging Mortimer. Now he recognised it as impatience. It was time, past time, to get to a telephone. He had to get on to Kepple, organise things properly. There was the possibility of using the guerrillas' radio, he supposed, but it was hard to imagine how to contact London with it, if they'd even let him try. Perhaps they could contact a telephone operator somewhere, through whom he could make a call. It seemed highly doubtful. On the other hand, if he found a way of leaving in order to get to a telephone, what might he miss while he was gone? Like the light of stars, news of this war would have to arrive late. News was always late anyway, even at the best of times.

Where did they plan to go next?

Again Jean Baptiste was uncertain, evasive.

"I need a proper contact, that's the problem," Mortimer told Celeste.

"We've stumbled onto this by accident," she said. "That's the problem. And the luck."

"There's Rio Camello next door, Mauritania has already

given up its claim on the Western Sahara, and now this. The whole desert could be repartitioned," Mortimer mused.

In a sense all the borders in the region were notional anyway. The Tuareg came and went as they wished between Mali, Niger, and Algeria. If there was a natural country in the heart of the Sahara, it was a Tuareg state. The idea wasn't so implausible. They could probably muster a population of a quarter million, more than in some African countries. And if there really was oil, even if there was only the natural gas that had already been found, they'd have enough of an economic base to boost the domestic product well past Africa's poorest. They'd need friends, obviously, but Jean Baptiste said they had friends. There was one obvious candidate for support: Algeria's longtime rival, Morocco. There would be a kind of justice in the two countries each financing a proxy war against the other: Algeria had the Rio Camello, Morocco would have the Tuareg.

Different men stopped by the house. Some merely wanted to drink a glass of tea with the foreign journalists, smoke their cigarettes; others wanted to preach, imagining perhaps that their words would be broadcast to the world. But none of them would tell Mortimer what the immediate strategy was. Had there been demands, had they been refused? No one would tell him anything. It was maddening. Mortimer scribbled everything down he could think of, but how was he to convey any of it to where it mattered? He would have to make a break for it, get Celeste's pictures and some copy filed soon. But he still needed more interviews.

And that was still a problem, evidently. One morning Hamed took an interminable time finding Jean Baptiste, and when he eventually did bring him, and Mortimer once again requested an interview with a leader, Baptiste tutted and shook his head. He kept on tutting, lightly, then sucked from a glass.

Mortimer changed tack. "I've got to get to Timimoun anyway," he said.

Jean Baptiste glanced at him in surprise. Then he shrugged. "All things are possible."

He said something in Arabic to Hamed, who at once shook his head.

"This is boring," Mortimer said aloud to Celeste.

"No, this is as exciting as it gets."

She was right. He knew she was right. And in fact it all began again soon.

17

They talked until late. She had been at the front line a few times before. "You keep out of the way," she said. "There is no line. It's a mess. No one knows what's going on. Gradually, or suddenly, it becomes clear it's over, and you get to see what happened."

She lay on her back staring at the ceiling. "*La plus belle des choses*," she began, then rolled towards him. "You know that? Sappho. For some the most beautiful sight is a regiment of infantry, or a fleet at sea; but for her it's to see two people in love."

The battle would have taken place the next day. More riders kept arriving that night, and it was with a battle yell of ululation that the camel troop set sail at dawn. But a khamsin blew up in the morning. No one could stand up, not even the camels. The Tuareg closed the eye slits in their veils and settled down to hibernate beside their dethroned mounts. Everyone hid their face as best they could. Mortimer's trousers rode up his ankles as he hunkered down, and afterwards a band of skin was worn raw, as if he had been manacled. The khamsin blew hard for two hours, then became weaker and intermittent, but it was enough to delay things for that day.

They slept out in the dunes. It was bitterly cold. Celeste huddled against Mortimer, until the two of them followed the Tuareg's example and pressed themselves against one of the camels. It turned its head, curious, and its belly groaned noisily.

Mortimer fell in and out of sleep all night. Each time he found himself awake, he heard deep, low voices.

At one point he woke to find the weather had passed entirely, leaving a night of perfect stillness. The shapes of the dunes all around were colourless, dark grey in the night, and the sky was bursting with swollen stars. The stars were so close you'd think they were not more than a hundred feet up; or less, much less, that you could reach up and strum your fingers through them, and they'd swirl about like blossoms on a pond.

Celeste was quite still at his side. Without moving at all, without looking at her, he realised that he knew she was wide awake; and at that moment he too became wide awake.

She was staring at him, her eyes gleaming in whatever little sheen they picked up from the stars.

"After this," she said softly, not whispering but talking in a low murmur. "I'm thinking what will happen after this."

"Taillot said the government will be good to the Tuareg. Too many people like them."

She hadn't shifted her gaze from him, her eyes both restful and alert. "I mean when we leave here. I mean us."

A faint alarm ran through him, though he couldn't have said what exactly he feared, except to be drawn out of the present circumstances, for all their danger. He didn't like to be reminded that the two of them would not always be here in the desert as they were now.

He said, "It's up to us."

She pressed her face into his shoulder. He shifted his arm so it was partly round her. He could feel her slender shoulder blade, her ribs, which seemed fine and delicate as a wishbone just then, and precious.

There was no wake-up call. Mortimer lifted his head and saw that nearby a number of camels had got to their feet, and that people were walking about on the sand. Jean Baptiste appeared with a trowel of glowing embers, bedded them in the sand, and made tea. It was still dark when the column mounted.

At this hour Mortimer noticed the bittersweet reek of the camels. The riders fell into single file. Mortimer watched the swaying of Celeste's camel in front of his, its haunches sinking from side to side as it climbed the dunes.

Someone had known precisely where they were when they stopped the previous evening. At the top of the first rise the plain of Timimoun opened out pale before them. They filed down the last flank of sand and entered a trot on the flat land, breaking out of single file and spreading wide. They were clearly heading for the town. Mortimer thought it would surely take them an hour to reach, but it all happened much faster. Instead of the pace slackening it intensified. Soon it became a canter, and Mortimer had to cling to his pommel with both hands. The great neck in front of him sawed back and forth, and there seemed a gulf before him. He dreaded falling and being left behind, and didn't dare look to see where Celeste had got to, though he wanted to.

Someone let off a gun. Mortimer saw palms ahead, and through them the dark wall of the town. The ground had become chalky white, the sky a dull grey. More guns sounded, there was no letting up, in a moment the whole troop was flowing under the trees and along the foot of the town wall. They galloped to the end of it, then circled out onto the plain, doubling back in a broad curve, and came to a halt a hundred yards off.

Mortimer discovered Jean Baptiste and Celeste either side of him, as if he alone had been unable to keep track of the others' movements. The great gates of the town slowly opened. The troop began to ululate, some stepped forward. A group of locals came running out on foot, and a number of riders called out, *hut-hut-hut*, tapping their mounts on the shoulder, and trotted into the town. Not long after, a gang of riders emerged with eight policemen walking between them with their hands on their heads.

Timimoun was then effectively theirs. It was so simply and harmlessly done that the whole procedure might have been nothing more than some annual ceremony. There was gun-fire behind the walls, but it was just celebratory, Mortimer guessed. Some of the riders who had remained outside cocked and raised their guns, then shot them into the sky.

It was an easy victory, and a small one. The town had only a handful of representatives of the state, and a couple of thousand inhabitants. The only casualty was a rebel who lost his fingers when his gun misfired during the celebrations.

It was also a short-lived victory. The police had evidently

got a message off before they were seized. Not an hour later a Chinook crawled by overhead, its twin fans turning so slowly Mortimer would have sworn he could see them revolving. The rotors thudded like mortar fire. Once, a beat of the engine cracked like a shell exploding nearby, as the sound ricocheted off the town wall. The helicopter circled the town, then droned heavily away.

Its appearance provoked much shouting and letting off of guns, but nothing that couldn't still have fallen within the remit of some elaborate ritual.

The rebels were pragmatists. They departed before the end of day with their prisoners, riding back across the plateau to the relative safety of the dunes.

At dawn three Sikorskys flew in. Mortimer watched them through Jean Baptiste's binoculars from the brow of a dune. They either landed or went away. Without a second thought, it seemed, the rebels mounted and made their way swiftly across the pan of clay, back towards the town. Jean Baptiste held back Mortimer and Celeste for a while, then agreed to allow them within half a mile of the town, and they all galloped off after the troop. They watched from a dry wadi while sporadic gunfire crackled and wisps of smoke drifted in the sky. The helicopters evidently hadn't left. One of them appeared, flying right over the town. It made a hurried descent, and as soon as it touched the ground just outside the walls, jumped back into the air, whereupon it was engulfed in flame, and black smoke poured from beneath the rotor. A moment later it sank down slowly, heeled onto one side, and Mortimer then heard the boom of its landing.

Celeste had been snapping with her long lens, and now

scurried out on foot for a better angle. Jean Baptiste shouted after her. She called back that she was all right, but didn't look round or stop.

Not long after, the two unscathed helicopters droned away to the east, and Celeste returned. The three of them remounted and rode slowly towards the town.

Celeste had ushered three of the riders towards the stricken helicopter, and had them pose on their camels before it, guns held over their heads.

"They'll like that shot," she muttered to Mortimer afterwards, as she was labelling the film.

18

The grenade looked like something from the pages of the *Commando* comics Mortimer had read as a boy, an old Jerry stick grenade with a cap on the end. It came rolling out of the town gate and tapped against one of the giant wooden doors. No one ever established who had thrown it, or why. It wasn't unknown for grenades to be part of celebrations among the tribesmen. Or boys might have got hold of it, Jean Baptiste thought.

It happened just after Mansour, the big Egyptian doctor who played chess, came strolling up the road, a stately figure under the palms, gliding between them and the wall in his long white kaftan, his face with its thick moustache looking serious in the sunlight.

He shook Mortimer's hand. "You are back in time to see our *news*," he said, and nodded at Celeste, who was busy photographing a group of boys playing with a gun. "You can tell them about this back in London."

Mortimer at once felt calmer and clearer in the man's company.

"I hope the desert was good to you," he said. When he looked at Mortimer with his slightly sad-looking bright eyes, and stood close to him, something went quiet in Mortimer's breast.

"My colleagues are frantic. Now they want to go home more than ever. I tell them that now more than ever we will be needed."

He walked on towards the town gates with the calm interest of a landowner making the daily round of his property, hands behind his back. Mortimer saw him pause at the gate thirty yards away, and engage a boy in conversation. Then the boy ran off, and the grenade appeared, rattling across the dust.

Mansour stood there alone beneath the high arch as it rolled towards him.

There was a split second when Mortimer knew what was going to happen, long enough for him to feel the ground tilt. When it detonated a group of men standing fifty yards off jumped. The crash seemed inordinately loud, and the sound ricocheted off the town wall as if being answered by further explosions timed to go off one after another. The men quickly realised they were safe and it was just some piece of celebration going on, and turned to look without moving, covering their momentary alarm by standing still.

Mansour had gone. A puff of smoke lingered, as of a car that had had trouble getting started, and one of the town gates had lost a ragged bite from its corner. At least a yard of lumber had been blown off. Then Mortimer saw Mansour lying on his front against the foot of the wall. The side of his kaftan was already dark, and on his back the cloth was dusty and dirty.

It took five of them to carry him into a house just within

the walls. Someone whipped up a rug and they laid him on his back on the earth floor. Already there was a bad smell, the sweet, fetid smell of offal.

Mansour's face was smeared with dirt but seemed otherwise unscathed, but his chest was in a terrible state. His kaftan had been cut up, revealing a dark glinting mess within. Mortimer held his breath and did not look closely. He ran off to fetch another of the Egyptian doctors.

The only one he could persuade to come was a tall, balding man who was walking around the yard outside his house, glancing towards the town centre with round eyes, and muttering to himself, shaking his head. In spite of his obvious fear he agreed to come and quickly fetched a bag of supplies.

By the time they got to him Mansour's face had turned yellow and there was a dazzled air in the room that Mortimer recognised at once as the presence of death. The doctor shook his head and said there was no need to examine him, though he did so anyway. They covered him with a headscarf.

"*Ça va?*" A man caught Mortimer's elbow. It was Jean Baptiste. "*Tu vois*, another operation. Small but successful." He pulled Mortimer away.

Mortimer stood in the doorway, in the shade of the building, just outside the glare of the brilliant day. It was late morning, very hot. The sand of the village was blinding, almost white. Across it fell the stripes of palm shadows. Palms and sand, palms and sand: the material of hot countries. He would often be among them now. Just now he remembered he liked a hot country: when he arrived in one, it was as if he pulled on some old and trusted jacket, a second skin.

He hadn't noticed Celeste in the room. She came out now, shaking her head. He put an arm round her, and she said nothing, but kept on shaking her head. Then she exhaled sharply, as if on the point of tears. "I'm sick of this. Sick of stupid, stupid killing. For what?" She shrugged him off. "I get hold of my camera, you get your notebook, and we think it's all so important. We don't see that we are the problem."

Mortimer's chest was a furnace. He felt he needed to be moving, needed a breeze to cool it down. But what he needed most urgently was a telephone: that was all he could think about.

"They've smashed their radio," Jean Baptiste told him. "They don't want word to get out." He looked seriously at Mortimer. "You must be careful."

If he didn't get to a phone today someone might hear of this and beat him to it, and all their work could end up going to waste. They needed to courier up Celeste's films too, preferably today. "I have to get back to El Menia," Mortimer said.

Jean Baptiste tutted. He stood tall, gazing out of the gate across the flat plain, which just now was the colour of chalk. The dunes in the distance at the far side were pink. A little way out a number of men and boys stood in a respectful line, near the fallen helicopter.

"You can't go that way. There will be roadblocks and they could shoot at anything that comes."

"But I must get to a phone. Or else it's all useless, a waste of time."

"You will go the other way."

"But there's nothing the other way."

"Sí." He frowned. "The frontier. Morocco."

"Morocco?"

"Four hours, less in a good truck."

Mortimer's mind clouded. He hadn't contemplated going into another country.

"But how will I find you again?"

And what might happen while he was gone? On the other hand, he had enough already for at least three pieces, he was sure of it, if not four, and time was of the essence. Any day a television crew might drop in out of nowhere, and he'd lose everything, all the surprise and momentum behind the ambush of the front page. Because that was where he was heading, he realised, surprised both to discover that this had been his secret hope all along, and that it felt like a real possibility now.

"They will negotiate now," Jean Baptiste said. "We believe so. It may be quiet for a little while."

It seemed implausible to Mortimer that the Algerian government would permit a handful of rebels to take control of a town, even a small one, and not seize it right back. But then Jean Baptiste said something strange.

"You must talk to Taillot. We have promised him. He has helped us and we have agreed. He has to know what you will print."

"What do you mean? What's it got to do with Taillot?"

Jean Baptiste sucked through his teeth. "It's difficult. He might be involved."

"Involved?"

"Elf Aquitaine, they are our friends."

Dimly Mortimer recognised that he was being told something unexpected, which would solve a number of riddles that had previously preoccupied him, before he had got caught up in the exotic adventures of the past few days.

"Please," Jean Baptiste went on. "Talk to Taillot."

Mortimer nodded.

"You must not print anything without talking to him. We have to know what the reaction will be once the news gets out.

The government might decide to send in everything they have. Taillot is our one sure friend. We have given our word that Elf Aquitaine can have the contracts, if we succeed."

Again Mortimer nodded, hearing the words as if they were being uttered to someone else, and recognising that they were the key he needed.

"If, or once, the Tuareg state is established," Jean Baptiste was saying, "that is the first thing we must do, get the oil flowing, with Elf's help."

19

A tanker truck had arrived the night before down the track from El Menia, and was traveling on to the border. It was the best they could do, a small dirty tanker which had perhaps once been white.

The driver, a fat man, his belly spilling out from under the hem of his T-shirt, folding over the waist of his trousers, slowly rolled out of town, with much churning of gears and hissing of the compression switch. He hadn't shaved in a good few days and his hands were grimy with oil.

"*La frontière?*" he asked, and cocked his head.

The radio screeched. It was a moment before Mortimer realised over the roar of the engine at their feet that the sound it made was music, some frantic Arabic concoction. The driver bounced on his seat, ignoring the potholes, crashing right through them. Except once when he braked hard and flipped through the gears, then wound off the tarmac, ground along the piste beside it for a hundred yards, bypassing a stretch holed with craters the size of cars.

He reached down and pulled a thermos from under his seat, splashed out a cup of thin grey liquid, which he held out past Mortimer to Celeste.

She took a sip then handed it to him. It was warm, spicy. He drank a little and handed it back to the driver. The man drained it in one go, then removed his hands from the steering wheel and mimed driving. "Land Rover? You don't have Land Rover?"

Mortimer shook his head.

The driver grinned at him. "Where are you going?"

"The coast."

"*Pas bon,*" the man said. "You should bring your own Land Rover. You can't cross the desert like this. If you do, the drivers will take you and do bad things to you. Or to your woman."

The man was silent awhile. "*Il faut faire attention.* There are bad people."

As long as they didn't stop, Mortimer thought, they'd get through this ride all right.

It was afternoon when they reached the border village. It was a small place of low mud homes, one of which, bare inside except for a table and two chairs, was the border post itself. The official, a man in trousers and shirt rather than the local cotton robe, but otherwise no uniform, or anything else to distinguish his office, stamped their passports, copied out their details into a ledger with a blue ballpoint pen, and said wearily, "*Bienvenus en Maroc.*"

There was a grey telephone on the table. Mortimer pleaded and pulled out his wallet, but the man held it up to Mortimer's ear and said, "*Vous voyez?*" The earpiece was stone dead. "The lines have not worked since September."

It was around three in the afternoon and fearsomely hot.

You could tell it was another country. For one thing, there were tin signs tacked to walls advertising Coca-Cola, Goodyear tyres, Marlboros.

The frontier official locked up his office with an aluminum padlock of a kind Mortimer had used on his bicycle as a teenager, and led them down a side street to a yard where a large truck with an enclosed back was parked.

The owner of the truck, a man in red and white robes with a dark purple headscarf, grinned and told them the bus would be leaving in two days for the coast.

"The bus?" Mortimer asked.

The man opened up the back of the truck and gestured at rows of leather straps slung across the interior. This was the bus and these were its seats.

For two thousand francs the man agreed to leave that day. But it was an hour before he had filled up with petrol, then driven around the town blaring his horn, picking up a few passengers, who could be heard laughing and chatting as they settled in the interior behind the cab, as if amused by the change in routine. Finally he pointed the bulbous bonnet of the truck out of town, towards the late-afternoon sun.

"Do we have to go to the coast?" Mortimer asked Celeste.

"There's nothing before Tarfaya," she said. "I'm sure of it. Nothing at all. Plus we can fly from there, or at least from El Ayoun, which is nearby. We could be in Casablanca tomorrow."

The sky thickened into a grey pallor. The sun itself appeared as a great red balloon above the level of the plain, and slowly sank into bands of darker and darker red as it approached the very edge of the sheet of land. Soon after it was gone the driver flipped the gear stick into neutral and switched off the engine and let the vehicle coast to a stop.

No need to park, out here on this tabletop of clay. Where the truck stopped was camp.

Mortimer pleaded and offered him money to keep driving through the night, but the driver wouldn't do it. He tutted and grinned and could not be swayed.

Celeste clutched his hand and told him it would be all right. They would leave at dawn and reach the little city before lunchtime. A few hours could surely not make such a difference.

"And look at this, it's beautiful."

It was true. A fan of brilliant orange had opened up in the sky. The whole plain had turned mauve. It was incalculably big. And utterly empty, without blemish.

Celeste's face looked more tanned than ever, a rich nut brown.

The other passengers had come prepared. A man who had brought along charcoal built a fire. A woman kneaded dough in a bowl, dug a pit in the earth, and laid three flat loaves in it and sprinkled sand over them. The man then shovelled up his glowing coals and tipped them over the buried bread, and set about making tea.

A star shone so brightly that Mortimer thought for a moment it must be a plane coming in to land. Then more stars appeared, until a snowfield spread across the night.

Mortimer switched on his torch and got to work in his notebook, figuring out how to work in the speculative involvement of an oil company in the insurrection. It was something Kepple would want corroborated, but it was priceless.

They were up early and on the road before dawn. It was good to be driving in the cool, dark air with a hint of dust in the back of the throat. Mortimer's limbs were filled with an early-morning freshness, a feeling of having stolen a march on the world. Soon the sky lightened. They glided along on the rumbling axles over the smooth plain with its mild undulations, and saw it grow from black to mauve. Beneath their feet the engine of the old truck chortled.

After the chilly night it was good too to be in that cab feeling the warmth of the motor. Mortimer was stiff with cold. It was a lovely place to be, high up on the old deep black seats, with the littered iron floor at their feet, and the big windscreen before them with its radial smears of desert dust, and Celeste beside him. There was only water to drink. Mortimer understood in a new way the necessity not so much of coffee or tea but of a hot drink in the morning, especially after such a night of hard, cold ground: it healed the body of nighttime.

The driver, who had wrapped his scarf back into place like a turban, offered Mortimer a cigarette. They were a cheap local brand, sweet, sickly blond tobacco, but he liked it all the same. With Celeste next to him in the cab, with dawn breaking behind them, and a desert breakfast of water and a cigarette, he felt good things in the air.

He thought of the four pieces he had written out and revised again by the light of his torch, and instead of panicking about how to transfer them to where they were needed as soon as possible, for the first time he quietly looked forward to when he and Celeste would roll back into civilisation, and he would be able to settle in a phone kiosk, or by a hotel bed, and spend an hour giving all the pieces to copy. Then there'd be the thrill of the phone ringing and it being Kepple, and all the big machinery of the press would swing into gear in order to take his material and get it out into the world. And this war, all this work he had been at times almost inadvertently, unwittingly doing over the past few weeks, all of it would emerge into the light and become real. It would get on the world's agenda: another problem now known, to be addressed if not solved.

Sure enough, in Tarfaya Mortimer couldn't wait until they'd found a hotel, but went into the first phone boutique he saw, got a pile of change from the old woman who ran it, and ducked into one of the five cabins and pulled the glass door shut after him. Kepple let out a long "Ah" when he heard his voice, clearly pleased to hear from him, and after a quick exchange of greetings transferred him to the copy takers, telling him to give them everything he had. He dictated all four pieces, then was transferred back to Kepple, who told him to call back in an hour. Then they took a beaten-up Mercedes taxi to the small, dusty city of El Ayoun, half an hour away, where there was an airline office.

Celeste labelled all her films and sent them to London by Royal Air Maroc's courier service. The next passenger flight out wasn't till Wednesday, three days away, but the films would go on the postal flight that afternoon.

They checked into a new concrete hotel in the centre of town, across the street from a noisy, dusty construction project. The room had a phone by the bed, but when Mortimer picked it up, there was no dial tone, only a faint hiss. Which at least perhaps meant the line wasn't completely dead. He clicked the button a few times, then a man's voice said in slow, lugubrious French: "*What number would you like?*"

"Well," Kepple said when he got through to him, "you've done it. You're on the front page. Just as soon as the films arrive we'll get them developed and see if we can't get a picture up there too. We'll send a bike out to Heathrow to fetch them. Congratulations. We're going to use everything, all the pieces."

Mortimer hung up and felt faint. He could hardly believe what he had just heard. Was this really his own life he was leading, and not someone else's?

When he told Celeste she gave him a tight hug and kissed him on the nose.

"And he says he'll try and put one of your pictures on the front page too, once the films arrive."

She smiled. "That's nice."

"Nice? It'll be fantastic."

She pinched his nose lightly. "I'm excited for you," she said, and hugged him again.

20

They strolled down to the port to find a place for lunch, and sat under an awning at a café-restaurant beside the harbour. They ordered brochettes, couscous, salad, "Spanch omlet," and two bottles of Fanta, two of Heineken.

The place was deserted except for a middle-aged white couple a few tables away. They got talking. The couple were English, it turned out, from Cornwall. The man, who introduced himself as Colin, had fine, fair hair and blue eyes with tiny pupils, as if they'd seen too much of the sun, and a weathered, wrinkled face. The woman, Vicky, was overweight, with a reddish, puffy complexion and uneasy black eyes.

"What brings you here?" Mortimer asked them.

"See that?" the man said, nodding towards the harbour. "That's what brought us here."

"And what's taking us out," the woman added with a

chuckle. "This afternoon and not a moment too soon, I can tell you."

"Now now, Vicky," the man said.

Among the fishing pirogues moored in the muddy water of the harbour stood a white yacht, the bare pole of its mast looking impossibly tall among the local boats.

"They don't call this the dark continent for nothing," she went on. "I tell you, I can't wait to see Mount Teide on the horizon. Las Palmas, that's the place for me. Whatever possessed us to come here I can't think. You'd never believe it's only a hundred miles away."

"How long will it take?" Celeste asked.

"Twenty-four hours at the outside. We'll be having drinks in the marina tomorrow night," she said, and giggled nervously.

"What are your plans?" Colin asked. "Don't suppose you fancy a trip to the Canaries? We've lost our deckhand."

It was Mortimer's idea. There was no time to think about it—just the momentum of their journey pushing them on.

"We'll get home quicker," he said. "From Las Palmas there'll be several flights a day to London and Paris. Come on. And you love sailing."

As he spoke he was conscious that they needed to talk again about what they were going to do next, where they would go. For the moment, when his stock was high at the paper, he felt he should get back there soon and see if he could consolidate his position.

She shrugged. "I've never done an ocean trip like that. I hope you don't get seasick."

They were sitting side by side on the hotel bed. From their

fourth-floor window they had a view past a water tank of the blue sea, looking impossibly inviting. It was irresistible. "I've never been on a sailing boat," he said. "Look at that. The ocean. We'll wash the desert right out of our hair."

"But now?"

"Why not? We are here, the boat is here, they need us. And we can figure out what we're going to do next."

It was fine enough when they first left port. Mortimer had decided not to take any Dramamine: he'd adjust quicker.

Vicky came bustling out of the companionway past Colin, who was sitting at the wheel in the cockpit. She ripped down a pair of trousers and a T-shirt that were drying on a line, shook her head, and hissed at him, "What are you doing? It was *you* that told *me*."

She disappeared back down below.

Celeste and Mortimer, seated up on the white fibreglass deck just in front of the cockpit, on top of the cabin, glanced at one another.

A moment later Colin said: "It's supposed to be bad luck to leave port with your washing out. I wasn't thinking."

The couple had been living in their boat for three years, yet it didn't seem to Mortimer that either of them was quite happy about it, as if they were still waiting to discover the point of their life on a yacht. In some ways it was as if they had never left home: the main cabin, a sloping-walled chamber with benches all down one side, and on the other a galley, then a built-in desk where the charts and pilot books and single sideband radio were all housed, was covered, walls and floor, in brown carpet. With its few china ornaments, it felt

like a cramped English living room. There was a sleeping
cabin up at the front where Colin and Vicky had their berth;
Mortimer and Celeste would bunk down on the benches.

They left their bags in a cavity underneath the seats,
against the sloping fibreglass of the hull.

It was a single-masted boat, a sloop, and not sleek, if anything broad in the beam. All round the big white deck ran rail-
ings of plastic-coated cable. There were various winches,
handles, and cleats all over the deck, and numerous pale, soft
ropes: all the age-old technology of sail. At the back was the
cockpit with the big chrome wheel in the middle.

Once they were on the boat and getting ready to go, it
seemed less of a pleasure cruiser and more like a serious piece
of equipment with a job to do. It was workmanlike, designed
with the purpose of accomplishing a task, not filling leisure
hours. Celeste walked around looking at the ropes and
winches, touching the mast, and gazing up its splendid height
admiringly.

The sun was shining and the sea was a rich blue. Sounds
of the land dwindled, until all you heard was the running of
water along the hull, and now and then a brief rumble of the
big red sails. Along the coast the town flattened itself into a
single line of white geometry. Here and there a mud-coloured
tower rose up, and a palm tree stood with its fronds like a cluster of roots. You could feel the strength in the breeze as the
boat heaved to one side. It began to rock. Both to rock and to
swivel. It nosed itself downward into each swell, swivelled a
little on its keel, and sprang back up, then repeated the move.
At first Mortimer was interested by this curious motion, then
became aware of a dull fear. Then he belched and felt dizzy. A
moment later he was leaning over the side ejecting a hot
stream of spicy vegetable soup. He watched it spatter into the

blue water and travel quickly out of sight. Another stream poured out of him, and this one hurt his stomach much more than the first. A third, smaller eruption came, which hurt still more. Then again his diaphragm clamped itself into a knot, and nothing emerged but a string of black phlegm that swung from his lips over the moving blue water.

When he lifted his face his head was spinning so badly he didn't think he could stand up. He clutched the rail at the side as the deck heaved back and forth under him, pitching this way and that. Every pitch sent a weight rocking back and forth in his skull. He glanced back at the now narrow line of the land, and yearned to get back to it.

Celeste's hand touched his back, and the sensation caused him to retch over the side once more. The boat pitched and again the weight heaved within his head.

When it had eased up enough to speak, he groaned and said he thought he needed the seasickness pills. But he couldn't for a moment imagine going down the ladder into the carpeted box of the cabin to search for them in his bag.

He heard Celeste moving away behind him, and uttered a silent prayer of thanks.

She returned with a mug of water and the little foil-wrapped tray of pills. But every one he took over the next hour jumped back out within a few minutes on a little gush of water, sometimes so soon after he had swallowed them that the water would still be cool.

Celeste shook her head and tutted. "You don't have to do everything, you know. You don't have to get on a boat just because it's there."

He groaned.

The rest of the afternoon he lay below with his head wedged against the carpeted wall, and tried to sleep. As long as he didn't move or open his eyes he found he could keep his stomach under control. When Vicky started cooking in the galley a few feet away, he breathed with his mouth open and held his nose. At some point he opened his eyes and saw that night had fallen outside the portholes. Later still he was woken by a bang up above, and felt the boat pitching about more violently. He could hear Colin shouting on deck, and the murmur of Vicky's voice answering him. He wondered if something was wrong and he ought to get up. The banging went on for a while, and one loud boom made the hull shudder. But he couldn't face lifting his head and opening his eyes and rising to his feet. He knew he'd immediately be overcome by nausea and wasn't sure he'd make it to the open air before retching.

When he woke again a low grinding filled the boat, and it was light outside.

Nervously he folded back the blanket someone had thrown over him, feeling chilled and ill, and stiff, and climbed into the cockpit.

Celeste was at the wheel staring contentedly ahead. "Hey you," she said. "Oh la la, you missed all the action. We're using the engine now. Did you hear that storm in the night? The mainsail ripped to pieces."

"Ripped?" Mortimer asked, surprised to hear that sails could do that.

"He had it reefed wrong."

Somehow it was comforting to be traveling under motor. It seemed more familiar.

Mortimer glanced out over the side and immediately felt sick again. A lot of waves seemed to be traveling in all directions rapidly, some of them rushing at the side of the boat, slapping it, then rushing off in some other direction.

"We're going back," she said. "So he can get the sail fixed."

Mortimer groaned and slumped down into the seat beside her and rested his head in her lap. She stroked his scalp. He couldn't remember ever feeling so cared for. Whatever ill assailed him, she would have patience for it, she would understand. She understood him: it was as simple as that. No one ever had before. It was wonderful luck, even while bobbing about on the Atlantic in the grip of nausea.

2 1

The problems started not with the tearing of the mainsail during the squall in the night, but when Colin pulled out his radio direction finder later in the day, inserted its earpieces in his ears, scanned the horizon with it, then consulted the charts down below, and discovered that they had overshot El Ayoun, and instead were near Dakhla, a port in the very south of the Moroccan Sahara.

Mortimer exulted to hear that they were near any port. It was clear that they would simply make for that one instead, and Colin thankfully agreed. Mortimer was so relieved to be on his way back to land, where he would not only get his feet back on firm ground but also resume his life, now uncomfortably interrupted, that he offered to take the wheel for a spell, and found that while holding the long chrome spokes he could watch the pitching of the prow and feel not the least trace of fear or sickness. Instead, it was exhilarating to have this great body of boat before one. He didn't even notice when land appeared on the horizon. Suddenly there it was: a thin green line and, when they were closer, a thin white line just beneath it.

Nor did he notice time passing. There they were now, not a mile offshore, with a cluster of tiny white shapes visible above the green line, which were houses catching the afternoon sun.

They had to find the mouth of a river that led into the port. According to the pilot book there was a sandbar in the river's estuary, which meant that from sea, even just a few hundred yards out, the line of white surf was uninterrupted. It was hard to spot the precise point where a boat could gain passage into the river mouth.

They could hear the surf now, a faint roar, and Mortimer's exhilaration grew at the sound of it. Then they spotted a water tower mentioned in the pilot book, and Colin decided to head for that. The river mouth should appear as they approached. Finally they saw it, a silvery sheet of smooth water beyond the mist of breakers, and a cluster of smoky-looking palm trees on the end of a spit of land.

To reach the river they had to get through the surf. But Colin wasn't worried. "She's built for waves," he said. Plus he'd grown up on the beaches of Cornwall, knew surf inside out.

"Just so long as it's deep enough."

This made Mortimer feel better still: if the sea here might be so shallow that the boat could even hit the bottom, then they were all but back on land already.

They got busy storing things below, locking up the cupboards, then Colin pointed the prow straight at the stand of palm trees.

Mortimer and Celeste sat on either side of the cockpit, each with a sheet rope Colin gave them, to control the jib-sail at the front. Colin was between them at the wheel. Vicky kept herself below.

The first breaker arrived slowly. It was as if it came to them, and not the other way round. Mortimer realised that a small cliff had opened up under the prow, a drop of ten or twelve feet. This cliff slowly moved down the length of the hull. At a certain point it would reach the midway point, and the boat would fall.

"We should be in bloody harnesses," Colin said loudly, as if admonishing someone.

The next thing Mortimer knew an avalanche of dazzling white snow was collapsing all around the cockpit. He looked at Celeste and she was flying high above him with her hair streaming and the blue sky behind her. A moment later she was directly beneath him, inches from dull grey froth. He himself would have dropped right onto her had he not been clutching the rails. Then there was a deep thud that caused the boat to stand still for a moment. Then it was moving again, and all around was a dazzling snowfield of hissing, seething fresh snow.

Celeste had moved. Mortimer looked up the boat but she wasn't there. He shouted to Colin and clambered on to the roof of the cabin, then peered down into the hold. She had vanished.

Colin shouted back and Mortimer jumped across and gripped the shrouds where Celeste had been sitting, and looked out over another sheet of new snow, effervescing in the sunshine. He scanned it frantically, then stared into the green face of a glass wall building itself, pulling itself clear of the brilliant froth, green as an empty wine bottle, tall as a house. He searched the gathering wall, and the emptying trough beneath it, that seemed to sink lower and lower, falling away as the battlement of water grew taller. There was no sign of her wherever he looked. Then Mortimer saw a shoe traveling through the water at what seemed an unnaturally rapid pace, back towards another eminence that was beginning to pull itself from the slanted sheet of white. It was a sneaker, and he recognised its rippled sole under a film of shining water.

He got his legs over the rails and jumped. He judged the leap just right, and at once his hand closed around the shoe. It seemed some kind of start. The water wasn't cold, and he lifted his head to look for her. At once blocks were falling on top of him, and he went under. In a second his ears and nose, his whole head was full of water, and he was in darkness, and a powerful turbulence had got hold of him, and he was being turned round and round. Still he held the shoe in his hand. Already his lungs were burning, his gullet was pumping, and he no longer knew which way the air might be.

Then for no reason he could fathom his head was out of the water. He heard himself gasp and gulp water and gasp again, and saw a tremendous hillside of green moorland streaked with runnels of grey snowmelt coming at him. He turned and lunged flat out away from it, but could get no purchase for the leap, stretched out flat without moving, and felt himself being rapidly sucked right into the very foot of the moving mountain. Once again he was in the roiling darkness. Powerful fish surged past his limbs, knocking them this way and that in their hurry to swarm by. This time he kicked and jerked himself and tried to keep away from them. They turned him over and over and his cheek scraped something like gravel and he heard—strangely, given the boiling thunder all around—a click deep within his skull, then once again he was mysteriously in the open air. He was out for longer this time, and no wall or mountainside was rushing at him. Instead, behind a far-off ridge he saw a TV aerial, or a white post, or a flagpole tipping this way and that. Then apparently from nowhere another wall was after him, had stolen right in behind him, and collapsed just before it reached him. He found he was stirring armfuls of dazzling white air as he tried to swim, and again he went down into the darkness and bumped against the gravel, this time with his chest as well as the side of his head, only it was smoother than gravel, and very flat, and he understood that it was sand. When the turbulence had passed he put his feet down and touched it with his foot and at once sprang up, sprang and lunged, and again. The bottom came a little nearer each time. Then he was trying to run, wading and jumping, and he could hear himself gasp and gulp horribly as he jumped and waded, still fighting through the seething and churning white even when it only came to his thighs, rushing to get clear of it before it dragged him back, which with every step it tried to do, to lasso his thighs and hurl him backwards off his feet. Then he stepped suddenly into a deeper pool that came up to his chest, and he sprang up at once choking in fright. Then it was calmer, the noise was farther away, the water was still and grey and ruffled with feathery ripples. He pushed through it and again got into shallower water where he could stand easily, and the water was down to his waist once more, then his knees, then it was all but gone. He was wading through ankle-deep mud, watery mud that swirled this way and that carrying froth on its back. He didn't trust it at all, and raced still to get free of it, and got free and at last was standing on a sheen of wet, hard sky.

The noise had moved off now, it had left him alone. He heard a trickle close by, and his right hand grew lighter all by itself. He looked down and saw he was still holding the shoe.

He saw her resting fifty yards away in the shallow waters. She had her face down, she was getting her breath back, so exhausted she didn't even have the strength to lift her face. He started to run towards her and fell over. He got up but his legs were jelly, his trousers heavy, and he stumbled again but kept upright this time, and ran on, stumbling and running, his hands clawing at the wet grey sand each time he nearly fell. He didn't know how he reached her, how he came to be kneeling at her side and struggling to lift her far shoulder and roll her onto her back. It was much harder to do than it ought to have been. Her legs knocked with each line of froth that rushed in towards them, and she groaned where she lay in the grey water with the fan of pale hair like fine hay spread around it. When he got her on her back her arms lay wide apart. Her lips were open and chalky blue. He put his head on her chest, calling out involuntarily. A shudder ran through her and she rolled on to her side under him. Water gushed from her mouth and nose.

It was still too deep here, the ripples splashed over her face. Quickly he got himself behind her head with his hands in her armpits and tugged her up on to the smooth sand gleaming like marble, like varnished wood. There on the smooth polished table of the beach he knelt over her, held her, and lifted her onto his thighs. She let out a high-pitched rasp of a choke. He rubbed her sternum, and she began to sob with every breath. He kissed her and undid her shirt, unravelled the long white cotton scarf from the desert that had wound itself round her neck, and kissed her again.

He collapsed next to her with his arms still round her warm, wet body. He closed his eyes and felt nothing but the warm soft weight beside him. She let out a long wail and turned her face into his neck.

Meanwhile, out to sea beyond the rows of white that

slowly traveled in, the strange pale boat floated quite still, except for its tall white mast, which tipped back and forth as if waving at him.

He didn't know how long they lay there, on the deserted board of the beach that stretched away empty in either direction. A pile of bushy clouds had congregated over the land to the east, and were brilliant white like steam in the late sun.

The beach shone and turned brown like a wet suntan. The clouds grew luminous, streaked with yellow. Still the boat was out there bobbing slightly back and forth.

"I've got your shoe," he said at last, and his voice felt as though it was being used for the very first time.

She groaned.

Later, a big local fishing canoe sailed past. The men stood up and looked at them and they looked back at the line of six figures in bright yellow oilskins gliding by. Later still, a white Peugeot pickup truck appeared on the brow of the beach and two policemen in brown fatigues climbed out.

The yacht was still there, anchored beyond the surf. The next morning when they came back down it would be gone.

22

They spent two nights in the town of Dakhla on that bleak, deserted coast, waiting for the consular officials to arrive from Casablanca. They had lost everything: her cameras, his notebooks, their wallets, passports, clothes. The British consul tried to arrange a wire of money to a local bank but it never came through. The first night the police gave them cast-off clothing that they were keeping in a box at the back of the station: a pair of crimson jeans for Mortimer, a long green corduroy dress for Celeste. They stood together in a storeroom rubbing themselves down with thin towels, and pulled on the baggy clothes and looked at each other and laughed. It was the first time they had, since they had dragged themselves out of the sea. Celeste had hardly looked at him all that time. For just a moment Mortimer felt a flicker of relief: they had been through the adventure to beat all adventures, and survived, and were still together. But he saw her face darken again, and his own fear came back. They were lucky to be alive. There was nothing good about it. It was fearful. He held her against him in her stiff unfamiliar dress, and she stood quite still.

The police gave them a plate each of couscous with meat stew. Four of them sat around in their sand-coloured uniforms while Mortimer and Celeste ate at a desk seated on steel chairs.

The whole town was bleached by the season of sandstorms. Dust coated everything. Palm trees, hoardings, houses, concrete blocks, the Peugeot trucks parked at the roadside, even the few people on the streets, everything was blighted by dust, faded to the colour of cloud.

There was a hotel with one star, a bleak modern building where the police put them up. The room had a telephone but it didn't work. There was water in the bathroom, and they both showered, and came out with the taste of dust in their mouths. A woman scrubbed out his shirt, and it came back smelling of dust.

Mortimer tried to apologise for having insisted they get on the boat. "It was a terrible idea. It was no fun being sick, for a start. Then I nearly get us killed."

"*I* do," she corrected.

"We should have just relaxed at the hotel for a couple of days, then flown." Yet even though he said that, he could feel that deep down he was happy to have had that experience: not just to know what it was like to be out on a small boat on the ocean, but to have experienced so intimately the huge force of the waves. It was another of the marvels of the world that you would never encounter unless you packed your bag and headed out.

He didn't so much feel guilty as sad to see Celeste so scared and defeated.

She didn't sleep. In the middle of the night he woke to find her sitting up in bed hugging her knees. He clicked on the lamp, which gave out a dim, yellow glow.

After a while she said, "I'm going home. I'm sick of being on the road. I've had enough."

He breathed heavily. "It's being in this room. Look at all this," he said. "This bed, the table, the walls, the roof, floor, staircase. So much stuff. Masses of materials. And we don't need any of it. It's a great big waste. All we need is sand and stars overhead. And a blanket."

She shook her head. "And the people we love."

He saw her chin begin to wrinkle. His heart sank. He put an arm round her. She stiffened and squeezed her eyes and began to shake. "I want to go home," she wailed, in a voice all but shorn of consonants, then wept in earnest, hunching her shoulders tightly, as if hoping to stifle her sobs. He let her shake in his arms.

When the crying had passed it was as if the room had warmed up and the lamp's glow become golden. "What a day," he sighed. "What a day."

They lay back, arms beneath one another's necks.

"What a month," she said. She turned to him. "Just think. If you hadn't seen me in the hotel in Algiers."

"If I hadn't decided to come down and get that drink." He shook his head. "And come and said hello. All because of a glass of pink milk."

They lay in silence. The town was absolutely quiet outside.

"Seriously," she said, turning half towards him. "I have to go home. Really I do."

Later, after she'd fallen asleep, he heard her moan in a dream.

The next day the consul arrived and the day after that they were in Casablanca. They sat in the lounge of a modern hotel drinking coffee. The hotel had a travel agency, and they were trying to resolve where to fly to. He had assumed she would come with him to London. She could meet the picture editors at the *Tribune*, and possibly they could fix up a regular contract for her. Sure enough, they had used several of her pictures, and one had been on the front page. They clearly liked her material. Then the two of them could be sent off together again.

"After something like that." She shook her head. "I don't know, I feel different. I need to stay at home for a while. Or at your flat in London."

"I told you, I don't have one now."

She frowned. "Well, where would we stay?"

"I guess at a hotel for a few nights. Or with friends. Then wherever they send us next."

He didn't like to see that she didn't know, or had forgotten, that he had no permanent home in London just now. It underscored what he hated to think of, that they had known each other only six weeks. He wanted it to be six months, six years. There was something indecent about it being so short a time.

She didn't reply. She was looking down at her coffee cup, slowly stirring it. Then she laid the spoon in the saucer.

"This is crazy. Here we are about to get on a plane and we don't even know where we're going."

"We're going to London."

"I mean—next week, or the week after, or whatever. Where will we be?"

"Well, how would you want to do it?"

"Go home. And stay there as long as I need to. Sort my new pictures, send the best of them to the library. Maybe make a trip to Paris to see some friends, a couple of picture editors. And I'll have to get new cameras." She paused. "And see my family."

She drank from her cup. "Normally, well, a lot of my life, I have been trying to get away from them, and from France. But now I need to go." She paused again. "I nearly died," she managed to say, before her bottom lip started trembling again. Then she sniffed, and pulled a smile. "It's OK. You can come and join me. Or I'll come to London. It's OK, really. Then we'll wait till the next assignment."

Even as she said the last words Mortimer could see a cloud pass over her face. He sank into dread. Was it that he didn't want to wait? He wanted no hiatuses now, but to keep on the move? So perhaps he could go to France with her. Idle a few weeks there, on her territory. That could be wonderful, possibly. Except he could imagine doing it for a few days, not a few weeks.

She shook her head. "I don't know what to say. I just want

to go home. And I don't want to make you come." She screwed up her face in a silent request for sympathy, and he couldn't resist embracing her. It never occurred to him that she might have been asking if he'd contemplate settling in France with her.

So he found himself alone on the flight to London.

23

Back in the city he discovered that he himself was the subject of a piece about the growing troubles in the Maghreb. Apparently all the journalists in Algeria had been sent packing, and he had been one of the last to leave, if not the last.

What he didn't know until he went down to Kepple's office the day after he arrived was that Celeste had taken many pictures of him on his camel, wrapped in a headscarf, and the Sunday supplement was planning to use one of them. Later, a woman rang him at the friend's flat where he was staying, and asked him a lot of questions. He was feeling so baffled at the bustle of London, with its thousands upon thousands of houses, and streams of traffic, and everything so weightily overbuilt, that he found he could hardly think about the desert, and answered her questions barely aware of what he was saying. That Sunday there was a profile on him. The writer had got wind of the fact that around the office he had jokingly been called "Mortimer of the Maghreb." They gave half the page to the interview, half to the photograph of him on a camel. He folded up the paper as soon as he saw it, read only the headline and lead paragraph. It was altogether embarrassing.

Celeste had also taken a number of classic shots that ran in the paper, as well as the magazine, and Kepple used everything Mortimer could give him. His were the first and last eyewitness accounts of the Tuareg Revolt; the most romantic war of the half century, people called it.

If it hadn't been for Celeste's shots, and for their both having been in the midst of it, and for the unusual circumstances under which they'd happened upon the insurrection, and for the protagonists' having been the tall and mysterious heroes of the desert, there would never have been so much interest. The coverage was out of all proportion to the story's importance. *Le Monde* and *Die Zeitung* went to town, with front-page photos and a series of pieces. They had staffers write up much of it but they couldn't avoid using Mortimer too, he was the one person who had been there, in the thick of it. *Paris-Match* did a photo essay of Celeste's pictures, and they too used Mortimer for a short piece.

It was all better than he would ever have dared imagine.

Kepple called him into his office. There was something about being in that huge room, with the typewriters hissing and whirring, the keyboards pattering, the people moving about, the white plastic cups of coffee on the desks, the trails of smoke rising up all over the room, gathering in a pall under the lights—this was the hive where the big events of the world were processed. It reminded him that there were big events, large forces at work out in the world. This was where the broad stage of human drama was written up. It wasn't so much that this place offered a kind of excitement, as that it was big. It had room for him. Here one might gain perspective.

"Congratulations, you're staff," was the first thing Kepple told him, in his little office walled with glass at one side of the big room. "Bill called down yesterday. 'Give the man a salary for God's sake.' His exact words. We'll have to think about where to send you next. Nicaragua's the obvious place."

"Well, I might need—" Mortimer began.

"Of course. Have a breather. A few more days off, whatever. You wouldn't have to leave till next week. We'll organise everything."

As Mortimer crossed the teeming room towards the exit, he felt a powerful exhilaration; or rather, simply power. A strong, calm feeling. Some current had got hold of him and was on his side, was carrying him. True, he was worried about Celeste just then as well: about the need to go and see her in France, to persuade her to come with him, be part of the destiny that was surely unfolding for them. But just then he couldn't conceive that things wouldn't work out. Everything was on his side.

Saskia had tried to make contact with him. She had left messages at the news desk, and at the flat where he was staying. She had also written a letter, saying she had read his material and he shouldn't hesitate to call her, should he want to.

That too seemed a confirmation of the tremendous goodwill that had strayed into his life.

"Let me cook you dinner," she said on the telephone.

And he couldn't resist. He was curious, more than anything, to know how it would feel to see her, now that he had crossed an invisible barrier, a barrier he never really believed was there, until he found himself on the other side of it. It wasn't exactly called success; more luck. Some people got on the right side of luck, and now he was one of them. And it was all because of Celeste, of having found love.

When he walked through the door of their old home, in which Saskia still lived, it felt perfectly safe, harmless. He could hardly remember how oppressive it had once seemed. She gave him a hug in the hallway, and that too felt familiar and unthreatening. Her body was slight against him, slighter than he remembered, and warm. Her face looked sleek and good. Perhaps she had lost a little weight, not that she had ever been overweight; or perhaps she was wearing a little makeup. A smile suffused her face, and he saw with pleasure that it was a smile of pride.

"You know, it's unheard of, this level of interest," she said. "You're a star, you really are. I always knew you would be."

He didn't stay for dinner now but drank three glassses of wine. When he left she kissed him in the hallway, a lingering kiss. He had to extricate himself tactfully.

"Not a good idea," he said.

She rested her forehead on his chest and shook her head.

24

Paris-Match wanted to send Celeste to Singapore.

"Come with me. Please. Just this once. I need you with me," she implored him down the telephone. "Please."

But he couldn't. "They want me in Nicaragua. Can't you come there instead? Let me talk to the *Tribune*."

Which he did. But Kepple said: "If the pair of you want to become stringers for us somewhere, we might be able to work something out. But you'd have to be freelance again. And in one place. We could perhaps use someone in Delhi. But I can't tell the picture desk to make her staff, or where to send her. It's none of my business."

He went to see her in France, in Pau, and spent three days there. He met her mother, a crisp, brisk woman with a silver bun of hair, and an uncle, a car dealer from Bordeaux who wore a well-cut suit of a shiny, soft, blue cloth Mortimer had never seen before. Even the sister with the four children was stylish, and slender. Mortimer felt dowdy and scruffy in his corduroy jacket.

Celeste was very happy to have him there. She was excited and animated, and took him to several bars and cafés, and up to a panoramic overlook a few miles above the town. It was a misty, cloudy day, the fir trees looking sombre among the rocks on the hillsides, and a river thickly hissing far below.

"You go," she said, and hugged him. She felt warm and good against him. "You go to Managua. It'll be OK. Really it will. It's right, of course it is. I'll come and join you as soon as I'm back from Asia. We'll see each other a lot, and soon. We'll work it out. Of course we will."

But there was something in her insistence, and her vagueness, that unsettled him. They hadn't worked anything out.

Even many years later when he thought about it he still couldn't understand, or even just remember, how exactly it had all unravelled.

She had been supposed to fly out to Nicaragua to be with him when she returned from Singapore. But three weeks later, she still hadn't even left France for the Far East.

"What's going on?" he asked her from his Managua hotel.

"I don't know." She hesitated. "I just can't leave yet. I don't feel right about it." He heard her sigh. "I belong here."

"But I thought you were going to go soon, then come here."

There was a long silence.

She inhaled, then sighed again. *"C'est difficile."*

After another pause she said: "Something's changed. Really, I'm not going to run around the world anymore. And when I come to Managua, what will I do? Maybe I'll sell some pictures. But I don't want to be doing this in five years' time. So I think I'd better stop now. This is my chance, when they all like my work and I can switch and do what I want."

He felt winded. He could hardly believe what he was hearing. "So when are you planning to see me?"

"Soon, soon," she said.

Somehow he felt he ought to have seen this coming. But what was he supposed to do? Move to Pau and write for the local gazette?

He flew back to see her again, and this time it was palpably different. She was still happy to see him, she couldn't help that: her whole body lit up at his side, he could feel it. Yet she was reserved too. And somehow the visit ended up feeling ordinary, like seeing each other was something they could do or not do. What was there left to discover? In which case, had their whole love been founded on novelty, and nothing else? Novelty of location, story, work, and ultimately of each other? So as soon as they knew one another through and through, the process had run itself out?

Or was it merely beginning? The mists of honeymoon had burned off now, and the real life together was starting? That was what he had wanted to believe.

But then he wondered: perhaps it had just been an exotic

romance after all—an elaborate and exhilarating one, but still, no more than that. Otherwise, how was it that he could be away from her, and miss her, yes, think about her many times a day, yes, but still manage to get on with his work, and still feel that in the end if he had to make a choice between her and his work, work would win? Surely none of these things would have been possible if he were absolutely, deeply, and necessarily in love with her. Surely you could trust love to make you, force you, to do what you most needed.

Then there was the phone call when she wouldn't answer his question about his coming to visit again. Instead, she said she wanted to write to him. She faxed a letter to his hotel later that day.

That too he should have seen coming. She had been seeing an old friend, and it was complicated. She needed to resolve that first. But the good thing was that she'd been commissioned to do a book—her very own book—on the shepherds of the Ardèche. There'd be an exhibition too, in Toulouse. She was happy about that, although she did still miss him, and would always love him.

Always? He couldn't bear to read that, or to think what it meant.

He missed her too, in a horrible way. He'd go to bed at night feeling sick as he lay down alone, every cell of his body yearning for her.

Weeks before, in the desert, Celeste had once said to him, "It feels like you're driving a tractor over my heart," after he had responded too casually to a question about what they'd do once they left the Sahara. "Should we be thinking ahead?" And he, not realising the implication at the time, had answered, "Let's not think ahead." To which her response had been silence. A long enough silence that he'd looked up from

the notebook he was reading through. She had had her back
to him. There was something about her posture, cross-legged
on the sand floor of their little mud house in the oasis, her
shoulders hunched. "What's up?" he asked. Then she said the
line about the tractor. And he realised what she had been asking, and instead of feeling tired, fed up with the problem of
coupling, with its endless capacity to derail one's plans and
slow one's life, as he habitually had with Saskia, his heart
melted. That was the right phrase for it. It was as if his midriff
turned to warm liquid.

Now he knew what she had meant about the tractor. His
insides felt as if they had been exposed to the air, his skin broken up.

So why didn't he jump on a plane and go and declare himself once more, and stay there if need be? Force the issue.

He didn't know. Somehow it seemed wrong. It seemed
there was another way. Perhaps that way was work.

He steeled himself for work. He told himself there was only
one way to go. You kept your arms sunk to the elbow in life so
you never had a moment to look back, you were too busy with
what was under your nose. And you kept moving. Two months
in Nicaragua, a month in Chile, two weeks in Panama, then
back across the world to the Solidarity marches in Poland.
Then back to Central America.

He had himself sent to Honduras with two passports so he
could get in and out of Salvador and Nicaragua without either
country knowing he visited the other. Six months in, he spent
a weekend in Mexico City with a Mexican newsreader, a tall
woman with freckles, curly hair, and large eyes, charmed by
his British accent, so she said. By the end of the weekend he

was fighting to disguise the fact that he could not bear to be touched by her. It was nothing against her; but he felt something vital within himself slip away, drain out of him, pass like water from a sieve, and the only chance he had to preserve it was to be alone, quietly, in a room on his own. Or else to be hard at work, hot on a trail; or else just to be struggling to keep up with events, scribbling and rescribbling in his notebooks, dinging the bell of his typewriter with dependable regularity—ten dings per cigarette. At that rate he knew he was in business.

Meanwhile, in Algeria, although the Tuareg Revolt dwindled to nothing, the country was set on its doomed course to chaos.

1988

1

Twelve years later, Mortimer returned to London from a Colombian earthquake, from a devastated city in the country's southern mountains, a colonial gem, a graph of white, grille-windowed Spanish houses now reduced to rubble with four or five figures' worth of bodies trapped under it—no one was yet sure how many had died. And even the dead had not got off unscathed: coffins in the cemetery had rammed the walls of the Catholic cubbyholes in which they were billeted, battering the masonry until they launched themselves into the street; one sarcophagus had even erupted from the living room wall of a house built against the cemetery and landed on a family's dining table, splintering it, and causing an elderly grandmother to die of a heart attack, thus joining her deceased husband who had happened to be in the very casket. Mortimer returned from that scene of carnage and devastation, of dusty faces, bleached moustaches, ghostly figures wandering through the pall of dust that hung like mist over the shattered city, to his London desk to find the new editor waiting for him.

"No time to unpack, my friend. We need you in Algiers yesterday. The city's exploding. We've got to get you in before they shut down again."

"Can't go home for a change of clothes?" Mortimer tried. "You're staying at the Hilton, they'll wash your clothes."

It was spring, the almond trees along the avenues of Algiers were in blossom.

The first afternoon he took a taxi down to the old city. Was it him—he was jet-lagged, had been traveling for twenty-four hours straight—or had the country changed? It was well over a decade since he'd been here. He had not walked two blocks when he felt he simply could not be out here on his own, without a guide. Although only two men actually approached him, one asking if he was looking for a hotel, the other offering hashish, he felt like a sitting duck, a marked man waiting to be ripped off, or mugged, or worse. Every pair of eyes bored into his back as he passed. The cafés full of black-haired men who looked up from their games of cards, the vendors lining the narrow streets, the loafers everywhere just standing about and watching—all of them checked him out. And he wasn't even in the medina yet; these were the narrow streets just outside it, its overflow, still wide enough for *petits taxis* and donkey carts to creep down.

He ducked into a relatively quiet café and took a table in the corner. The waiter was a silver-haired man in a black waistcoat, and Mortimer felt safer within the orbit of a man in some kind of uniform. But the waiter spent a long time eyeing him up from the zinc counter, with its trays of upturned glasses, before he came over and took his order. In the end Mortimer's mint tea took such a long time to arrive that he put twenty dinars on the table—far too much, he was sure—and was just about to leave without his tea, had already stood up and begun walking to the door, when he heard a clamour outside. Men were chanting, and loudly, and coming closer. In no time at all the chanting was very loud, and a column of men came briskly up the little street, causing all the vendors outside to pick up their boxes and trays and press themselves against the café windows, darkening further what was already a dark interior.

Mortimer went over to see what was going on. Just outside, a young man in a black leather jacket attempted to lift his tray of pastries from the ground, to save it from the tramping boots of the marchers. The first men stepped over it, then one put his foot on a corner and the tray jumped, scattering all its thin cakes into the dust.

The men came through thick and fast, five, six, seven abreast, shouting their chant, storming through the old town. The heart of the procession came by, a wooden litter carried on the shoulders of four men. Mortimer's eye fell on one of the pallbearers' throats, its tendons flexing as he too shouted the song. The volume swelled as the litter passed. In it, laid on rushes, wrapped in a flag, recognisable for what it was by the little peak at the rear where the feet were, travelled a corpse.

Perhaps it was an everyday funeral. But there was something so angry in the air that it felt like a crowd intent on an enemy. It pressed on towards the medina, many more following the body than had preceded it. After the last of them, the chanting lingered a moment in the streets, then was gone.

Mortimer stood at the grimy café window as the normal sounds returned—of footfalls, the clack of checkers, the chatting of men's voices—and found he was clammy with sweat.

The waiter brought over the tea but Mortimer was already on his way out.

Without looking back he walked to the seafront, where he could find a taxi.

What had been the matter with him years ago, charmed by all this chaos, envy, poverty? Everywhere, he saw unscrupulous eyes intent on getting what they could from him. As he sank into the seat of a Mercedes *grand taxi*, still faintly redolent of its original leather, he thought, Thank God for the Hilton. When they stopped at a sprawling mess of an intersection, with streets coming in from every angle, and no vehicles seeming to pay any attention to the rules of traffic, his heart jumped into his throat, and he glanced at the lock on his car door. It was only when he crossed the hotel's big marble lobby and heard the soft ding of the elevator arriving for him that he began to feel safe again.

Up in his room he had a long hot shower, feeling uncommon gratitude for decent plumbing and sanitary ware, for a private bathroom in a spacious room. Though he wished they had larger towels. He couldn't quite get one round his waist, and had to shuffle to the bed with one draped over his shoulders, holding the other round his thighs.

He lay on the bed listening to the hum of the air-conditioning, while outside beyond the boulevard in front of the hotel the sky grew pale over the sea as evening approached.

In a while he lifted the bedside receiver from its cradle.

The double ring tones of the English phone were restful and pleasing in the ear, reminders of a world of order and good sense, a world in which one could relax, breathe more easily. It occurred to him to wonder, as he lay there with the earpiece beside him on the pillow, what it was about that world of the old Arab town that seemed so forbidding, so foreign, and so much like an enemy territory. He had just been in Colombia, surely no less foreign, if anything more hazardous. Yet there he had not once felt so out

of place. Or was there really a surge of anti-Western sentiment roiling about the narrow streets? This whole region, so
different from the regulated and calm one he could hear
declaring itself with its tidy, soft double alarums at the far
end of the phone line, seemed endemically warlike and hos-
tile, not just to outsiders but even to its own. Every town had
its old ksar, its fortress. This had always been a land where
to stray from your allotted terrain was to err into enemy territory.

But then, where on earth would that not be true?

Perhaps he was getting too old for the field, too jumpy.

"Greetings from the Maghreb," he said, and forced a
chuckle. "How are you?"

He heard her sigh. Her first utterance to him. His wife:
Saskia.

He had been away ten days in the Andes, then been sent
straight on to Algiers without even collecting a change of
clothes, and all she could manage was a sigh.

He swallowed his irritation.

"Mrs. Levinson had a go at me," she said.

Mrs. Levinson? He racked his brains and remembered:
one of the boy's teachers. "Really?" was all he could manage.

"She called me at work. I shouldn't have let Johnny go to
school with that cough, can you believe it? He's thirteen. I
had the Nigerian attaché on the other line. Anyway," she
checked herself. "How are you?"

But she asked the question as a formality, with no trace of
interest at all.

"OK, OK," he said rapidly, to get off a subject that held no
interest for her. "Relieved to be in a decent hotel."

For the first time, it crossed his mind she might not be
happy that he was back in Algeria.

"It's mayhem here," he said, hoping to dispel any notion of this being a trip down memory lane.

"That's what we've been hearing." By "we" she meant the aid agency for which she worked.

There was a pause. Then she said, "Actually, I wanted to ask. You couldn't swing a trip to the south while you're there? There are a hundred thousand Malian refugees in southern Algeria. It should be in the nationals."

"Can you fax me something?" he said, reverting to professional ground. "Hold on." And he got up to fetch the fat fake-leather folder of hotel information.

When he got back she too said, "Hold on" and went to find paper and pen.

Outside the window, a pool of opal sky was being swamped by a bank of cloud darker than smoke, so that it seemed like night itself coming in. He felt all the more reassured to be in a comfortable modern hotel room far above the teeming city, lying in the glow of three pairs of fake gilt carriage lamps.

2

Mortimer's career had gone from strength to strength. Back in 1976 the paper had changed his contract and put him on a megalith of a retainer, as Kepple called it, and made him their "world correspondent." Ever since he did a Latin American series for *The Washington Post*—reluctantly the *Tribune* had assented, there being nothing in his contract about transatlantic exclusivity—that won him a Pulitzer, other papers had opened the door to him.

Several times over the years he had nearly got back in touch with Celeste. He had meant to, planned to, decided to, even written letters. But then thought he should rewrite parts of them, and kept intending to, but put it off until gradually the impulse would sink away and the weeks became months, and finally years.

He and Saskia had staged their recovery two years after he'd been in the desert. He was sent down to Conakry, Guinea, in West Africa, where the iron-fisted dictator, Sekou Toure, had decided to crack open the tight seal he kept on his country, and allow in a little foreign investment. The whim hadn't lasted—he didn't like to share—and he'd soon slammed the door shut again. But it so happened that Saskia too was sent down by her aid agency at the same time. A lot of aid people had come down. The two of them had had a fling, then more. Afterwards, every time he came through London he saw her. And her child: she had a young son, by an American diplomat who had run out on her, who in fact already had a family.

He'd walk or take a taxi down the old street where they had once lived together, and feel a growing, calm pleasure to be back. He'd remember their old joke when he saw the doorbell that said "Press" on its white ceramic. "Press? I'm press."

Eventually they had even married again. They had done it quietly in the registry office—quietly, that is, until the boy started whining, then bawling when she strapped him in his pushchair.

Mortimer had found it hard to adjust to life with a toddler; or rather, the Western way of living with one. The cot, the pushchair, the large toys—there seemed so much paraphernalia, all of it designed to keep the child away from its mother.

The net result was a screaming child. He couldn't help noticing that in the third world, where children were not religiously put to bed at seven o'clock on their own, the babies seemed never to cry. They lived on their mother's backs.

He found himself disagreeing with, even disapproving of, Saskia's way of doing things. Yet it was none of his business, not just because she didn't want it to be, nor because the child wasn't his, but because he came and went so much. When the child had croup it had been Saskia's mother who was around, who had come to stay for three weeks. Mortimer had been in Mozambique, then was sent directly to Sri Lanka. Sometimes he got the feeling the household ran more smoothly, and that Saskia was happier, when he was gone. For months on end she seemed to have little for him except impatience and annoyance. And she became ever less guarded about showing it.

He knew he was a dismal kind of partner. But he couldn't see what he could do to become better, short of changing his profession. He made a point of bringing back gifts from every trip—some local toy or costume from the market for Johnny, once he discovered how much the boy enjoyed dressing up, and for her a cosmetic he knew she used from duty-free, and a rug, a sculpture, a small painting. Fortunately she liked ethnic art. Though whenever he strayed into ethnic dress of any kind, whatever it was would vanish into the wardrobe never to emerge again.

Sometimes it was lovely to come home—the boy eager to see him and get his present, which over the years moved into duty-free electronics, and Saskia welcoming him with a smile and a joyous time in bed, where it would be both warmly familiar and exhilarating after the abstinence. But more often he would have the sense he had walked in on some troublesome scene that his presence would only make worse. And on top of that, though their sex life had never been explosive, after the blow of a child, it had never recovered. Sometimes when he was home he felt like an interloper, an unwanted guest; anything but the returning champion that just occasionally he'd have liked to fancy himself. It seemed that any good feeling he managed to rouse through his professional endeavours he could count on her to crush.

Now and then they'd get a babysitter and he'd take her out to dinner, and she'd dress up a little, and a shine of affection, or better, would return to her eyes.

Most often when they went out it was to dinners, functions, parties that one way or another had a bearing on his professional life. She would accompany him when she could, being ever on the lookout for funds and exposure for her agency. But it was a sadness to him that she seemed to have lost any pride she had ever had in the accomplishments of her partner. Sometimes he even wondered if she wasn't somehow resentful of them—as if given more freedom, more encouragement, she could have done the same; even, occasionally, as if she were actually envious. It wasn't always pleasant to climb into bed beside her.

But then he could always draw comfort from his work: he knew he could not have asked for a career that had gone better.

3

Lying in his hotel room now, in Algiers again after so many years, drying off on the warm, damp towels spread over the bed, and experiencing just a little prick of a chill, which prompted him to pull on his trousers then resume his position, he gazed at what he could see of his reflection hovering in the dark glass against the blackness of the Mediterranean night: pale brown slacks, the white bulk of the torso, the high ruddy forehead, a forehead that now more or less reached all the way back to the crown of the head. He hadn't shaved lately—he would often stop while away—and just now had a short grizzled beard.

It wasn't the look of his expanded body but something else that unsettled him. He became inexplicably restless, with an uncomfortable constriction in his chest. He decided to finish dressing and go down to the bar.

The Hilton bar was crawling with journalists. A bearded young man from *Paris-Match* who Mortimer had met a couple of times before offered him a beer, then asked if he'd like to ride with him the next day in the Mercedes the magazine had hired for him. He wanted Mortimer to drive so he could shoot from the car window. "You know the city," he added.

"It's been a long time," Mortimer said. But he was happy to oblige. It would save him having to rely on taxis.

Then he ran into two old acquaintances he'd once worked with years ago in television.

"That wouldn't be Mortimer of the Maghreb?" a gravelly voice asked. It was Harry, a news producer at the BBC. "You've had a few meals since I last saw you." He spluttered an alcoholic laugh.

Mortimer patted his belly. "Best part of the job, the varied cuisine. You haven't changed at all."

It was true. Harry still had the same red, ageless face, a bit less hair, and a few more wrinkles, but Mortimer would have recognised him at once. Not so his sidekick Jimmy, though, the cameraman, who had lost most of his hair and whose face had reddened to the same hue as his boss's. He sported a pair of thick, ginger sideburns now.

"You two aren't still working together?"

"Why not?" Jimmy asked.

"If you can call it work," Harry growled. "It's not like it used to be. Christ, never mind you, soon even we'll be out of a job."

Mortimer had worked with the two of them on his very first television stories.

"These days," Harry went on, "all you need is some film student with a video camera, you hook them up to a satellite antenna, and away you go. There's no skill left. Just point and shoot."

"What are you talking about, Harry? Let me buy you a drink."

Harry swirled his whisky glass, drained it, then set it down. "Reporting as you and I know it is over. The punters want to see it as it happens. Don't tell me you hadn't noticed."

"I hadn't noticed."

"History unfolding before their eyes–type thing," Jimmy added.

Mortimer shrugged. "News can't go out of style. It's the nature of the beast. What'll it be, whiskies all round?"

"Our kind of news can. Cheers. On the spot, live feed, it's the way everyone's going. Anyway, what the devil have you been up to? Apart from eating."

"I take it you don't read the papers," Mortimer replied.

"Not if I can help it. They're all junk too these days. Columns and whatnot."

"Well, here's to old times," Mortimer said.

Later, they had a well-lubricated dinner of couscous and kebabs.

4

The next morning, in a dazzle of hangover, Mortimer drove through a bright spring day towards the convulsing centre of the city, with the French photographer beside him in the passenger seat. They headed straight for the medina.

Had he been alone, would he have done anything differently? Sometimes he liked to think so. It hadn't helped that the car had been that gleaming Mercedes, of all things, a symbol of Western power, Western carelessness.

When they stopped at a junction Mortimer said, "Last time I was down here it was also with a *Paris-Match* photographer. Celeste Dumas."

The man smiled and nodded. "Sure. She's a great photographer. She moved on from journalism. She's done well for herself. You can't go into a poster shop in France without finding one of her pictures. Shepherds, peasant farmers, goats, and mountains, that kind of thing. She's good."

Mortimer crept across the intersection, and up a smaller street away from the sea.

"Do you know her?"

"I've met her."

"She and I, we went right down into the desert," he said, driving slowly up the street.

"I'd love to do that," the man said softly. "One day when it's safe again."

They hadn't yet reached the medina, just the narrow streets near it, when they hit trouble: shouts echoed among the buildings, then they reached a corner and heard the roar of a mob. Halfway down the block they saw them, youths shouting as they ran down a cross street, carrying things. Mortimer couldn't make out what they held, in the brief moment before he looked back over his shoulder to reverse the car, but he had the unmistakable impression that most of them had objects in their hands.

He couldn't tell if it was the commotion in the streets, or hearing about Celeste, but something had disturbed him. He had that same constriction in the chest again, and felt impatient, irritable.

They cruised around, trying to gauge where the heart of the action was, and how to approach it, and how closely, when a column of protesters rounded the corner into a street they were crawling down. Mortimer at once turned the car, a five-point turn, cursing himself for not simply having reversed, only to find another brisk phalanx filing along the next cross street, blocking their exit.

There was nothing for it. He drove slowly towards the column. Only when the car was twenty yards off did it attract the attention of the crowd. A crop-headed young man seemed to smile at Mortimer, pointed, and shouted. Then three or four youths, perhaps students, Mortimer thought, filtered away from the main procession, jogging towards the car. For a moment Mortimer thought they had gone right past, their attention on something else, until a sharp, loud knock on the roof made him bounce in his seat.

"*Vas-y, vas-y,*" shouted the Frenchman beside him.

How to drive through a crowd: there was a proper speed for it, just fast enough to show that you meant to keep going, slow enough to let them get out of the way. Which they did. They paused, waited for the car to pass, and Mortimer drove through. Perhaps most of the crowd hadn't yet realised that this vehicle was legitimate prey, at least as far as the radicals were concerned. But the youths were still shouting, and someone caught on and gave the roof another slap, loud enough that Mortimer thought it must have been delivered with a hard object.

"*Dieu, Dieu,*" the Frenchman said, looking round as they drove away. He shook his head. "Do you know how lucky that was?"

"What do you think? Park and keep out of the way?"

"Not here," the Frenchman exclaimed.

They crawled down the street away from the medina, passing a group of three photographers who were jogging down a block. Mortimer slowed and offered them a ride but they all declined. Then they ran into an angrier, faster crowd, a mob farther down the road to violence. They appeared behind the car, rounding the nearest corner.

Mortimer looked back over his shoulder. The crowd were shaking their fists, ululating, slapping their wrists in some local gesture, and filled the narrow street. The odd stone and bottle flew towards the car, nothing too serious. If the rioters had really wanted to damage the vehicle, Mortimer sensed, they could have done a lot worse. But there was no telling what might come next. Perhaps they knew now who was in the car, and wanted the foreign journalists out. The very presence of the Western media would be emblematic of everything the Islamists despised about the current government, with its readiness to get in league with the profane might of the West.

He wasn't taking any chances, and started to drive while still looking back, watching the crowd behind. Someone started running after the car, drawing back his arm to launch some kind of missile. Mortimer put his foot down, and turned forwards just in time to see a man clad in a white djellaba and a grey, wool skullcap launch himself into the road. At first Mortimer thought the man must have been pushed, or lost his step. The Frenchman screamed, "Watch out!" Mortimer saw the man's face, screaming too, the cropped white beard, brown teeth, sparkling eyes, creased cheeks. He jabbed the brakes and swerved but too late. A double knock came, first an axle-jarring jolt, then a thud as the forehead delved into the windscreen.

Mortimer stopped and began to open his door, but the Frenchman shouted, "*Non, non.* Go!"

He looked back and saw a lot of people running at the car.

"Go, go!" shouted the Frenchman again.

Without thinking, he closed his door and accelerated, felt the car break free, lurch forwards as if suddenly lighter, as the man slid off the bonnet. The last thing to go was his hand, apparently attempting to clutch at the windscreen. The car bumped over something in the road.

The one good thing was that the glass didn't shatter. Or perhaps it would have been better if it had. Mortimer would then have had to stop. But there was only a misty web of splinters where the head had hit. Mortimer heard a lot of shouting close by, just outside the car, and above the roar of the mob behind, the whine of the powerful, well-tuned engine was inaudible.

At the first corner the tires squealed on the smooth cobbles as he made the turn. The big car travelled slowly round the bend. Something made Mortimer glance out of his window. He found himself staring straight into the large blue eye of a camera lens. A baldheaded man with reddish sideburns and a video camera on his shoulder was stooping to get the shot of the car's driver.

Mortimer looked back in amazement, for just long enough to see the cameraman train his lens on the car as it drove away, then lift his contraption off his shoulder and proceed to run down the street, away from the advancing mob. Mortimer's startled face must have been the last thing he shot, before the riot exploded all through the streets of central Algiers, and the foreign journalists had either to flee the country or to go into hiding.

"Bloody hell," Mortimer said. "Did you see that? He was filming us."

Mortimer had seen cameramen get like that before. Once in Sri Lanka he'd watched a tall Argentinian wait until an angry crowd had closed around him, until he stood with his machine by his head like a rock rising above a tide. He'd got lucky, that Argentinian, the mob had had other things on their mind. All the journalists saw him later at the bar of the hotel they were staying in. There hadn't been the backslapping and rowdy toasting one might have expected. Rather, people kept their distance, talked in lowered voices. Partly, it was jealousy: that man would have the best footage, no question. But also theirs could be a dangerous game. With every new risk some hot-blooded hack took, the danger rose for all of them.

The Frenchman pointed ahead. "There's the future."

Halfway down the block a large white Mazda van was parked at the curb. It had a telescopic hoist on its roof with a satellite dish at the top. The dish was tipped at the sky, the point of its silver antenna beaming into space.

Mortimer didn't recognise that the bald cameraman had been Jimmy until he saw, in the window of the van, Harry the producer's face. Their eyes met. Mortimer lurched with a shock of recognition.

"Bloody hell."

"Live feed," the Frenchman said. "They watch it back in Lyons as it happens. Our game is over."

"Balls," Mortimer said, accelerating down to the boulevard that ran along the foot of Algiers's hills. "Video was supposed to kill the cinema." He shook his head. "What did that idiot think he was doing, jumping a moving car?"

"They don't think."

"They could use us, we're not the enemy."

They sped east towards the Hilton.

"Was it bad?" Mortimer asked. "Did it look bad?"

The Frenchman shrugged. "*Pas tellement.* But that's not so good," he said, nodding towards the shattered dent in the windscreen.

The Algerian's grey cap had attached itself to one of the wipers. "Get rid of it," the Frenchman snapped. Mortimer switched on the wipers. The cloth hat waved back and forth, clinging to a join in the blade's mechanism as the rubber scraped over the broken glass.

The car cruised rapidly along the avenue, the shadows of the blossom-covered trees flicking over it.

1996

1

Mortimer was in a taxi again, he was forever in taxis these days, and never did he seem to have to pay for them. He'd reach into his wallet not quite sure what he'd find, certainly a few crumpled ones, a five, with any luck a twenty or two, though he'd be preferring to hold on to those just a little longer, you never knew when they might be called on for a tumbler or two of Ballantine's Finest.

He got out at his local, on Seventh Avenue, and pressed into its welcome dark. Five-thirty: he was a little early.

It was OK to live as he was, in one long ragged celebration, or commiseration, as long as one had a target, a destination, a point at which one could get off because one had to, in order to return necessarily to the desk and the keyboard. But for many months now he had not had that. Years. It had been Clive, an old friend and colleague from the *Tribune*'s features page, now "consulting editor" for a glossy, who had got him over to New York as a "roving editor," whatever that was. He had organised the visa, the sublet, the modest but decent retainer, which ought to have been enough to cover his basic costs but wasn't. The idea had been that on top, he would receive a generous fee per story.

So far it hadn't worked out. What was to have been his first story, on the drugs war in Colombia—"A war of sorts," Clive said—was pulled from Mortimer's fingers and given to some young blood from Atlanta.

That had been four months ago now. Just this afternoon there had been a message on Mortimer's phone machine from Clive about another possible story he'd been hoping for: "I'm sorry, Charlie," it said, "that story isn't going to work out after all. Can we get together tomorrow or something? Give me a call?"

Mortimer suspected what it meant: he had been in New York for months and still not a single story; his retainer couldn't go on forever. Clive had gone out on a limb for him.

Yet why hadn't things worked out? He was as good as he had ever been. It seemed it had nothing to do with his skills, and everything to do with luck. Or not luck exactly, but having the world on your side. When he had started out as a young man, he had loved the world; then he had felt the world start to love him. And look where it all ended up.

When Clive had first called him in London and offered the position, Mortimer had leapt at the chance to get away. It had seemed that at last he might escape the swamp his life in London had become. It wasn't *his* life anymore. It was someone else's, and somehow he had mistakenly been transplanted into it. This other person wrote nothing but reviews of restaurants, and of stray fashions that swept through the capital. They didn't travel at all, ever, except for the cab rides that trundled them to their many meals. They drank wine ceaselessly. And when they weren't drinking wine they drank whisky with a little water. They didn't like many things. They tended to thunder at the keyboard complaining about whatever struck them as new and unnecessary.

Fads and food: these were his subjects now. What they wanted was a cantankerous old colonel, and that was what they got: a sodden old colonel of the press, retired from the field.

"At least you've got the build for it," an old colleague remarked when he heard Mortimer was doing restaurant reviews these days.

"I've had a bit of training," Mortimer conceded.

The rushed and meaningless columns for the *Standard* would feel already soggy with the next day's fish and chips even as he banged them out. He wasn't sure what to call it but something unpleasant made its home in him; despair, or loneliness, or chaos. Its effect was to hurl him headlong down the face of a wave with a churn of anxiety and fury in his belly.

Nor could he believe how fast time was flying these days. He kept waiting to be sent back to the pine-clad valleys and dusty cities where a man like him belonged, and couldn't understand why it wasn't happening.

After years Saskia had finally left him, again. Which was to say: thrown him out. He had come home drunk one morning with what looked like an egg stain down one lapel, to find his bags literally packed for him in the hall. He had stared at them and thought, Hello? A trip somewhere?

The note was on the kitchen table: *I can't bear this any longer. Please don't be here when I get back.*

Even then, seeing his sentence of banishment, he had felt not dread or guilt, but curiosity. At least this was something *new*.

. . .

After the Algiers accident, some of the hacks had had a field day with him.

"Once dubbed Mortimer of the Maghreb by his colleagues, British journalist Charles Mortimer is at the centre of an international controversy over the role of Western news reporting."

It was the video age. Within seven minutes the images had been in Atlanta, all over the world. Jimmy, planted by fate on that street corner in Algiers, had been filming live. It was golden stuff for him: a dramatic scene from a country in collapse, a car knocking a man flying, then a long, slow close-up of the driver, apparently showing no remorse, no inclination to halt the hit-and-run. And of all people it had been the distinguished reporter.

There his face was, the jowls grizzled with a few days' growth, the wild spray of hair well past due for a cut around the expanded forehead, the broad, mottled nose, and the startled, grey eyes.

But most editors had conceded that Mortimer had had little choice but to flee, with Algiers collapsing into violence all around him. However, that incident had primed everyone for his great error the following year, 1989, when he pronounced so fatally wrongly on the fate of the Soviet Union. That truly had been the beginning of the end. Thereafter, he was no longer a war reporter, a true journalist.

It was the *Standard* who came along after that and first offered him a column. "Can't bear to see a good man go to waste," the woman said. She offered to put him to work writing about restaurants. "Are you serious?" he asked. Then told himself: I'm a professional. If they want arugula and Montepulciano, that's what I'll give them.

2

Later that year, he had received a letter from Celeste. She'd sent it care of the old paper, who had forwarded it.

What a lot of asses they are. Anything to get their names out there. Anyway, I was glad to hear news of you, even bad news. I've read your stuff now and then. It has been so long. Again and again I have wanted to know what has happened to you, but also been scared to know, I don't know why. Have you ever wondered about me? It brought it all back, hearing of you, seeing your face. I hope it is all right for me to write to you. Surely it is. We are adults. On est adulte.

Let me know if you're ever in Paris, I'll come and see you. But don't worry. Just if you can, if you'd like.

Thinking of you, Celeste.

The letter also told him that she had two teenage daughters, her husband, Eric, was a psychiatrist at a local hospital, and they lived, along with two donkeys, a few goats, and a lot of geese, in an old farmhouse she had restored in the Ardèche. She hoped he got through this nonsense quickly, and didn't let it bother him.

It bothered him for a start that even in France they had evidently heard about his downfall. But that was only the start of it. That letter had been just what he didn't need.

. . .

He did go to France, and he oughtn't to have done. He went shamefaced, hangdog, pretending to himself that he had been planning to go to Paris anyway in order to do some research. A few weeks after he received Celeste's letter, he wrote back telling her where he'd be staying.

She called him.

The strange thing was that the sound of her voice, far from alarming him as he'd expected, or plunging him into old feelings of guilt or panic, or making him worry further about what a mess he seemed to have made of his life, simply made him smile. Once or twice in the years after they split up they had had a little sporadic contact, but it must have been fifteen or sixteen years, he thought, since he had actually heard that soft, breathy, yet musical timbre of hers in his ear.

"*Bonjour,*" she said, with a playful lilt. She was clearly happy to be speaking to him. At once—in the face of everything that had been going on, his public shame, the growing resentment Saskia bore him—at once an unexpected joy welled up in him. And he found himself smiling, telephone in hand.

"How are you holding up?" she asked.

He could tell that she too was smiling.

"Much better this morning," he declared. "It's damn good to hear your voice."

She chuckled. "Me too," she said, in a little confusion. "I mean, it's good to hear yours too."

It was such a lighthearted experience, that phone call, that it seemed easy and natural that they agree to meet the following week, when he would be in Paris. The only problem, she said, was that it would be hard for her to get to Paris after all, as one of her kids had exams, but would he like to come and visit? The new train could get him there in two hours, and they had plenty of room.

He hesitated a moment.

She said: "Eric would love to meet you. And actually he is very busy that week, we will have plenty of time to talk, to catch up."

And he thought to himself: this is not about a long-lost romance into which new life may be breathed. This is about restoration, recovery, the need to get a little perspective. The long view: that's what's required at such a time, and that's what she's offering. So he went.

When he stepped off the train on to the platform, where only one other person, an elderly woman, disembarked, he had the sense that he physically felt her at the end of the station wall before he actually saw her. She was standing there in a camel coat, a scarf round her neck, and her arms crossed. He walked towards her, and had the unnerving sensation that the platform had developed a gelatinous surface, that he couldn't trust each footfall not to squirm about and upset his stride. Then for a moment it was as if his soles didn't even quite make contact with the ground, but hovered on an uncertain cushion of air.

It was a cloudy morning, and it had been raining. The very air seemed impregnated with grey. The trees beyond the station were black, and the tarmac of the car park outside shone.

Celeste was much darker than he remembered. Her face had a rich, nutty tan. But the eyes were exactly the same, and so were the bones under the skin, the shape of her face. He registered that she had more wrinkles, especially around the eyes, and her dimples had deepened, but he did not exactly see these things. He saw straight through them to her real face, the face that no amount of time could change.

They embraced, and he noticed how warm her body felt, in spite of the chilly day. Or perhaps because of it. And her cheek against his, as they briefly kissed each other, was somehow simultaneously both hot and cold, as if a chill lay on the surface of her skin, but beneath it her face was warm. It was surprising, and somehow wonderful, to notice these things.

She said that she had a bottle of wine in the car—a big Citroën estate car—and thought they might drive to a scenic spot and raise a glass to old times. He thought he detected a nervousness, or a guardedness, in her, and promptly agreed. He added: "That sounds great."

But he wondered if after all she didn't want him in her home, and perhaps had not even mentioned his visit to her husband. Or maybe after their drink she would take him to their house.

He slung his overnight bag in the back of the car and they sat in silence while she steered out of the station, then out of the small town on to a smooth new road that wound down the valley they were in.

"Well, thank you for seeing me," he said.

"Thank you for coming." He saw her smile in profile. She glanced at him and they both laughed. She put her hand on his knee for a second. "It's nice to see you."

"You too," he said, then felt a little foolish, as if he had said something quite unnecessary.

After another pause they both began to speak at the same time, and stopped, and laughed again. Then they both waited for the other to talk first, and neither said anything.

"You first," he said after a moment.

"No, you."

And again they laughed.

"So how are you?" he said finally.

And the question seemed embarrassingly lame, and somehow formal, after all that preamble.

Finally they turned on to a lay-by high up a valleyside,
then drove down a track through a pine wood for a quarter of a
mile, and parked in a clearing. There was a narrow deep gorge
at the end of the little space, and you could hear the thunderous roar of a river a hundred feet below. A metal bench had
been erected near the ravine, and Celeste had thought to
bring a sheet of plastic to put on it, along with the bottle of red
wine and two paper cups. She had opened the cork earlier
and shoved it halfway back in the neck.

"It's funny," she said, once they were seated, "all that stuff
that happened to you in Algiers. I mean, it's not funny at all,
it's terrible. But that it should have been in Algeria. It brought
everything back to me. I have been thinking about getting in
touch for over a year. I hope you don't mind."

He responded automatically that of course he didn't mind,
and then noticed that far from not minding, he was delighted.
He couldn't have explained how or why, but to be sitting here
with her in this improbable place—having just stepped off a
train, on a dreary day in the small mountains of south-central
France—felt like the most natural thing in the world. He even
had a curious sense of something he could only call belonging. As if all the problems, efforts, and striving that his life
ordinarily seemed to consist of—and the boredoms and irrita-
tions—had all quite naturally abated, because at last, however
unwittingly, he had won through to where he belonged.

This is ridiculous, he told himself; but it is nice too, so I don't mind. And even that—the capacity to accept the situation and how it felt, along with its implausibility—even that felt like a curious blessing he was being granted.

They raised their glasses and looked at each other, and Celeste held his gaze with her eyes that were green and blue, and also flecked with rust, with straw, with what looked like gold in the sombre daylight in the woods.

"So," she said. "This is crazy. Me dragging you down here."

"You didn't drag me."

She sighed. "I feel I want to tell you about my life, tell you everything, but I don't know where to begin."

"You're a big success."

"What about you? Look at you. But that's not what I mean. I mean, what happened to us, and what happened after."

There was something about the way she said it. It wasn't just the implicit certainty that whatever they'd shared had been important; she accepted it as a God-given fact. So much so that without even checking with him, she went on: "Sometimes really I don't know if I ever got over it. Sometimes I used to curse myself for not going with you. To Nicaragua. And even this, to see you now, this is a great privilege. I mean, I have had a good life. Touch wood, so far. I love my husband and my children, and my home, my work. I have friends all over. I sell my pictures, everything is good, it's not just some shallow, petit-bourgeois life, it's a good life. Good. Eric is a good man, a tender, sensitive, intelligent man. And helpful. We can talk about almost anything. We laugh a lot." She nodded to herself and frowned slightly. "We love each other." She chuckled. "But you and me. We never finished. I think that's what it is, or was. A sense of incompleteness. It took a long time for that to fade in me. That feeling. And for years and years sometimes it would come back. Why didn't I go with you? Was I right that I needed to settle down? And then all this stuff happening to you in Algeria, where we were. I'm sorry, I just thought, I must see him. It is late enough. My elder daughter is doing her *baccalauréat*; Ondine, the younger one, will do hers in two years. They are nearly grown up. And maybe, well, you must be suffering now, this cannot be easy, all this nonsense, and I thought maybe, just maybe I can help you somehow. I'm sorry I'm telling you all this, but I don't know how long we have, and when we will see each other again, there is no time for formalities. Can it be a bad idea? How can it be a bad idea? How can it?"

She fell silent and looked at him a moment. As soon as she looked away he felt that he had been wearing a smile on his face all through her speech: a mix of surprise, of pleasure, and something like wonder had called the smile forth. The lightness of his heart had grown and grown until his heart was just about ready to float into the sky. It was a sensation he hadn't known in decades it seemed.

But she looked away now down into the ravine. He glanced at the side of her face, and wondered if he ought to have been smiling after all. He could still hear her question: How can it be a bad idea? She meant to see him, of course. Could he reach out and take her hand? That was what he wanted to do, what perhaps also he ought to do. But just as he was deliberating, he saw a mottling of tiny wrinkles appear on her chin. Then her shoulders hunched silently, and she shook a little, and a full tear ran swiftly down her cheek, undulating a little over the minor folds of her skin. He watched the tear make its track, and the strange thought came to him: that tear is what happened to my life.

She began to shake her head gently as she wept. He put his

arm round her, and she let him, but equally she did not respond to it. He felt her cold now, stiff within his embrace. He sat there holding her, letting her cry. He didn't understand why she was crying; at least he didn't feel like crying himself, but he felt something very serious was going on; something serious for him, as well as for her. In a curious way, he didn't feel that he had to understand what it was: it mattered more just that this be happening.

Then on an impulse he squeezed her hand and leaned close and kissed her wet cheek. He kept his lips there, and held her tight, and mumbled, "It's OK, it's OK," repeatedly. Even that he didn't really know why he was saying, but it felt true, and right.

When he thought back to this moment later, he realised that one remarkable thing about it had been that in spite of being presented with this copious volume of feeling from her, he had not felt in the slightest bit alarmed. He had just wanted to be there with her through her suffering.

And it had turned out to be quite brief. After a while she shrugged and wiped the back of a hand over her face, then rummaged first in one pocket then the other, found a tissue to wipe her cheeks with, and blew her nose noisily. Then she let out a kind of laugh that was also a sigh. He touched her cheek with his hand. After all these years he felt that he could. And apparently he could. She smiled, and leaned her face against his palm.

That, for him, was the fatal moment. The years seemed to crumple. It was as if you folded a piece of paper so the two farthest edges came together. The years didn't vanish; they simply had never been. It was suddenly plain that nothing of any importance in his life had happened between this day and the last time he saw Celeste. The whole intervening period had been so insignificant that some part of his brain—or worse than that, some universal law—had simply not acknowledged those years at all. They were just chaff, and blew away in the wind. And this, here in his hand now, was the grain: the only thing that mattered.

He had the strange sense that even this experience with Celeste, begun all these years ago, and perhaps now resuming, didn't matter terribly much. The important thing was that it was real. And everything else was not just false, but in some baffling way nonexistent. This alone: her in his arms, her face cool and wet with tears against his palm, her warm body wrapped in its coat, and the pretty scarf about her neck, and the fine-boned limbs that he knew to be contained within all her warm and pretty clothes—only this person beside him, and the clearheaded way he felt with her just now, only this was real.

"Come on, let's have a drink," he said. And again she laughed—if it was a laugh—and they lifted their cups, with a design of diamonds in various colours, probably intended for a child's birthday party, and drank. Even the cups seemed significant, a symbol of childhood, and therefore of the passing of the years. They too helped to shrink time, shrink the length of a life. Life was after all not so very long, he felt; nor so very far: wherever you wandered you never could get very far from yourself.

When she got up she had already composed herself, and he knew what would happen. They hugged a long time, standing beside the bench. His mind seemed to go soft and blurry, and he lost all track of time and in the end he never knew how long they stood there, nor how long they had been at the bench. But when she dropped him back at the station, as he knew now she would do, he discovered that five hours had passed. He felt that he had no idea at all what that meant. Was that a lot of time? Or very little? She kissed him on the lips and thanked him several times for coming, and he thanked her for inviting him. He managed to say: "I think I never stopped loving you." The words formed by themselves and pressed their way out of him. He was glad they did.

She said, "Shh," and put her fingertips to his lips. Her fingers tasted cool and unbelievably fresh, like dew on a petal at dawn.

She leaned her forehead against his and rocked her head gently, and whispered, "There is too much to lose now."

And he agreed with her and felt she was absolutely right.

All through the train journey back to Paris, and then the plane back to England the next day, he was carried along by a curious lightheartedness. For a few days he could think of virtually nothing but her. He seemed to have another mind, another voice in his head, along with his own—hers. He had conversations with this voice, he laughed with it, he made declarations to it, he commented on things he saw, and she responded.

One afternoon when he ought to have been working in his study at the house, Saskia came home to find him grinning at the kitchen table: sitting there with a grin on his face, for no reason at all.

She glanced at him with a smile. "Let's hear the joke."

For a moment he had no idea what she was talking about. He frowned, and that was when he realised he had been grinning. At which point he smiled again, and laughed. "Just daydreaming."

Saskia touched his hand and said, "It seems like an age since we've seen you smile."

Then gradually Celeste's voice faded. Instead, her face

began to loom in his mind. Somehow whatever he saw, he saw her too. At first it was her happy face, then it wasn't; he began to see the frown she had worn just before weeping on the bench by the ravine, and again at the station when she said goodbye to him, and told him there was too much to lose.

One day he had a frightening thought: what if all these years she had in some way longed for him, and felt that their love had never been completed, but now for her it was complete? He had come down and helped her close the door. But that was her door, not his. Somehow while shutting hers, they had opened his. How else to explain the way he felt? Sometimes for half the day he would feel a physical pain in his midriff, a yearning for her so intense it really did hurt.

He called her twice. The first time she was cheerful and polite, and brief. He guessed she wasn't alone in the room where she'd answered. He let a few days pass and tried again, in the middle of the day, when he hoped to catch her on her own.

Before he could stop it he found himself blurting: "Celeste, I'm thinking about you all the time. I just don't know what to do. What should I do?"

She was silent on the line. Then she sighed and said, "It's all my fault. I'm sorry. I should never have asked to see you. We both have our lives, our marriages and kids, whatever, our work. I'm sorry. It was stupid and selfish of me. I was curious, I wanted to see you again, just for me, for my own benefit. I didn't mean to upset you. I'm sorry. Please forgive me. And forget me. Please. Maybe I'll write to you. Maybe not. Perhaps we mustn't be in touch, it'll ruin everything."

Mortimer was astonished to hear these words; they were so melodramatic. Were the two of them really caught up in some kind of romantic drama? Somehow it seemed scarcely credible. Yet the way he felt surely suggested they were. Or could be.

After that phone call, at first he felt curiously relieved. For one thing, it was almost as if she felt as he did, that the price of closing her door on their past was to have opened his own. And he knew now he had no choice but to forget about it. It was good to know where he stood, he told himself.

He managed to acquire a second column in the paper around this time, and got very busy. He was out to dinner at some new restaurant, or at an old favourite, virtually every day now. He drank ever more heavily. On the Lethe-like tide of drink that he allowed to take over his life and carry him off, Celeste shone as a beacon for a while, then he was simply too far from shore, and she dwindled, and went out.

3

It was Saskia, his ex-wife, who urged him to take up the New York offer.

Over a year had passed since his abortive trip back down to the Western Sahara. New York would be something new.

After Saskia left him, he'd call her now and then, and sometimes write, always hoping they could meet. Eventually she had agreed, and occasionally they'd meet in the park.

All his life, parks had plunged him into a mood of miserable docility. It was something about the grey tarmac paths threading among the damp lawns, the tea-coloured ponds, the anaesthetic air, the pretence of peacefulness: parks never were peaceful, they possessed the unease of shirkers, she thought. But now he liked the park. They met there a few times, and he always looked forward to it. They'd do the things one did: sit on a bench watching ducks scavenge about the pond; stroll down paths; and talk. Parks were good for conversation.

It was a cold winter this year, and the trees were black and bare. He liked it anyway: the kids stuffed in coats so stiffly they could hardly move, the ducks congregating around the diminutive, plump figures whenever they had bread to distribute. There was one toddler he saw a few times, recognizable by his yellow duffel coat, who used to trot towards the birds and send them scattering with gusts of wind as they flapped their wings. Every time they fled, the boy screamed with delight. It was nice to see.

He and Saskia sat on a bench and watched these momentous goings-on.

The sky was the same uniform, drab grey it had been for weeks. It was as if a shroud had been pulled over all the stark land, and henceforth only buses, cars, and trucks could live in it, gasping their plumes of breath.

He told Saskia about the New York offer.

"You see," she said. "There is life for you still. Someone still wants you."

He grunted.

"It's just what you need. Don't be an ass."

They walked back to his place in time for the six o'clock news. It was the first time he'd induced her to come. Perhaps she felt safe, with the prospect of his leaving town again. The first two items of news were domestic: teachers, the Treasury. Mortimer groaned. Then he said, "Ah, here we go." The third story came up: a new coup in Liberia.

"We're now going live to our correspondent in Monrovia," the anchorman said.

"As you can probably see behind me," the reporter opened, "another angry crowd has been gathering here in Constitution Square. If it's anything like yesterday—"

The man broke off his commentary as a surge ran through the crowd. There was a rumble of wind blowing over the microphone, then silence, then someone distinctly said, "Fuck," and the screen went black.

"More live feed," Mortimer said.

"Breaking news," said Saskia.

"Breaking wind, more like. They're not reporters, there's nothing to it. First it was poetry—free verse, whatnot. Tennis with the net down. Then architecture, putting all your plumbing and supports on the outside for all to see. Now it's news reporting. Who'd have believed it? Free reporting."

"Not that you're an old codger."

"Who, me?" She managed to raise a smile in him.

He got up and poured them each a glass of yesterday's wine, then returned to the sofa.

Just then he couldn't understand how he had been sidetracked. Men as old as him were still out there reporting. What exactly had he allowed to happen? Here he was sitting on his sofa with a glass of wine in his hand while the world was still in as much upheaval as ever.

He went back to the kitchen to make a start on dinner. He had bought salmon steaks, which he remembered she liked. He drained the all but empty wine bottle into his glass and opened a new one. A fax from the New York magazine had come in the afternoon, while they'd been out at the park, confirming the terms of the offer. It lay, a shining scroll, on top of the oranges in the fruit bowl, and caught his eye as he drew a kitchen knife from the block and began to chop a carrot.

This was what life consisted of now: a roll of fax paper, oranges, a knife, four carrots, and the granite kitchen counter that the last owners had installed. "Should last two generations," the husband had said when Mortimer looked the house over, and the wife had hummed her assent. "Nothing like granite," she said, as if Mortimer might have been the kind of buyer who would rip everything out and overhaul the place. He hadn't touched it. He had owned it over two years now, and it still had had no more attention paid to it than his student digs. Even the picture hooks were still where the vendors had left them, some now graced with the odd painting Mortimer had acquired through bequests, or as gifts from friends who painted. Many hooks still pegged out rectangles of bleached wall. When the sellers had asked if he might be interested in buying their weighty old sofa bed, he had jumped at the chance, and asked if there was any other furniture they wanted to get rid of.

He overcooked the salmon. It came out from under the grill charred on the outside, pale and firm within. It flaked on their plates, dry as dust. She ate most of hers anyway.

Halfway through dinner she said, "It's simple, you need to find something else to do. You need a change of scene."

She left right after dinner. He had been hoping he might somehow induce her to stay. He had to admit, though, that the idea of living abroad for a while kindled a flicker of liveliness in his frame.

When the taxi from JFK rumbled across the grilles of the 59th Street Bridge high above the East River, and Mortimer saw the sabres and cutlasses of the world's mightiest army glinting in the afternoon sun, clustered together on their strip of island like a fortress, his heart had exulted in the high sunshine above the silver water of New York.

The very first afternoon, in the corridor of the magazine offices, people had grinned and welcomed him with fierce handshakes. *Good to have you on board. We're lucky to have you.* Right away the editor herself had had Clive and him into her office, a large room with a set of golf clubs in one corner and two banks of windows giving over the city gloriously far below.

"Well, welcome," she said. "We're all *very* excited about this." Then: "Let's think up some ideas. It's good to have three or four on the go. Don't you think?"

And the two of them, the two old English hacks, had almost fallen off their chairs to agree with her.

In the corridor Mortimer had asked Clive: "What's going on?"

"They don't forget a Pulitzer here. You're a coup."

And Mortimer had shaken his head, wondering once again whose life he had accidentally stumbled into.

But the stories hadn't come his way. And meanwhile he'd had a couple of scares.

His apartment wasn't much to write home about: a dingy one-bed at the Chelsea Hotel, with floorboards that squeaked and undulated as you walked, and black wallpaper that might once have been chic but was coming away at the seams. But it was on the eleventh floor, almost as high as the Chelsea went, and the view over broad 23rd Street was invigorating, contemplation-inducing.

One morning he'd woken to find a black-fringed hole the size of a football in his blankets, and on the floor the smashed remains of both a terracotta ashtray and a tumbler of water.

He must have fallen asleep smoking, set the bedclothes alight, and doused them with the water, all without remembering any of it.

Another time something jumped in his chest and for a full minute he couldn't draw breath. A hand squeezed his heart and pulled it from its usual place, making all the sinews go taut. When he came to, his heart was thumping and his head hurt so badly he didn't dare move. It took him an hour to get to his feet, find his coat, and make his way to the elevator.

The doctor admitted him for a night, and the cardiologist saw him two days later to discuss the tests.

"While we're in there we'd probably better go ahead and make it a quadruple," he said breezily. "You'll be better off in the long run."

Was it urgent?

"Take it easy and you could keep going as you arc for a good few years. It's more a question of risk. And how active a life you want to lead."

Active, Mortimer thought: was that the word for his life now?

He decided it had better wait until he got back home to London, though when that would be he didn't know. But he was thankful he had listened when Clive told him to get American health cover.

Just about the only place that felt like home was his local bar after two whiskies.

He gazed now at the rich gold light on its windows, which any minute would be gone, as the sun sank behind 23rd Street. It seemed a kind of miracle that the sun had found its arrow shot to the bar at all, among all the immense buildings. Then the shade arrived, slowly, then quite briskly, swallowing up the fields of golden light that the windows had become.

He drained his drink and picked up the three-day-old *Times* that was still lying on the bar top, with its one piece of real news, the notice of Celeste's death, and tucked it under his arm. Bone cancer, it said. He wondered how sudden it had been, he thought that was one that could be swift. He reeled slightly on his feet, though that was neither from the drink nor from his own health issues, but from shock. She was gone off the face of the earth. Soon he too would be gone. Soon enough all people would be gone. Really, he didn't know what to make of it at all. Except that somehow—however missed and bungled it had been, even with the two of them messing it up, or with him doing so, him failing to go to her when she had pleaded with him to do so—nevertheless the love they'd had still somehow made death less important.

Outside, night was falling and the sky had receded from the tops of the tall buildings. If he'd only known any of Celeste's family well enough he'd have written to them, maybe even gone to see them, for whatever end that might have served. But he didn't. Perhaps he'd write to her husband.

Yet something had to be done.

He swayed a little on the pavement. He had missed love, he now saw, not just with Celeste but with his long-suffering wife too. He had messed up his career, the thing to which he had given everything, and now Celeste had died, and he himself would probably die before too long. And he didn't know how to forgive himself for his professional errors, instead he had been living in a daze of remorse.

He went back to his apartment and sat by the window. The metal heater tutted against the wall. Cars hissed by down below, eleven storeys down, the black tarmac gleaming in their lights. Across town a few signs winked on and off. At this height, there was a softness about the city. Through the door into the bedroom he could see the lamp glowing by two stacks of books. He smoked a cigarette, exhaling against the windowpane. The stream of smoke ballooned then rose slowly, indecisively up the black glass.

Beyond the window New York sighed and hummed beneath him, and sometimes wailed quietly.

He was in the wrong place: he knew that now. Even if he himself couldn't, there was a place that could forgive him, a land beyond error and restoration.

It was an alarming thought, but perhaps the thing was to go back to the desert, one last time, to the dunes, to the place where one might really meet oneself, or God even; where there was nothing but fierce, searing love. Funny that when the stage was empty, that alone was left.

He got up and went to the cupboard. His heart began to race as it used to in the old days. Life was not a gift but a loan: one never knew when it would be recalled. That was a reason for courage, even for recklessness, for anything but caution. Faster and faster his blood ran, he could just about hear it crashing through the veins. Already, as he fetched his bag and threw it on the bed and opened a drawer and commenced packing, already he could feel the desert all around him. This was what he had been waiting for. It was as if just outside the dark walls of his room, there the desert lay, dark orange, with a milky evening sky hovering over it, and a sunset coalescing in the smoky west. He could already see it, already taste it. And the silence of the desert. His heart knew that too. And beside the crackling campfire there sat his one true companion, on the sand, the firelight licking her face.

He wouldn't let himself stop to think. First thing in the morning he would be at the travel agent's with his bag, ready to go.

4

He was sitting by a watering hole in the desert. They had put out from Tamanrasset in a Land Cruiser. He could remember all of it—how he'd got there, the look of the young driver, whose name was Abdul—he could remember the way they'd driven through the night and once seen a column of vehicles in the distance, the beams of their headlights like faint brush strokes in the darkness, and Abdul had told him: *"Contrebandiers."* Mortimer had reflected that there was no cover out here for a smuggler: no gullies or defiles to creep along, no forests, nothing but the vast, unmappable space, and that was all they needed. They hid in the magnitude.

But he could not remember how he came to be here. Surely he had never reached Tamanrasset.

It was midday, and they were sitting with a group of nomads who had come to water their camels at the well. Abdul had known of the well. It took him a while to find it. He had homed in on it, rather than driven straight to it, as if he had some cartography of the desert pre-installed in his brain; or else a magnetic sense for water.

The nomads were sprawled on the ground under a thorn tree with black boughs, while their camels stood nearby, each with a rein tied to a foreleg. One of the men had of all things a canary stashed in his robes. He took it out and showed it to Mortimer. Celeste would have enjoyed that. He could see her wanting to take a shot of the man and his bird. She would have stroked the back of its tiny yellow neck and smiled. *"Jolie, très jolie."*

The man growled out a phrase in his incomprehensibly deep voice.

Abdul, squatting nearby, translated: "He says the bird will sing if you give him a cigarette."

Mortimer went and fetched a couple of packs, which he found in his bag in the Land Cruiser, where he knew they'd be. He also pulled out a slice of bread from the food box, thinking the bird might enjoy that. When Mortimer set the things down on the ground the man didn't move for a while.

When he did finally pick them up, Mortimer thought: Such fine fingers the desert nomads have. They are ascetic, sun-cured people.

It was true. The man's fingers were very fine. He tore off a crust and gave it to the bird, which was still sitting on his open palm. The bird thrashed the bread about to break it up.

A web of shadows spread over the men, cast by the dry boughs of the small, black tree they sat under. Mortimer noticed the dull gleam of rifle barrels on the ground among the men's robes. Perhaps they were fighters who had left some other revolt, and were already home again, in their endless dwelling place.

"Where have they all come from?" Mortimer asked, wanting Abdul to relay the question.

Abdul sank to his haunches. After a moment's pause he spoke to the men in Arabic.

Some of them looked at Abdul, then at Mortimer. One man, with short black stubble and shining white teeth, growled an answer.

"He says from the north. I think they are all from different places."

A man in a white turban muttered something. Then another who had seemed asleep, lying in the dust with his black scarf draped over his face, rolled onto an elbow and spoke in a deep voice that resonated in the pit of his belly.

"Yes," Abdul confirmed. "They come from different places. This man has come from Mali, this man from Assamaka. They are Tuareg, from all over here. From everywhere."

What Mortimer wanted to know was what they were doing here, at this one tiny well in the middle of five thousand miles of emptiness. Where were they going? Why? And who had built the well anyway? When? No one lived anywhere near here. Except, in a sense, these travelers did, in as much as they lived anywhere. The whole desert was their home, they roamed it according to their own buried notions of necessity.

The man with the bird bent close to it and whispered something. The bird shook itself, fluffed up its chest, and began to sing, craning and puffing its neck, releasing a full chorus, an intricate stream of warbling and cheeping with too many notes in it for the human ear to catch.

Celeste would have been delighted. "But that's wonderful. A canary in the desert. May I?" She would have lifted her camera.

And if the man made no response, she would have left it. Mortimer would have noted that he himself would probably have done the opposite, and admired her for her restraint and tact.

"Shall we have lunch here?" Mortimer asked Abdul.

Abdul tutted quietly, and turned to look at the car.

They drove for another hour, then stopped to eat, and dozed in the shade beneath the car through the early afternoon. Then they drove again, still westwards, towards the sun, and the sand sea where they were headed.

The sun was getting low when they pulled up in another hollow similar to where the well had been. Two of the small black trees grew from the stony ground.

"C'est bien," Abdul said. "From here it's just an hour to the piste. See that hill over there?"

Mortimer nodded, though he didn't know which hill Abdul meant, nor what piste.

Abdul fetched a machete from the car and began to dig around in the dirt, until he found a length of dry root. He tore twigs and bark off one of the trees, and made a horseshoe of rocks. When his fire was crackling with translucent flames, he used the tip of his machete to open two cans of pasta, which he emptied into a pan.

Mortimer climbed one of the humps of earth nearby to see what view there was.

The sun had just set. There was a milkiness to the evening sky. The diminutive hillocks among which they had camped rolled away to the west, dissolving into an undifferentiated mauve. Perhaps over there the land once again became flat.

He had an urge to take off his shoes and socks. At first the ground seemed a little cool in the evening, then quite warm, then he couldn't tell whether it was warm or cool. It was prickly against his tender soles.

Why had he always loved empty places? A radiant mist of orange spread up the sky, a startling sight, a richer, brighter colour than one would ever have thought possible, a neon glow. Its fringes fanned into a pool of jade, which in turn gave way to an iridescent dark sky, a canopy that came right up over Mortimer's head, over the whole bare planet.

For a moment he could feel Celeste's warm breath against his cheek, in his ear, and smelled the smell of her hair, and of her skin just after she'd undressed, smelling like a garden after a rain shower. It was as if she were here, invisible to his sight but perceptible to every other sense. He had slipped into another world, the world of then. And she had been waiting for him, had found him as soon as he reappeared.

Then there was just the empty desert, a ramp leaning against the red wall of sunset.

Softly he could hear the clink of Abdul cooking, and once he caught a crack and hiss of the fire itself. Soon they would spread thick blankets on the ground and bed down under the broad sky. Mortimer could not imagine a better covering for a night than the dark sky, nor a place he would rather sleep.

By the time he walked back down the little hill, his footsteps crunching like toast, the world had grown dark enough to make out the fire's glow under the pan, its sheen on Abdul's dark face. Around their secret camp the boulders and slopes of clay loomed and shone.

PART II

Castaway

Harry Burton had had to get away from the island of Inagua. Ironically, the island's name was derived from *lleno de agua*: full of water. Inagua was full of water—inland lakes—but all of it was brine, sea water, salt pan. Salt, salt, salt. Not all the beer in Christendom could kill the thirst Inagua kindled.

And this bloody place, Blunt Island, next island in the chain, was no better. Pittstown Point Landings, the hotel was called. Harry had had enough of these itsy-bitsy names. Points, Bluffs, Landings—the Bahamas were full of them, yet the people who lived in the settlements were slow colossi, whale-like humans, ponderous, sleek, gentle but vast in bulk.

Give him a decent name: Nottingham, London, Hull.

He opened his eyes and stared at the fan above, which, infuriatingly, had a rhythm. Swish-swish, swish-swish. Bloody thing needed a service, it wasn't balanced right. He glanced round the room, which he had entered drunk late last night after four hours in the bar that formed the centrepiece of the bleak little hotel. Trudy, the manager, had walked him down the path to his "cottage."

It was nothing like a cottage, of course: a plain motel room, but without the air-conditioning. Swish-swish.

The sun was already up. A hideous shadow of a palm tree lay splayed on the blind amid an orange luminescence. He rolled onto his side. For a moment things seemed unbearable: to be hungover in a bare white room on the tip of an island with a population of two hundred dreamy souls, surrounded, imprisoned, by hundreds of miles of lurid tropical sea. To be here for a *holiday*, and all because he so desperately needed a break from that other island on which he lived, where he spent all day in a Nissen hut among mountains of grey salt, arguing on the telephone on behalf of the Morton Salt Co. (which couldn't care twice about its lonely Bahamian operation), and where he spent all his evenings drinking in the "lounge" of the company guest house, a place like a giant bathroom, tiled on the floor and, in a bizarre misunderstanding of Western interior design, tiled halfway up the walls too. He had spent too much time in that lounge. Apart from three depressing prints of tropical sunsets on the walls, just in case you forgot where you were, the only adornment to the room was four motionless figures in the corner: whisky, gin, vodka, rum, standing there like sentries, reproaching you. Some nights he'd have company, though not company he would have chosen: a Japanese scientist visiting for a week, who communicated fine via graphs and calculations but spoke not a word of the mother tongue; an official down from Nassau, some heavy morose local whose office had only swollen his taciturnity; an American contractor. These last were much the best, it went without saying. They could put down a few and tell a story, were even on for the odd side trip to Topp's Restaurant for a touch of local life, maybe a bit of a flirt with Josey the tall waitress. Harry wasn't above sharing. Then the slump into bed to the roar of ancient air-conditioning mingled with the clatter of the town generator, a background of black noise that was the last thing you heard at night, and the first upon waking. Coffee and eggs served up by the hefty Viola or her equally hefty daughter, and a trip to the head—fruitless more often than not, with all the "rice 'n' peas" they stuffed into you—and out to the Chevy Blazer, the one thing the job gave him with which he could say he was satisfied. At least he had a decent truck.

So Harry's workdays went.

Check out Blunt Island, people had said, on your next leave. It real lay-back, man, you go like it. It *fine*, man. Which meant highly desirable. But he should have known all the locals said that of anywhere or anything about which they had no particular reason to disapprove. He should have understood them, and it, and himself. He *needed* Miami once a month—the cars and streets and concrete buildings and traffic lights—just to remember that there was a real world out there, a world in which he, Harry, made some kind of sense. A world into which Harry could fly with his walletful of gold plastic, the hard-earned rewards of his years out of touch, beyond the reach of normal life, his years on rigs and mines, under tin roofs, in cots, in bunks, in canteens. What good was all that mounting heap if you didn't tinkle it around from time to time?

Pittstown Point Landings, Blunt Island. The only thing that had ever *landed* on Blunt Island had been a few kilos of Cali's best, back in the days when the narcos still used the Bahamas.

Then an unexpected gust of generosity blew through him, as he lay blearily in bed. Give the place a chance. Go on, who's ever heard of Blunt Island? It's remote, they're trying. At least the beer is cold. He who expects nothing is never disappointed. You just might, he told himself, have a nice little stay here. And it's only three days.

He was thinking of Trudy, the hotel manager. She was neat and slim, with short, tidy blond hair. American. She probably trimmed her pubes. All American women did, at least in the magazines. He would like that. The first thing she had said to him, when he checked in, was something about her divorce of two years ago. And she was hardly going to have met a new beau down here.

The thought of her gave him the impetus he needed to get to the shower, which turned out to be the same plastic cubicle as in the Morton company guest house, and sprayed out the same stinging froth. They were more like cappuccino machines. He had had hopes of a thick plunge of cold water, a stream to carry away not only last night's hours at the bar but the last few months of his life too, all the salt of Inagua.

Hopefully, with a new idea in mind, namely a dip in the fresh morning sea, he slapped a towel over his shoulder and opened the front door. For some blurry reason he was half expecting to feel a bracing morning chill. Instead there was only the uniform tropical warmth. It was infuriating. Couldn't the weather do anything other than warm or hot?

He stepped onto the concrete porch of his cottage and made his way down the path. Two lizards streaked across in front of him, and one, three paving stones away, crouched bravely, staring him down, its throat pulsing. The sea lay just a few yards off. As always, it was a vivid blue, with streaks of sickly green. But this morning it was more lurid than ever, as if a photographer had spilt the chemicals in the darkroom and come up with a grotesquerie of tropical colour. Feeble waves slapped themselves onto the beach, then gave a brief slurp, like someone sucking from a soup spoon, as they withdrew. He could imagine just how warm the water would be—like swimming in urine.

Ahead a palm tree was flapping about in a breeze that he couldn't feel, and sunlight flickered back and forth across his face. He felt giddy, and turned round. Depressed, despondent, feeling sorry for himself, Harry trudged back to his room and fell onto the bed.

A holiday. Week after week of work on a hot desert island, then three days off, a long weekend, and what does he do? Madly, he flies to another hot desert island.

Then he remembered that he hadn't yet started the day, and felt a little better: breakfast. First things first.

On his second outing he came across Trudy squatting in a pair of shorts by the side of the path.

"Hi," she called, rather too ebulliently. The enthusiasm in her voice reminded him that he was the only guest.

"Morning," he answered, with more verve than he intended.

"I'm trying to turn this damn thing on," she said.

Sooner than he meant, before he had even thought about it, he had gallantly sunk to his knees beside her and was reaching into a drain, straining to open a stopcock hidden inside a length of piping.

"I have to turn it off at night or the kitchen floor floods," she said apologetically.

He got it open and stood up feeling much better, as if he had done something constructive for the day. "There," he announced.

She thanked him effusively. "Come on, I'll fix you some breakfast."

He followed her down the path, inexplicably struck dumb, watching her legs. They were a soft, creamy brown, as if new to the sun. She must have been forty, but she was well kept. Perhaps a little too well kept, too prim, altogether too healthy for his taste; he guessed she might be a Midwesterner. Yet he couldn't take his eyes off her legs and the twin shapes enclosed by her shorts.

He took a stool at the bar and waited for her to produce a cup of coffee and "the works," as she called it, meaning eggs and bacon. Apparently the cook was coming in late today so Trudy was fixing it herself. He listened to her bustling about the kitchen. It was a soothing sound, and lulled him into a reverie of a home somewhere, a familiar home that at first he couldn't place, until he realised he was thinking of his student digs in Manchester. With a sudden chill it came to him that that was the last place he had ever lived that he could call home. Fifteen years ago. A surge of self-pity struck, at the thought not of his itinerancy, but of the innocent zeal with which he had travelled out to Botswana for his first posting. The roar of the yellow bulldozers, the clatter of the generators—sounds that had become the backdrop of his life—the dust-filled air, the strong sun, the beers with the lads in the hot nights—it had all thrilled him then.

Trudy came in to fetch ice from the bar's big refrigerator. When she opened the door, his eye fastened on the stacks of misty brown bottles inside, and another memory swept into him: he found himself remembering the bottles of chocolate milk they used to sell in Spain, where he had gone on holidays as a child. His father would buy him a bottle at the café on the beach, and the waiter would click off the top with his opener. At once Harry would catch the smell in his nostrils, a thick, malty aroma that filled him with excitement. He would watch the waiter glugging the thick grey drink into the glass, then he would lift it, ringed with froth, to his lips. He could taste it now. He felt his eyes moisten.

Trudy called, "Won't be long," in a cheery voice.

The coffee came first, then the eggs, and finally Trudy herself.

She sat down opposite him at the table she had laid, with her giant Koffee Kup in hand. Which was awkward. Much as he appreciated her friendliness, he knew himself well enough to know that breakfast was no time to practise his charms. He asked if he could borrow the newspaper at the front desk, even if it was last week's. She didn't take the hint.

"Did you sleep well?" she asked. "I put you on the beachfront specially. There's nothing like drifting off to the sound of surf, I always think."

He nodded with his mouth full of salty bacon, while buttering a piece of brittle toast, which snapped under his knife. He forced himself to swallow.

"It beats the town generator on Inagua." He laughed hoarsely.

"What's that?" She stared at him with an expression at once blank and uncomfortably penetrating.

He had to explain about the generator in Inagua. It fatigued him to have to spell it all out, first thing in the day. He lowered his eyes to the sunny eggs, and tore them open with his knife tip. A spasm of warm longing for their rich flavour ran through him.

"So what brings you to our lovely isle?" She raised her Koffee Kup, hiding her face.

"Holidays," he said, snickering ironically. "I thought a nice dose of R and R was in order."

"You've come to the right place," she said brightly. "Nothing but R and R here. Unless of course you're a fisherman."

Which he wasn't.

"Tell you what," she went on, lighting up. "I have some

errands today, but how about a flying-fish fry-up tonight? I'll tell Maureen." Maureen was the absent cook. "Sound good?"

He hummed his accord, chewing a mouthful of toast. It not only sounded good, it sounded, as far as he could tell, like a date. A faint anticipation stirred in him. He nodded. "Wonderful," he got out, pleased also because now that they had a plan for later on she might leave him alone with his breakfast. Moreover, he thought he detected the possibility of a long-overdue bowel movement.

Sure enough, Trudy announced, "Well, no rest for the wicked," pushing back her chair. She smiled at him in such a way that a smile was unavoidably summoned from his own face. As she walked across the room he resisted temptation for a moment, then gave in and eyed her buttocks as they moved away, encased by her shorts.

After breakfast he went back to his room to masturbate, then decided that he really must do something till lunchtime. But what? Perch on the scorching sand and watch the wavelets? "Stroll" along a potholed road through the burning heat? Sit in a tin-roofed shack known as the Tea Room sweating over greasy too-sweet coffee? And what about after lunch? He had the entire day to kill. In Miami it was easy. You could wander along the shorefront, then take a seat at one of the sidewalk cafés and watch the models go by while sipping iced coffee. Or lie by the hotel pool, or take a stool under the palm bar. He could even finally have looked up, as he had been meaning to do, one of his old college acquaintances, who was living near Miami with his family. But here?

He felt another attack of his blues coming on. He had left home fifteen years ago, and arrived nowhere, and now it was too late to arrive anywhere. He was one of the cursed of the earth, doomed to roam the globe, passing wherever he went the houses and gardens and climbing frames and family cars of the earth's inheritors. A decade and a half already. Twelve-, eighteen-, six-month contracts had eaten up his years, his chances.

Have a swim, have a swim, anything, something, but get out of this room, he told himself.

He walked around the hotel, following the paths among the twelve identical cottages. It was a sad place, every bit as impersonal and unloved as any motel on an interstate. He guessed it would have been built in the sixties, in the Bahamas' heyday, when private pilots used to fly themselves and their girlfriends down to swinging clubs all over the islands. Now the place was graced only by occasional visits from sports fishermen. The coast of Cuba lay eighty miles away, and in between was the West Indies Channel, where the marlin fishing was said to be good. Harry sauntered into the hotel lobby and idly flipped through the register, still with plenty of pages to spare in a volume that went back to 1975. It was full of comments such as: "Great fishing!!" . . . "We'll bring him in next time!!!" . . . "352 pounds of pure fun!"

He changed into a pair of bright orange shorts and tried slipping into the warm ocean. He lay on his back under the blue sky. Wasn't there anywhere in the world where the weather was good but not so bloody hot? Somewhere like the English summers of his youth? He remembered long days cycling around the city park and down back streets with his long-lost friend James, then diving into the brown canal to cool off, and how the water used to have a warm film on the surface but cool dark depths beneath. He and James would kick about, sending up plumes of white spray, then swim slowly down into the coolness with their eyes tightly shut. That was good weather. Not this baking, sweaty heat above a bath-warm ocean.

He swam out thirty yards, took a breath, and let himself sink down into the sea till his feet touched the sandy bottom. The water was warm all the way.

He was grateful when a breeze got up and the palms rustled. He lifted himself from the waves to greet it.

The mail boat came in later on. Harry wandered into "town," a handful of huts dozing among trees, to watch the boat unload. Every pickup on the island, all ten or twelve of them, had congregated in the shade of the great old iron vessel with its crumbling mildewed deckhouse. A crew in yellow hard hats were busy disgorging load after load of gas cylinders.

The locals, with and without pickups, had gathered in force. Some were evidently awaiting passage—women in their best straw hats and dresses beside old suitcases tied up with belts and string, men in slacks and white shirts, one old man wearing a pair of heavy black-rimmed glasses without lenses, as if glasses were part of a man's formal attire. Others watched the cargo coming ashore with a keen eye, awaiting goods. After the gas cylinders came huge string sacks of onions, potatoes, oranges.

There was something relaxing about the scene. It was hard not to like it—the rusty old ship, the twinkling blue harbour, the quietly excited crowd, the noisily bored shipworkers, all dressed in singlets, who kept up a continual shouted banter while they manned the derrick, guided the loads, loaded the pallets. Harry perched on a bollard at the end of the quay and wondered what it would be like to be one of the locals travelling away, up to Nassau and beyond. They'd see their little island become a tiny strip of green on the horizon, then vanish. Night would fall over the wide ocean, and they'd wake up in the Nassau Channel, flanked by a world of concrete and braying car horns. He wondered if they would be homesick or thrilled. He decided it would depend on their age.

He remembered, for example, his own first trip away from home, down to Lyme Regis, and the indescribable thrill of reaching a new town where his family would be staying for a whole week. It was like suddenly having a new home at your disposal, with all its streets and shops and walks and alleyways to explore, though it was better than a home because it was temporary, you could leave it if you wanted. He had felt a similar thrill when he first reached Africa. When the plane landed and the taxi took him through the bristling city, all sparkling under the African sun, he could barely believe his good fortune that this would all be his for a year.

New places were different now. They weren't so new. Harry found himself noticing the suburban homes, the satellite dishes, and whether there were one or two cars in the garage, a swing in the garden. All countries had turned into places to bring up children. Some were arguably easier than others, though it was largely a matter of taste. Harry was only forty-two, which wasn't old, of course, but more and more often the men Harry worked with were younger than him yet already had two or three children, and he noticed increasingly that wherever he worked people talked about the same things—schools, colds, the price of kids' clothes—whether he was in Accra, Aberdeen, or Angola. It was as if there was nowhere exotic left. Exotic was just a memory.

Through the late afternoon Harry sat alone at the hotel bar nursing Johnnie Walkers. At quarter to six, bang on cue, yet another sticky tropical sunset began to spill across the world like undiluted orange squash.

Trudy walked in. "Mind if I join a weary salt miner?" she asked, pulling off a pair of yellow rubber gloves, which she draped over the back of a bamboo bar stool before climbing on. "Must be thirsty work, huh?"

He removed the cigarette from his mouth and, in his suavest voice, amid a cloud of smoke, and full of gratitude for the distraction, drawled, "I'd be thoroughly delighted. It's thirsty work just living in these parts. What'll it be?"

She fanned at her throat vaguely and laughed. "Thoroughly delighted. You Brits. Only you can talk like that." She glanced at her watch. "Why, thank you. I'll have a beer. It is six o'clock, practically."

She *was* a pretty thing. With her tidy, short blond hair, possibly dyed, and her neat little shorts and tennis shirt, and that soft tan on all her slender limbs, she was altogether adequately desirable.

"Ahoy there!" Harry called out, towards the empty doorway behind the bar.

"Maureen!" Trudy echoed beside him, with a laugh, as if they were really having fun.

A moment later a slow island woman emerged. "Yer call?" She stared at her boss implacably.

"Drinks, please, Maureen. Mr. Burton will have another whisky, and I'll have a beer."

Without a word, the woman set about the order. She lifted a great block of ice from the refrigerator and hacked at it with a screwdriver, sending chips of ice flying about the room, some of which landed on the bar top, where they quickly melted. Then she stooped, rather gracefully Harry thought, despite her bulk, to pluck the top off a beer bottle on an opener under the bar. Finally she unscrewed the top off a fresh bottle of whisky.

"Cheers," Harry said.

They knocked their drinks together.

"Ever been our way?" he asked.

Trudy had a sip and wiped her mouth. "You know how it is. Any time off, you head straight for Miami. But I'm dying to come and see the flamingos."

Everyone had heard about the flamingos of Inagua. Inagua was nothing more than a ring of land encircling its great salt flats, where fifty thousand flame-pink birds fed and bred. They were about the only reason anyone ever visited the island, except for the salt miners.

"The flamingos are a wonderful sight," he said. "And that's not all, you know. We've got five thousand wild donkeys, descendants of the asses of Roi Henri Christophe." He pronounced the phrase with relish, having read it innumerable times in his *Fodor's Guide*, extracting from it every ounce of glamour it could yield.

"What?" she exclaimed, overdramatically, not the reaction he had expected.

"As you may know," Harry drawled on, "Henri was King of Haiti. He shipped his gold over to Inagua when the French attacked. Donkeys carried it. But the gold was lost." He swirled the drink in his glass, making the ice clink, thinking that it was deft of him to have introduced a romantic note so swiftly yet stealthily. Before she knew it she'd be dreaming of buried treasure and falling into his arms.

She was frowning at her drink. "The donkeys *swam* over?" she asked, in a kind of whine.

He explained that they had been shipped across the hundred miles of sea from Haiti. But he felt irritated. She was too bloody literal. No passion.

"Well, what happened to all the gold?" she asked.

He shrugged. "It's still out there somewhere, I suppose." A solitary ray of golden sunshine found his left eye. He leaned out of it.

She looked at him and raised her glass. "Well, let's go find it. Here's to Henri's gold. What are we waiting for?" She was smiling. It was a nice smile, sincere. He raised his glass to it. Maybe the old Burton magic was working after all.

He said, "Tell you what, when you come over, I'll give you a guided tour in my Blazer. We'll find the blasted stuff."

For some reason she found this hilarious and rocked back on her stool, knocking off her rubber gloves. He at once slipped to the floor and picked them up for her. He hadn't noticed until now, bending down beside her, that despite her trim figure she had a good bust. The words of an old Australian mining colleague ran through his mind: "Mines beat bloody rigs. Pussy galore on shore, mate!" Harry let his face fill with a smile of modest gallantry, and carefully settled the gloves in the lap of her red shorts, folding the plastic lengths over at the finger joints.

She sat very still, clearly pleased, and said softly, "Why thank you. I didn't know there were any gentlemen left in the world."

"It's the one bloody thing Britain does still manufacture," he said, seating himself again.

She gave him a look. He wasn't quite sure what it meant, but felt he should return it, which he did, with interest. It seemed to be the right thing to do, because she let out another peal of unexpected hilarity.

He answered with a low chuckle, a kind of snigger he had grown accustomed to using on Josey the waitress on Inagua.

Trudy said, "Well, we may not have any gold here, but we have got paradise. There ain't anything to do except enjoy yourself."

Her accent seemed to have shifted. Perhaps he had been wrong in placing her in the Midwest; she sounded more like a Southerner now. Southern girls were a lot of fun, he remembered knowing from somewhere. They had the right attitude.

"I'm always on for enjoying myself," he said. After a short but awkward silence, he added, "So how long have you been down here?"

"Eight months, and *lov*ing it. Peace and quiet, getting away from it all."

"Do you get many visitors?" he asked, though he already knew the answer.

She shrugged. "People come and go. Suits me fine. But sometime I'll be ready to move on. Move back, rather."

Harry raised his eyebrows in what he hoped was a curious and mildly concerned expression. "Back to the States?"

"Find me a little place in Arkansas, up in the Ozarks. A farm I can settle down in for the rest of my days. A place my grandchildren can visit."

She tipped up her beer bottle. Harry tried to calculate how old she must be to have grandchildren already, but was distracted by the sight of her throat as she drank. He didn't expect her to have caught the sun under her chin, but the skin down there was golden in the late light. A nodule of bone flexed in and out complicatedly, turning out then reinstating a small pool of shadow. As he watched, a yearning grew in the pit of his stomach. There was something lovely about seeing the equipment of this human body doing its job so efficiently, and about being so close to it. But there was more. She stirred a vague sense of recollection, of recognition, as if they might have known each other long ago.

Perhaps that was what *he* needed: a farm in the Ozarks, a destination, somewhere to aim for, a cottage in the Cotswolds, a farmhouse in Wales, a bungalow on the Wirrel. Somewhere he planned to end up. But he wasn't sure you could have that without a permanent woman. What could be lonelier, after all, than sitting by yourself up a rainy hillside in Britain while it got dark outside at four o'clock?

Trudy emptied her beer bottle and settled it on the table with a sigh of satisfaction. "All *right*. Well hell, let's see how that fish is doing."

She sidled off her stool and walked around the bar and into the kitchen with an eagerness in her carriage, her back upright and bust held forward. It was nice watching her. Harry decided he liked her. It felt good to like someone. They might see more of each other. It could become something regular. She on her island, he on his. There was no reason they couldn't meet up every weekend, for example. Two professional people out here, they needed one another's company. He could move out of the guest house and rent a villa, somewhere with satellite and AC and a big sitting room where the two of them could unwind, joking, reading the papers, after their respective weeks of labour. It could turn out to be the perfect arrangement—a woman on the next island, not too close but close enough. They could have a real courtship, give each other plenty of time to get used to the change. He had fallen at that hurdle in the past—rushing things and then panicking and wanting out.

He pictured them in a white villa on a hill. There weren't any villas on Inagua, or hills for that matter, but where there was a will there was a way. Then, when they felt they had done their time in the Bahamas, they could see what the next step would be. With her American passport and his British they could go anywhere, once they were spliced. It would be the best reason for people of their age to marry: a practical reason, solid enough to spare them embarrassment, as well as the sprinkling of romance, of course.

Trudy reemerged from the kitchen and announced, "Maureen says it'll be a while yet."

A loud hiss filled the bar, followed by the unmistakable soft click of a gramophone needle landing on a record. A loud chord, a drumbeat, a man gleefully singing out, *Ah feeling to wine on something* . . . It was the usual island music, which Harry heard interminably on transistors all over Inagua, only this time it sounded strangely appealing. It made you want to tap your feet, swing your hips, and click your fingers. There was something about the strumming guitar, the hop-popping conga drums, the insistent cowbell, that infected your muscles.

"Another drink?" Trudy called.

She poured them both a whisky, then tore a packet of Marlboro out of a carton. "We may be a small island, but we've got cigarettes, we've got whisky, we've got everything you need." She handed Harry a fresh drink, clunking her own against it. "Down the hatch," she declared.

They danced. Normally Harry hated to dance, but before he could object she had whisked him out of his seat and placed herself in front of him, shaking her hips. She had learnt to move like the islanders, swinging from side to side. She leaned back and set her legs apart, either side of Harry's thigh, just as the island women did. At first Harry was embarrassed—nothing was worse than foreigners who pretended to be locals—but she had a way of moving that brought a smile irresistibly to his lips. Her loins took on a life of their own, rotating and pulsing back and forth. Once she backed against him so he could feel her warm behind. Another time she held his neck in her hands and quite distinctly pressed her pubic bone against his. He started to shake his hips too, grinding himself against her. She whooped with delight, grinding back. Then she got into a kind of Latin dance, whirling him round and round. He laughed along and trilled his tongue.

Afterwards, seated at the table, Trudy leaned forwards and touched his arm. "You're something, you know," she said. "Forget about mad dogs and Englishmen. Dogs and mad Englishmen, more like." Her hand was hot on his bare arm, below the sleeve of the tropical shirt he had changed into earlier.

Maureen emerged from the kitchen bearing a platter filled with strips of battered, fried fish. She shuffled across the floor and deposited it on their table. "Dinnertime," she said in a lazy, tired-sounding voice.

Trudy had been chilling a bottle of Chablis, which Harry insisted be put on his bill, but she wouldn't hear of it. While they ate, Trudy talked about *Masterpiece Theatre* and how much she had always wanted to go to England. Harry dropped numerous hints that he would gladly take her. After dinner she suggested a stroll along the beach. It all went like clockwork.

Who is Harry Burton anyway? A global man, highly trained, bulky, stiff, ruddied by tropical suns, he is glimpsed in airports, at poolside bars, behind the wheel of Land Cruisers in hot countries. He long ago severed the ties that bind. He needed to break free, and having broken free finds himself not a citizen of the world, but no citizen at all. The world adjusts, and no longer needs him. When this troubling recognition dawns on him he ignores it: he's just a little low. Another night with Josey down at Topp's Restaurant, or with Marie over at Madame Nelly's, a decent screw, a night with the lads, whoever the lads happen to be, and all will be well. But after years of looking askance at himself, years of flinching at the sight of Volvos full of children and lights in living room windows at night, Harry realises that the dream he set out to fulfil has become grim truth. The juice evaporates from the fruit and nothing can bring it back.

Harry stirs in his sleep beneath the swish-swish of a fan. A warm knee presses against his thigh. He rolls over and his hand grazes a pubic bush. At once he rolls back the other way. He cannot hear the woman's breathing, but thinks she is asleep. He slips out of bed and into the bathroom, assuming he needs to pee, but finds that he doesn't. His head aches. In front of him is the dark bathroom (he doesn't want to turn on the light), his dim, swollen shape in the mirror, and the familiar dissatisfaction with the day coming. He will have to sleep with her again tomorrow night, it will be impolite not to. Then he will be gone. He drinks from the tap. The water tastes like a swimming pool. He slips back into bed as quietly as he can and lies a long time staring at the fan overhead, waiting for sleep to carry him away.

Old Providence

"Oh *God*," Rothman Case muttered as his daughter parked the car outside the gallery. "This is ruinous, murderous. How did you ever persuade me?"

She switched off the engine. "Stop being a prima donna. You'll love it, you always do."

"I never do. And this is different and you know it." He let out a long series of coughs. "Oh good God," he persisted, as if even now there might be some hope of getting out of the evening ahead. "What if I got appendicitis again, for Christ's sake, or if the old liver finally gave out?"

She dabbed at an eyelid, peering in the rearview mirror. "Appendicitis *again*? Break a leg," she muttered.

Rothman, a stiff man, bulked to the full by late middle age, though not obese, planted his feet on the pavement. "Better get it over with I suppose," he enunciated deliberately, adding "Ha!" for no apparent reason, out of alcoholic bravado perhaps. He stood on the curb and glugged from his flask, flipped the cap, and had it back in his breast pocket before she finished locking the car.

He caught sight of himself in the glass doors of the gallery. The impression was of universal gleam. A gleaming face, a gleaming shirt, even his black trousers seemed to gleam. The glamour of the night was apparently upon him. He had stepped, it would seem, into the limelight that was duly his. He directed an imperceptible nod of thanks towards the mirage in the glass that was him, buckled up his mood, battened down the furies, storm-sheeted the miseries, and allowed the waiting doors to be swung apart on his behalf. His daughter alighted on his arm as he took the first step, and he felt the two of them make precisely the entrance required.

Jackson Mitchell the critic was first to approach, gliding through the crowd, glass in hand as ever, cheeks flushed as ever. "Oh but this is most *de*finitely the one we've been waiting for. By George."

Rothman smiled involuntarily. But the "by George" unnerved him. It was unlike Mitch the Bitch to euphemise his expletives, on or off the page.

"Paintings of Providence. Wonderful, wonderful. Want a little taste, eh?" Mitchell giggled in his high-pitched wheeze, pulling a catalog from his coat pocket. The back page was covered in scribbles. "Seldom has London," he began in his incisive tenor, reading his own prose, "had such cause for self-scrutiny as it did last night, at the opening of blah blah blah. Nothing shames the art world," he delivered with Hitchcockian emphasis, "like the arrival of a master."

"Fuck off." Rothman waved him away. "Arrival?"

"Knew you'd do it sooner or later. Always did. You're a *force*, dear boy." He uttered the word in such a way that Rothman could not help but smile, under pressure partly of flattery, partly of the man's absurd camping. "And every single one of them gone already. A positive pointillism of red dots. By the way, who *was* she?"

Rothman raised an eyebrow and didn't answer.

"Well." Mitchell glanced at his watch. "I'll be out of here in five minutes to catch copy. That'll be in the morning edition."

Then Chaim, the gallery owner, was at Rothman's side,

along with Kachinski and de Jongh, and suddenly it seemed odd that Mitchell should have been talking to him *à deux*. Perhaps Chaim knew that Mitch was planning on kissing arse, had given him a minute to deliver the good news himself. Mend bridges, so to speak.

"Fuck off," Rothman called once more over his shoulder as he was escorted into the main hall, aswirl just then with the well dressed and the ignorant, and with the delicious, reassuring scent of expensive women. For which thank God, Rothman reflected: in the end it was the old pleasures that held a man together.

Next thing he knew, cameras were flashing and he was caught in a scrum of naked shoulders, a shrubbery of champagne flutes, and a blaze of light. Too much light. He bellowed out his daughter's name but she didn't hear, she didn't come, and meanwhile his shoes became light and began a two-step of their own, and the light grew brighter, and as it did so he grew more aware of the painting hanging to his right, he thought it must be *Maria IX*, a big dark canvas with the face looming out of it. The eyes in the face seemed to attach themselves to the side of his head and pull . . .

Maria cradled his head in her long Latin fingers. Such fine fingers the Latin woman has. What the devil was Maria doing here? They'd said their goodbyes long ago. Maria's eyes shone like the rain: like pebbles in a stream.

"An out-and-out triumph, old boy. Every single one gone."

The older one got the more the asses felt it incumbent upon themselves to call one "boy." Who was this one now?

Ah, Chaim. His daughter's fellow. Not half bad. Rothman attempted to let out a ribald cackle but it didn't sit right in his throat.

Where were they now? Somewhere dark, somewhere illumined, as far as he could see, by a phalanx of red candles whose light licked over a bowl of glossy fruit. Ah yes: the black mass of the groaning table, the still life of dinner: they were *dining*, of course, some eight or ten of them. A white tablecloth, a meal well in progress, an empty chair at the head, no doubt his, for he was slumped in an armchair, it would seem, unlit cigarette in hand.

"More wine," he heard himself bawl. And: "Where's my supper?"

Chaim, good egg, faced him on a dining chair, straddling it like a cowboy, his elbows on the back. "Wine for the maestro," he called out.

Someone produced a brimming beaker which Rothman seized and promptly poured into his lap.

"For God's sake, Daddy."

Ah: Virginia. Good girl. "You're a good girl," he might or might not have said aloud to his daughter.

"What *are* you doing?" she asked.

He looked up at her but not for long. She was a frightening sight: eyes with the glint of steel, of all-sobering clarity.

"You shouldn't be drinking."

Chaim smiled up at her. "I'm keeping an eye on things."

No use carrying on like this, Rothman thought. Got to straighten the old self out, get back to work. The best days are the days we work, Maria used to say. Too right. They were the *only* days.

And Maria was beside him again, Lord knows how,

stroking his cheek, explaining with the touch of her slender fingers that he had got it all wrong, it was all terribly simple, one just had to be humble and diligent, nothing else. Diligence was goodness. To live somewhere pure, with good air, good light, and to work.

Virginia got him home, scolding him on the way for being foolish and obnoxious, for drinking on the pills, on his ravaged liver: why couldn't he simply enjoy a night of success, why complicate everything? And Chaim was in the back of the car, coming along to help. The two of them would hoist the old fool to bed, have a little nightcap, compare notes, that sort of thing, and hey presto, the two-backed beast would be at work.

"I mean, Daddy," she went on, "why you can't just leave things be? All anyone wanted you to do was smile and say thank you."

Outside his flat he said, "I need to get away. You have to get me away." But even as he said it he didn't believe it. After a certain point in life there was no getting away.

He was up early flagging a taxi to the studio, dosed with aspirin, sertraline, ribavirin, and coffee. The high hall of the studio, with its great dusty window overlooking, if one could have got up a ladder to look out, the Piccadilly line at Barons Court, had never looked emptier. For once the place was tidy. Judy, his assistant, had evidently been in. The big table in the middle caked with decades of paint had nothing on it but a stack of art books. A fleet of rags hung bone dry, clean, over the sink. The two easels stood empty and the big armchair, cushions puffed, waited between them.

The pleasant sigh of morning traffic reached his ears. He sighed too. A subterranean tremor shook the floor as a tube train passed.

It was good to get the canvases out of there at last. Or was it good? The place was unnervingly empty. What was a man to do now? The only thing he could think of was to pull the flask from his pocket.

The new show had been his daughter's idea but had happened through his own carelessness. He was a fool to have listened to her. What was left now? His private store, his own little treasure chest, the one true store he had carried through life, was plundered, its lid unhinged.

Three months earlier, one late afternoon while he was finishing up his last series of *Chair* canvases for Chaim, Virginia had caught him at it. Alone in the studio, he had gone to one of the stacks, as he sometimes did, flipped up its curtain, and pulled out the three canvases lodged there. Then he ripped up a strip of carpet on the bottom, inserted his finger in a hole, and lifted out the baseboard. Hidden under it were eleven canvases. He reached up to switch on the light overhead and peered in, finally lifting out two, studying them both in daylight, and replacing one. The other he carried to an easel.

The picture was straightforward enough. From a profusion of foliage the face stared out at you: a dark woman, her face a geometry of lines, bones, complexions, all suggesting a disquieting and more or less unfathomable mood, a mix of resignation, despair, hope. A deal made with passion, with disappointment too. A trad picture, but good, chock-full of the right stuff. A solid chunk hauled from the sump, authentic to its core. Marred only by a gauche stroke here, a jejune line there. No question: Scavello and the other dealers who had looked at it twenty-five years ago had been wrong, blinded by the fashions of their day, incapable of seeing true work when it stared them in the face.

Something of Frida Kahlo in it, he thought. And of Gauguin too, of course. But mostly it was him, Rothman, through and through. Or rather her, Maria. Maria as she had embedded herself in his mind, glaring at him from the profuse nature embracing her.

He went over to the sideboard, hunted for the right palette. Which Judy had cleaned and scrubbed the best she could. It would have been better if she hadn't bothered. He bent down for a box of oils, squeezed out titanium, chromium, returned with a pair of brushes to the canvas.

He began with a ghost of a stroke. By God, he thought, but the damn thing was done after all. The eyes were particularly good. Bright and sombre at once. Remarkable how they held the viewer. Rothman let out a cough that was also a sigh, a laugh, even a sob. Who the hell had done this picture? Who had that young man been? Rothman didn't know whether to laugh that such a talent had existed or weep at its squandering.

Then he had heard the door downstairs. Footsteps climbed the staircase. At once he picked up the picture, but before he was even halfway across the room he realised he would never make it to the stacks in time. He returned to the easel, angling the canvas away from the door just as the rising steps brought his daughter into the room.

"Oh it's you," he said. "Afternoon, dearest, or is it evening?"

"You're here late," she said. Her hair was swept back and she looked good, fresh faced, touched with cool autumn wind.

"You didn't expect to find me here?"

She reached into her bag and tossed an attractively plump envelope on the table: his week's pocket money. If you couldn't run your life yourself you could do worse than have your daughter, if she was a capable woman, do it for you.

"What are you working on?"

It had been bad luck. But at the time it crossed his mind that perhaps it was good luck. Was he really going to keep these pictures hidden forever? She came round the table towards the big window and stopped behind him. She said nothing for a moment. Then: "Oh my. What is this? It's so unlike . . . Are there others?"

"Done before you were even born, my dear."

"Let me see them."

And it being a beautiful afternoon of late sun, and Rothman having just finished the last of the *Chair* pictures for the contract with Chaim, each of which he knew would fetch a comfortable five figures—riding as it happened on the crest of a glorious daylong hangover, he had acquiesced. Why not after all? This was his daughter. What harm could there be? What exactly *was* he planning to do with them?

"But Daddy—" She was apparently speechless at the next three he took out.

A train rumbled past, trembling through the floor.

"I'm calling Chaim right now."

"Whoa, hold on a moment." Yet he couldn't help smiling.

"You have to come and see what Daddy's done," she said into the receiver. And Chaim came straight over. They got all eleven canvases out, leaning them against the wall, propping them on books, up on the easels, until the whole studio was filled with Maria's dark face and the darker foliage of the island on which he had loved her, and with her breasts and torso, the perfect taut plateau of her stomach, her deep delta. Rothman's head began to spin. He was sick in the toilet.

Chaim stooped and peered and screwed up his face. He paced backwards and forwards, cocked his head, sighed, chuckled, hummed. He tapped gently here and there at clots of paint. "Well," he mused, and, "Hmm," and, "Yes, yes, interesting." Then he gave Rothman a big hug. "Where have you been all my life? I'm putting everything on hold."

Before Rothman knew what was what, it had all been arranged, he wasn't even allowed to touch them up. "They need nothing at all," Chaim declared. "I'm not letting you near them. What a departure. When did you *do* them? This'll be one in the eye for the critics, eh, who think they've got you pigeonholed."

It had been an accident waiting to happen. As the weeks went by Rothman felt worse and worse, drank harder and harder, until finally the night came and he collapsed in front of everybody in a ruinous, ridiculous, sozzled heap, as he would later put it.

The day after the show Chaim bought them lunch, Rothman and his daughter, at Little's.

"All gone, every blasted one of them. Time for a holiday, I think. Are you serious about going away?"

"What?"

"Last night you said you'd like to go away."

"Oh that. Of course I'm serious. A man needs . . ." He trailed off, racking his brains for what a man needed.

"I've been thinking—"

"An island. That's what a man needs. A bloody perfect island."

"Quite, quite."

"Chaim's got the perfect place, Daddy."

Rothman frowned.

"Unless you're working, of course."

"Got to give the old eyes a rest once in a while."

Why not? Yes indeed, he would go and have a haircut, buy some new clothes, and off they could all go on holiday with Chaim.

"To every man's island." He drained a tumbler of Rioja. "To *away*."

"Daddy," Virginia began: an ominous note. He slumped in his chair. "You can't go around collapsing on us, you know. I've made another appointment for you."

He shrugged; he grumbled; he wanted no doctor but the alchemist, the alkahest, the ultimate dissolution. "No need, no need. Thanks anyway. All I need's a holiday. Quite right."

So it was that just three days after the Providence show opened Rothman found himself supine on a horsehair mattress in County Clare, falling in and out of sleep.

An owl was hooting somewhere out in the night. He could hear it when the wind went quiet. To how many creatures was it given to look behind themselves? he wondered. To the owl with its pirouetting neck, and to the long-necked ruminants, the slow cow, the jumpy horse, the skittery sheep. To how many was it not given? To the fish, with their sensitive tails, and the stiff-necked biped to whom had been given the inner eye, which was all he could look back with.

When he woke again, out of the window he could see the ewes in the field sitting down like a flock of birds. Broad daylight already, sunny.

Rothman studied himself in the bathroom mirror. Ringlets of grey and white hair framing the temples, the bald pink skin overhead, the bulbous shiny nose of his Hungarian forebears: a grotesque face. Hazel eyes that had become permanently untrustworthy. Grotesque because false — a half smile moulded into the cheeks kept the eyebrows raised. It was the face of a man who had been in the public eye too long, the mask of a *personality*. Which was what he had become. The Painter of Roads and Chairs and other Everyday Articles. One either had a personality or gave it up to become one. Of the many wrong paths an artist might turn down, success was the hardest.

He lathered up his cheeks. He was of the sideburn generation. Funny how some things stayed with you. He had journeyed right through life with a pair of sideburns, once brown, now silver.

Coming down the narrow staircase he glanced out the window again: green elbows and shoulders of land, a veil of mist driving across them, a muffled thunder of wind in the rafters. You couldn't hear the sea from here but you could see it, grey and boiling beyond the field. That was Ireland for you: weather that turned on a dime. It had been sunny just now, and already it was cloudy. A stand of reeds shimmered in beating wind.

A mistake, obviously: Ireland had never been *away*. Ireland was just more of the same, the same old axis of booze and rain and candles and landowners with flats in Eaton Square who bought art, at least they *bought*. Ireland was just part of the grounds, even if you were flung up on the cliffs of Clare. No one around here had any idea what *away* meant. He couldn't bear to look outside. This was not, had never been, where he belonged. Pills and booze and good galleries got you by, and women too, of course, but they would not have been necessary elsewhere. His head hurt. There was a stone in his chest.

In the kitchen he mixed up a Disprin with a splash of Powers and a dollop of fresh-squeezed orange juice from a jug on the table. A farmhouse table at which were seated daughter, daughter's lover, Chaim, and a lady wearing a blue scarf.

Chaim, curly-haired, bright-eyed—eyes somehow too bright, as if permanently made up for the stage—got to his feet. "What'll it be? *Oeufs jambon?*"

Rothman didn't want to have to look at him. "Whatever," he growled, and thwacked the cork back into the Powers bottle.

"Daddy." His daughter's voice.

"For God's sake let me die in peace."

"You're not dying, but if you keep on like this you'll kill yourself. This is Mrs. Williams." She meant, he knew, the woman with the headscarf.

"Mrs. Williams, how do you do?" Rothman didn't turn round. He drained off his glass. It went down awkwardly, stinging his chest.

"She's come to see you."

He set the glass down. "You mean, I think, that she's come to see *about* me."

The poor woman buckled up in her scarf said nothing. Jesus and Mary, she'd be thinking, but this one'll be a handful and no mistake.

"From where do you hail, Mrs. Williams? The outpatients wing at Lisdoonvarna Hospital? The Samaritans?"

"Cork General Hospital."

He turned. She had eyes of the coldest blue, bearing straight at him.

"Cork indeed."

And a sharp nose and no lips at all. She wasn't a nurse, she was a monster. What had happened to the exotic women in his life, the suntanned arms and long nails that he, being a man of mixed origin, preferred? You travailed through a desert of concrete, glass, and stripped pine, and this was where you ended up, in terminal discomfort overseen by women without lips, with chips of ice for eyes.

He sat on the edge of the bed, shirt unbuttoned and lying around him like the petals of an old flower. Mrs. Williams prodded and palped with cold, fleshy fingertips the blubber of decades that had settled on him like silt. When she hovered over his liver he jumped. Then she pulled out an ear trumpet, at which he peered down his nose.

"Still using those things over here?"

She ignored him.

The wind rumbled, restless under the roof. The thing to do would be to sit on the black rocks and watch the waves come in. But even they lost their mystique eventually, they too suffered the ceaseless knock and rock of existence just like oneself.

"I suppose you'll be telling me we have to toddle off to hospital. Well, I'm not going, so put that idea out of your mind."

Mrs. Williams paid no attention but fastened the bell of her trumpet to his upper chest, where its cold rim sank into his flesh. She listened for a while. Her stiff dress rustled as she breathed. Then she straightened up, shook her head, and tutted. "And why not, might I ask? Lie down."

He lifted his feet off the floor and tenderly introduced his bare back to the chilly counterpane. She raised up first one leg then the other, then did the same with his arms. Irish notions of nursing, apparently. Then she sat on the edge of the bed and looked down at him.

"You'd better stay put in that case. You shouldn't be up at all. I'm calling the doctor."

She put her hand on his chest. And for just a moment in her palm's stonelike coldness he felt a flicker of peace. Snapped on like a light: quiet, stillness, a suggestion of joy: and off again.

Maria once more: Maria with her eyes like Marlene Dietrich, eyes that rested on you and saw through you. Maria understood him, always had. She looked straight at him and he knew full well what she was thinking, she didn't need to say it, she might as well have been shaking her head and tutting.

Maria had gone on and made a life for herself. Women were good like that, they knew how to settle for second best, for the bird in hand, understood as men never would the value of a suitable match.

"No, no, no, you fool, I'm not talking about Ireland," he had trumpeted at Chaim over lunch at Little's. "Who needs Ireland? Ha. The island. The Island of Providence. Home of the provident adventurers who put their bows to the west and their trust in . . ."

Chaim hadn't understood a word. It had been a mad idea anyway, that they might all troop off to a forgotten atoll in the western ocean. Chaim had gone and bought the tickets to Cork or Shannon or wherever they were. Tipperary, for all he cared. It was the wrong side of the ocean, wrong side of

Cancer. Or was it Capricorn? That was the particular error of which his life had consisted: the wrong side. And now the demons who governed this side had come along to claim him, planting their pitchforks in his liver like the flags of the vanguard. Soon they'd advance to the spleen—or had they had that long ago?—and the kidneys, lungs, and heart. What was left of it. They were taking him piece by piece, and he was powerless to resist. He had long ago given up his last toehold on firm ground. He had built on sand, and now the tide had come in, here it was, an iron-black tide carrying him off on the shoulders of its breakers.

This was not a place he could manage sober. He bellowed like a whale. What was he doing under a ceiling of white wood with the wind howling through it, the wind that had come from the right place, from far, far to the west, that was hurrying to the wrong place, the lands of Tartar and Viking, of the unforgiving civilisations? The land of mercy was where he needed to be, in the western sea.

He bellowed his daughter's name.

"Ah God, thank God you're there. My dear, my dear."

Mrs. Williams had a sponge in her hand, she was sponging his brow. Stinging water on his brow.

"My dear, you have to help me. I won't get through this you know unless, unless . . ."

Providencia. No one knows where it is. Isn't that a curious fact? They all think they do, and then if you ask where, they say: the Bahamas, Rhode Island, Cape Cod, anything but the right place. Old Providence, the locals call it.

In de Caribbean de very bes' is de beautiful island of Providence, the calypso men sang.

They were right too. *De very bes'.*

They had arrived in Maria's father's plane. Rothman had

never forgotten the first glimpse of the island below, floating on the sea's brow. Was it really there? A hazy diamond of green, framed by the plane's wheel and high wing. His head reeled. The whole island was in view, a bundle of green hills, a sparkle of livid rocks in the luminous sea, a chipped nugget draped in verdure, incorruptible, preserved in a thousand miles of brine. Salt, the scourer and purifier, kept it safe. Then they were circling over white and black reefs, reefs like tears in a canvas, and over lagoons of an almost sickly turquoise, and beyond them the island became a lot of monsters tussling under a green carpet.

Providencia, Maria called it, being half Colombian. Gauguin had sailed past on his way to Panama. Rothman's stomach lurched as the little plane jumped off a rock in the air, free-falling until its wings snared in elastic.

Old Providence. Island of the provident souls who sallied forth from Plymouth soon after the Pilgrim Fathers to find a better world; and though blown off course by hurricane, driven south by storm, had nevertheless found their promised land.

Rothman was twenty-nine, had just had his first show in New York. "It's your Saturn Return," Maria said. "Everything coming together for a new dispensation."

His fellowship from the Brooklyn Academy, his having left the stuffy Royal College for good, the dazzling new world of the New World, the broad horizon of post-abstract, post-pop, the white heat of his experiments in lithography— she was right, it was true, he was only twenty-nine but had touched his prime already, the flood would soon be full. And with him, beside him, Maria, the beautiful daughter of Colombian-American parentage who would be his wife. She was a daughter of El Dorado, of fabled wealth, giving her all to the starving talent of a man with eyes like dark stars, as she liked to say.

The plane wheeled. The island was a tumble of mossy rocks now. Above, the big grey head of the volcano brooded, the head that—pathetic fallacy be damned—knew what was what. That for now allowed the rivers of green to pour down its flanks and the villages' twinkling roofs to adorn its skirts but that one day would decide enough was enough and shake them all off.

So this was Old Luis's home.

"You know Luis?" she had asked.

"But of course. From Madrid. When I had that scholarship to the Prado School. He taught ceramics."

"I forget." And she gives him that smile of hers which melts his breast. She nudges his shoulder. "But you have lived everywhere already. You're not old enough to know so many places, so many people."

"It was just college, nothing more."

"And how long will you stay with this one?"

"This one?"

"*Sí, querido.*" And she touched her own breast. "Am I just college too?" Then she laughed and tapped his nose with an erect fingertip, hid her face in his chest.

"Let's start with a week," he said. "A whole week in bed."

Which is what they had done. Her father's house, a Caribbean gingerbread of the old style, had a veranda, a porch, and a four-poster pocked with woodworm. Rothman stocked the house with coconuts, bananas, guavas, mangoes, stalks of sugarcane, a loaf of sand-bread, and rum. A machete too, the island's universal tool. You could do nothing down here without one. And a flotilla of hibiscus and heliconia. They slipped the painter mooring them to time and for seven days drifted on their bed. The more they talked, the more they had to say. The more they loved, the more desire flared. He rode her body as his own. They raped each other's mouths, talked with skin, tongue, limb. Meanwhile, outside, the savage sunsets and neon dawns came and went, and the night skies chalky with stars. The sickle of the new moon affixed itself to the sky's sheet. The sea turned vermilion each evening, then night blue. He was a young artist in love, and he could already hear the canyons of New York clamouring for his work.

At the end of the week Rothman woke up and thought: Work, damn it. Time for work. And he stumbled up to the shed behind the house at first light, fuzzy-headed and heavy-limbed from the love orgy, doped with her scent, and commenced to paint again.

It was all very well, this seeing things with the soul's eye, as the Colombians called it, but the more the soul's eye saw, the less the eyes saw. To imagine was to be blind.

"At least let me get outside, for God's sake," he wailed at his daughter.

"Mrs. Williams won't like it."

"Screw Mrs. Williams. Wrap me up."

Donegal tweed, that was the stuff. A hairy coat that weighed as much as a man, making a great prickly bear out of you.

An afternoon of wind and sun and rain. He sat on the black rocks with Virginia at his side watching the waves explode. Fifty yards away they flew against a ledge, sending up towers of spray like snow, which blew over the ledge and spattered down, then streamed off over the Irish turf in mist. They sat and watched, he hunched over his stick, she leaning back with her hair blowing about her face.

"Fifty-six," he said. "It's not a bad age."

"You could have another thirty years if you wanted, and you know it. Happy years too."

He squinted at the walls of flecked water coming in, tumbling over themselves. The Irish Sea. The North Atlantic. It was a beastly, unfriendly sea, it had no time for people.

"Happy? I've used myself up."

Even if she couldn't, he could see what he meant. There was only so much a man could do. There was no point pretending and letting yourself grow ever thinner in body and work. Better to stay plump till the end, assuming you had the choice.

He didn't know what to say. There was nothing to say. It was remarkable he had lasted this long, with so little moral ballast on board.

Soon the rain came once more and they got up to go. He had taken only a few steps back up the beach, kicking at the sand, when the hip seized. They had to get the car and steer him to it, then drive him up the track to the house. He sat in the passenger seat gasping.

"Ridiculous. A warm climate is what my bloody bones need, not this freezing rain and wind. Whoever thought of living here? We're not made for this kind of weather, none of us are. Whoever thought of this for a holiday? We're not Vikings, you know, not anymore."

"You should be thanking Chaim for having us."

He tried to respond but couldn't. Chaim turned on the windscreen wipers. Whine-clunk, whine-clunk. The Britannic symphony. Patter of rain, whine of wiper. Why had he ever come back? Two good years he had had over there in the New

World, two of the best, the only two good years of his life. What had the rest been? A ride half asleep, half drugged, swaying about on time's back.

The steaming palm trees after rain, the whole island giving up its cargo of fragrances to the trade winds, the old bus with its wooden seats and no doors or windows, no walls even, lumbering around the island first one way then the other, climbing in and out of potholes. And the islanders weaving along the lanes on bicycles, on mules, asses, and ponies, with always time for a game of dominoes, a glass of rum, a healthy beer. And the straw-hatted farmers calling out their accelerating crescendo of *"Anda, anda, andale!"* to the skinny mules that plodded round and round the gears of sugar presses, while the farmers themselves, long reins in hand, stooped beneath the spindly arms of the mills as they turned, feeding in the stalks one after another, making the brown juice splash into buckets. And the two of them, she and he, bending under the mill spokes to where one farmer stood, and him whistling, *wheet-wheet*, and the horses stopping, and him dipping a coconut shell down into his bucket. "Try it, señorita, what do you think? Better than Coca-Cola, no?"

And he, Rothman, drank too—*"Para el señor"*—and sure enough it was the drink of health and longevity and fortified the very soles of your feet.

"Lucky us," she had said, clutching his hand on the beach as the sky turned lime green and the sea blood red and the sun zipped itself away.

Why were we doomed to make the fatal error? We were not. Doom was an excuse for stupidity.

Her father had bought the house long ago. He had been meaning to come down for years but never had time, too busy shuttling between his offices, mistresses, and haciendas, between Bogotá, Miami, New York, Caracas. "Just don't start importing anything," he advised them. "If you hunt about you can find all you need on the island. They're wonderful carpenters. What they don't have they'll make for you. But go easy on the island art," he advised. "It can be . . . *un poco fuerte*."

High on a hill, with porch, peeling blue paint, and red tin roof, the house had four rooms and a view over Freshwater Bay with its stand of royal palms. Now and then a boy on a horse might canter under the trees through the surf. With the shutters opened up, the trade winds fluttered through the house, riffling her papers (she was working on her thesis on Cortázar), rustling the sheets, stirring the festoon of mosquito netting gathered over their bed. Which they hardly needed, what with the breeze on their hill.

"If Gauguin had found this place on his first trip he would have done without the syphilitic South Seas."

Maria shrugged. "He was a young man, still curious. He would have left."

"It could only have got worse. Curiosity is a euphemism for restlessness, which is a euphemism for incurable insatiability. He would have been a fool to leave."

But sure enough he himself, Rothman, had left. And ended up a depictor of chairs. The *Chairs* had been Chaim's idea. Not a bad one, he had thought at the time. Shrewd chap, this. There was no end to the polysyllabics the asses could slap about when considering the *seat* and its absence, the implication of corporeality, the iconicity of the quotidian. Et cetera. What does a vacant chair *signify*? A kid with a dictionary could do it. The longer the words were, the higher the checks went. But the truth was, you could no longer bear your own fatal humanity so you painted chairs instead, and idiots bought them and made you rich. You meant to stop getting rich, to go back to your true subjects, but truth was always just after the next show. Then gradually you got sick through and through, body and soul, and survived on a diet of pills until the pills themselves started to do you in. Then you took pills against the pills, and more pills against those pills, and pretty soon there was nothing left of your own biochemistry, your own metabolism, your own body; or, in fact, of you.

At least he had had the Maria pictures. Only pictures he had ever done from memory. Though of course it would have been better if he had never needed to do them at all.

Maria stayed boxed and packed, all eleven canvases of her, for twenty-five years. Later, he might slide one out now and then, when the studio was deserted, sit before it under the giant window, then shuffle over to the sideboard littered with rags, palettes, bottles of turpentine, and the five big jars of brushes, rummage about for the right palette, and maybe add a touch here and there. The eyes were the hardest thing, those dark eyes, like wet pebbles but dark, and shining with a stern compassion. How much you could find in an ordinary woman if you only looked. And she had made him look, she as no other.

They planned to build a studio for him higher up the hill. Meantime, he worked in the palm-and-plywood shed at the back of the house. Every morning he would unclip the bolts and fold back the entire wall, opening it up to the southwest, to the bay and the jungle tumbling down. He would see the Black Sister out to sea, a granite rock where the frigate birds roosted. The little fishing boats would be scudding out under their scraps of sail to the reef. When the wind came from the west he would hear the reef, a distant thunder deep in the ear.

One morning he went out with two fishermen, brothers called Armando and Raimundo, who once they were near the reef threw their anchor rock over the stern and uprooted their driftwood mast. Masked and finned they drifted down forty, fifty feet through the clear green water, swimming as slowly as astronauts until they touched the sandy bottom and began to gather shells. They'd come up as slowly as they descended, heads tilted up so the masks flashed with the sky's reflection, their green string bags bulging behind them. They taught Rothman to clear his ears and tip himself head over heels and swim down with them, though by the time he reached the sandy bottom he'd be bursting and have to swim straight up again, while they with their dolphin lungs got to work below.

Raimundo and Armando provided his first island set, a series of oils done each afternoon from sketches he'd made while out with them on the boat.

One time when he touched the seabed he scrabbled about in the sand and his hand closed on a clam shell. When they opened it they found a pearl attached to the flesh, a grey bead the size of a pinhead.

"I'm going to give you this," he told Maria, unwrapping the handkerchief in which he had kept it. "But not yet." He had plans for it; to have it flanked with chips of diamond, set on a band.

Each afternoon looking out from his shed he would see

the sky turn to flame as the frigate birds gathered like bats about the burning pillar of their rock.

And there was old Luis, a Spaniard of ageless middle age who back in Madrid used to talk about the islands off the Spanish Main, and one day had finally packed his bags and gone, taken up with an island girl. They lived two bays and three hills away, with a parrot and a three-legged dog. He sported a leonine white beard and gleaming bald head, and with his suspicious eyes fancied himself piratical. He even wore an eye patch, referring obliquely to a fishing accident *en el mar*.

Once, Rothman showed up during siesta time and found Luis reading the paper with no patch to be seen.

"Have to rest the eye," he mumbled, waving at his face. He called the girl. *"Conchita. Ven!"*

Conchita, clacking with braids, tall, black, clad in nothing but a loincloth, traipsed out onto the veranda. She saw Rothman, smiled at him, and turned away. Her breasts, slightly angry with one another, as the French put it, gleamed in the sun. They looked like bronze. Rothman couldn't stop looking at them. She was a living sculpture, a miracle of form and function. No wonder old Luis had settled here.

She approached Luis from behind, bending over him in the hammock. She opened her hands, stretching wide the elastic of his eye patch, announcing her intention with a kiss to the top of his bald head, and slipped the mask into place. Throughout the procedure Rothman was unable to prise his sight off those nipples, thick buds of chocolate, and the flesh that supported them. Her breasts looked firm like the flan they served down in town, firm and soft at once, magnificent.

Luis's house, a modern villa, was covered throughout with his own canvases, hurried daubings of virulent colour; the tropics had gone to his head. "I paint, I read, I write, I make love," he said. "And I eat fresh fish, fresh fruit. This is the healthiest place on earth. Everyone lives into their nineties. It's the *Shangri-La del Caribe*."

Inevitably, of course, Rothman had fouled his Eden. It was so simple a thing, so farcical he could hardly believe it would have had the potent effect it did. A pair of knockers knocked the tiller out of your hand, and next thing you knew you were headlong down the face of a hurricane.

Conchita. One night she clacked out of the dark house onto the terrace, tipped back her head, making the beads in her braids clack and shush, and smiled at Rothman with an emphatic sigh. It was hard to know what that sigh meant. Perhaps it was just a stray piece of island emphasis. The locals liked to be emphatic like that, speaking as if the language were a drum to beat. But perhaps it was more.

Nighttime. Rothman had come out to suck on a Cuban and look at the moon. His bride-to-be and his old companion in arms were both inside at the table. He heard Luis laughing a long deep private laugh: an absurd man after all, but somehow inspiring, perhaps because he had truly cut himself loose from all ties. Though it hadn't necessarily been good for his work.

Conchita clacked up beside him and leant against the wooden rail. "*Dáme*," she said. Give me.

She sucked deeply on the cigar. Her cheeks lit up in the flare of the tip. A lustrous red-brown, smooth as brass.

"You must let me paint you," he said.

She demurred, inevitably, but it was equally inevitable that he should persist, insist, devise a portrait of the two of them, Luis and His Girl, in order to overcome her reticence. He made it a picture of that moment with the eye patch. It was inevitable too that one day Luis would be too tired or lazy or gripey to stroll up the winding road to Rothman's shack, that she should therefore come alone. Nothing else could have happened but that she should stiffly, awkwardly, yet somehow passionately accept a glass of rum and crushed mint after the sitting, that under the pressure of his eyes and hands she should acquiesce, comply, agree, hike her skirt to midriff, and sit on him, first one way, then the other, and grunt and grind her way to a peak that caused a bloom of sweat to break out on her sternum; then that she, being an obliging island girl, should smear that sweat together with the coconut oil she had rubbed into her skin earlier, which her exertions had now brought to the surface again, into the valley of her breasts and sandwich him.

Which was when, true to farce, Maria appeared in the doorway. She had finished her day's work on Cortázar and gone shopping, and now came bearing a tray of fruit and punch, refreshments for the two toilers after art.

A little farce was a dangerous thing. It was Conchita who saw her first. She made no sound but bowed away, retreating with her arms doubled insufficiently round her. She fumbled through her sprawl of discarded scraps of clothes, bending double to pull them on.

Rothman lifted his head. One of his hands had already fallen listlessly to his bereft shaft. He said, "What? *Qué?*" But he didn't need to go on, he could feel the trouble that had entered the room. He glanced back to confirm it.

Maria, after a moment's stunned hesitation, did the only thing she could: dropped the tray where she stood and ran out.

He was young, in his stride, not about to let her slip through his fingers. Fumbling with his belt buckle, shirt flailing, he skipped over the rolling mangoes and shattered glass and ice, raced out the gate and down the track.

Maria must already have reached the road, a fact he noted with surprise, and indeed as he neared the road barefoot and unbuttoned, he heard an engine pulling away: their scooter. She had already disappeared round the first bend.

Cicadas chirruped. The sun was hot still, though through the palms he could see a bloom on the sea as the afternoon eased towards evening. A cockerel crowed. A light breeze lifted itself through the fingers of a dead coconut frond at the roadside. The scooter hissed away into silence.

Rothman felt embarrassed standing there. That more than anything else. He was a fool. His eyes darkened, he felt the blood in his face. What could he do, though? He would have to wait for her, that was all. Had the bus been running perhaps he could have boarded it in the hope of finding her somewhere round the other side of the island. But she could be anywhere. And the bus wasn't running, it had broken down two days before.

Conchita's head appeared a hundred yards up the track, peering out of the yard. He realised what she wanted to know, and beckoned. She came shuffling briskly downhill in her sandals, elbows crossed over her chest.

"*Ay dios.*" At first it seemed she intended to walk right past him, but she stopped a pace or two beyond. Shaking her head (clackety-clack) she said, "*Ni una palabra a Luis. El me matará a mi. Ay dios.*" Luis would kill me if he knew.

She stepped to and fro, kicked a stone. Her legs the colour of wet sand. It was shameful to see such a statue of a woman reduced to the ridiculous.

"Enough melodrama," he said. "We're only human after all. We have our weaknesses, we live in error."

"In sin," she corrected. *"Pecado. Todo pecado."* She looked into his eyes, imploring reassurance.

He said: "You're lovely."

Her eyes filled for a moment with the tenderness that had opened her legs in the first place. At least one thing might still be done decently: the farewell of these two briefly acquainted bodies. He stepped towards her and kissed her on the lips.

Head bowed, she scraped across the torn-up roadway and down a sandy lane to the beach, perhaps wishing that she did not have to exit his life quite so soon.

Back in the house he removed the flowers from a pitcher, rinsed it, and mixed up a lot of punch. He drank a couple of tumblers straight down and sat smoking on the veranda with a third.

The problem, he reflected, was not so much what he had done as Maria's actually having seen him do it. That was what would traumatise a Latina.

But if you fell in love with an artist, what did you expect? He was a man of the senses. Yet he knew how it would wound her. It would be the ultimate betrayal. And even to suggest that it meant little, was just a stray cupidity, would be a betrayal too, implying that their own lovemaking was not the demiurgical undertaking that it in fact was.

The sun flared over the island and died. The night that followed was the longest of his life. What began as a gnawing anxiety grew into a wild panic that saw him confusedly rummaging through his clothes, pulling out a suitcase to pack, leaving it open, empty, yawning on the bed beneath the mosquito netting, which somehow in the course of the night fell into the open jaws of the case. Why a suitcase? By morning he couldn't remember; probably he had sensed somehow that she had already gone, leaving everything, passport, wallet, clothes, and all, and fled to the mainland. And from there who knew where?

At first light he hammered on the door of the shack that was the post office (a yellow *"Correos"* sign hung from a shutter). But Señora Carmen wasn't opening up yet. He slumped against the door, and when finally he heard her slide back the bolt and open the door he almost fell in. Then he found he had no money on him and she wouldn't let him use the telephone without a down payment. She inhaled sharply and shook her head. "No credit, no call, see the sign there?"

When he returned with his wallet he realised he didn't know where to call. He tried her mother's house in Long Island. No answer, why would there have been? Her apartment in Manhattan—also no answer. Then the island's phone went down.

Panic gave way to gloom. He thought of Luis, an older man, and could only imagine him devastated, were he ever to know. Would Conchita be able to pull off a lie? The island was her home, she had found a man here to appreciate her for what she was, to bring to her the aesthetic of the big world. Rothman had been playing for bigger stakes than he had realised. As the sun rose it was a sky of steel that arched over the little green island lifting itself from the sea. Love of such a calibre as his and Maria's could not be trifled with. When you had all nature on your side, as they had—all his nature, all hers, and all the nature around them—you had to prove yourself worthy.

He drank rum for breakfast, then sat by their gate and waited and smoked and lied to himself that she would come back. But he was not a man who knew how to wait. She'll be back, said Armando and Raimundo. A lovers' tiff, nothing more. A man must sometimes wait. *Un hombre tiene que esperar.*

But five months later she was married to a man who owned an Argentine bank; and Rothman, back in New York, left honest painting behind for good. That was the folly of youth: its dangerous solemnity had a power beyond its years.

Those first few days alone on the island he knew with a young man's melodrama that it was over. Hadn't this end been inevitable from the start? But life and work had to go on, they could not be stopped for long. The river of a life ran on, if not one way then another. A man was a man, an artist was an artist, there was no shame in fulfilling the desires of eye and body. Why then did he think of nothing but her face, her limbs, her fingertips, day and night?

This is no way to carry on, he told himself, and would briefly feel on top of things. It was in one of these respites that he decided: only one thing to do: paint her out of my system. No doubt while he was hard at work she'd walk in the door. He went into the studio with a saucepan of strong coffee and a box of paints. In five days he had finished a canvas and thought he was done, but no sooner did he begin to clean his brushes than another intention presented itself, a bigger one. In the end he worked for five straight weeks with hardly a break.

When finally he left the island he packed up the eleven paintings up and took them and himself back to New York. Which was no easy matter, without Maria's father's plane to collect them, nor the fare for a charter. He had to take a banana boat to the next, bigger island of San Isidro, an overnight journey, then a steamer down to Barranquilla on the mainland, where he waited five days for a third steamer up to

Miami, where he boarded a train up the east coast. It took three and a half weeks. But it was a healing journey, he told himself. The young artist with his first masterly works in a box beside him makes his way back to the woman he loves, who surely will be unable to resist being won back.

But she was able. She had a moral muscle, denied to Anglo-Saxon women, that simply could not permit what he had done. "I saw you," she spat when finally he trapped her on the telephone in the Madison Avenue apartment.

He paused, surprised. "But I know you did."

"Ha!" At least that was what it sounded like, a shocked exhalation. "You and your floozy, kissing goodbye."

Maria had not gone down the hill but up. She had run uphill towards the grey head of the volcano. She had seen him kiss Conchita goodbye: that on top of everything else. She had gone up the farmers' tracks to the very crown of the island, then down the other side to the airport, where a local air taxi bore her away.

At that moment it all seemed ridiculous, excessive. Too much bloody earnestness, the phrase ran through his mind. His *floozy*. Surely she couldn't really mean that. That pitch of corn. But he fought back the feeling. "Please let me see you."

A long pause. Then: "It's too late," uttered in a soft voice, too calm.

That scared him. "Too late?"

She sighed.

And of course the man in question was not an impecunious talent but a banker, or more than that, an owner of banks, a man with his own plane and haciendas, a man from her own world, more or less, who would give her proper places to live and all the rest. Rothman called again the next day to ask to see her, but she had gone on a trip.

He didn't unpack the pictures for a week, just sat with them in the bare room of his shared apartment on West Broadway. Then he sent them up, still boxed, to Scavello's, and waited by the phone. A day, two, four went by. Finally he had to call himself.

"Hmm. Maybe a wrong turning here? This sort of thing is out of date, you know, you can't expect to attract the same attention. In this game to be with it we have to be ahead. To walk you run. That's why we did well before, in the first show. You were pushing the envelope, challenging our *concepts*, making us think about what art *is*. Carry on where you left off, I say."

So he did. He boxed up the canvases and thought a lot and shipped them and himself back to London, where he embarked on his first tarmac images. "The Road Show," they called it, studies of Britain's road surfaces. The show was his first big British hit. And at the opening he met Lady Daisy, the countess's daughter who would mother his one and only child, Virginia, then leave him for a rock drummer. Never again would he permit oils to seduce him.

Mrs. Williams from Cork cleared the house of alcohol.

"What?" exclaimed Chaim. "Have a heart."

"If I didn't know better I'd think you were trying to kill him off," Virginia said. "What else can we do?"

"Let him down gently, for God's sake."

"The man's not got long if he carries on the way he is," said Mrs. Williams.

All day Rothman sweated and bawled, then slumped into a dosed abyss. The next day he woke clear as a bell in a pool of lucidity.

Righto, he thought, pulling on his heavy trousers, making his way down to the kitchen in the early light. He made coffee, fetched his sketchbook, a box of charcoal, a rag, stuffed them all in his coat pocket, and opened the door.

Outside was a world transformed. The gale that had been blowing the last three days had abated. Heavy dew lay on all things. The green sweep of fields sparkled as with wet paint. The sea, at last, had shaken off the turmoil of grey and was deep blue, speckled with whitecaps.

He levered himself over the stile and stumbled across the boggy field down to the rocks. Across the bay Ireland stretched away like a green shadow, ending in a little grey pinnacle. The horizon trembled like a taut string. A ewe bleated up on a hill.

I'm here, Rothman thought. I'm actually here. Meaning: alive, noticing things.

Squelch went his boots on the sodden grass. The breakers roared. Deep inside some blowhole the waves thumped and gasped. And he smelled the tired old smell of the sea, of salt and stale seaweed, which instructed a man in a way he could not refuse to unloose his worries, lay down his burden.

Rothman sat on a broken stone wall. How much of his life, he thought, he had hidden behind a slab of paint, peering round the edge occasionally. Was it sad to have ignored the million daily calls to canvas in favour of one lodestone from the past? At least he had avoided staking his name on junkie heiresses drooping in Bayswater light. He may have opted for Chairs and Roads, but he had not given in to the climate of fatal greyness that many had, had kept his little bottle of sunshine intact. Except no longer.

I am here now in a wet country by the sea, he told himself. This is my life. It scared him to realise how seldom he could have claimed the most rudimentary awareness of his surroundings.

❖

Rothman heard a friendly *pop*. He opened an eye. Chaim was squatting beside him, Powers in hand.

"Got something for you." He grinned, his face screwed up in a gargoylelike grimace.

Rothman stared at him, groaned, and reached for the bottle. Cool in his hand, unreassuring, perhaps not quite what he wanted after all, but he'd be a fool not to accept a dose anyway.

Beneath all its packaging there was nothing *in* the Old World, that was the problem. Whereas within the New there beat a young heart which lent all newcomers its vigour, to which he had once been privy. Why had he turned his back on it? Crassness, self-deception, compromise. A wanton spilling of the basket of strawberries held out by the hand of a good woman.

Out on grey Westbourne Grove two weeks later, back in London, it was raining again. The taxis, the buses, the young couples went by, huddling under their umbrellas. *British United Providence*, one umbrella had blazoned on it. Under it a girl in a green mac clung to the arm of her young executive. She had blond hair, a rain-washed face. The two of them huddled beneath the shelter of their mortgaged future.

One could do worse than that after all, Rothman ruminated. Get a mate, a job, a mortgage, then settle down and procreate. One couldn't hope for any kind of final fulfilment;

just to get through life, as they, the streaming couples out in the rain on their way to lunch, under the shelter of BUP umbrellas, were doing, would continue to do, was no bad thing. Anything nice, ultimately, was better than whatever was not.

The tinkle of liquid poured over ice brought him back from the window. Chaim's sitting room was big and deep, a room of low furniture and tall walls, hung all the way up with recent art. Rothman avoided looking at it. It was all junk, all the modern British trash of which he himself had been a prominent producer, with his Knives, his Shoes, his Foam on Beer Glasses, all his studies of the "quotidian." How little real content could you have: that was the game. The vacuous masquerading as the clever. The more vacuous it was, the cleverer it was thought to be.

"What they call a Dutch martini," Chaim said, handing him a glass. "Genever and vodka. And a pickled onion."

Rothman downed his in one. "Disgusting." He scowled. Then raised an eyebrow. "The second always tastes better, eh?"

"That's the spirit. Screw those bloody hacks."

Jackson Mitchell had printed another story, this time asserting that Rothman was past it, over the hill, in terminal alcoholic decline. His working days were over. All he could do now was salvage daubings from his distant past.

"The buggers just say what they like. Best thing is to ignore them completely, *n'est-ce pas?*" Chaim said. "Anyway, it's time you and I put our heads together about your next contract, old bean. I've been thinking about 'Brushes.'"

It was while he was in the bathroom that Rothman noticed something unusual. All his Maria pictures were lying high up on a little gallery above the hand basin. A wooden ladder fastened to the wall gave access to the loft, and he climbed a few rungs and reached up just to make sure. It was them all right.

"What are *they* doing here?" he asked Chaim.

"They're on their way to the buyers," Chaim answered. But it was odd: first the show had ended strangely soon. Now the pictures, long since taken down, were here in the gallery owner's flat.

"They'll be off soon."

Rothman left feeling vaguely disturbed, to meet a gang in Little's, where, while he stuck it out, someone commented that the pictures at his last show had been snapped up and out the door so fast people hardly got a look at them. It wasn't customary to pull them off the walls as they sold, surely. Rather a departure, those pictures, from what one heard.

"Not at all," Rothman growled.

Next day he called Chaim for a list of the buyers.

"No can do, I'm afraid. But we've banked the draft all right. You'll be getting a fabulous check any day."

Then he called Virginia. "What's going on?"

"You've been drinking," she answered. "I'm not talking to you when you're drunk."

It was true, he had been drinking, but he wasn't drunk.

"Will someone just tell me what's going on?"

She was silent at the other end. A warm, breathy silence in the receiver. He heard himself exhale, a soft rumbling in the earpiece.

"Chaim thought they'd be better off out of the way."

"But they've been *bought*, for Christ's sake. Why are they all in his flat?"

"They have been bought," she said. "Yes."

He was quiet a moment. "So?"

"I'll come round."

Which she did. To say: "What does it matter? The things are sold, it's all aboveboard."

Except it wasn't. Rothman could see that a mile off.

"Who the hell bought them?"

"Some wealthy South American."

"Of course they're wealthy. But who?"

"An Argentinian minister."

In silence she watched him drink a glass of wine. He screwed up his nose. "Argentinian?"

She sighed. "He's married."

Rothman stood up. He poured out another tumbler of wine.

"He didn't want his wife's body splashed all over town. And she wanted them too. She wanted to have them."

Rothman began in a singsong: "Well why didn't anyone *tell* me?"

"Chaim was going to. She offered him a big bonus for getting them down fast. He was afraid you'd disagree, I suppose. And to be honest, everyone says how good it is that you've been consistent all these years. Chaim was worried about that."

A mouthful went down the wrong way. Rothman gasped, spluttered, and shook his head. "Well, no more bloody contracts with him. I've done enough chairs or roads or bloody brushes for one lifetime. I'm an *artist*," he said, but he couldn't help putting a sarcastic twist on the word.

Suddenly he badly wanted his pictures of Maria to go out into the world. Instead of which they would remain imprisoned in some basement in Buenos Aires. Chaim had never even done a catalogue of them. But they were his true representatives. Even at his age, with his name, Rothman was still stumbling around outside the citadel, begging to be let in. It was the wrong way round. It was he who had the power, who ought to be living behind the shining walls, while the likes of Chaim prowled at the gate. But he hadn't realised that. Too early he had made it his business to drink and dine with the enemy. Especially drink.

Downstairs, he opened the door on to a street just then enflamed by a brilliant low sun—a street of gold, with the silver cars rushing up and down it. He stood looking at it, just outside his door, with no idea which way to go, towards Hammersmith or away from it. As he waited there—or not so much waited (there seemed to be nothing at all that could possibly dislodge him from his static position) as wavered—he heard footsteps coming down the stairs behind him. He remembered that his daughter was still up there. At the thought of her, at first a habitual relief and gladness touched him; until it came back that it was she who had persuaded him to open up his private store, who had instigated its plunder. Even she was lost to him now. He couldn't forgive her. He was truly bereft.

"Daddy," she said, stepping down onto the pavement and reaching for his hand inside his coat pocket. Her hand was cool and almost erotic in the warmth of the coat. He stood still, he wouldn't look at her. He felt the cool palm close over his fist.

"I've been robbed," he told her.

"But they're paying massively. You can do what you like."

He snorted. "All my life. I've let them do it."

A thought flashed into his mind: perhaps it was possible there might be one advantage to his having lost all that work; just for an instant he saw a glimmer of a kind of freedom, a productive kind, almost a desire to produce more work. Not only that but there was even a subject that suggested itself, a *real* subject, the first real subject he had thought of in decades. And as the thought of it, or rather the feeling, the clarity of need to pursue it, came upon him, he felt his limbs and torso wake up as they hadn't in so long, flushed as if with springwater, or as if lubricated with clear oil. The subject was his daughter: he had never properly addressed it, just as he hadn't properly addressed any subject in three decades.

He turned to glance at her. She was looking at him. Her eyes were gleaming with reflected sun. It was like looking into luminous amber. Something jumped in his chest and he started coughing. He turned away, catching a glimpse of a western sky like a cauldron of gold before he doubled over.

Darien Dogs

Rogers did not remember coming aboard. He lay on the hard surface listening to the voices swooping round him. Black voices on black wings.

Yeah man, you lucky we pass.

Lucky we stop, man. Ain't easy to stop like that.

They were talking a language he had once known. He didn't know what a language was now. It was sounds made in the back of the head. It was something you heard and you knew you knew why you were hearing but just then you couldn't remember the reason. It was bright light in a steep stairwell. Sunlight on a deck, sunlight in a hatch. The sound of men eating, the clatter of plates, a screech and boom on a television mounted above.

Take a lot a fuel you want to stop fas' like we did back there. You see? So man, where you from?

Leave the man alone, Silas.

Don't talk how that Silas does talk.

Likely the fella could want to know who ship he on. That we ain't no Colombian pirate boat running no drugs or nothin.

A cup a water and a bunk, thass all the fella need.

He need a doctor, man. Look at them scrapes.

He needed the IV. Get the IV.

Somebody laid a blanket over him. The blanket was night and it was warm. Rogers could feel its weight all over his limbs, light and heavy at once like a fur coat, prickly with stars. The night bled into his mouth. Melted into his throat like ice. Like ink. Could be he was drinking ink. Surely ink would go down the throat like this, slick so it clung to your gullet.

Then he was gone.

I

1

"You want AC?" the taxi driver asked in indeterminately accented English.

What a question. Ten minutes out of the plane and Jim Rogers's shirt was already dissolving into his skin.

"AC twenny-fy, no AC twenny," the driver went on.

"*Claro que sí*," Rogers snapped. What kind of country was this? It didn't even have its own language, it didn't care who occupied it. Brits one year, Yanks the next, Spaniards the year after. And the taxi drivers charged for air-conditioning.

The car, a mid-seventies Lincoln, was of the vintage that favoured the colour burgundy. There was a long line of them at the Mario Rosales Airport. Rogers sank into its velvet upholstery and with something like relief felt the ancient suspension sag into the first pothole. The suspension of America, the potholes of Latinismo: two things he thought he knew how to love. Panama lay ahead, a whole week of it, but at least he was out of New York, away from Sylvester Securities. Sylvester's: the seal and stamp of his shame. What a *name* for a bank— you could just hear how shoddy and low-budget they were.

The driver buzzed up the windows and switched on the air-conditioning. A clattering of maracas burst forth under the hood, and steam poured from the vents. Rogers wondered if he ought to have economised after all.

He watched a fan of banana bushes move past, coated in a sheen from another world, and thought: I'm a ruin, a shell of a man. Lately he'd been suffering terrible attacks of panic, misery, dread—he wasn't sure what to call them. The smallest setbacks shook him with annoyance, rattled about inside him. And at the same time, things—objects, sights, smells—could find no purchase in him. There was nothing left in him for them to get a toehold on.

Take those spindly palm trees. They were probably beautiful, their fronds glittered like metal, like knives, in the equatorial sun. But he couldn't say if they were beautiful. He could barely have said if they existed. Maybe they were just figments of a dream. When consciousness was backed into the blackest corner and only the tiniest chink of light still reached you, how did you really know if you were awake or asleep, alive or dead? It was as if he had woken at three in the morning in the depths of the circadian trough, only this trough went on and on. All the bright fields of the mind closed down one by one until all that was left was one gorge, which you gradually fouled with your daily presence.

Now, now, he told himself. Don't go that way, don't let it start.

Maybe the change of scene would do him good.

A bus pulled out in front of the taxi, a big old American school bus painted a riotous mosaic of colours. Smoke billowed from under the fender. At the back window the hairdos of five schoolgirls bounced up and down: ponytail, braids, plaits, all of them black. When the bus braked, the heads bowed away from the window, then bobbed back into place. Rogers was cheered by the sight. They were poor, obviously, those girls, but he could see them smile and giggle at each other. There was something obscurely comforting about a land of poverty. Perhaps it reminded you of a simpler way of living.

The taxi driver said, "You got some pretty girls where you're going."

Rogers didn't answer.

"Great girls," the driver repeated, as if Rogers might not have understood. "Chicas. You looking for chicas?"

Rogers shrugged involuntarily.

The man growled out a laugh. Rogers glanced at the rearview mirror and saw that the driver was staring at him. "The Geisha Sauna. Good place. The girls they've got—*good ass*." He uttered the final phrase in English, with much relish, and a protracted cackle.

These third world types, they had no concept of personal space. The word "intrude" wasn't in the lexicon. There was nothing remotely embarrassing, apparently, about discussing sex with a stranger.

Yet Rogers found that oddly comforting too.

The city was nothing but concrete. Concrete transmission shops, concrete stalls loaded with papayas, concrete high-rises pale in the distance, and everywhere the unmistakable smell of the cheap Caribbean, a smell composed of rotting fruit, diesel fumes, and urine. This was the real Caribbean, nothing to do with beaches and Bacardi. It was a land of Indian businessmen, Syrian traders, Chinese storekeepers, of graceful black cabbies with wrinkled notes wadded in breast pockets, of Range Rovered whites in button-downs, of small-time salesmen prowling the ports with their briefcases of catalogues. It was a world of mildew and oil drums, and concrete. Rogers felt something almost like nostalgia to be back in it.

He surveyed the fetid scene and wondered: could this really be the setting for his great comeback? He had got wind

of a chance to steal a march not just on his so-called colleagues at Sylvester's, not just on the market, but on the very
multinationals themselves. Rogers had had to visit the desk
manager three times in his glass office to get him to listen.
Twice he was brushed off with a "Later, Rogers," like an office
boy, until finally the man said, "We're sending you down to
Panama," as if it hadn't been his idea all along.

And it was a good idea, just the kind he had been waiting
for: a chance to lead a consortium of banks. They would
finance a new pipeline. The beauty of it was that the line was
short: less than a hundred miles. Short, hassle-free, and build-
able in less than three years. Yet it would link the two great
oceans. All you had to do was look at a map to see its beauty.
The Isthmus of Darien, the snake of Panama, the gateway
between the two worlds: you could either say that land had
been illogically and inconveniently placed where, by all that
was rational, there ought to have been no country, no land at
all, only open sea to allow the passage of free trade. Or else
you could seize the opportunity. There was still only one way
through. With its choppy blue channel of warm water Panama was nothing but an inverse ferryman, the ferryman's toll-
booth. Pierce it, puncture it, plumb it into the world's oil
trade, and you could be picking up fees on millions of barrrels
a day. And with the Gulf the way it was, the timing couldn't
have been better. It was a miracle no one else had thought of
it. But then Panama was a closed shop: you had to find the
right way in.

Yet when the taxi man pressed a button on the Deluxe
radio and a salsa tune jangled from the speakers, the music's
optimism didn't infect Rogers. He felt nothing, none of the
spark and clarity that in the past used to presage a good deal.
Rogers was unhappy with many things: his age—halfway—

appalled him; his marital status—zero—sickened him; and his job—which was all it was now—had shrunk to banana republics, the nowheres, the armpits of the continent. Latin American accounts were the dead end, the sump of the business.

Yet he couldn't help liking Latin music. Every time he heard it he would catch a whiff of his first few months in New York—the odour of traffic, of pizza, of a perfume called Kosaku worn by a girl called Monica, and the detergent smell of the tiny never-used kitchen in his apartment: they all came back to him, together with the tremendous hopefulness of those early days in Manhattan. Surely those had been the best months of his life. Monica had hailed from the upper-upper east side, the Spanish quarter. He'd had his school-dance fumblings before, his moody college loves, but nothing to prepare him for the love of a hot-blooded Latina. On the first warm day of March her many uncles would set out tin tables on sidewalk and fire escape, and clack down their dominoes, dewy beer bottle between the legs, while their transistors filled the city's hazy atmosphere with a dawn-to-dusk background of Latin rhythm—popping congas, dinging cowbells, screeching trumpets, and above all of it the high-octane, high-stave, highly excitable Hispanic male vocals. Monica taught him the dance steps right out there on the sidewalk, to the amusement of her uncles. She painted her nails and her lips blood red, and in the bedroom dominated him in every way until the final moment of submission, whereupon she would become a helpless victim of passion. It was very flattering.

But all that was long, long ago, in another life.

The first thing Rogers did in his room at the Hotel Panama was step out onto the balcony and smell the air. It was thick, rich, a balm, full of tropical heaviness. Across the car park sat a squat brown building with a curly neon sign on the roof: "Geisha Sauna." He took one look at it and with a heavy heart acknowledged that he would not be able to resist its sordid allure. There was simply no reason to.

The girl said she was called Paulina. She spoke Spanish with a mellifluous accent he hadn't heard before, a flow of words perhaps devised specially for use in the little room where she led him—the death chamber of love, he reflected, with its white-sheeted bench. When she agreed to the acrobatic posture he suggested and commenced to tackle him, the tangle of emotion he had carried with him from New York fell slack, unbinding him. He expected a tremor of vague guilt—this wasn't something he had done in a long while, after all—but felt only a flutter of gratitude. He buried his hungry face in her, mumbling something about "love."

And she was lovely. Afterwards, relief administered, he lit them a cigarette each, sighed out a column of smoke, and studied her face. She could have been Oriental. She had strong cheeks and warm, intelligent eyes, and a smile of curiosity played on her lips as if she were interested in him, as if he pleased her.

He asked where she was from. Sitting on a stool with her bare legs drawn into her chest, she cocked her head, blew out smoke. "San Blas," she said.

"San Blas?" He imagined some market town where they grew grapefruits and coffee, somewhere she had gone blind with boredom before delivering herself into this noncity, neither suburb nor downtown, of plastic and concrete. Panama, really, was nothing but a shopping mall, to which the label-struck of all Latin America came for their Dior and de la Renta.

She frowned. "You haven't heard of San Blas?"

Rogers shook his head. This sort of thing could be a bore—having to hear about My Country, *mi país*, pronounced with an emphatic caesura. Latins could get maudlin about their homeland, he thought, their *patria*. But she was pretty. He propped himself on an elbow.

"Tell me about San Blas."

She hesitated, perhaps thinking about money.

"I'd like to hear," he said. "Charge me whatever." Yes, he might be down on '90, '91, '92, but he still had deep pockets, he could dip and dip and the well would not at once run dry. The material of his trade, if you could call it a trade, was, after all, money.

Her cigarette hand rose to her lips and she paused as she inhaled. Then she smiled, revealing good teeth, perhaps a little big in the middle, though that added character.

"San Blas is a different world," she told him. "We have no illness, no poverty, no hurricanes. People live a long, long time."

He raised his eyebrows. "Like how long?"

The girl whistled and shrugged. "We have our own doctors, they keep us well with their songs. A hundred, a hundred and twenty, that's normal."

"With their songs?" She was obviously some tribal girl from the pages of anthropology.

"Our doctors sing to keep illness away. Sharks too. If any shark comes near, they hear the song and go away. Sharks are like dogs, we call them sea dogs. The doctors know what to tell them, and they stay away."

He watched her as she talked. She was very watchable. The flare of her cheeks, their copper hue: she must be an Indian, a real native. But a pretty one, nothing like the heavy people he had seen out west in the States. She spoke languorously, crossing her knees, resting her wrists on them, fingertips lifting and dropping as she spoke, like some nightclub socialite. She was lovely, her belief in folklore was charming. For the first time in months, Rogers kept his attention right on what was before him. She was worth it. He felt vaguely sad that she should be living in a soulless city—sooner or later it would infect her and she would forget about the shark doctors back home—but he was also excited to be sitting, or reclining, here with her.

One of her shoes dangled from a toe. She swung it about. "You should go to San Blas," she said.

"You should take me."

The truth was, he felt like asking her to dinner. She was bright, he could see that already. Something in her eyes matched what was left of his own intelligence. He didn't know what protocol there might be to seeing a prostitute outside her place of trade, but he didn't care. His heart beat harder as he said, "I'd like to see you again."

She smiled. "Come back later."

"If I didn't have a business dinner I'd take you out."

"Another night, hombre."

He could see her eyes cloud over. Which made him all the more determined to set something up, something other than a further appointment on the white bench. "How's tomorrow?" he tried.

"I'm here."

Rogers didn't know if that meant she was busy, or available. "Could we go out for dinner?"

"Why not?" She smiled again.

"Let's make it a date." He was unexpectedly pleased. Maybe the week wouldn't be so bad after all.

He roused again. She put a finger to his lips and pressed him back down, climbing on board. He trusted her—her turn to show him the native ways, the San Blas formulas. Which she did. She swam over him like a dolphin, roosted on him like a bird, raced him like a pair of horses to the line. She was very convincing.

2

Once, and not all that long ago, Jim Rogers had had everything—a huge income, an office in the sky, a girlfriend whose face graced the continent's highways and its palaces of darkness. His three cars, of German obsidian, Detroit's best chrome, and one piloted by an angel of English gold, slumbered in the underworld beneath his home. His home had been a palazzo hoisted atop a stone-clad pillar of industry in a historic district. From his balconies he could see the light beating off the Hudson River and all the flatlands of America groaning into the sunset beneath their burden of iron.

Nor had he been one of those men imprisoned by their wealth, encumbered by sections of sod, piles of bricks, acres of rippling roof sheltering ranked machinery. He didn't own his wealth, he was paid it. Month after month, in the checks came. To go every day empty-handed into the office, free on this earth, and emerge with a slip of paper in one's pocket that had the right numbers on it—that was truly to live by one's wits, as a modern-day hunter-gatherer. He made it a point never to put down. The cars, for instance: from the figures that flew in each month lesser figures winged off to take care of them. His life was a flight of figures.

Year after year, he wore his wealth lightly for indeed it weighed little. The crash of '87 saw him sway on his pillar but not topple. He had laughed to feel the breeze of risk on his cheek, then tightened the belt by one or two holes.

Rogers's partner had been European, like him, but of ancient, long-distilled stock. Royalty flickered distantly in her blood. She had fled the Sorbonne after three weeks, hopped on a whim to America, joined a modern dance studio, and changed her name from Kandele to Candlebury. Five years on, when Jim met her, the lowlands of Benelux still hovered in her voice like an aroma.

Sometimes he wondered if they had treated each other well because they came from different countries and met in a third, never quite shaking off a certain diplomatic protocol.

Somewhere he had read: *a lost soul groping in the darkness of remembered ways*. That was right, exactly. To be lost, as he was now, was to remember the time when you were not lost, and to dream, or despair, of recovering it; but either way to look back. And he had also read about love being a rock, and if the rock is cleaved then either half dwindles, corrodes in the air. You know by that litmus if it has been real love. And he knew that yes, his had been true love and he had thrown it away. Happiness—which was the same as his soul—had shrivelled up in him like a dead spider. Three years had passed since he gave her up, three years of disaster, disaster metaphysical, moral, material. Morgan's had moved him from Far East to Middle East, then London, then Latin accounts. Then they dropped him entirely, and he had had to scramble onto a stool at Sylvester's.

He tried to be a good man, a flexible man. He knew fortune was a wheel and wheels spun. He had had to give up the loft, had moved to the West Village, to a narrow three-room railroad with a strip of a view of the Empire State and a friendly Colombian across the hall who invited him in to watch Mexican football matches on cable. Occasionally they got a UEFA match too. The place was cheap enough that he could save.

In the hotel car park clouds of insects whirled about the lamps, cars gleamed, and from a pair of poles two translucent flags hung limply above a coarse lawn. There was something about a lawn in the tropics, and a city of concrete: they acquired glamour in the heat. Here in the warmth you could believe that even if you were no longer the success you had once been, you were at least still a man making his own way, you still had some kind of chance.

An oilbird flapped out of the darkness, disappeared into a palm tree.

Reentering the tropics always gave Rogers a buzz, even now, after many trips, after two years of Latin accounts. Every time he came down he still couldn't help enjoying the first fragrance of night blossom in humid air.

The Panama Pipe Corporation had taken a back room at the Casa Frattini. Or rather the company's ghost had. The PPC didn't really exist, it was just a name and an all but empty bank account. That was why they were gathering: to see if they could make it exist.

Rogers's flight caught up with him. When his lobster bisque appeared, dizziness swamped him. He guzzled his Chablis, doubting it would have the power to inebriate but hoping it might plant his feet on the ground.

The company was what you got at such dinners. A Swedish ex-dish in her fifties with cropped blond hair, from a Scandinavian bank; a Señor Carreras with bald head and injudiciously solemn countenance who was the official host, being high up in the Bank of Panama; Señora Carreras too, who patted the corners of her mouth with her napkin after every forkful; and a slick young banker called Jean-Louis Codrin with wavy hair and expensive loafers, Carreras's sidekick.

Of the five men and two women who made up the party, Sylvester's would be wanting him to watch the various bank executives, but Rogers was interested in Albert Jones, an improbably named Argentinian with a flushed face and bouffant of white hair. He had put together the consortium of Latin investors and was close to Milagros, a Colombian of immense wealth renowned for his "clean nose." Milagros, ultimately, was the man one needed, and the way to him was through Jones. Rogers and Jones had talked on the phone a few times, and Rogers had steered him to a friend on the trading floor for some low-commission sweeteners on the Nasdaq.

Twice Jones sent Rogers a curious look across the table, a smile at once supplicating and smug. Rogers wasn't sure what to make of it.

Jones spoke English fluently, with a richness no native speaker could muster, fluting his way through the syllables as if the language were Brazilian, a delight to listen to.

Tournedos Rossini, lobster Thermidor, poulet à la Kiev: it was that kind of place, nothing but famous dishes. The least one could do was bury it with one's credit line. That was the point of a dinner like this, after all: to eat well, then be the one who paid for it. Sylvester's policy: it is better to give than receive hospitality. Rogers had the platinum trump up his sleeve. Soon he would excuse himself and slip it into the maître d's palm.

In the lavatory the ventilation hummed. A tiled floor and dark wood cubicles gave an Iberian touch. Rogers looked at himself in the mirror and felt exhausted. He was exhausted. He was approaching forty womanless, childless, and not moneyless exactly but with less money, much less, than ever before. He was a man with troubles, a man who needed to sit through dull dinners in the hope of pulling off a deal worthy of his past, worthy of his aspirations, what was left of them. And that was another worry: his aspirations were dwindling fast. All the more need to pull something off now, before they disappeared altogether.

The floor tiles swayed, flexed, became spongey, settled again. He was tired of his aspirations. What was the point of them? So the folks back home could say, My, isn't he doing well? So his onetime fellows in rainy Blighty could look wistfully across the ocean and follow the dazzling trail he left behind him? What was glamour anyway but something you were bound to lose? He remembered the glamorous dinners in the early days in Manhattan, dinners clustered with the up and coming, all attracted to one another by the mutual flicker of success. They were long gone now. Or rather not they, but *he*. He was long gone. Whatever you did, however bravely you swept across the hills and fought your way up the gleaming towers of downtown, sooner or later you started losing your hair, succumbing to male standard pattern, while your stomach swelled and success drained from you like lymph.

Rogers scooped his hands under the tap, not as cold as he'd hoped, and lifted a bubbly handful which defrothed into a tiny dribble before it reached his face. His cheeks prickled.

Albert Jones walked in while Rogers was drying his hands.

"So," Jones said. It was a question. He looked up from an industrious scrubbing of the hands, the water roaring, and stared at Rogers that way he had, half appraising, half appealing.

Perhaps he was gay, Rogers thought. He didn't know what to do. "Cool," he said, to say something.

Jones smiled. "When in Rome . . . What do you think?" He sniffed, tapped his nose with a knuckle.

"Good idea," Rogers answered, before he could stop himself. "Do as the bloody Romans. Wonderful." He injected a trace of cockney into his voice, a touch of Claptonese. Foreigners sometimes liked that in an Englishman.

"Here." Albert Jones held out a closed hand. "Welcome package."

In a locked cubicle Rogers opened up the little envelope. It was a long time since he had had any cocaine, and for just a moment he considered pouring it down the toilet. Then he thought: why not? He exercised too much restraint, he had forgotten how to let go and get on a roll. He pulled out a credit card, a bill, and stooped to the cistern. Nothing like the good stuff. And these people tonight, they were partners, future partners. He had nothing to fear. They were all on the same side in the fight against moneylessness, against the indifference of the world. Their job was to take a mountain, a cliff, a bay, a forest, and make it *mean* something. It was up to human beings to inscribe their meaning on to the world, and the number-one language was money: sterling, balboa, inti, cruzeiro, whatever you called it, it all amounted to the same thing. No one *needed* tournedos Rossini medium rare, no one *needed* Porsches or Connoisseur Class, except to give a little indication, an index of what they had; except to talk their talk in the one universal language, the *idioma del mundo*.

Rogers's sinuses felt hollow, almost visible, they were so happily defined. A smile affixed itself to his cheeks and in the back of his throat the wonderful chalky taste settled in. Why didn't he do this more often?

Back at the table he was aware of a long silence. Finally, when he himself was about to break it, Albert Jones put his hands on the table and said, "Well, shall we?"

Jones's hands were hairy, and very clean. His ruby-studded ring left a little dent in the tablecloth.

Outside, as the others slipped past car doors being held open for them — *"Gracias," "Tak," "Merci"* — Jones suggested a nightcap. He cocked his head by way of beckoning, and strolled up the road with hands in pockets, expecting Rogers to follow, which he did. Halfway down the block the high-pitched wail of a locking system rang out and a Mercedes blinked its lights.

They drove fast under high white buildings and palm trees orange in street light. When they stopped, a stiff night wind had got up. Rogers's trousers flapped, the car door sprang from his fingers, slamming shut, and a paper bag raced past his ankles.

Down red-carpeted steps, through a red velvet door. Jones nodded at the doorman. Inside, in dim light, golden flesh strapped with black lace, white nylon. The eye required a moment to adjust, understand.

"OK?" Jones grinned. He led them past the bar, freighted with mirrors and bottles and chrome, to a corner cubicle.

A bottle of dark rum añejo, four bottles of Coca-Cola, their caps snapped off by a waiter, an ice bucket, a packet of Marlboro, unpeeled, half ejected from their cartridge.

Jones said, "You can do what you like here."

"In that case . . ." Rogers laughed, then felt a little foolish for laughing. He pulled out his gift pack and cut some lines in the lee of the ice bucket. Jones chuckled in that suave, suntanned way of his.

A second waiter came up and asked Jones if there was to be anything special tonight. Jones shook his head and said, "Just something nice."

A moment's unease hit Rogers. They were bankers, throwing a rope of trust from ship to ship on the high seas of business. That was fine. But there was something else with Jones, something Rogers couldn't put a finger on, that wasn't quite like a banker.

They clinked glasses. Rogers took a long pull. "I have to tell you, I still don't get why the oil companies won't come on board."

Jones shrugged, glanced to one side as if looking for someone. "Like I told you, they've been scared off."

"But by who?" Rogers's drink was sweet and cold.

Jones shook his head. "The government doesn't want to rock the boat. You've seen the margins. If the government hikes the canal tolls for tankers, which they've been threatening to do for years—"

"Then the line would be a godsend."

"Yes and no. We're talking three to five years to build this thing. That's a lot of tolls. But I'm not talking about the Panamanian government. It's the Casa Blanca. No US president wants to risk any commotion so close to the canal. Sixty years ago they had a war on their hands, the Cuna War. They're afraid. The region is sensitive. There's the environment, there's the locals, there's Colombian guerrillas just next door. All that, with the canal right in the middle of it."

Rogers shrugged. "So?"

"So you need cowboys to pull off a stunt like this." Jones raised his glass and chuckled.

Rogers nodded and drained his drink.

"You really can't move this stuff fast enough. Once we're up and running they can't *not* jump on board."

A girl came over, a dyed blond whose bottle had managed only a pale rust, the best it could do with what must have been a spectacular oil-black mane. She wore bustier, suspenders, boots, the whole catalogue, and planted a shining black heel theatrically on the table.

Jones hissed in Rogers's ear, "Colombiana. Pretty, no?" He looked up at the dancing girl, who had pulled herself onto the table top and was swaying to the salsa music.

"The best are the Colombianas," Jones explained seriously. "All the pretty ones come here to get their pussies on the Yankee dollar." He let out an impassioned giggle, his face creasing up.

Rogers was surprised. It was the kind of remark you heard from morose taxi drivers. Rogers felt a certain fondness for Panama. He thought of the country's tenuous S resting under the tropical sun, the link between north and south stretched thin like a piece of taffy. There was surely something romantic about it, it ought to be granted its share of prettiness.

"What about the pretty Panamanians?" he asked.

Jones shrugged. "What about them?" He cackled, then paused, coughed, realising he'd got the joke wrong, and said: "What pretty Panamanians?" He laughed again.

Rogers took a long draw on his drink. He would need drink to pull off conversation like this.

Jones leaned close. "Actually," he said, returning to a serious tone, "some of the Cuna girls, they're lovely."

"Cuna?"

They were having to raise their voices over the music. Jones smiled up at the dancing girl, who moved with bewitching attachment to the beat. "San Blas," he explained. "They're from San Blas."

Since walking into the club Jim Rogers had been wondering how soon he could plead jet lag and hustle his way back to see the sauna girl. He had already decided he wouldn't wait till the next day. He would propose right now, tonight, that Paulina come and spend the night with him. Maybe he would even try to fix up a *Pretty Woman* deal. Be my wife for the week, I'll pay you handsomely. It wasn't every day you got a chance to hang out with someone who came from the tribal world, if she really did, and who was that pretty. And bright too. He even felt an urgency about seeing her. How much would she want? It didn't matter. He imagined her unfolding his shirts, tutting over his thick socks, snapping out his Italian ties. The important thing was to keep the impulse alive.

"To rum and coke," Rogers said, raising his glass.

Jones cackled, tapping out a heap of powder from some hidden phial and handing a straw up to the dancer, who squatted, bent to the table, snorted through the straw, then straddled his face. He flicked his eyebrows. "*Sabrosa mujer.*"

Drink slipped down an ice channel in the back of Rogers's head. He reached the cold bloom, the flush, the fresh ice bucket of the high.

On the way to the door Jones took hold of the inside of Rogers's elbow. Rogers liked the mild intimacy. They were two men exploring the realms of pleasure together, of entrepreneurial expansiveness.

"Can you keep a secret?" Jones looked closely at Rogers. "I think you can."

"Of course." Rogers enjoyed feeling close to this man he hardly knew, this bouffanted voice from the telephone.

Jones reached into his jacket and handed Rogers an envelope. "Look after this. No copies."

Rogers caught himself frowning. A small frown. He swept it from his face and slipped the envelope into his pocket. Jones's eyes lit up, a beautiful pale hazel.

Outside, the doorman held open the door of an old white Lincoln. Rogers gave the man a screwed-up five. Panama ran on dollars. It was not a place to be if you were counting your money. He loosened his tie and sank into the sinking velvet of the old seat.

3

The girl at reception brought him a Heineken. She wore a miniskirt that both gave nothing away and was sufficient advertisement to anyone looking for it. After a couple of swigs, Rogers sat forward in the armchair to which he had been directed and engaged her in conversation. She sat behind the glass countertop filing her nails.

"You should come here carnival time," she said in a bored voice. "You know cumbias? Cumbias all over town."

Rogers nodded and said he did know, and loved, cumbia music, and perhaps she would teach him to dance the cumbia when he returned.

She said of course she would, mustering a ghost of a smile. It was late, the girl evidently could not summon the kind of bonhomie such conversation called for. He sensed she would be happier to sit and file her nails in silence, musing to herself. He imagined that nail filing must be one of the great muse-inducing activities. He guzzled the beer then went to the bathroom.

Inside the envelope Jones had given him was a single sheet of paper folded in three on which a diagram had been printed. Rogers recognised it at once as the intended course of the pipeline, the curves, the straights, the pump stations. Notes had been handwritten beside each section in neat English. The uppermost section, in the north, where the dock and plant would be, was circled.

It was odd to receive such a document on paper, and handwritten. It wasn't good news, he saw that at once. Jones had told him they were clear the whole way, but it was obvious that they weren't. That northern section, labelled "36-A, 36-B," had no deed title written beside it, instead only a big question mark in a square, and a reference to some kind of legislation. *Acto 347IIc de 1939*. He crumpled the envelope and dropped it to the floor, then folded the paper and slipped it into his wallet. He would have to ask Jones about this.

Paulina had changed into an emerald minidress that buttoned up at the front. It suited her. She smiled sweetly when she saw him, coming forward to take his hand and offering her cheek. As soon as they were in the room he knew he had done the right thing in coming back, and also in not coming earlier. He had taken care of business and now he could take care of her.

She held his wrist, looked at his watch, and said, "Hombre, it's late. Just for you I can stay longer."

He squinted at her. "Just for me?"

She shrugged and smiled. "Did you have a good dinner?"

He sat on the edge of the massage bench and took off his

tie, then moved to a small yellow sofa he hadn't noticed last time. Words flowed from him, water from a reservoir. "It's not every day you find someone you can really talk to," he said. "You're a fool if you don't see more of the person." He felt it as he said it. She was beautiful, she came from an unsullied world; he did want to see more of her, badly.

She stood with her back to the door. He liked seeing her standing there against the door, as if she didn't want either of them to leave. It softened the business aspect, which was somehow graphically represented by the door. He was amazed at how being with her sobered him, cut through the drug's upholstery.

He told her he had a suggestion. She looked at her nails and blew on them as if she had been painting them. Which encouraged him. Perhaps she had been sitting here alone all evening doing her nails. "A suggestion I hope you like."

She came over and kissed the top of his head, her legs brown and gleaming in the low light. She had beautiful slender knees. She folded her arms against her chest, making her breasts rise under the cloth. "What is it?"

He felt a light come on in his chest and he told her. He said he'd pay anything but wanted her to quit working for the week. He'd look after her, buy her clothes, whatever she wanted. Already he imagined them going to the Valentino store and abusing the credit cards. People like her, poor beauties in poor countries, always got less than they deserved, and here he was with a chance to redress that. And a chance to be with one more real beauty before he himself finally slumped into hairless, bellied, terminal middle age. It would almost be like an affair, a real relationship.

She stroked his cheek. "If you would like," she said. *Si te gustaria.*

He nodded.

She continued looking at him. "*Yo te gusto?*" You like me?

He nodded seriously.

She said nothing but bent forward and planted a kiss on his lips.

Walking across the hotel car park Rogers wasn't sure whether to put his arm round her. Would it seem sentimental, or decorous? She walked confidently beside him, apparently not bothered whether he did or didn't.

It was good to be strolling through the warm dark at midnight beside a beautiful girl while the city sighed around them. For a moment, approaching the marble ocean of the hotel entrance, Rogers felt himself crumpling under the need for more of the drug. But in the confines of the elevator, their voices muffled in the small space, a kind of peace returned. He took her hand—she had slender, long-nailed fingers—and conducted her into the quiet corridor, past the heavy door, which opened with a click, into his quiet room.

She wanted nothing to drink, just Sprite. He didn't even need to call room service. He snapped the tag on the little brown fridge and poured out a glass, cracking ice into it. Then he picked up the half bottle of Moët and raised his eyebrows. She said sweetly, "Well, if you're offering," and he was touched to understand she had been holding back, not wanting to be any trouble.

He left his jacket on the desk by the window. She was quiet, perhaps a little overawed by the situation, and was more comfortable once she had him on the bed and had popped off his shoes. She pulled off his socks the long way, by the toe, then kissed his feet.

"How long have you been in Panama City?" he asked.

She knelt by his face. Her thighs golden. The original cigar maiden, native girl from the land of tobacco. Walter Ralegh himself must have rested his cheek on such a thigh while puffing a rubbery roll of leaves.

She leaned over him, hair falling like rain on his cheek. She kissed him, put a finger to his lips. *"Estoy nueva,"* she whispered.

She was unbelievable. The girl from the junction of east, west, north, and south. He had heard about Amerindian tribes who taught their girls the full Kama Sutra before they were allowed to marry. Perhaps she had been through something like that. She gathered him into her arms and rolled him like a tobacco leaf, then raised him on her palm, in her fingers, blew smoke through him. His eyelids glittered with sun-strewn water, his skin stretched on warm sand, and his ears filled with the pounding of surf.

At 6 a.m. there was only one other man in the hotel sauna, a baldheaded guy who sat with his skull lodged into the corner, some victim of sleeplessness hoping to heat himself into a coma, perhaps. He didn't stir when Rogers came in.

The smell of sweat and something sweet cloyed the air.

Rogers had woken into a pool of lucidity. The first thing he had seen, the beautiful face on his pillow, its cheek slightly concave in rest, had moved him inordinately. And dawn had been astir, brushing the fringes of the curtain with snowy light, an untropical light that reminded him of England. A wave of nostalgia had seized him. Perhaps he was finally coming to realise that he was an exile. Perhaps it was time to go home. He imagined how much he would enjoy his native land's soft grey air, walking over its rain-drenched lawns. In some strange way this girl brought it back to him. She too, after all, was from a real place, a real home, San Blas, where the witch doctors kept everyone safe from old age and sharks. He didn't normally miss his homeland. It was one of the successes of his life that he had left it. Yet now he thought of taking her there, of how she would like that. Perhaps what he had been waiting for all along was just this: a chance to go home with a prize on his arm.

The man in the corner of the sauna groaned and shifted his shoulders, adjusting his weight against the dripping tiles. Rogers's nose poured sweat: last night pouring off him, a stream of hygiene.

When he got back to the room he noticed the quiet, the emptiness, at once. The rumpled sheets, the jacket on the blond-pine chair, the quiet in the bathroom, a towel left damp on the sofa. She had gone. No note. He searched the desk, the bedside table, on the TV. Perhaps she couldn't write.

He wasn't worried, all in all. For one thing, he hadn't paid her. She would surely be back. There must be some prostitute's tenet about never leaving the scene of the act without the money. As he thought of her his chest filled with clouds. They had not had sex but made love, slowly, warmly, intoxicated not with drink but with warmth, with mutual fascination. Surely she couldn't have been faking it when she traced her fingers over his torso, down his legs, at a snail's pace. Or when she rested her cheek on his chest reminiscing about her childhood on the lagoons of San Blas, in the hammocks and dugouts and longhouses, confiding in him about the places she wanted to go, the work she hoped one day to get as a location manager for a television station. There was something pretty about that ambition. They hadn't slept till late, very late, talking and making love by turns.

No, he needn't question it—it happened from time to time, a hooker and a client.

His fingers tingled when he pressed a five into the hand of the uniformed boy who brought the breakfast tray. Scrambled eggs, Marlboros, coffee for two. He ate fast. Fruit had come too, wonderful slices of tropical fruit from nature's laboratory. He loved this part of the world today with a new love.

He hung yesterday's blue suit in the closet and peeled out today's Saint Laurent, a relic of his good old days. When he was ready—showered, shaved, tied, shod—and feeling better than he could remember in a long time, he went to the desk to pick up his wallet, then, realising he had left it in his blue jacket, went to the closet and searched the jacket and found first one inside pocket empty, then the other. He checked the side pockets too, and the little breast pocket, even though the wallet couldn't have fitted into it. He took the coat hanger out, slung off the trousers, and checked them. Then he checked the jacket again. He looked under the bedside tables and in their drawers—one red Bible each—and under the bed and in the bathroom and behind the mirror—empty glass shelves. Then he checked on the balcony with its bare glass table and two slatted chairs, and in the bathroom again.

He had to accept that the wallet had gone.

He called down to reception and hung up before they answered. He called Albert Jones's office without asking himself why, and hung up when the machine answered. Which gave him the idea of calling Janet at the desk in New York. But he felt that he needed to do nothing, just sit still. Except there was no time for that. Seven o'clock: one had to move, move along, if one was an unloved salesman on his way through middle age, with success evaporating from him like dew. The young filched it from your pockets while you weren't looking. While you were worrying about your hairline, your slackening belly, your dwindling gym life, they leapt into the seat you had just vacated.

He left a message for Janet about the credit cards. He could survive off the hotel bill until tomorrow, when replacements would arrive. The cash? Cash came and went. But he would have to try and find the girl. No question about that. He didn't want to think about Jones's damn piece of paper, but it wasn't the kind of thing you let go walkabout.

He snapped open the curtains on a flowing morning. Shadows raced across the city like smoke, the shadows of palms, clouds, buses. A few things were golden: half a building, a flight of high windows, a sapling dying down the block. A vulture went by, high up. The underside of its wings glistened like tinfoil. After all, a man could misspend his years and still recognise beauty when it glided by.

Seven-thirty a.m. The Geisha Sauna's tinted-glass door was locked. He buzzed and buzzed into the darkness within.

4

The Panama Pipe Corporation did not yet have its own offices but met in a suite high in the Bank of Panama. Rogers managed to avoid Jones all morning, even in the breaks. Except once, in the bathroom.

The hiss of plumbing, a faint smell of bleach, a lingering trace of urine — the smell of an institutional toilet. For some reason it brought back a feeling of New York in the early days, when he had first moved there: the morning walks beneath the granite crags, the air like mountain air, the subway vents steaming, the little coffee-and-doughnut places rattling up their shutters, and the water towers of the high buildings catching the sun. He had loved New York then. There had been no better place on earth for him.

Someone walked in while Rogers was peeing, crossing behind his back to one of the cubicles. The lock clicked. As Rogers shook himself, Jones's voice reached him. First a low chuckle, then: "*Qué tal?* Good night?"

"*Excelente*," Rogers answered, projecting a smile into his voice.

Jones flushed and emerged in one commotion while Rogers was drying his hands. "You must let me have back the document." He looked up and pulled a smile. It was hard to say what it meant.

"Of course," Rogers said. Under that gaze he could say nothing else. This was a man one wanted to agree with. "We'll have to talk about that, you know. I understood we were clear the whole way."

"Nearly the whole way." Jones shrugged like it was no big deal. "We'll talk. But I must have it back now."

"After lunch OK?"

"Why not now?"

"It's at the hotel."

Jones wiped his hands. "Why jou didn't bring here?" He stepped closer to Rogers, his eyes narrow, then turned away. Jones snapped the towel roll down and swore under his breath. He looked at Rogers. "Is not mine. Jou know that. We don't play games."

❖

Rogers cried off lunch.

A middle-aged woman wearing a black skirt and clinking bead necklace opened up for him at the Geisha Sauna. He reminded himself to be polite and smile at her, but she turned before he could, clinking away ahead of him, revealing an absurdly long slit up the back of her skirt. No one else seemed to be around.

"Is Paulina here?" Rogers tried. "Excuse me for interrupting, señora," he added, though he didn't seem to have interrupted anything.

The woman raised her dark eyes and studied him. He felt ridiculous, chasing a prostitute like this. His cheeks burned.

"*Se fue,*" she said. "*Ya se fue.*" She looked down at a diary. "You want to make an appointment?"

The thought had not occurred to him, and stirred his loins. "No, that's fine," he mumbled. The woman shrugged sulkily.

"She went back to San Blas," she said, vaguely lifting and dropping a hand.

San Blas. Where the hell *was* San Blas?

He told the taxi to stop at a newsstand and jumped out to buy a school map of the country, the only kind the vendor had. Rogers opened it up in the back of the car. It showed none of the terrain, only the administrative regions, all in the cartographer's dreary pastels. San Blas was a pink strip along the north coast.

Panama was a narrow country, and on his map it looked like San Blas could hardly be more than sixty miles away, an hour or so on the road. He had to keep Jones sweet at all costs. Not to mention the risk—which in fact seemed to him remote—of scuppering the deal with a careless leak. All in all, he ought just to go ahead and take the taxi up there right now, and miss the afternoon session. All they were discussing was the South American loan plan. He knew these small Latin towns. It wasn't hard to find people. Even if Paulina was not her real name, he could probably track her down—the *bella* who works in Panama City. But then again, who knew how many towns and villages there might be in the district called San Blas? One on the map, what looked like the largest, was actually called San Blas. But did that mean she was necessarily from there?

"How long to get to San Blas?" he asked the thick-necked driver, who was busy accelerating past a truck belching smoke.

The driver braked. "San Blas?" he asked, letting out a long "Er . . ." He concluded the sound with a concerned "*Qué?*" and a frown in the mirror.

The truck roared beside them.

Rogers repeated the question. Only then did he look down at the map again and see that San Blas ran most of the length of the north coast between Panama City and Colombia. It couldn't fail to be the very region where the pipeline's route had run into some kind of problem. Probably just some farmer or rancher who had previously said yes and now changed his mind, or wanted more compensation.

"You mean San Blas *islas?*"

"San Blas. Just San Blas."

The driver speeded up again, glancing at Rogers in the mirror. "San Blas is the other side of the mountains," he said. "An ugly road. *Muy feo.* You need a Land Rover."

"How long does it take?"

"To get to San Blas? That depends. *San Blas islas . . . o toda la región?*"

"Just to get there," Rogers said.

The driver mumbled to himself, swerving past a school bus.

Jones was waiting in the lobby of the Bank of Panama. He sideswiped Rogers from the elevators and walked him towards the polished black marble of the rear wall, where their two reflections flashed as they approached. Jones fluttered his fingers in the universal gesture for *gimme.*

"It's gone."

Jones stepped close. "This is not funny. It doesn't go. It doesn't go anywhere. This stuff is not public knowledge, you know that." He plunged both hands deep into his pockets and swivelled like a dancer on the polished floor. "Come on. Enough joking." His breath was warm and fragrant.

Rogers was familiar with this Latin temperament. He did not like to be its brunt but it didn't scare him. "Someone stole it. They stole my wallet and went to San Blas."

Jones uttered an expletive that sounded like *Hotspur.* "San Blas? Quit joking."

"I'm not joking. Why would I be joking?"

"Why? *Hotspur.*" Jones pulled a grimace and pirouetted again on the gleaming floor. "So who was it?"

"A girl."

"When?"

"Last night. After I got back to the hotel."

"Why you think she went to San Blas?"

"That's what they told me."

"Who?"

"The people she works with."

Jones rested his eyes on him. They sparkled. "A chica stole your wallet. Tell her she's giving chicas a bad name." He shrugged, then enunciated: "Well, we will have to go and get it back, won't we?"

"I'll go. I know who I'm looking for."

Jones shook his head. "You don't know who you're looking for. You don't know anything. We both go, there's no other way. Tomorrow morning, first thing."

"Why not now?"

He inhaled audibly. "You have to leave this to me, man. You don't know this place. All the flights are in the morning."

"The flights?"

Jones tutted, examining Rogers's face, then moved away towards the elevators.

Dawn, 5:45 a.m. As the taxi rumbled down a back street Rogers saw a coconut fall, something he had never witnessed before. No wind, no provocation, it simply dropped, a lethal nugget, from a spindly palm in a wasteland between two concrete hulks, landing without a bounce.

Rogers felt strangely excited. Salsa was playing quietly on the radio, soft sunshine had begun to suffuse the city, and he felt unaccountably free. Free, and heading off into the sunny unknown, a million miles from home, wherever home was, with a roll of large-denomination bills in his pocket that Sylvester's had wired through. He remembered how, when he first moved to New York, every morning he had been thrilled to think that while England had already been up for five hours, America like an irresponsible younger brother still had its head on the pillow. He used to walk down through the canyons of the city, the gulfs of shadow, while the high floors of buildings were struck gold by early sun. And all the subway vents would be releasing their bright steam into the morning. And meanwhile his deals had kept getting bigger and better. The only limit to Rogers's achievement had been himself. The world had offered him all its scope and it had been up to him to occupy it. He had never worried, never hurried, just worked the long hours and lived by the law of least effort. And the universe had returned with its abundance. Which was not only financial. He remembered one summer evening meeting a redhead dance student in a SoHo gallery; not three hours later, after a well-sluiced dinner at the Odeon, she was performing the splits on the edge of his Le Corbusier while he knelt before her raising a ruckus of moans. That was the way to live: man the hunter, man the pleasure giver. Man stomping down the walls of the present to ambush the future. If you didn't live that way—this was the maddening thing—the only alternative was to allow yourself to be led by the nose. It was one or the other: lead or be led. Somewhere deep down he couldn't help feeling that it oughtn't to be like that. Surely it was possible to feel calm, content. Or were those the very feelings nature deployed to keep the followers dumbly following?

"Going to the islands?" the taxi driver asked him. "Nice place. You're gonna like it."

"Is there anything to do?"

The driver laughed. "Man, you don't go there to do anything. There's nothing there but the Indians."

Rogers arrived at the small downtown airport in time to see
a black-windowed Mercedes pull away. The weather was perfect: the tall buildings across the runway orange and beautiful
in the dawn sun, the air warm on face and arm. And he still
carried an absolving glow of physical satisfaction, even now,
twenty-four hours after Paulina had left him.

Rogers clicked his biro to write a note to himself and
noticed that the pen's barrel was stamped "med U.S.A." He
had never noticed before: Medusa! He and the Medusa were
heading off on an adventure. Coconut and lobster galore, if
what the girl had said was true. It was good to be traveling with
just a holdall, in short sleeves and slacks, to be getting away
from offices and computers and business, getting out into the
real world.

The terminal was thronged with twelve-year-olds, all with
lank black hair in Beatle bobs, dressed in extraordinary theatri-
cal clothes. They might have been some school drama expedition, except that the female kids, in blue skirts and
fluffy blouses, barefoot, their ankles roped with beads, had
babies strapped to their backs. They weren't twelve-year-olds
at all. The men, in baggy trousers and crumpled bowler hats,
pressed at a counter behind which an official paced about,
periodically thrusting strips of green paper into the forest of
hands reaching out to him. Despite his white shirt and thick
spectacles the official was visibly of the same stock as the rest
of them, with his long black hair and modest stature. The
place was more like a post office in some Soviet Asian republic than an airport.

Albert Jones appeared, wading through the throng. "*Jose
Maria, ven!*" he called out.

The spectacled official came to the end of the counter and entered into a leisurely chat with Jones as if the boisterous crowd in the room didn't exist. Then the two men disappeared through a door.

Rogers waited. The crowd was in fact quite orderly. Everyone seemed to be in a good mood. Rogers couldn't remember the last time he had been in a room full of such good humour. It was like some happy, sober party, filled with a babble of anticipation. Like the last day of school. Albert Jones reappeared in the doorway and beckoned to Rogers.

In a small back office a man with a greasy mane of ashen hair sat at a metal desk. Jones introduced him as Señor Carlos. "This girl," he told Rogers. "Tell Señor Carlos how she looks."

Carlos didn't look up but held a pen wavering over a table of figures.

"The girl?"

Jones and Carlos chuckled. A third man joined in the laughter. It was the white-shirted official from next door, standing in the doorway, watching with arms folded.

"Average height," Rogers said. "Slim, black hair."

"Pretty?" Carlos asked seriously.

Rogers shrugged. "Sí."

"You think she flew yesterday?" Without waiting for an answer, Carlos brushed back a lock of his grey hair and grabbed a microphone off a radio set, turning up the speaker so it filled the office with a crackle of static. He exchanged some noisy incomprehensible remarks with a man on the other end, then hung up. "It's impossible. None of the pilots can say. Could be Porvenir, could be Tigre, could be El Corbiski, could be anywhere."

Rogers couldn't imagine how that brief communication

could have established anything so categorical. Carlos tapped his pen on the desk in a series of little clicks.

Jones coughed into a fist. "Well, what are we to do now?"

The official shrugged extravagantly, eyebrows joining in, and sent Rogers a sympathetic look. The clerk from next door, still enjoying the excuse to ignore the crowd behind him, followed the conversation with interest, uttering little exclamations of agreement and concern.

"The greatest volume is of course to El Porvenir," Señor Carlos continued, running a hand back through his long hair. "Very few go to Corbiski or farther down."

Jones fiddled with something—keys, change—in his trouser pocket, his knuckles pressing out the cloth.

Carlos asked mournfully: "You don't have a name?"

Albert Jones said: "Paulina. So she says."

"Paulina?" The man brightened, but Rogers could tell that it was only because here at last was one tangible detail, not because he knew anything that would help.

Jones coughed. "She's his girlfriend." He glanced at Rogers. "At least, you understand. A chica."

Carlos nodded vigorously.

Rogers felt like breaking out in an embarrassed giggle. All of this, this search, this caucus of masculine heads pondering a problem, had been occasioned by his lust. He had been caught with his pants down.

In one smooth, quick motion Jones tucked a folded bill under the writing pad on Carlos's desk. The man picked up his microphone and again filled the room with a roar of static, in the midst of which voices hovered like ghosts. It was impossible to understand what they were saying. After a while he set the microphone down and raised his palms in a gesture of caution. "No one knows for sure. But maybe, *maybe* Inadule." He shrugged. "But it depends how she looks."

Jones clasped his hand across the desk. "*Gracias.*" He turned to Rogers. "Dark and pretty, right?"

But Rogers had already let himself out of the office.

As soon as Albert Jones emerged, Rogers seized him by the elbow and walked him out into the car park. "You want to go a step further with this, you're going to tell me what's going on with San Blas."

Jones spread his arms wide in a Latin gesture of compliance, truce. Hey, the arms said, your call. "Whatever, it's fine, whatever jou want." Jones stood like that a moment, defenceless, then cleared his throat and took Rogers by the arm.

"Well, this is hardly the time or place," Jones said, "but what the hell."

Suddenly they were two businessmen again, strolling arm in arm, very Latin, charming and brotherly. They walked among the ailing cars strewn about the lot, which might or might not have been taxis waiting for rides. A few men who might or might not have been their drivers were drinking coffee from paper cups, and a teenage boy was selling fruit juice to local women from a giant plastic cooler.

"I said we were clear the whole way. Well, not anymore. Ninety-five per cent of the way," Jones said brightly, "there's no problem. We have options on the deeds, et cetera. But ninety-five per cent is not much without the last five." He contemplated the ground. "It's complicated. Let me give you an example. You want to drill for oil on one of your Indian reservations out west. Somehow you have got hold of a good seis-

mic and you want to go in. You think you can just do it?" He
shrugged. "Here in Panama we have something special, unlike anywhere else. The real Caribbean natives, they are still
here, and they are still Stone Age, and in 1938 your government and my government gave them their own autonomous
region. You might as well call it another country. Their own
laws, they don't pay taxes, they do what they like. And what
they like is to live in bamboo huts and paddle dugout canoes
and swing in hammocks and collect herbs from the rain forest.
For their own consumption, of course."

Jones paused, swivelled on the heels of his loafers. They
began pacing back towards the little airport with its green
tower.

"They're into ecology, the environment. They own a strip
of the coast and all the islands. They see what has happened to
the forest on the other side of the mountains. Gone. Not there
anymore. Basically, you want to do anything coast to coast,
you can't avoid them. You knock on the door, you say, can we
build a pipeline please, they slam the door. No, no." Jones
wagged a finger, tutted.

There was something comforting in Jones's paternal Latin
ways. Rogers even prompted: "So what do you do?" He liked
this man, he couldn't help it, he liked this project, he liked
the sound of these people and was already imagining how they
too might benefit from it. It was good to help indigenous
people, why not, let them come on board in some way. Wasn't
this the way forward, the world fragmenting into tribes each
with its own stake in the giant playground of the global
market?

Jones paced carefully, each foot placed as if the shoe were
made of glass. "You have to go to the back door, which we did,
you have to talk to somebody one on one, find out what

they're interested in. Suppose there was one chief on your reservation who wanted, let us say, to build a new gas station. You need an excuse to get the right equipment in, and you also need the right contract."

"How do you mean?"

"Like with some useful clauses. National interest, that kind of thing, things the lawyers can play with, interpret the right way once you're up and running and they try to close you down. So we found someone. Of course. Milagros, he knows somebody somewhere. Excuse me. Everywhere. A certain Cuna chief, a *sahila*, as they say, who is open to discussion. He wants to build a small marina for yachts. Then his people can sell ten times as many *molas* to tourists." Jones chuckled. "So this *sahila*, he told us he thinks he could get plans for his dock passed. So we come in with him, we help him out. That's enough, it's all we need to get the diggers in. But let him get wind of what we're really up to—" Jones spread out his hands, miming an explosion.

"These people, they can be a pain in the ass. They think they're special, everybody tells them so. Tourists pay to see them paddle their dugouts and wear their crazy clothes and dance their dances—the most boring dances you've ever seen, like stomp-stomp-stomp—and there are these German tourists and such, these do-gooders from Scandinavia and Canada, standing around paying for the privilege of using their video cameras, nodding and talking about the wisdom of tribal peoples, all that crap. I tell you, if they would let somebody come in with them, there's a fortune to be made. A nice big eco-resort, you could clean up. But they'll never get it to- gether. The only way to help people like that is to do it with- out them knowing."

He stopped smartly and turned to Rogers. "Now the guy says he needs more time to persuade the elders, the council, or whatever they are. That's the problem. So we're going there to kill two birds with one stone. We need to pay a visit to our *sahila*, and we have to make sure the girl just took the money out of the wallet and threw everything else away. See? The last thing we need is for word to get out among all the Cunas."

Rogers started walking again, frowning. "Why didn't you tell me all this earlier?"

"It wasn't a problem earlier."

"And why put it on paper anyway?"

"You read, you burn. It's the safest way. That's what we do here."

Rogers felt the ground sway. He was thinking that if once a man found his path then strayed from it, all was lost. You paddled away from the shore and ended up anywhere.

"How many of these Cuna are there?" he asked, to ask something.

"Twenty thousand. It's a small place, a lot of small islands. But the depot will be offshore, three or four miles out. Once the pipe is in, they don't even know it's there."

"Except the ships, the stations, the quays, the staff housing, and everything else."

Jones shrugged. "That's why we're going there now. We can't afford not to. If we're lucky the girl can't even read. First thing you've got to do is give her more cash. You OK for that?"

"The first thing we've got to do is find her," Rogers observed, feeling suddenly depressed. "How far are these damn islands?"

"No distance, twenty minutes. But there are three hundred of them, maybe fifty inhabited, and twenty airstrips."

"So we charter and work our way down."

Jones tutted and twitched his head. "That's not the way here. You got to listen to me. Everything, you need the chief's permission. You go to the next island, you get the chief's permission. You eat a sandwich, you get the chief's permission. No private planes, only Cuna Air. Which is why we're here."

Jones beckoned that way he had, inclining his head, hands in pockets. "Come on," he said. "I have a plan."

5

They had a beer in the bar on the airport roof even though it was only seven in the morning. Rogers's mood got lighter and lighter; he felt like celebrating; it was that good to be on the move, to be going somewhere new. Then they strapped themselves into tiny seats in a stuffy airplane and his mood swung the other way. It was awful that he was welcoming this side trip from a side trip, that his life had no centre, had had the heart ripped out of it. What in hell was he doing visiting hookers, then *chasing* hookers, of all ignominies, and getting caught up with coke-crazed businessmen? And what was he doing here, strapped into a midget-sized airplane seat made of tinfoil?

The little plane scuttled to the end of the runway, where the drone of its propellers turned to the sound of a fan. Rogers pulled open his collar, sodden already at the early hour. He felt an attack coming on. Strapped into his little seat, he was powerless to fend it off.

The meaning of his life had dissolved, clearly. That was the only reason he could be so interested in a hooker. He had hoped to secure a deal down here that would bring in a quick forty or fifty right away, with much more to follow, and instead he was on a wild-goose chase, and something in him prevented him from simply getting out and going home. If there was any money at the end of it, it would be less, less, less. That was the way his life went: less instead of more. Less sex, less money, less love, less desire even. Sometimes he wanted nothing other than to want something. Or the big blank, of course. Sometimes he just waited and waited to be run over, drowned, dropped from the sky. But disaster shunned him, it wasn't interested in those who didn't care, only those who did. Buildings toppled, terrorists blazed, fires fell from heaven all over the earth, but always at a safe distance from him. Hell at work. It occurred to Rogers that perhaps on these torrid islands he might meet the devil. That would be something. To come face to face with his tormentor. And yes, he was suffering pointlessly. His misery was maybe chemical, maybe philosophical, but not practical, not realistic. It was inexcusable.

As the plane took off, the white office blocks of the Zona Banquera came loose from their moorings and drifted by. Beneath, a brown beach swung past, less a beach than a mudflat. Rogers felt the pull in his head as the plane banked. He watched the filaments of thin breakers rolling slowly in across brown water onto brown mud. The sun winked at him from an oily bend in a river. Then they were already flying over the green and grey mountains, serious small oppressive mountains, and a moment later a great metal sheet was visible ahead, shining like brushed chrome. It was the Pacific. He could see vague black arms reaching into it and a dapple of cloud shadows stretching away towards Darien.

Then he thought: The devil was you yourself. It was you who said there were no second chances. It was you who deprived yourself of the second chance with your myopia, your fixation on the one lost chance. For the man who lived in the now, who did not look back, there were endless chances.

He had a dizzy spell, leaned back in his seat, and closed his eyes.

Christmas '92. He had bought Candlebury a set of earrings. Two jewels hanging from gold hooks. Simple, beautiful, expensive. She cried when she unwrapped them, and he choked up too. He was sure that without knowing it he had intended them as a pledge. Next time just the one: solo, solitaire, on its band of gold.

He was fortunate, he espoused the good, made his home in the positive, and reaped the rewards. Every month the checks grew larger. Top new broker of '92, clearing seven-fifty. A prince of finance at the prince of ages: thirty-three, the bloom of youth still on his cheeks, and the sap of knowledge in his limbs. He had learnt a kind of inner patience too. Call it peace; why not? He loved sitting at home knowing Candlebury was next door doing her yoga, or chatting on the telephone. He learnt to love the smell of her incense, and opening a bottle of organic *vino nobile* while hearing the light bubble of brown rice cooking. He liked adding seaweed to their stir-fries and shopping in overpriced stores with wooden floors and sacks of grain and walls of vitamins. He began to love, he realised, health. Health itself. He quit smoking.

Candlebury left the Graham chorus line, stopped modelling, and joined an avant-garde hula group who did cutting-edge movement therapy. They were not a big hit except on the workshop circuit. She bought a sequencer and composed music for them. Rogers would come home to the big place in the Heights to which they had moved to find it awash with her ethereal choruses, aglow with etheric light bouncing off the harbour. He'd see the cluster of spires on Wall Street across the slate-shiny water, and know their home floated halfway to heaven.

When the first fall of the nineties hit he welcomed it. He lost money and all his clients lost money and his commissions dropped from nine to six points, and on smaller sums, but he felt it was right. The world was being purged, all the bad stripped out. The pouring on of hyssop, the scouring of the Lord.

Candlebury called it these things. They passed monastic evenings on the floor of their big room with a tall church candle burning by the window, which threw back their reflections, and they considered that all they needed was dry ground to sit on and fire for light and warmth. As they saw themselves in the dark window, so they really were. All they needed was right there, hovering in the glass.

But the losses had unsettled him more than he realised, and twelve months later, it was all over, he had ruined everything. First he jumped an aerobic blond—a spin, a tumble, someone who should never have occupied more than a few hours of sport, but whom instead he started seeing two or three times a week. Before he knew it Candlebury had found out, and she left for Hawaii, for a New Age camp hosting an inner-child seminar, where she said that she would think about what to do. He was scared, but guessed it meant she wouldn't leave him. And she didn't. But next thing he took a gamble and used information he shouldn't have. An unidentifiable recklessness had taken him over. He moved twenty percent of his own portfolio into a company a client of his was preparing to take over. He shouldn't have done it, he did it without even wanting to. Though he was never definitively implicated, there was an investigation. He was yanked off the Asia desk and dumped on Eastern Europe. They wanted him to get involved in debt restructuring. They thought an ex-trader, which is what they made him, would be good in there, with special know-how. They sent him to London in February for six dismal weeks of training.

That was the real end. The ceiling came off the world. The tent came down. No more illusion, no more shelter. All the bland daylight that he and Candlebury had chased away with candles and romance had been gathering like a cold tide outside the door, waiting for a chance to flood back in. He didn't want to go to London, he didn't want to be involved in Eastern Europe or debt.

In London he started smoking again and spent long hours in the pubs attempting to resuscitate ossified friendships with bankers he'd known years ago. There was a queasiness to get-ting together with old friends you hadn't seen in years. Nei-ther of you quite wanted to know what had happened to the other, in case it was too bad, or too good. In the swamp of beer and cigarettes and rain his new life crumbled. Everyone in London seemed to drink and smoke too much. One drunken night he slept with a woman in a navy suit and, it transpired, lacy underwear. Her mouth tasted like an ashtray. She lit up as soon as they finished. It depressed him no end.

The London rain washed the magic out of him. By the time he got back to New York he was sickened by himself, by his weakness and failure of faith. But equally he couldn't bear to hear how Candlebury's angels had guided her to the place where her inner spirit-child was to be born, on the shore of an island called Wowie or something similar. How did love run out on you like this? How did it run out like a clockwork toy? Did it have to? Did one make it? Or did it truly do it by itself?

He supposed, if he really thought about it, that he imagined there would be something purgative, cathartic, in these stray encounters, that somehow he would puncture a bubble of misdirection, find himself properly back where he belonged, in Candlebury's arms, longing to remain there.

Then Candlebury decamped to Hawaii again. He unravelled further. He drank, he smoked, he guzzled espressos. He sent her flowers and a letter. He wasn't sure she even received them. The only address he had was an office on Maui called "First Space–Sacred Space," which ran the workshop camp she was attending. Eventually he got a five-page letter from her written on lined notepaper explaining that although she loved him it was mostly on the earthly plain, and therefore their relationship could only hold her back in the divine work she had to do during her time on earth. Therefore, much as she continued to love his spirit, they must part and stay out of touch. It hurt her no end, she said. He didn't doubt that it did.

The long night followed. Weeks spiralled on weeks, eddying to the ground dead. Always you hoped to find in your hands once again the cable, the lifeline, but it wasn't there, it never was, you had to make your own way now. Error grew on error, mistake compounded mistake, and while you dreamt of redemption the satanic agents got busy erecting the bars to keep you just where you were, thirsting for deliverance. They liked you that way, craving change, forever deprived of it. You became a sleepwalker sleepwalking through a bereft world, clockworking through friendships, sex, work, everything.

When they moved him off the floor he had a flutter of anger which deepened and delivered him into the dark place through which he trudged. No one could join you there. When he came home from work to his small apartment in the West Village all he wanted was to sit at the counter by the kitchen window staring into the gulf of city night, nose pressed to glass, forehead cooled by the pane, eyes lost in the burning constellations. His girlfriend, if he happened to have one at the time, might touch his shoulder and he'd mumble something which meant: Better not bother. Then came the Latin fiasco. At that point, of course, he ought to have done the noble thing and quit. Shown them there was only so much dishonour he would take. But a working life wasn't exactly a matter of honour. One had mouths to feed, for example, if only one's own. And soon they dumped him anyway. And he had had to scramble for a stool at an unknown bank called Sylvester's. And they too put him on their Latin desk.

He'd think of Candlebury, picture her married to some truck driver or didgeridooist in Hawaii, think of the moral integrity her life must have because it couldn't afford not to. He'd wish with a fresh intensity, as if it were a new discovery, that he had married her, that he'd opted for the life of the soul, not the bank. Every triumph in the bank, not to mention every failure, was another wound to the soul. Amazing that you could get so far down what had appeared to be the right road only to discover that you had lost the one thing worth keeping.

At eight or nine o'clock, when the taxi clicked homeward over the jagged avenues of downtown, he would experience trouble, no other word for it. As the car bounced and rocked, his stream of thought tutted over submerged rocks, thumped over the boulder of a man having thrown away the best thing life had given him. The time when a life could go this way or that had passed. You might realise you had made wrong choices, but it was irrelevant to realise it now. Your only hope was to advance as rapidly as you could along the road ahead, however mistaken. And having seen one's choicelessness, having more or less accepted it, then to find the market shrinking and sinking, to find oneself shifted from the Far East to Eastern Europe to Latin America, watching younger hounds leap into one's place; to see that one had not only selected a course that with hindsight one would not have chosen, but that it was harder, slower, and longer than one could ever have guessed; to find that instead of being rewarded for one's compromises and flexibility, one was effectively being punished, as obstacle piled on obstacle. What was the good of going on if the road was so mistaken? *A lost soul groping in the darkness of remembered ways.*

Well, come on, for Christ's sake, he would tell himself. This has a name, the name is depression. It depressed him no end to be depressed. Sometimes he thought he might die soon, and assumed it would be violent: a Colombian with a gun, a gang of teen warriors. Would he mind? Hardly. There was more too. After two or three years of these thoughts, you had to admit they offered their own perverse solace. At first he had liked to believe that life could not possibly go on as it was. But hell's preference was for persistence. It liked an unpleasant track. It had found one in him and sought no cataclysm. The endless postponement of resolution: that was hell. But then he'd think: stop exaggerating. You've got a job, a roof, money in the bank, at least some money—you call that hell? And he would feel guilty, but chastened, fortified. He could put the madness aside and participate again. And then wake up at four in the morning knowing that he was not, unfortunately, exaggerating. The stakes were very high. They could not be higher. They were called *your life*. And his had gone down the tubes. Week after week, month after month: gone.

He wondered if it might be better never to have been happy, not to know what one was missing.

As his fortunes dwindled, he had turned into a lackey. Or perhaps it worked the other way round: he had turned into a lackey, and therefore fortune had withdrawn her favour. But how had he become a lackey? What had toppled him off the pedestal? How did a prince of finance become a worm? Rotted from within.

Recently he had caught himself staring at a brown suit in a shop window. A brown suit. Uniform of the doomed, of the advisers and sub-brokers, attire that went with blue-carpeted offices out on the G and N lines, under a river or two on the R. Next he'd be having lunch down the block at the big Coffee Shop with a Difference, the Brown Derby, where the waiters wore bow ties and said, "Can I offer you a preprandial cocktail, sir?" "A what?" you were supposed to reply. To which they'd say: "A little eyewash before you attack the menu." Or some such.

Then along comes Panama, with its P, for pipeline, potential, prosperity. No wonder he jumped at the chance.

The little plane shuddered and began to descend. Rogers opened his eyes on a different world. A leopard-skin sea lay below, a silver sea dotted with cloud shadows. Except they weren't shadows but islands, thousands of tiny islands. The engines whined, his ears creaked.

A circle of silver palms moved under the wing, followed by a congestion of thatch floating on the sea. In the middle of the thatch was an open space, a dirt yard. In it Rogers could see naked brown children staring up, each figure pegged to a line of shadow. He glimpsed the plane's crucifix blurring over a roof. Then it flickered over the sea, over sheets of aquamarine and mint green.

He felt a pang of jealousy. Why couldn't he live some-where like this, in a straw hut in a warm sea, with nothing to worry about except the gathering of coconuts and the catching of lobsters?

A man with a gleaming belly of hairless springy flesh, wearing nothing but a dwindling pair of shorts, ferried Rogers and Jones in a small steel boat from the airstrip to the next island.

The water, blue like a pot of paint, ruffled by the breeze, slapped against the prow, sending up buckets of warm spray that landed neatly, tirelessly on Rogers's back. In no time his shirt was drenched. Jones grinned. Rogers smiled back. Jones raised his eyebrows, and just then a bucketful bypassed Rogers and slapped Jones full in the face. His brow furrowed and he allowed a pained smile into his glistening cheeks. Meanwhile, in the stern the pilot silently gazed ahead, planted firmly as a tree trunk in his seat, as if he had learnt over the years, over the generations, over the millennia, to make the sea his ground.

All around lay islands, some close, shimmering with silky palms, others farther off, in receding shades of blue, grey, black, the farthest just charcoal dashes on the horizon, but all of them bathed in a Venetian haziness. Here and there Rogers could make out a gleam of thatch among the trees on some island, and two islands appeared to be nothing but bundles of thatch, like floating medieval compounds. Bright patches of white sail crossed the lagoon. Here and there a canoe made its way from place to place, a figure in the stern ducking and pausing, ducking and pausing as he paddled along. This was a neolithic Venice, a waterworld of canoes and floating homes, the people traveling by dugout among their waterborne houses and villages, the flotilla of multicoloured islands. The iron mountains of the mainland closed off the rest of the world like a wall. Rogers felt, as he looked around, that this wasn't just another country. Countries were all much the same—straggling developments along the airport freeway, the high-rises of some kind of downtown, the villas of a suburb. But this was like arriving in another world, a world still in its original form, existing as it had first been built. Rogers couldn't exactly understand what he felt, except that it excited him. What was this watery suburb, who were these people in their dugout canoes? And why did the scene look so happy? Which it did. Somehow the sea and mountains and islands and dugout paddlers all seemed to belong together.

II

6

"We gots big porpoyce out by the reef," declared Señor Luis.

He was a fat old Indian in shorts and dirty baseball cap and thumped out each syllable of his tourist monologue. The owner of the Hotel Inadule, he lay slumped on a bench in the hotel's yard, one stumpy leg crossed over the other, entertaining his two new guests with his resonant voice.

Along the tin eaves of his hotel, palm fronds rustled listlessly, unable to decide whether to agree with the wind. The fronds had presumably been installed up there to add a native touch. The two plain wood buildings were all empty now because such guests as there were had left for the day. Without differentiating between his usual clientele and these *hommes d'affaires* who had come on a mission, Señor Luis was giving them his normal spiel.

"We gots three hunnerd sixty-fy islas. Yeah. One for every day," he said.

They were sitting in the heart of the village, in the heart of the island of Inadule. Up above, a tall palm shivered in a breeze, its leaves glistening. Sweat ran down Jones's forehead. Rogers was still drenched from the boat but could already feel the suffocating heat. Neither of them could muster the determination to stop the old man wasting his breath.

"You say you want to get to Chichimen?" the old man finally asked.

Jones nodded and said, "Sí, sí," without looking at the man. "We need a boat, pronto."

Señor Luis turned away and blinked in the sunshine.

Rogers was fascinated by another man, who sat slumped in a kind of shack across the yard. He thought it must be a rudimentary shop. The man had long lustrous hair and appeared to be wearing rouge. When he caught Rogers looking at him he lifted his face from his crossed elbows and sent him a broad grin. Rogers looked away in embarrassment.

Two pretty little girls were playing cards in the dirt, in the shade of a bamboo wall. They slapped their cards down one after another. Now and then one would shriek, gather up a pile of cards, and they'd begin again.

In a while Jones stood up. Señor Luis continued to sit with one chunky leg resting on the other and droned on. "Yes, yes, no problem, I get you a boat. The señor doesn't want *molas*?"

Jones gave Rogers a look, then said rapidly: "Sure, let's get some *molas*. Good idea."

Señor Luis whistled through his teeth.

The longhaired man with the rouge lifted his head again, then slapped round from behind his shack in a pair of flip-flops. He wore a bright pink singlet and a towel wrapped round his waist. Without a word he sauntered across the yard, dragging the heels of his sandals, and down an alley between the bamboo houses, pausing to glance back over his shoulder with a tilt of the hips.

"Go with the mans," Luis told them in his voice like emery paper.

As they got up Jones murmured, "Can't come here without buying *molas*."

"Why don't we just tell them why we're here?" Rogers asked in a whisper.

Jones tutted.

"I have a plan. We're going to talk to Don Ramon."

The houses, woven from rushes, with their high palm roofs, were like the longhouses in pictures of Amazonian villages. Inside, through the doorways, Rogers could see naked children playing on the earth floors with sticks, with empty Coke cans, deflated footballs, scampering around among dirty clothes and clay pots. Women swung in hammocks, talking softly as they worked at embroidery in their laps. The houses were all semipermeable. Somewhere, it was hard to say where, a girl was singing in a thin, plaintive voice. Someone else was shaking a rattle. Rogers looked around trying to determine where the singer was, and stepped in a puddle of warm, brown water. He thought: this is a place to go barefoot.

The singer turned out to be a girl of ten or eleven with a long black ponytail, swinging violently back and forth in a hammock in an empty house, with a baby clutched to her chest. When Rogers appeared in her doorway the girl stared at him a moment without stopping. The baby sat mesmerised, eyes glazed in the dark, transported by the rhythmic singing voice and the centrifugal tide in its skull. In the semigloom of the hut the girl looked a little like Paulina. Perhaps she could even be her younger sister, Rogers thought.

Jones came alongside Rogers. The hut darkened. "They sing all the time," he said. "If you can call it singing."

Their guide came back and peered over Rogers's shoulder too. He called out in Cuna and the girl paused, laughed briefly, then carried on her singing.

The man touched Rogers's forearm, a warm, light touch. "She's telling the baby when he grow up he'll be strong and catch a lot of fish and paddle a long way in his canoe. It's school. He has to learn."

Rogers said, "You start school young here."

The man gave a little shudder and patted his cheek. "Otherwise who knows what might happen."

In a small yard several women sat on tree stumps, sewing. It seemed that whenever they had their hands free, the women got busy with their needles. One was hanging washing on a line. Rogers imagined that it would take forever to dry in this damp, hot air. But his own shirt was beginning to stiffen already against his back, after its soaking on the boat. All the women wore gold nose rings half showing at the nostrils, and on their ankles and wrists gypsylike strings of beads.

The man said something which sounded like, "Got two for."

Immediately all the women left off what they were doing and ran silently into the doorways around the yard. One by one they emerged carrying wooden racks draped with squares of colourful cloth. Each woman's rack had a pole which she planted on the ground, holding it like a battle standard. "*Comprame, comprame,*" a chorus of whining voices rose up all around. "*Sólo fy dollars.*"

Fy dollars. Several others picked up the refrain. *Sólo cinco.*

Rogers was alarmed by the sudden bustle and backed off, bumping into the rack of a woman he hadn't seen behind him. She grinned over the top of her wares, seeming to take his bump as a sure sign of a sale, and sheepishly added her own note: *Sólo fy.*

Jones coolly plucked out his wallet and extracted some bills. The chorus amplified at the sight of them, but once Jones had pointed out the four *molas* he wished to buy, each hanging on a different woman's rack, the voices subsided.

Rogers followed his example and endeavoured to pull off a single note from the roll in his pocket. After an embarrassing flutter of several bills to the ground, he managed to get down to one, a fifty, then randomly pointed out several *molas*, losing count, unsure if he had ordered impolitely few and adding two extra. One of the women took his money and disappeared into a hut without being pursued or harassed by any of the others. When she came out again she gave him a ten-dollar bill as change.

Meanwhile, another woman took hold of his arm and before he realised why, she had wound a long strand of beads round his wrist. He was amazed at her dexterity. She snapped the end of the thread in among the beads. When she asked three dollars for it, he couldn't refuse. He wasn't even sure he could have got it off.

It was a hard day, a day of waiting. And hot. No wind reached them. Rogers envied the Cuna men who went about almost naked. His slacks clung to his legs, his shirt to his back.

He decided to go for a swim, and glided out between two little jetties, each of which had a peaked outhouse on the end, like something from a Chinese painting. A cloud of minnows drifted beneath him, glittering, a silver shadow. Even just a few yards out, a calm pervaded the world. The sea looked like silk, flat calm, and the hazy, milky air was filled with the soft sounds of the little village afloat in time, the sounds of humanity at peace with itself: children laughing, someone calling out for help with something, a knock-knock of wood on wood from someone at work.

Rogers felt at peace too. A moment of delirious happiness swept through him, he felt sure things would change for him, change in a good way, though he had no idea how. This world seemed instinct with hopefulness, as if the people carried hope in every muscle. It would infect him too.

Señor Luis, a stump of a man, a well-planted, stocky rolling bean of a man, a man neither hurricane nor tidal wave could upset, was on his feet when Rogers returned to the hotel yard.

"Right, right," Luis called. "This man, he go take you, he know where to go."

Another Indian, sullen, dressed in a singlet and an Esso baseball cap, sat on the back of a bench, elbows on knees, hands clasped in front. He glanced at Rogers, then turned away and spat.

Rogers had never understood the language of spitting. What did it mean? Did it mean anything at all?

"You haves to pay," Luis added. "He gonna take you."

Jones drew himself up, loafers neatly together. "He knows Chichimen?"

Señor Luis frowned. "Yes, yes," he said in a bored voice. "He know all about it. Hundred dollars."

"*Bueno*," Jones said.

To Rogers it sounded like a lot of money. Perhaps it would be a long trip. Or else Jones didn't want to rock the boat. For all they knew, their business might already be suspected, they might already be watched men.

Their pilot climbed into a waiting canoe and fired up the outboard. Jones and Rogers clambered down into the boat. Rogers, alarmed at its pitching, felt increasingly encumbered by his urban clothes and shoulder bag. As they motored out, they saw all around the shore the canoes waiting on log rollers, their prows tipped clear of the water. They, their ranked savage prows, and the intermittent outhouses on stilts at the end of the little jetties, were the first and last thing you saw of the island village. They gave it an exotic, menacing look from outside. Gradually the island shrank behind them, coalescing into a single impression of sunstruck straw topped by thin palms.

Many islands passed, some tiny, sustaining a single solitary palm tree like desert islands in a cartoon, others large, showing as distant ink stains on the horizon. Here and there among the glistening palms of the closer islands a golden roof caught the light. Otherwise, the islands formed blocks of watercolour, from iridescent green to faded blue, troubled grey to charcoal black, and as the boat forged through the open waters between them, they seemed to rearrange themselves constantly along the skyline, scuttling back and forth like beetles.

Rogers fell into reverie with the motion of the boat.

Fifteen minutes of fame are not as important as fifteen minutes of adventure, he was thinking. A beautiful woman and a beautiful home were not after all enough, if one possessed them for their beauty. Beautiful people were boring in the end. All the lanky young men with peroxide crew cuts, the skinny small-bottomed girls strutting the sidewalks of SoHo with their ballerina necks and dolls' faces—they amounted to a city's wallpaper, that was all. They prettified the environment. One day they'd be fat or bald or ugly or all three, and even then they still might believe nothing mattered more than those glorious years when they had had their day, when they had strutted the avenues in the gorgeous company of one another, and believed the city belonged to them. Now they had the real estate and it wasn't worth a fraction of what they'd had, they might think. But they would be wrong. Beauty was the wrong god.

He too had been duped. He was a fashion victim of a sort, had led a life, or tried to, effectively sheltered within the pages of the glossies. He had never touched anything real. It was inevitable if you made Wall Street your home. Clouds of perfume, veils of designer clothes, forests of mannequins had blocked his view of the real world for so long now perhaps it was better not to wake up to it.

Rogers got used to the intermittent drenching of the ride. Anyway, the water was warm. He wished he had a hat, though. The thrumming of the engine in his seat, the sparkles on the water that made one squint, the gentle heaving of the boat, all lulled him.

He remembered a time as a kid when he and the Jericho Street gang had dropped over the wall from Billy Thornton's, all four of them, into Mr. Watson's garden. It was early autumn and Rogers was back from two weeks in Cornwall with his family. The gang, previously a loose consortium, had formalised in his absence.

They were looking for worms. Rogers was going to have to eat one. That was standard practice among gangs. Billy Thornton had found a garden fork and was raking through the soil, holding the large implement just above its tines, awkwardly scraping the lumps of soil behind the bean plants, then breaking through them with his fingers.

Eventually, inevitably, Billy found a worm. Until then Rogers had not worried or really even thought about the trial ahead. Whatever the others had done he could surely do too. And on the other hand it seemed unreal and improbable that it would really come to it. Now Billy had a worm dangling from a prong of the fork and he was excitedly saying, "Come on, come on, take it." With the result that all the others hissed at him to lower his voice. Which was unnecessary. Mr. Watson's house was far away across an expanse of blue suburban lawn, beyond a hedge.

The worm was long, rosy, quite fat, and hung limply, as if dead, until Billy waved the fork about, whereupon it writhed energetically, almost succeeding in freeing itself from its prison in the air. "Come on," Billy said.

The others were silent, watching. Rogers stepped closer. "Put it down," he said.

Billy Thornton tipped the fork over the flagstone path, making the worm drop in a self-contorting knot. The others moved closer. "Ugh," one of them said.

"Shut up," Billy told him.

Rogers knelt in front of the creature, one knee on soil which quickly dampened and cooled his trouser, the other on the path. The worm was in a frenzy, desperate to find earth. Rogers put his hand towards it, thinking he might at least take the step of picking it up. It occurred to him then that if he was about to eat the worm he was also about to kill it, in which case the matter was between him and the worm, no one else. He didn't want to eat it any more than it wanted to be eaten. If neither he nor the worm wanted it to happen, then why proceed?

He tore a stalk of dry grass from the path and after several attempts which the worm was keen to resist managed to prod it beneath the animal's body, somewhere near the middle.

"With your hands," Billy said.

"Bare hands," someone agreed.

But Rogers simply flicked the worm away among the beans. "You can keep your silly worm," he told them. "And your gang."

Distantly a lawn mower droned, a car hissed by on the street. The others started calling him a sissy, a coward, none of which he minded. He had guessed by now that none of them had really eaten any worms. Except possibly Billy Thornton, he was just ill-tempered enough.

On Wall Street he had sometimes thought of that day as a key to his early success: listening to no one, making your own decisions. Now, in the boat, he saw the episode in a different light. There was a warmth to it that had escaped him, something tender. It no longer even seemed especially significant, just in some way nice. He had behaved gently, like a monk.

Of all the islands strung along the horizon, one began to expand from a charcoal smear into a breadth of vivid green. That was clearly the one they were heading for. It was like seeing your destiny emerge from vaporous suggestion into solid form. As they came off the bigger waves and onto the swells running into the island's lagoon, a sudden peace, and more than that, awe, swept over Rogers. The green, feathered water, the distant line of a reef beyond—the whole scene had something timeless, immemorial, about it. It was like motoring into some picture, some fantasy world, the world of a visionary painter.

Four figures appeared on a steep beach by the shore of the green lagoon. It was late afternoon, the palms struck by sidelong light, enflamed by the last of the sun, tossing their heads like horses in a reef breeze. Rogers studied the figures, his heart in his throat, and couldn't make out if any of them was the girl.

He tripped as he dropped into the surf, soaking his trousers. The people on shore all laughed. When he waded up onto the dry sand they were still grinning. But there were only three people after all. Perhaps one had gone inside a hut, or perhaps there had only ever been three.

An old man with cropped white hair and a few stumps of broken teeth swayed about on a walking stick wedged in the sand. Another man wearing a torn green polo shirt stood nearby with arms crossed like a totem pole, much the tallest Cuna Rogers had seen, wavy-haired, with an expressionless face like a tree trunk. The third figure was a woman with an ageless face, who chatted away, it wasn't clear to whom, undoing then tightening a wrap round her short sleek body and letting out a high-pitched giggle.

Just then, walking up the shore of a diminutive island lost in a corner of the Caribbean, Rogers could not believe that the pipeline was a real venture. Here they were, two men of finance stepping barefoot on to a desert island. This was not the way pipelines got built. Pipelines were surely a matter of boardroom tables, gala lunches, limousines meeting ministers at airports. Or maybe they did in fact begin like this. That was possible too, and the limos came later. Who knew the earliest origins of great schemes?

The woman stepped down the sand jerkily, with a limp, and seized Rogers's hand. Her grip was strong, yet soft, warm. Talking in the local language, she led him up to the small old man, still balancing on his wooden peg.

Perhaps he was in charge. The old man smiled, his eyes creasing up. "Yeah, I'm Don Ramon," he said. "You come to Chichimen Isla." He removed a knobbly hand from his stick and held it out for Rogers.

The man's eyes sparkled. The sight of that buried smile made Rogers impatient. He had an inkling everything was going to take unnecessarily long. Where was the girl? They ought to just find her and be gone. And as soon as they had disembarked, the boat reversed off the beach and motored straight out of the lagoon. Rogers could see the little craft now, climbing the face of a wave, appearing in outline against the sky, then vanishing. Its gurgle was soon swallowed by the distant roar of the reef that showed as a white line a few hundred yards away, roaring like a waterfall.

Don Ramon dislodged his stick and shuffled up the beach, beckoning. "*Bienvenidos, Señor Albert,*" he said.

7

Inside the nearest hut a veil of smoke hung over what looked like a decades-old fire of smouldering coconut husks. A second old man sat in front of it, fanning the embers with a sheet of woven palm, producing a flurry of sparks and a crackle of fat, as a rack of grilling sardines dripped onto the fire. A line of smoke climbed towards the stained roof.

It seemed chilly inside the hut. Altogether, cold and dark and smoke-blackened and messy, strewn with odds and ends—a broken table with four labelless bottles, a pair of spread-eagled inside-out trousers, half a Frisbee, sweet wrappers, broken coconut husks, two thin old hammocks, three lopsided palm stumps—the hut was not welcoming.

Don Ramon dropped onto one of the stumps and sat gazing out the door.

"May we?" Jones gestured at the other seats.

"Sit yourselves down," he said neutrally.

The three sat in silence, listening to the lapping lagoon and intermittent cracks from the fire. Half a mile offshore that reef, which lay at the edge of Cuna territory, still roared like distant thunder, like an avalanche on the other side of a mountain, like a hum in the back of the mind. Beyond it was the open sea.

Rogers coughed and quietly asked Jones: "Does he know why we're here?"

Jones seemed a big man now that they were squatting on the logs. He cleared his throat. "Most pitifully and regretfully," he began in his best Castilian, using a tone of almost ironic deference that Rogers had not heard before, "it has been too long since I have been able to visit the land of Kuna Yala." He pronounced the last two words emphatically, like a native in a Hollywood movie.

The old man hawked out the door and stared at Jones a moment, eyes sparkling.

"We're still here. We always have a hammock for you."

"Thank you."

"Yeah," Don Ramon droned. "Things trucking along down here *just* the *same* as ever." He spoke in a singsong, going high on the "same."

Jones unzipped his holdall and pulled out a small black carrier bag with a gold V on it. Rogers recognised it as a Valentino bag from some fashion boutique. Jones handed it to Don Ramon, who grinned and said, "Yes, yes," and put it on the ground between his feet. "Anything you need, you let me know."

Rogers glanced at Jones. "You know these people?"

Jones shrugged.

"You've always been supremely helpful to us," Jones said, reverting to his textbook Spanish. "Just now we find ourselves in a quandary, this señor and I. A bit of a quandary."

"Yeah man," Don Ramon said, in a West Indian–sounding growl. "So what's up?"

Jones frowned and smiled at once. "We're looking for someone. This man, a trusted associate of mine, he wants to find a girl. Some girl he met. Wants to see her again. He's . . . well, he likes her."

"She a Cuna girl?"

Jones nodded.

"Yeah, some of them real nice."

"She's lovely, so he says," Jones went on. "Called Paulina. Met her in Panama City."

The other old man who had been squatting in front of the fire now brought over three of the cooked fish. The fish arrived on a circle of white plastic with numbers round the edge, an old clock face. Where did that come from? Rogers wondered. It was as if someone had demolished a department store and these people had filched whatever scraps they found in the rubble. The real source, Rogers guessed, must be the sea, the tides, the Walmart of the waves bringing in the flotsam of modern life. Don Ramon began to munch on a fish, eating it whole.

Rogers heard voices outside. It was the woman and the tall man. Rogers could make them out through the palm-frond wall. The woman giggled in a delighted squeal.

"Paulina you say?" Ramon asked, plucking up another fish by its tail. "We'll find her. Ask around, like you say. Could take a few days." He bit off the head.

Rogers had the feeling just then that to see the girl again would be to make himself doubly a fool.

Don Ramon continued to eat his meal. Rogers asked him where he had learnt his English.

"I work in the Zone ten year, then Pop die and I come home. Seventeen year I haven't left the island, not one day."

He nodded and hummed. "We got four thousand palms here, twelve peoples."

He looked like an old Chinese man, in his ragged, filthy slacks held up with rope. The lined face, the creased eyes—you could see he was of the original race that had crossed the Bering Straits from Asia twenty thousand years ago. His forebears had presumably wandered the continent, until one band, his, had pitched up on this island with their canoes and palm houses, and had been living here ever since. Home to four thousand palm trees and twelve human beings. Fourteen tonight.

"Paulina," Don Ramon repeated, and wiped his hands on his trousers, as he was evidently used to doing, judging by the state of his clothes. He glanced at Rogers. "So you like her." He looked away. "So what's she like? A *gordita*?"

"She's slim, quite tall."

"A *flaquita* then. Works in Panama." He said something to the other old man, who got up from his broken plastic chair by the fire and sauntered out the door. "Yeah, we'll find her for you."

"You know her?" Rogers asked.

"Yeah, yeah," Don Ramon answered, in a voice suggesting nothing but apathy.

Jones pulled a cell phone from his trousers, snapped out the aerial, and dialled a number, then walked outside. Don Ramon didn't show the kind of surprise Rogers would have expected at the appearance of a cell phone in the Stone Age. But from outside there came another long peal of laughter in the gathering dark of the lonely cay. The woman was still out there. Her voice rose in pitch and speed, until it sprinted off a cliff of a punchline and she let out the biggest cackle yet. A deep thump of a laugh joined in, emanating from the chest of the tall man. It seemed that these two were not going to enter the hut, but carry on their own little get-together outside.

There was a moment of silence in which Jones could be heard saying, "*Sí sí sí, Colombia.*"

Colombia was not far. Perhaps Jones would be able to call there directly. Rogers wondered why he would want to.

There was a click, which Rogers guessed was Jones snapping shut the phone, then a lot of beeping and buzzing as he apparently tried dialling again.

Then a naked man walked into the hut. He strolled up to the broken table, drank from a plastic jug, leaning right back to tip it up, and let out a belch. A cotton wrap hung over his shoulder and he wore a tight singlet over his chubby torso, but otherwise, down below, he was stark naked, openly displaying his bald brown genitalia, the drooping shaft of which was the size of a small banana. He had the same long wave of hair the rouged man on Inadule had had. He unfurled his wrap and snapped it round his waist, then shuffled across the room, brushing past Rogers and Don Ramon, mincing out the door and onto the beach. He spoke rapidly to the woman, and the two of them then traipsed off down the sand. Rogers made out their retreating figures through the palm mesh.

What was it with these camp men? Was there one on every island? It was unusual enough to encounter such exaggerated effeminacy at home, but among these simple tribal types? Rogers began to feel uncomfortable. These people were weird, they had a screw loose. Not only that, but they were just going about their daily business, making no visible allowance for their visitors. Nothing was being done for them. Night was as good as fallen. Where were Jones and he supposed to sleep, for example? No one seemed to care. What were they going to eat? No one had added any more fish to that fire. Quite the reverse. The old man had pulled off the charred glistening bodies of the sardines and laid them in a cracked Frisbee, then broken up the fire. And how on earth would they find the girl among all these islands?

When Jones came back in, Rogers asked him, "Get through?" As he spoke, he felt like the unpopular boy at college asking yet another dreary question. What did he care if Jones had got through to anyone? Jones shrugged and sat down.

Rogers began to panic. It alarmed him to be facing a night of discomfort. He came under threat of another attack, a harsh one, he felt himself turn sour inside at the thought of being bitten alive by mosquitoes, of freezing on damp sand, of going to bed, whatever bed was, on an empty stomach. Years ago he had backpacked and roughed it, and on tour with Candlebury he had spent the odd makeshift night curled on the mats of dance studios after late rehearsals. Once he had slept in the aisle of the dance company bus, driving between Cincinnati and St. Louis. He had slept on the carpeted floors of crowded motel rooms too, letting her share the bed with her female colleagues. And these in retrospect had been some of the most enjoyable nights. But that was all years ago. Now comfort was necessary to him. It sickened him to realise it, because he knew that really he didn't believe in comfort, never had, yet it was too late to stop living as if he did. Why? Because everyone else did. Because why else work in a bank for fifteen years? Because how was he, one solitary individual, supposed to succeed in living a life that actually made sense, when no one else did? That his career had bellied out, to put it politely, that he no longer enjoyed any of the flights of luck, of intuition, that he used to, that he never got on a roll and let himself go, creaming thousands in minutes, blowing them on limousines and dinners—that that kind of life was over didn't exactly bother him. He was approaching forty, after all. You couldn't keep living like that forever, perhaps. But one way or another he had grown accustomed to comfort. And not just accustomed but attached. Comfort assuaged the soul. Why was the soul tormented, though? Because that was life for you. You neared forty and maybe you had done all right, had done the things you planned, but most likely you hadn't, most likely you had turned off the right path a long time ago only you hadn't noticed, or had chosen not to notice, until pretty soon you couldn't fail to notice, and by then you had lost loves, brides, mortgages, portfolios, and it was too late to do anything but shrug and say: So I have disappointed myself, life goes on. And it was easier to maintain that kind of attitude in *comfort*. That was the point. A man of a certain age and predicament needed his dinner, his armchair, his cognac, his firm bed. He needed mollycoddling, whether as reward or solace. Why? Because he felt like a fool without it.

He thought of Candlebury again. She was remoter than ever, a silhouette, a permanent profile in his mind.

But it wasn't just the prospect of a chilly, sweaty, itchy night that bothered him. It was also the constant din of the reef offshore, thundering faintly like a half-forgotten memory—like the ruler line at the margin of the page, the dark beyond the edge of consciousness.

Jones picked up a stick and doodled in the sand between his bare feet.

Rogers felt something nip his ankle. He brushed the skin with his hand then decided to put on his socks and shoes. He picked them up and went out and sat on one of the logs they used for rolling the canoes up the sand, and spent a long time dusting off his feet. Someone lit a lamp inside the hut. The whole building lit up like a lantern, striped with light, a tiger-skin dwelling. The water of the lagoon was black except for fringes of white on wavelets slapping the beach.

Rogers calmed down. Whatever problems he had, they were not physically present right now. If his life was a mess then he must tidy it up. It was possible to do so. But that idea produced another plunge, for it was equally possible to mess up one's life to a degree where it was beyond tidying.

He got himself under control again. All he really needed, he thought, was a break from worry. A streak of phosphorescence shot through the lagoon nearby like a shooting star, and he decided to take it as some kind of auspicious augury.

8

The longhaired man who dressed like a woman said, "I'm Jorge." He gave a little shrug as if to prove it, then led them to the hut where they were to sleep.

It had only one wall. Dry fronds hung down from its roof. The boom of the reef ran right through it, and you could hear the waves breaking on the beach, coming in larger here than on the lagoon side.

Jones brushed a hand through his hair. "This is an old house."

Jorge spun around. "*Qué?*" he said, resting one foot on the other, arms crossed in front.

Jones hesitated, then said softly, "When was the house built?"

"This house?" Jorge limp-wristedly batted his mouth, shrugged his shoulders, then held a hand out, palm downwards. "Since I was that high."

The man was not just outrageously camp, but camp in just the way you might find in the West Village. Same gestures, same persona. It was uncanny.

There were two hammocks. Rogers tested his weight on one. It was thin, thin in every sense: the fabric threadbare, barely stronger than an old tea towel, and barely the width of Rogers's shoulders, not wide enough to contain him. Without even trying to raise his legs into it he could see that it wasn't going to be long enough.

Oh well. Perhaps he'd sleep on the beach. Perhaps he'd figure out how to untie the hammock—though that looked unlikely, judging by the huge knots at either end—and simply spread it on the ground. Perhaps he'd just be up all night. There might be a certain pleasure to that: a vigil on a lonely little island in the farthest corner of the Caribbean, in a total backwater, a real desert island.

Rogers said: "You'd think the hurricanes would have pulled this place down by now."

Jorge answered with sudden animation: "The hurricanes never come here." He shook his hair away from his face. "When they try to come we all go on to the beach with pots and pans and bang them, we make as much noise as we can. The hurricane hears us and goes away." He gave a lame smile and let a kind of shiver run through him.

Rogers cleared his throat. "You scare it away?" He was rather appalled by the man.

Jorge let out a high giggle that cascaded into an emphatic "No, no, no! We tell him where we are. A hurricane is a bad pilot. He's got lost. When he hears us he knows where he is and goes away. He's just trying to find his way."

Rogers shook his head and glanced at Jones. But Jones was already rocking in his hammock, facing the other way, hands clasped behind his neck.

Suddenly Jorge let out a falsetto whoop and doubled up with laughter. "I forgot," he exclaimed, like it was the funniest thing imaginable. "Do you two *caballeros* want to eat some fish?"

Supper—four small grilled fish and a lump of yucca—arrived on a cracked, worn Frisbee. The woman brought it over, and gabbled away in rapid Cuna as she set the meal on an old crate. From inside her clothes she produced a bottle of Maggi tomato sauce. She cocked her head, spreading her hands, then stomped out of the house with her brisk limp. Rogers felt a spasm of gratitude.

They ate with their fingers. The fish was delicious, tasting faintly of coconut, and even the yucca was sweet and creamy, like a giant sweet potato, and had been cooked to the perfect consistency so you could break off chunks that melted in the mouth. He had not realised how hungry he was. "All we need now is a beer," he said.

Jones passed over a handkerchief for Rogers to wipe his hands on. "I've got a cigar," he intoned like a question, reaching for his bag. He unzipped a side pocket and fumbled inside. He lifted out a little cardboard box not much bigger than a matchbox, which rattled as he passed it to his other hand, then returned it, with another chortle of its contents, to the pocket. Then he extracted two slender cigars from the bag.

Was that a box of nails? Rogers wondered. Screws? Staples? But why bring them here?

The conditions didn't bother Jones. That was the difference between third world man and first: in the third world even the wealthy had had some experience of discomfort. They still possessed some sinew of endurance lost to civilised man. You noticed it only when circumstances called it forth. Jones now acted as calmly and stoically as a man who had known innumerable sleepless bus journeys, who was used to eating watery soup off market benches beneath which he would later sleep. He rummaged in his bag, unbuttoned his shirt, hung it from a nail on the house pillar, a nail which he found as readily as if he had known where to look, and pulled on a Yale sweatshirt. The more at ease Jones appeared, the lonelier Rogers felt.

The sweatshirt seemed like a good idea. Rogers pulled out a bundled-up windbreaker from his bag and the two men rested in their hammocks, not talking, puffing on their panatellas while the thunder of the reef grew, invading the shelter like an advancing storm.

At a certain point—an hour or two later—Rogers realised that this was night already, night had arrived and they had gone to bed. They were simply going to half sit, half lie in their diminutive hammocks all night long. His cigar had long since gone out, and he didn't want to disturb Jones for a light.

A storm did in fact arrive in the night. It announced itself with a soft flicker like a strip light trying to turn itself on. Then it murmured from far away, detaching its voice from the low roar of the sea. A series of explosions clattered forth, falling down the sky like fireworks, and an angry flashing began: a sharp crackle of a retort, followed by a gurgle like the sound of someone clearing their throat, but heard through a stethoscope.

"Jesus," Rogers said quietly, wondering if Jones was awake.

Silence. Then Jones's voice, low and clear. "Beautiful, no? They have the best storms here. Won't be long."

Rogers didn't know if that meant long in coming, or in staying. He got up and walked out through the palms to the strip of beach. The darkness fell open, revealing a cloudscape of enormous thunderheads. They looked like a painting. Scared, Rogers returned to the shelter. And just in time, for the wind had died down completely, replaced by a cloying stillness, an unnatural warmth, out of which exploded a hissing roar.

Rain fell hard for a quarter of an hour, a deafening surf crash that eased suddenly. Then a tap-tap of drops from the roof found Rogers's cheek. When he rolled his head out of the way he could feel the drops drumming on the taut cloth of his hammock, gradually drenching it. Half the night he couldn't tell if he was asleep or awake.

Morning. Outside, the palms made a kind of forecourt as in some ruined hotel, littered with pebbles and old coconuts, as if the servants had long neglected to sweep. The air was milky, sunless. A curtain of oyster-shell clouds hung around the horizon. The place seemed oddly familiar, ordinary, reminding Rogers of an abandoned construction site, as if nature and industry came up with the same moods when left to their own devices. The sound of the reef brought back the night, disturbing the morning with its troubled note.

There was no sign of Jones.

Rogers's limbs were stiff in a way that seemed to suit the cloudy morning. He stripped off and swam in a channel right off the beach. The water had no morning chill. He looked at his pale brown shoulders, the colour of milky coffee in the turquoise water, and thought he'd like to see them go nutty brown, become the shoulders of a lean man living in a lean-to on a coconut island. What a thought. And what was there that really would prevent it?

Rogers spotted a white sail against a distant island. Just then he heard a creak, and turned round in time to see a canoe, fully rigged with mast and patchwork sail, scuttling down the channel towards him, not twenty yards away. He paddled back and stumbled up the beach.

Four people filled the craft, a woman, two children, and a man in the stern holding a paddle vertically in the water. They all stared at Rogers as they passed. No one said anything. The man joggled his paddle. Rogers heard the wind scuffle with the sail. The apparition was gone as quickly as it had come.

He walked round to the lagoon, where Don Ramon's hut was. There was no sign of anyone, except for one small figure sitting motionless in a canoe far out on the water. Whoever it was must have been fishing.

Back in the hut Jones was swaying in his hammock. Rogers asked to borrow his cell phone.

"Battery's dead."

"How long are we going to be here? I've got to call New York. I haven't spoken to anyone since the day before yesterday."

Jones didn't reply. A distance seemed to have grown up between them since they arrived on the islands. Jones had turned into a tough man of few words. He even looked different. His snowy hair matched his leathery face in a new way, and his tan no longer seemed a salon product but the result of a tough life. He had shed his boardroom manners as easily as his suit. Faint dimples had appeared in his face too, making it look weathered. It reminded Rogers of a drunk Colombian he had once met in a bar in Barranquilla. He began to wonder if things had got out of hand. It was all very well to have a bit of fun and lose the suit for a couple of days, but here he was stuck on an island in the middle of nowhere with no means of transport, with a man he hardly knew.

Jones sat up in his hammock, rocking himself gently back and forth with his feet. He looked at Rogers. "Nice place, no?"

"I guess," Rogers said.

"A man could build himself a nice villa here, a dream house. Retire. You think about retiring?"

Rogers thought about it, and no, he didn't think about retiring.

"I guess that's for later," Jones went on. "All I really want for now is to get myself totally legit. I'm through with the war."

"The war?"

"This is Panama, man. No one's legit until they're rich enough to be, then they get out of the battle zone. Don't play naive. Where do you think people put their money down here? In banks? No, you go buy a stake in a transit operation, five times out of six something goes wrong, but you only need it to go right once in six. Russian roulette, man. Blam, when that baby hits, it hits big. A thousand percent easy. You give me ten thousand dollars, it may take me a year and a few tries, but I'm going to give you back a hundred grand. And that's allowing for the fuckups. Everybody does it, everyone's in a consortium. Only thing is, the more you put in, the more control you want. It's only natural. But you get too close, it gets hairy. We're not talking guns down here. More like subs, torpedoes, rockets, the whole deal. This is a war, that's why they call it a war."

Rogers didn't know what to say. The man was obviously talking about drugs. But that drug runners had submarines?

"Yeah, everyone's in on it, even the fucking Russians. Used to help out M-19, the Marxist guerrillas in Colombia. They made a lot of contacts there. Half the cocaine that got into the US used to come in Russian subs, at least part of the way. Undermining the enemy. Anyway, I'm through with it. I want my returns another way. That's why Carreras brought me in. I know the scene. I know the players, how to deal with them. This island, for example. Why you think we're here?"

"I thought we were looking for the girl."

"I know these people. They used to put me up from time to time when I was waiting for a drop or whatever. This is a nice, quiet place, well out of the way. If anybody's going to help us, Don Ramon will. He knows everyone. They all know each other down here."

Rogers frowned, feeling even more alarmed. "Why should he help us?"

"Why not? He always gets something from me. He and Jorge. He hates to leave the island, so he says, but there are things he misses. Marlboros and whisky and steak. I used to keep him stocked up. Other things too, not for him but his *friend*."

Jones put an enigmatic emphasis on the word.

"Friend?" Rogers had to ask.

"Jorge and Don Ramon—" Jones flicked up his eyebrows. "Jorge likes things, magazines, cosmetics, makeup, that crap. All the fashion stuff. And clothes. I used to bring a load of

Dior and Lancôme every time I came. Keep him sweet for Don Ramon."

"You're kidding me."

"No way, man. That's what they do down here. They have two kinds of women, it's a traditional thing."

Rogers exhaled slowly. This was all more information than he needed. He had had his suspicions about Jones, it was only natural when you dealt in this part of the world. But that the man should be so open about it—he didn't want to hear it. And that Jones was in cahoots with these odd people only made Rogers more desolate.

"Anyway." Jones tipped himself out of his hammock on to his feet. "Time to check in with Don Ramon. See if they've figured out who she is."

Which they had.

"Yeah," Don Ramon said, when they had settled on the tree stumps in his hut. "The girl you're looking for, we calls her Nikiri. Nikiri is a turtle."

The old man glanced at Rogers. "She a bad girls. You catch a turtle, leave it one minute it's gone. Look slow but man they fast. Only way to keep a turtle once you got him you got to turn him on his back. That's why we call she Turtle."

"You know where she is?" Jones asked.

Don Ramon glanced at him. "Maybe. We go find her. Got to get a boat ready. Go looking."

Rogers wondered what it would be like to see the girl in the flesh, to be face to face with her again. She could hardly be happy to see him. But what about him? Why wasn't he angrier with her? She had defrauded and robbed him, yet he felt in a vague way that he owed her something, as if her actions had been justified and his hadn't.

"Reckon she's a long way down Kuna Yala. On Rio Tigre," Ramon went on.

"Where's that?"

"One of the last islands, man," Jones explained. "Practically Colombia."

The rest of the morning passed slowly, as they attempted to organise a boat. There wasn't much Rogers could do to help. His watch, normally reliable, stopped at ten to eight. He walked round the island. The side that faced the mainland was warmer and scruffier. In the distance rose a dark-grey bank, the forested Isthmus of Darien. Old coconuts littered the beach, along with a waterlogged dugout and cracked sheets of fibreglass from some old launch. Dried weeds that looked like pine needles had been brushed by the waves into little arcs, like hundreds of disembodied eyebrows.

He felt oddly excited, like a kid on summer holiday. They had figured out where the girl was, now all they had to do was get there. Meanwhile, he could explore the island. *Explore the island*: were there any more exciting words? He couldn't think when he had last been on an island. And he looked forward to seeing the girl again. Who knew what might happen? He could even decide to drop out and marry an island girl. What a way to do it, here in the aboriginal Caribbean. It wouldn't be like opening up some Rum Runners' bar in Antigua with burgers and Bud on tap and a steel band on Friday nights. This was the real thing, more Crusoe than Crusoe, a whole society living like Crusoe except they had been doing it for thousands of years. They had none of Crusoe's cupidity, all his ingenuity. How could a man get rich here, even if he wanted to? He might hoard coconuts and dried fish, presumably, but why bother, when they were in limitless supply anyway? In fact, he couldn't imagine anyone wanting to grow rich here. There was just no need. Their husbandry was subtle and secure. They didn't hoard because they didn't need to.

There was a second homestead round the other side, three or four huts just like Don Ramon's, with a rudimentary bamboo table beside a blackened outdoor fire pit.

As Rogers passed it a man in black satin shorts appeared in the doorway of one of the huts. He glared at Rogers. Rogers waved but the man didn't respond, and after a moment he went back inside.

Then a little boy came out chewing on a wooden doll. He smiled at Rogers. He couldn't have been older than two or three. The same man scooped him up from behind with a skinny brown arm, and pulled him back in the hut. Then the man reappeared alone.

"Who you looking for?" he asked.

Rogers was taken aback, and literally stepped backwards, catching his breath. He was about to answer, No one, when it occurred to him that it might be worth a try, and said, "Paulina. I think they call her Nikiri here."

"Nikiri? She ain't on the island here. She over there." The man nodded towards the east, either at the next island or down the chain of islands.

"You know her?"

"Sure. She with her father. He works for Don Ramon with the palms there. They got ten thousand trees on the island. Lot a work."

"You know where she is?"

The man looked at him. "Sure. She just there. Next

island. She come a couple days back. You find her there. Achutupu, Pelican Isla."

Rogers didn't know what to make of this information, and decided to ask Jones about it later. He wandered on round the island.

Jones had changed into a pair of shorts and a red T-shirt. He stooped under his hammock and reached for his bag just as Rogers shuffled into the hut. He zipped up the top of the bag, but halfway along he had to stop to push a small tube out of the way. Rogers saw it. Perhaps it was some kind of pen, or some kind of scuba gear, or even the tip of a collapsible coat hanger, he thought. Except he knew exactly what it was: the barrel of a gun, an old-fashioned Lugerlike handgun. And Jones had tried to hide it. Why? Rogers knew people in New York who carried guns. He wouldn't be surprised to learn it was customary in Panama City. Briefcase, wallet, handgun. Spectacles, testicles, wallet, and Walther. Why hide it?

On the other hand, Jones had packed his bag. That could only be a good sign. Rogers imagined leaving the island right away, and thought that already he would feel a certain nostalgia for it. "We off?" he asked.

"Sure are. They've got the boat together. Let's go. Pack your stuff."

Rogers was about to tell him what he had heard from the man on the other side of the island, but decided to keep quiet for the moment. If Don Ramon had a reason for not letting on where she really was and instead sending them down to the far end of the archipelago, it might be better to wait until they had left his island before mentioning it.

They sat on log rollers by the lagoon. Rogers felt like a lad on holiday idling time away. After a while Carmelita the woman and Jorge the effeminate one came out onto the beach and stopped in their tracks. They whooped and waved, then disappeared into the farthest hut.

A faint buzzing, the buzz of a fly, detached itself from the thunder of the reef. A small boat appeared in the mouth of the lagoon, a canoe without a mast, its prow riding high. When it was a few yards offshore Rogers saw what a strange-looking man the boatman was: white, not as in Anglo, but utterly white, with skin like paper and bloodshot eyes.

Don Ramon emerged from his hut, a derby hat perched on the back of his head. Rogers asked, "Is he all right?"

"They calls that a moon boy," Don Ramon said. "Shouldn't be out in that boat, they don't likes the sun and the sun don't like them. They got a short life, those people."

The man was wearing a red baseball cap that exaggerated his unearthly complexion. He brought his boat into the beach just hard enough to lodge it on the sand. The stern began to drift as Jones, without a word or a wave, waded straight out into the water, shoes and all, and clambered aboard. Rogers followed him, slinging his bag into the trough of the boat. The boatman withdrew the prow with a rev of the motor, then let it idle a moment as he changed out of reverse gear, and they began to move towards the mouth of the lagoon.

Once the boatman had ridden them out of the lagoon and into the calm waters of the island chain, where the green water gave way to blue, Rogers turned round from his place at the canoe's prow and said to Jones, "I don't know if I believe Don Ramon."

Jones smiled a little patronisingly and shrugged. "What does it matter?"

"I mean about the girl." He told Jones what the other islander had told him.

Jones squinted across the waves. "Which island?"

"Somewhere called Pelican Island."

They had been traveling only ten minutes but already Rogers was disoriented. It took him a moment even to figure out which green oblong was the island they had just left. It had a blue half to it, presumably farther away than the rest, that confused him. There were three or four islands that could have been the one the man had meant, each a dash of grey-green, smoky in the morning sun. As he stared at them, the sparkle on the early sea dazzled him and became too bright.

Jones tapped the boatman's shoulder and waved his hand down. The man eased up on the throttle, which made the small engine sputter, falter, and die, and the dugout glided silently through the wavelets.

Jones was sitting in the middle of the tiny boat with his elbows resting on his bare knees. Silver hairs covered his legs. Rogers stared at them and wondered if he had totally mis-judged this man's age. He had assumed he was only a little older than himself. "So what's all this about?" Jones asked.

The boatman meanwhile was busy at the outboard with the cowling off, wrapping the cord of rope round the spindle. He gave it a sharp tug and the engine coughed.

"Well, that other guy, like I said, told me she was staying just on the next island, with her dad."

"How did he know?"

Rogers could only shrug and add, "He seemed to know exactly who I meant."

Jones frowned. "Rio Tigre is like the last island in the

chain. It could take us most of the day to get there. Especially at this rate."

The albino boatman had failed again to get the motor started. Now he removed its metal manifold and adjusted a nut with his fingers. The boat pitched as he tugged the cord again. It started at the next try, and he kept it revving high in neutral, pouring a stream of blue, fragrant smoke and spitting gobbets of water. The man's pale hands shone under a film of wetness.

Jones spoke to him in rapid guttural Spanish. Then he turned back to Rogers. "We better try. Don't want to waste the day." He frowned again. "But I don't get it. What's up with Ramon, if it's true?"

The boat began to move again, and the boatman swung the prow till it pointed at one of the low smudges of green lying on the horizon.

This is bloody heaven: the thought surprised Rogers. A wave of elation ran through him. He didn't know people lived anywhere like this. Scuttling between the palm islands across a sea they knew as well as the backs of their hands, in tree trunks that grew for free in the woods, powered, many of them, by wind that blew for free. But it wasn't the freeness that got to him. It was just this happy world, all the islands strung across the warm sea, and the people able to scurry to and fro in their canoes: it all seemed so perfect, so well designed, so ideally thought out. They'd hang out on the beach, in their huts, then take a little trip across the blue water under the sun, and be back in time for sundown. And they had all they needed.

It stirred a vague memory in Rogers, perhaps of childhood holidays on the beach. It was as if he had once known that life could be this good, this happy. Sun, sea, beach, palms, boats, fish, hammocks, thatch roofs: why did these seem to be the ideal and always intended ingredients of life? It wasn't so much that life here seemed happy, or that the people did, but that he himself did.

When he thought of the girl, his stomach collapsed in excited dread. He sensed that in some way all his good feelings were connected to her. He was looking forward to seeing her badly enough that he could hardly bear to think about it, felt sick when he did.

Which made no sense. She had ripped off his wallet, screwed him two ways for money. Talk about sentimental: to fall for a hooker who robbed you. It was lamentable. But then again, he hadn't exactly fallen for her. He reminded himself of that and felt better.

The island they were aiming for grew until Rogers could make out the individual trunks of its palms, gleaming like stalks of straw. But the engine kept faltering, gurgling and threatening to die, then finding a new spurt of power for a while before again faltering. It took a long time to cover the last half mile. As they approached the shore, another dugout with a triangle of dirty white sail crept along the beach, coming closer and closer to where they seemed likely to hit land. Finally the boatman drove their canoe hard up on to the beach. It glided for a moment over the sand with a deep shush, then abruptly stopped. Rogers pitched forwards and stumbled onto the beach just as, a few yards offshore, the sailing dugout went scudding by, carried along by the slight breeze at a pace that seemed if anything faster than their own motorised transport had managed. Rogers could hear the wind in its sail.

A man was standing in the stern, holding a paddle as a rudder, and wearing a pair of glasses with thick black rims and a dark office suit, but no shirt. Rogers watched as the boat slipped past, and the man called out in a hoarse voice and skipped up to the mast of his vessel and plucked it out of its socket, folding it down sail and all among his passengers.

A few yards on, the boat slowed. The man with the suit and glasses jumped out, up to his chest in water, and steered the craft in, giving it a shove to drive its keel onto the beach. It hung there, the length of it drifting round towards the shore.

"Yes sir." The man lifted an arm to hail Rogers. "You're looking at Henry Rawlinson."

In spite of the Anglo name, in spite of the unexpected attire, with his mop of black hair and sleek features the man was visibly a local.

"You sirs need a guide, I am at your service. I expert in Cuna culture and territory. I born here," the man explained, "and I work in the Zone fourteen year and now I back making my researches into Cuna culture and history. What can I do you for?"

Jones already stood on the beach brushing down his shorts and was ready with the obvious reply: "We're looking for a girl called Nikiri."

"Yes, you come to the right place, man. She just across the lagoon, I go fetch her, meet you round the other side."

"The other side?" Jones asked.

"Where the village is. You go see."

With that, the man heaved his canoe off again, with its three passengers, and scrambled among them to hoist the mast. The makeshift sail flapped until he hauled on a line and it filled.

Jones and Rogers arranged with their boatman to meet them at the other side of the island and walked off, leaving him fiddling with the engine.

The village turned out to be four palm shacks, with only one person around, a tall Cuna with a dark smooth face like polished walnut. He introduced himself as Achu, then bent down to resume his work untangling a small blue net. "That a bait net," he informed them, in case they wanted to know.

Rogers and Jones sat on the sand to wait. "Looking good, no?" Rogers said.

"Maybe," Jones muttered. "What the hell is up with Ramon, sending us off to Tigre?" He spat neatly, landing the gob in the froth where the ripples dissolved into the sand. "When she gets here, I'm going to leave you to sort things out. I've got business with our *sahila*. Then I'll come back and get you. I'll bring you to a council meeting." He rubbed his face. "I've got a good feeling about this trip, you know. There's nothing like being on the ground, in the field. We could tie it all up once and for all."

The prospect of being left alone here alarmed Rogers; then he thought with anticipation of being alone with the girl on this atoll. Except who knew how she'd feel about seeing him?

"I don't need to tell you you've got to give her more," Jones said. "First thing you do. Make sure she knows she's OK with you."

Rogers took a stroll up and down the beach. This island was if anything closer to the roaring reef that bounded the Cuna territory.

9

It must have been close to noon when the dugout arrived under sail. It glided into the lagoon slow as a galleon, deep-bosomed in the water even though it was so tiny. Then, once close, it seemed to skitter into the beach like a toy. Only when the strange office man steering it scrambled up the length of the craft to whip the mast out of its socket, letting the sail collapse any old how, and jumped off to guide it up against the sand, and the other passenger, who sat smiling ahead all the while, stood and turned round, revealing a fine rump clad in a pair of tight black cycling shorts—only then did Rogers realise that it was really her, and as in a dream discovered that he was about to step into the kind of experience he would no longer have believed could come his way. She had arrived. She had come laden with smiles and bicycle shorts and a little red knapsack containing a bikini and a bottle of almond oil.

Rogers knew by her first smile that she was happy to see him. She was a Cuna, an Indian, this was her homeland, she was answerable to none.

Rogers imagined Henry Rawlinson's and Achu's eyes to be on him when he embraced her. Perhaps this was like El Salvador or Cuba, or pretty well anywhere Latin, where there was no better catch for a girl than a gringo passport. Except he doubted that.

She seemed to have accepted her summons without question, wherever she had come from. It was hard to understand. But then these people were hard to understand. They seemed both childlike and more mature than Westerners. When Rogers later struggled with a canoe paddle, he felt like a little boy who ought to know how to use one by now, at his age. When his feet pricked on washed-up flotsam, he felt that he had the tender soles of an infant. And when that night the girl began to teach him things about a hammock he would never have imagined, he felt like he and everyone he knew lived up a side track off evolution's main highway.

. . .

Paulina led Rogers to the last of the huts, a little way from the rest, and screened from them by a stand of almond and sea grape trees. The first thing Rogers did was pull out two hundreds and fold them into her hand.

"I owe you this," he said.

She sent him a heartwarming smile, thanked him, and put the money in her little knapsack.

They sat in the sand outside the hut. She lit herself a cigarette and ran the match through the sand in front of her, drawing a star. "I shouldn't have done what I did," she said.

Rogers couldn't take his eyes off her neat, dark eyebrows; the complexion around them was so smooth and edible looking. He wanted to tell her that of course she should have.

"There was a reason," she went on. "You know I had only just started that work. I need money for my father. I'll have to go back soon. It's complicated."

"Is he unwell?" Rogers tried, surprised by a warm concern.

She tutted, drew on her cigarette. "It's nothing like that."

After a moment Rogers asked: "Do you still have the wallet?"

"Of course." She smiled. "I forgot." She reached for the knapsack.

He felt an instant of relief just to see the wallet again. That was a number of hassles deleted in one go. He glanced inside, saw that Jones's paper was still there.

"Hombre, I just took the money. I have it here still. I'm sorry. I was in a hurry, I was desperate." She shook her head and looked to the horizon. "I have to get a thousand dollars for my father."

Rogers nodded. She already had the three-hundred-odd

that had been in his wallet, plus the two he had just given her. He himself had a further eight still in his pocket.

"Twenty years my father has been working for Don Ramon. Can you believe it? And now it's his turn to be the *sahila* of our island. I don't want Ramon to stop him. But he has to be paid off."

"Is this the Don Ramon I know? From Chichimen?"

"Hombre," she said quietly.

"So all that's left is another five hundred dollars?"

"Why do you think I went to Panama? They told me I could make that in two weeks."

Without a second thought Rogers reached into his shorts and counted out the bills. "Here."

She took the money thoughtfully, folded it, and clasped it in her hand awhile. Then leaned over and kissed him on the cheek.

"It's nothing," he said, though she hadn't expressly thanked him.

They sat in silence a moment. Then Rogers asked, "So you didn't mind how you got the cash together? You didn't mind that work?"

"It's easy. We're not like you people. We get older lovers when we're young. We have to, or we can't get married." She shrugged. "And I met you." She kissed him again, on the lips. Rogers felt that his heart was not in his throat but his skull. He could feel it throbbing against the bone cavity, and his brain seemed to be melting.

In their three days together they never again mentioned the wallet. These people didn't care the way others did. He had the feeling that whatever he asked her, she would smile and say yes, why not. It wasn't that she didn't understand. Perhaps it was him, and the island had lulled him into a rhythmic sea dream into which she slipped as easily as someone joining him in a hot tub. Life here was a dreamy dreaminess, a lullaby of sea and waves and palms. The islands rocked in the cradle of the sea. Here no one thought too hard but lived by perfect intuition.

Yes, yes, yes: all uttered with that ironic smile. How did she get away with it? By being a beauty, by being an island girl, by living a life where all that mattered was getting the next plate of fish, of which one was assured as long as the seas stayed clean.

She had glided into shore smiling, head erect, and jumped into the water as soon as the canoe's prow dug itself into the beach. She had performed the leap gracefully, allowing the momentum of the boat to propel her, and everything she did followed with the same grace.

That first night they lay side by side in their hammocks. She held his hand and gently pulled, causing the two of them to swing in unison. Now and then they would get out of sync, and collide with a soft tingle-producing thud of rump on rump. She had brought a candle with her, which guttered on a stump by the back wall. Giant shadows flickered and flapped across the thatch roof.

He said, "I really wanted to see you again." The words flowed easily from his lips. He was lulled by their lovemaking, and more than that by an irrefutable feeling of love. He longed for her and at the same time felt the thrill of a longing fulfilled. He was happy. He would have liked to rest his brow on her breast and listen to the thump of her heartbeat, have it carry off his worries, drum them out of his bloodstream—give himself a transfusion of her clear, calm blood. She was young, unspoiled. He lay his cheek against the taut cloth of the hammock and looked at her—those immaculate sleek cheeks, the fine mouth, and that faint smile that always seemed to show in her eyes. As if he slightly amused her, and as a result caused a reservoir of affection to be tapped. As if he could already sense the kind of love she might have for him, a caring, amused one, with a tenderness at the core that could be fanned into passion.

They took care of the dilapidated shelter. He tied up a driftwood board for a shelf, rolled a useless but beautifully smooth branch a hundred yards along the beach, letting it stand as a sculpture outside the hut.

In the morning she came out blinking into the palm-dappled sunshine with a black and white Valentino scarf tied round her waist. It looked good against her brown limbs. She watched him with hands on hips as he attempted to sweep up the grove between the hut and the beach using a palm branch. She tutted, shook her head, set a knife between her teeth.

In a matter of seconds she had shimmied up into the head of a palm, where she sawed away until a frond cracked, shushed to the ground. As he watched her up there, crouched among the fronds, nimble as a monkey, he realised he could not remember the last time he looked at a slender female thigh from such an angle and saw nothing sexual in it, rather just the limb of an agile creature, skilled and lithe.

Back on the ground she stripped the backs off the leaves, pulling a sinew that came away in thongs. Five minutes of squatting, tugging, cutting, holding things with her teeth, and she had made a new coconut broom.

She seemed small, standing there at the foot of the tree, yet a decisive presence. He felt awkward and self-conscious as he gave her a hug by way of thanks. But she received it, along with his awkwardness, with her usual placid smile. It was impossible to upset her.

This was the house they shared for now; he would sweep it clean.

Rogers had no way of contacting Jones; he could do nothing but wait for him to return from his business with the *sahila*. Then presumably they'd return to Panama City and press ahead with the negotiations, knowing they were good to go on the ground. But it was strange how staying here on this little island, all lust slaked by Paulina, and a glow of love kindling in his belly, he couldn't muster any feeling about the deal: if it came off, well and good, but if not, so be it. It hardly seemed to matter, a small and remote affair.

He let himself drift along with the life of the little community. It turned out that Paulina's father was Achu, the tall Cuna with the smooth, dark face. He took Rogers fishing.

Achu's boat was a hefty bole with a chunk missing from the stern. He spoke some Spanish and Rogers tried to make a joke about whether a *tiburón* had chewed the canoe. Achu told him he needn't be afraid of sharks.

They rolled the boat down on its roller until the log was all the way up at the prow, whereupon they had to drag the boat the last few feet, cutting a deep groove in the sand. Rogers was relieved to see the craft had some kind of keel. But it wasn't much of one. Every move he or Achu made set his heart thumping.

"Yes, man," Achu began when they were bobbing out on the clear green water. "Nikiri been working her butt off for me in Panama. She a good girl, man."

It struck Rogers as an unfortunate expression: but then he asked himself why. Even if the man had meant it literally, which wasn't implausible here, there was no shame attached to sex in this community. You couldn't change what the human body wanted, all you could do was take care to provide it.

The big Indian nimbly walked up the boat, stepping right over Rogers with hardly a pause, and picked up a lump of grey rock in the bow, heaved it over. The water swelled around it and the yellow rope attached to it thrummed rhythmically as it fed over the side, then went still.

First Achu uncoiled a line, fed the hook through the eye socket of a minnow, then tied on a rusty bolt. He knotted the line round his big toe, cocked for the trigger tremble, then set up another line for the other foot.

Rogers used fingers rather than toes. He'd feel the tremblings on the line, soft, electric tingles, and whip it up hand over hand only to find the bait fish gone or half gone, and sometimes only its head remaining on the hook. Then one time as he started hauling in he couldn't believe how heavy the line was. He could barely pull it in, especially with his fingers being wet. He thought the line must have got trapped under a stone, and tugged it hard a couple of times, let it go, pulled again, and the weight was still there only this time he felt a livid tugging. He hauled harder, faster, the line slipping in the creases of his knuckles. He had been trying to keep the line tidy but now, in his panic, created bundles of knots on the bottom of the boat.

A glitter in the dark water, then he saw the fish itself just a few feet beneath the surface like a silver leaf. He lifted it clear, wriggling, and dropped it in the hold. It was beautiful, silver tinged with orange, and not more than six inches long. Its spiky dorsal fin rose and fell like a fan opening and closing as it gasped for breath. Then as the boat tipped the fish found itself swimming in a puddle that Rogers had failed to bail. It flinched, recomposed itself, and twitched about the boat. Then once again, as the water sloshed to the other end, it found itself high and dry on its side, and fluttered furiously.

Rogers was delighted and horrified at once. It was a long time since he had deliberately killed anything except a mosquito. One forgot what it was like.

Achu said, "That one stings, be careful of the spines."

How could he be careful? He had to dislodge a barbed hook from inside the fish's skull. There was a crunch as he tugged it out.

Achu brought in a chubby parrot fish a foot long, sweeping in the line in long loops that sailed neatly to the floor of the canoe as he discarded them. In a second he had the hook removed, rebaited, and lobbed out again, while Rogers was still recovering from his first triumph.

At night Paulina sang to him. She rehung the hammocks side by side and taught him the rich and various Cuna love lore that took advantage of the slings.

In his few days he began to learn the island ways—how they erected a new house, knocking up a lashed bamboo frame, then simply heaving up the already woven walls of palm; how they scampered up trees to cut coconuts and tied them by their stems into bunches of four; how in the corners of the huts they stored piles of green plantain and yucca from the slashed fields of the mainland, which they'd swapped for coconuts with the Cuna who brought them over, piled high in the bottoms of canoes; how they grated the fresh copra to make coconut milk, and boiled the milk to make oil. He counted the uses of the coconut tree and reached twenty. When he asked Paulina about it she shrugged and said, "Hombre, who knows? One hundred uses? One thousand?" One way or another, it was food, shelter, heat, and even light to them. They made wicks out of the husk hairs, floated them in bowls of coconut oil.

But that wasn't what mattered. What mattered was how it felt to live on a beach. To be ten miles from land, to be so roundly accepted into the world of sand and sea, to see your shoulders turn coffee brown, and to feel the vigour of the sea unfurl within you from some hidden place where it had been stowed all along: that was to come alive.

It wouldn't occur to these people, he thought, that food could be anything other than fresh. Nothing remarkable for them in a meal that had been growing on a tree or flickering over a reef two hours before.

The only thing Rogers found hard was going to the lavatory. He didn't like to squat in the lukewarm sea to excrete, nor to see his dung bob up beside him. But the alternative was to go inland among the palms, where quite apart from the harassment of the insects there was always the risk of being discovered by one of the inhabitants. And there was something particularly unpleasant about the smell in that dark tropical warmth. Almost as if the smell was welcome there and suited the environment, which only made it worse.

Rogers got the story of the little villages here and on Chichimen piecemeal from Paulina. She knew Don Ramon and his entourage well. In fact she regarded Don Ramon as an enemy.

"Twenty years he has kept my father here," she repeated. "He has to look after all the coconut trees here. They are Don Ramon's."

It was hard to think of the scruffy old Don Ramon eating off broken Frisbees as the cruel *latifundista*, but Paulina did. Apparently many years ago Achu, her father, had fallen in love with Paulina's mother, now dead, a woman who had been betrothed to Don Ramon. Ramon had invoked an ancient custom whereby on her death Achu had been obliged to make up the theft, as they saw it, of the bride. Meanwhile, Don Ramon had himself anyway grown estranged from his own wife, who lived on another island, and had taken up with Jorge, the excitable homosexual on Chichimen.

It was like a light opera, Rogers thought, or perhaps a soap opera; a folkloric drama of the kind that might have amused an Enlightenment court. Delightful because the protagonists lived in concord with their environment, were made of the very same fabric as their world, constituted of salt water, coconut juice, and fishbone. When he was fishing in the canoe with the blood and scales scattered about him, the smell of fish oil on his fingers, the odour of death and the sea in his nostrils, Rogers would feel that he too was entering the embrace of this world.

Every evening Achu would saunter over to their hut with a

frayed tea towel over his shoulder and stand just outside the eaves in the last of the light, conducting a stilted, formal, and somehow necessary chat. Then he'd make his way to the well under the trees and in the grey light strip his long, sinewy body and wash it with fresh water scooped from a bucket.

Around the same time, when the sun had retreated and the water was thick as paint, Rogers would go for a swim, marvelling at his shoulders being dark already as wood against the green water. Every evening they seemed darker, a wonderful deepening colour, as if he were a creature of sand, made of sand for sand.

"Why don't you come to America?" he asked her one night. Surely everyone wanted to come to America. He himself had longed to, and been glad that he did.

"America," she said, turning her head slowly, and looking out the door as if to catch a glimpse of the continent.

She could come and live with him, why not? And if there were visa problems, well, they could just go ahead and marry. He didn't see why not. He could handle it, he wouldn't ask too much of it. Was this all that he had been missing, the company of a calm woman?

She pulled his hammock close and kissed him.

He liked the island best at noon when the palms stopped shivering. The sea became the optical equivalent of a tree full of singing cicadas—a dazzling light that deafened the eye. Nothing moved. The stillness would crawl up him like warm water.

He looked out from their shelter at the sea of ancient masts, of ships and tenders, dugouts and yawls, the pirate's silver anvil, the merchant's bowl, and reflected that there was nothing to date the scene, not even he himself. Three nearby islands hovered on the horizon, blue, black, grey, hanging there like dreams you couldn't quite remember, or quite forget, like dreams waiting to be dreamt.

Now and then a coconut would thud to the ground. Half a mile offshore the reef roared: the thunder at the edge of the world. The girl might sing a song. If he asked her what it was about, she would laugh and say it was a song for wind—if the sea wind blew then the mosquitoes wouldn't get out of their beds—or a song for fish so they would not go hungry. Once she told him a story about her uncle who became a shark. She would swim out to meet him when she died.

Several times at night immaculate thunderstorms arrived. They'd sit on driftwood logs while fantastic cloudscapes erupted from the night, hovering and flickering overhead. He would consider: this is a good place to be, under palm thatch on a sandy island, as explosions pealed from the sky like gunfire, like flak. When the rain came they'd retire to the hammock and make love to the water chime of droplets streaming from their roof. She was an expert, a maestra of love in a sling, hooking it behind the knee, beneath the thigh, for expansion, contraction, rhythm, and tension. When finally they slept the night would be warm and still, and he'd hear the reef thundering in the back of his mind like a memory of safety.

He woke one morning and discovered that he didn't know what day it was. He was alarmed, then delighted. He couldn't remember ever feeling that before—the day of the week simply made no difference.

He began to imagine how easily the island could feel like home. This was a world that in its very fabric wanted to hold and nourish you. The plainness of its mornings, the chalky dawns, the need to get up and swim and go fishing, the somnolence of the afternoons when it was best to lie still and listen to the slapping and running of the sea and hope the wind was coming off the sea not the land, to keep down the biting insects — all this felt like home, like a world he had been built for.

1 0

One morning a speedboat appeared in the lagoon. Rogers couldn't quite believe it was really there. The gurgling, smoking vessel of white plastic didn't belong in this world of sand and wood. Its presence seemed to defy the laws of physics. It came like an apparition, smelling strongly of exhaust, a sweet, exhilarating smell.

He stood staring at it, rooted to the spot. Only when it turned and began its approach towards the beach did Rogers realise that it could mean only one thing: Albert Jones was back.

Dread opened up in him. He didn't know what to do, but felt a pressing need to do something. In his dazed, island-lulled condition, and with the quiet roar of the reef as if permanently implanted in his ear, he couldn't figure out what it was.

He turned and ran back towards the hut. He met Paulina coming down the track through the wood.

"Jones is here," he told her. "You've got to listen to me. He's going to want to take me to a council meeting. Is your father a *sahila* yet? — now that you have the money —"

"As soon as he pays Don Ramon."

"Did you give him the money?"

"Of course."

"So he and I will go over to Don Ramon's so he can pay it.

You stay here. I have to sort some things out. But hide. Don't let Jones see you."

She smiled and shrugged.

"Go into the interior of the island. He's crazy. I don't know what he might do."

"This is Kuna Yala, I don't need to hide."

"You do. Please."

She smiled and cocked her head like it was a game and she would humour him, why not. She shrugged and kissed him on the cheek and sauntered away.

Rogers ran back to the beach.

Albert Jones called out to him from the boat. He beckoned from his seat, one hand on the gleaming chrome steering wheel as the boat's stern drifted towards the sand, spitting from two exhaust pipes. "Get your stuff, let's go."

For a moment Rogers couldn't think how he knew this man. The silver bouffant and white shorts and clean brown body sprinkled with curly silver hairs seemed to be part of the boat. He, Rogers, had been living in his sea dream; now the land had come to wake him and he didn't recognise it. His chest tightened and he became aware of the blood in his veins—especially once Jones tossed him a can of beer. When he levered the top with his big-nailed finger and heard the explosive gasp of aluminum and smelled the smell of beer the dread came back. He shouldn't be leaving, it wouldn't be as easy as he thought to get back. And that wasn't all.

Rogers left the beer on the beach and ran into the first hut, where Achu was just getting ready to light a fire. "You have to come with me. We'll go to Don Ramon first. I'll explain. You're a *sahila* now, I need you to talk to the other *sahilas*. I'll tell you everything on the way. Hurry please."

Achu stood to his full height and walked out. "I did hear

the boat," was all he said, and Rogers wondered that a man could go on a journey with nothing but the shorts he stood in. No bag, no briefcase, no wallet even. Just his bones and flesh and skin.

As they climbed into the boat, Rogers told Jones: "This is Don Achu. He's a *sahila* and friend. We need him. And I left something on Chichimen, I need to swing there first."

Jones looked at Rogers and was about to say something. Then he lifted his shoulders and said, "OK, we've got time." He reached back and shook Achu's hand. "Achu?"

"Don Carlos," he said. "They call me Achu."

Jones raised his eyebrows, then in English said to Rogers: "Achu's not much of a name round here. It means dog."

As the boat roared out of the lagoon, squirming on its trajectory then settling into a true course, Rogers stared back, transfixed by the V of its wake, by the flattened hood of bubbles at its apex. The shape was so like something he knew. When he realised what it was, saw the watery shape take the form of Paulina's vulva, he looked away embarrassed, then kept sneaking glances at it. It was mesmerising.

The first swig of beer reminded Rogers where he was now: back in the brassy world. He looked at Jones's back. A plastic man who belonged in his plastic boat.

Rogers wanted to jump off, anything to get back to the island. He imagined how he'd swirl about in the bubbles, then swim to the nearest island. He'd make it. He could wait till they were passing some islet. The dreaminess was still there, and as long as he could stay in touch with that it would carry him to safety.

"Here's the deal," Jones shouted over the engine. "The chiefs want to meet you. They're holding the council meeting tonight, on Rio Tigre. We're building a dock for them. We get that through and we're OK. We've got the contracts drawn up and ready to sign."

Rogers listened to the voice but his mind was still hearing the boom of the reef, still floating in the little island's lull.

At Chichimen they found Don Ramon sitting outside his hut on a log roller. "Yes sir," Ramon called as they climbed from the boat. Without a word Achu went up to him and handed him a folded wad of notes. Don Ramon took it and looked up at the man, then got up and walked into his hut. Jones followed him, and emerged a minute later.

When they were back in the boat, roaring along with the great barrier of mountains always to their right, Jones beckoned Rogers up to the cockpit.

"Who is this guy?"

"The girl's dad."

"Why is he here?"

"He's a *sahila*. He's on our side."

Jones frowned. "Ramon says we shouldn't trust him. I don't like it. He should take a hike. We don't need anything rocking the boat right now. We're good as we are."

"He won't rock the boat."

Jones cut the throttle right back and said, "Something up with the propeller. Hey," he called back to Achu. "Can you see anything back there?"

Achu peered over the stern. Just as he bent low, Jones slammed the throttle forwards, and the boat surged, tipping Achu neatly into the water.

As they gathered speed Rogers hesitated a moment, in the grip of unknowables, and seeing that he could not know just then what was best, but aware that Jones still needed him—he had the American angle to bring to the table—he stepped up on to the side and jumped off too.

A shiny, dark surface hit him in the face, and he was pad-dling in seething white, and the sound of the boat had gone, replaced by a tremendous hiss. He turned. Achu was already calmly swimming towards a bright green island close enough for the mesh of its palm trunks to be distinguishable. Rogers paused, searching for the boat. It was far away, a little white box moving above a little jet of wake. Its shape changed as he watched, elongating. It was veering to the right. Then it diminished again, and a star settled right in the middle of it, on what must have been the point of the prow. He couldn't hear it at all. He kept swimming.

When the boat was getting close Rogers tipped himself up and sank headfirst. He swam slowly in order not to waste his breath, and guessed Achu would be doing the same. The boat sounded like a little toy now, a tinny drilling passing overhead. He saw the white fork travel over him like a zipper, blurred. Water got in his nostrils and he looked down again. Under-water, he carried on swimming in the direction of the island. Five strokes, six. When his lungs were aching and gagging he let himself come up. The boat was all but inaudible now, a faint ringing in the ears. He exhaled before he broke the sur-face, came up into the brilliant day long enough to inhale, sank under again, hanging just below the surface so he could rise to take another breath, and another. After the third, dur-ing which he glimpsed Achu's small head sinking under the surface ahead, he resumed his slow submarine progress towards that nearest island.

Jones in his speedboat skated over the surface in figures of eight, loops and curves, a shiny little chunk of Panama City searching, searching, not knowing where to go, winking in the sunlight on the broad blue sea.

Rogers rolled in the shallows of an empty beach, raising

his head to breathe, lowering it again into the green water. When he looked again, he could just make out the speedboat, glinting far away.

Achu was already standing among the palms at the edge of the beach. Rogers got up and joined him.

"What do we do now? We need to get to Rio Tigre."

Achu didn't answer, but set about gathering sticks and dried sea moss that lay scattered on the sand. When he had enough of a pile, he set to with two sticks, drilling one against the other with his palms. Rogers had always believed that method of starting a fire to be near impossible except in archaeology textbooks, but in a little while, smoke drifted from where the sticks met, and quickly Achu fed moss to it, blowing hard, in fast, deep breaths. The moss kindled and sparked, and a smoking line travelled across the bunch. Achu piled more on, kept blowing, and soon Rogers heard a crackle and saw a small pale flame lick across the parched web.

He gathered more twigs to feed it.

It was late morning by the sun, perhaps a couple of hours later, when a sailing dugout came scudding along the beach.

"I see the smoke," its pilot, a man in glasses, called out.

It was Henry Rawlinson again. "Yes, I see the smoke on Delfina Island, I thinking, nobody live there. What's up? You gentlemen step aboard."

"Rio Tigre, fast as you can," Rogers said, adding: "If you possibly can."

Henry was happy to pass the day helpfully, it seemed.

Rogers reckoned that in a good wind the sailing canoe might average five knots. He knew Rio Tigre was the last island, but the whole chain was only a hundred miles long, and they were already some way down it, so it couldn't have been much more than ten hours away. If the wind kept up they'd surely make it in time for the night's council session. And anyway, surely if new information arrived, the council of *sahilas* could reconsider a decision.

But it seemed not.

"It's a matter of principle," Achu explained. "There are seventeen *sahilas*. If they put their name to it, they can't go back."

Jones would have them signing tonight if he could.

As they rustled along the coastline, past the many islets, Rogers told Achu: "You'll have to use your vote tonight. And your voice."

They passed dugouts with sails, dugouts being paddled, and island after island. Sometimes grinning families sailed past them. Rogers began to enjoy the ride, the sunshine, the silence of the boat. What a week, he thought. He had possibly fallen in love, he had lived a neolithic life, learnt to live on a desert island. And now he was gliding along the coast of Darien in a Stone Age canoe.

He soon dried off in the hot breeze. His shorts and shirt felt stiff as canvas.

In the late afternoon, when the light was beginning to grow rich, and the sun laid a glittering highway across the dark sea, they reached a far-flung island all on its own. Judging by how far they had come, they must have been close to the Colombian border. All the island's ranked canoe prows bristled from the shore. It was a thatch fort, a Viking camp.

Somewhere on the south side a concrete wharf had been half built. Tied to it, a beaten-up barge sagged in the water under the weight of piles and piles of supplies, heaps of orange sacks and onion sacks, stacks of boxes. Among all the produce on deck unshaven men dozed in hammocks. Sailors. A small army of sailors. In the prow of the boat a mountain of green coconuts bleached in the sun.

The men shocked Rogers. They were fat and their facial hair was a surprise (he hadn't looked at himself in a mirror for some time) and they were altogether big. Big and coarse. With a sudden discomfort he realised they were his people, Westerners.

"They come from Cartagena to buy coconuts," Henry Rawlinson informed him. "They buy them green. The people here buy clothes and shoes and pots from them."

Big people, ugly, fat, without any grace at all, completely lacking the Cunas' lightness of touch and build. Rogers stood in the sunshine in the middle of a concrete plaza beside the quay, shocked to realise that it was these men he had been planning to help. His job was to get behind Jones and help him open up this paradise to fat, ugly men who had no idea how to treat themselves, much less a desert island, who could only come up with roaring engines and beer and plastic trinkets to sell for green vouchers exchangeable for more beer and motorboats. This, right here, was the very point of civilisation's drill; here, where the men of finance were preparing the way for the men with hard hats and survey sticks; here, where Balboa first saw the Pacific and knew he had found not the East Indies but an unknown continent, and gave birth to the Atlantic market of iron, of chains and cauldrons and human bone. The jigsaw towers of Manhattan, Milwaukee, Cincinnati, all the concreted prairies and drained swamps sold over and over, owed their beginning to this very meeting of Colombian and Cuna. And what had it all achieved? A wake of ruin, of bereft children, miserable mothers.

They idled away what was left of the day in a longhouse

with just three scrawny hammocks in its cavernous dark. Tall wooden drums and giant panpipes leaned against either wall, waiting for some ceremony to call them forth. Rogers wondered when the people used them. He had heard little of Cuna music. Now and then a child would peer in from the street, stare at the strange men, and go away. It was more like a warehouse than a home, an abandoned place with a few relics left in it.

In the evening they moved through the hurricane-lit village to another longhouse. This one was filled with a haze of tobacco smoke hanging above rows of benches, on which sat a crowd of Cuna men, all of them smoking pipes or cigarettes, and chatting away, raising a thick murmur of sound. At the front three elders swung in white hammocks chanting to one another in high-pitched voices. The mumbling and chanting together made a kind of music.

As soon as they walked in, Jones was at Rogers's side. "What happened to you, man? What's up with you?" He stared at Rogers, his eyes gleaming in the dark. "Have you gone fucking crazy? I thought you must have drowned. What are you doing?" His face was close to Rogers's, and Rogers could smell his thick breath. "Anyway, you're here. This is our chance. Don't fuck with it." Jones led him to a bench.

An old man in a chair at the front pulled his pipe from his mouth and began talking in a muffled voice, addressing the floor a few feet in front of him, and gradually everyone fell silent. Then they all laughed. The old man had apparently cracked a joke. He stood up, as if getting into his stride, and began to find a rhythm in his speech. His voice was a masterpiece of rhetoric, even if you couldn't understand a word of it. It climbed imaginary staircases, sprinted over cliff edges, plummeted to valley floors, climbed all over again. Here and

there, in pauses, you could hear the soft bubble of men sucking on their pipes as they waited for the next punch line, and
the hiss of the one hurricane lamp hanging on its nail at the
front, casting a sharp glow through the room.

Eventually the old man sat down. Then one of the three
elders in hammocks, a toothless man who could have been
cousin to Don Ramon, without getting up, without even lifting his head from the pale strings of his hammock, began to
chant again. He finished with a curious singing coda, a series
of rising curlicues of falsetto, then carried on swinging as
calmly as if he had been silently listening all along.

Jones sat beside Rogers on the bench with his arms folded
across his chest, immovable. Rogers could feel Jones's bony
knuckles digging into his side. Finally Jones prodded him and
murmured in his ear: "Tell them you're happy to be working
together with the Cunas. It's a big honour for an American
company to bring its expertise. Big honour." Then he prodded
him again and told him to stand up.

As he stood, Rogers realised it hadn't been Jones's knuckle
he had been feeling in his side, but something smaller,
rounder, and harder. In the shock of realising what it had
been, he found himself repeating Jones's words. Then he sat
down again. A man with a dark shiny face gave him a cigarette, and someone rang a bell at the back of the hall.

Rogers had been in a daze, numb and automatonlike. But
at the sound of the bell an acute sadness welled up in him. He
thought of Paulina, a beautiful woman forced to bring herself
to the ugly city, and of the awkward advantage he had taken of
her, and of how he felt towards her now; and a boiling, angry,
active sadness drove him out of his seat towards the chiefs in
their hammocks. He stood before them and spoke his mind.
They lay there swinging as he talked, giving no sign that they

heard anything he said. He told them that neither he nor Jones were to be trusted, that their plan was to deceive the Cunas and profit from them.

When he finished still no one said anything. One of the elders glanced up at him with a lively, animal eye sparkling in leathery folds of skin, and struck a stick on the floor. There was a murmur among the benches. Rogers looked round just as Jones arrived at his side. Again he felt the barrel tip in his ribs.

"You come with me." Jones grabbed his arm and pulled him to the back of the hall, then outside. As he left he glimpsed Achu rising to his feet to address the assembly.

Rogers wanted to explain to Jones, convey why their plan was a bad one and must be abandoned. This place could not possibly survive having a pipeline stabbed through it. It was a delicate world. He started speaking, but Jones only jabbed the gun harder into him, making him wince.

He walked Rogers down an alley to a strip of shingle among the houses, where a dugout was waiting, with the albino man in the stern. They climbed in and the albino began to power the canoe out with choppy heavy strokes of a paddle. In a while a pale hull suddenly loomed out of the darkness pushing a plume of white water in front of it. It sank and settled into the black water just ahead of them. Jones reached up for the boat's gunwale and scrambled on board, followed by the albino, who as he climbed up pushed the canoe away with his bare foot.

"No, no," Jones snapped. "Don't let it go. He's coming too."

Rogers threw up the dugout's painter, still vaguely hoping he might win Jones round. Someone up on the boat wearing a black commando hat caught the rope. Rogers recognised now that this wasn't the same speedboat Jones had had earlier, but something bigger.

Jones told the man to tie up the canoe, then shouted down to Rogers: "You shouldn't mess with what you don't know." He held out the gun. "This is fucking real," he cried over the boat's gurgling engine. "Do you realise how big this deal is? Do you have any idea of the kind of money involved? This is the kind of thing that changes the world, amigo, changes it forever, makes it a better place for all of us. You really think we can't find other investors? Someone like you should fuck off from where you don't belong. You could have had a piece, my friend. You should learn to keep your fucking nose clean."

The big launch began to roar, pulling the dugout after it.

Rogers, who hadn't eaten all day and was still dazed by the long hours of sun and by all that had happened, sat in the bottom of the dugout gripping either side of his wooden torpedo, which slid and slithered and tipped and sprayed him from its snub end as it shot through the water.

Finally they cut him loose and roared off with a parting shout he couldn't make out.

Rogers knew that all he had to do was determine which way was south and go that way, towards land. They hadn't come far. He would soon reach shore. He had a paddle. And he was in the safest place in the world, on the warm black sea under the blanket of night, within the encircling reef.

The buzzing of the big launch had already taken itself into silence. Quiet. Black sea. The sound of surf pounding somewhere, noisily drawing breath. He would go towards it.

He paddled through darkness. The sea rippled under him, carving long easy swells, tremendously long gentle slopes that went up for a hundred yards, then down, so gentle you could miss them in the dark.

Suddenly the surf was louder. He had been dreaming. And the paddle, as he dug with it, struck something under the water and flew out of his hand. He turned round and the canoe wobbled and already the paddle was moving away, out of reach, and was nothing more than a pale gleam in the water. He could see it but only just. He got to his knees to dive in after it but thought: What about the canoe? Supposing it drifted too far for him to see it in the dark? It seemed preeminently unwise to leave his vessel. So he decided to dive while holding what was left of the boat's painter. He wrapped the cord round his hand and leapt. Time was everything, the paddle was moving away, already he had lost sight of it, and as he dived he wondered if the rope was long enough, wondered how short they had cut it, and the next thing he knew a flashbulb had exploded in his shoulder. Then something was running over his back, something long with coarse skin. He spun round. It was just the canoe. But his shoulder had gone ice cold now and he had lost all sense of direction, had no idea which way the paddle had gone.

The rope was still attached to his hand, though. He tugged on it and the dugout turned and came smoothly towards him, as if gliding on runners, so that he had to dodge it.

He had never known it be so hard to climb on board. With one arm out of action, he had to lodge his elbow over the prow and try to kick his leg over the side, all without capsizing the trunk. It didn't work. He tried innumerable times then hung still, getting his breath back. His chest felt heavy, and stung badly. Perhaps he had grazed it against the wooden side. He passed himself hand over hand to the stern. It wasn't easy there either. There was nothing to get a foot or knee on, being right at the end, and the only way was to drag himself, heave by heave, right over the wood, which made his chest rage and burn even more. But he managed it.

He rolled onto his back and lay still in the bottom of the boat. Ripples lapped against the hull in a way that at first he found irritating, then soothing. But still, to be floating in a dugout without a paddle—it was unbelievable, and all night long too. At least it was warm and he would soon dry off.

Meanwhile, his chest was gently bleeding. He looked down and ran his hand over it. It was covered with little slits. Soon they coalesced into a single dark patch. The side of the boat must have done it as he dragged himself over. There was nothing he could do except lie still and hope the cuts congealed quickly. He didn't want to inspect them. Better not to know. One leg ached, his shoulder was still completely numb, and his chest stung. But that might be a good sign, a sign of shallow wounds and things on the mend already. Just cuts.

The worst thing by far was that the boat leaked. Perhaps it had struck a rock while he was out of it, loosening a tin patch that had been nailed in. He lay in a cold gutter of water. By heaving himself into the bow he was able to keep most of a gash in the stern clear of the surface, but he could see the crack gently seeping. Sooner or later he would have to figure out something to bail with, if he could manage to move. But he was drifting off, finding it hard to remember where he was. Thank God he liked sushi. Later, when it got light, he could try to fish. Though how he'd gut a fish without a knife, or catch one without a hook, he didn't stop to think.

The water stirred, the canoe shifted. The thunder of the reef had abated. His heartbeat steadied. When it grew light and he could see where he was, he would paddle for shore.

For now, he folded his hands high on his chest, above the wounds, and waited for dawn.

He woke up in his apartment on West Thirteenth. It seemed a lovely place, small, just the right size for him. How lucky it was that he had no children yet, that there was time still for all that if he wanted it, that his and Candlebury's had been a clean break. In a sense he had even yet to begin his real life, there was still time, he could start all over again, for real, he could leave Wall Street, move into some entirely different field, and concentrate on things that mattered. He longed to sit again in his black leather armchair and watch a soccer match with his Colombian neighbour. That man had short hair. A number two, he guessed. He could see the lovely strip of dust-rich sunlight that lay across the dark kitchen counter at a certain hour of the morning. He would look at it and imagine he could almost hear it, it was that peaceful a sight.

It was the hardest thing, to admit a mistake. He had made a mistake. He had lost Candlebury. He had allowed them to lose each other; he had lost her because he had lost himself. And he hadn't been able to admit it, neither part of it. To accept that he had steered his life up the wrong creek was to say he should still be with her; which he hadn't the heart to say. Equally, to admit he had erred in losing her could only mean that the new life he had sought after her was also mistaken; which he could not bear to consider. But it was the truth. And although there was no chance now of winning her back, he could own up to the loss, and mourn it finally. More than that, he could own up to the meanness, the selfishness in him. He had treated her carelessly, callously. So what if he had been miserable himself? It excused nothing. Now, within the embrace of the small life he had inadvertently created for himself, he could face up to that. And suddenly he felt that with that acknowledged, he could really be all right. Which meant happy. He was astonished by the realisation, and felt a buzz in his limbs.

It was all because of Paulina. She was right for him. How she came to be so, a girl from such a different world, he couldn't say, but she was. He missed her, but more than that he was happy to have found her.

Why wasn't he worried? Despite the aches in his flesh, he felt flushed through with achievement. Then it occurred to him that feeling this good might mean he was about to die. Even that didn't dent his mood. If he was on his way to the end, so be it. He could enjoy that too.

It was hard to believe he really was where he was, adrift in a boat hardly bigger than his own body. It was hard too to know how bad the situation was. Many islands lay nearby, and plenty of dugout traffic moved between them by day. Someone would surely see him in the morning, and anyway he was floating, thank God, within the reef. At some point if the worst came to the worst he could simply swim to the nearest island.

He thought of Paulina with a twist of longing. He knew she would be all right. She was that kind of woman: strong, and she knew her world well. He would have to find her right away, as soon as he could. Would she want to come to New York? It was a possibility. And what if not? Perhaps he'd set up some kind of business down in Panama. Or perhaps she would just end up being a beautiful episode, his rescue.

The matter in hand now was to get to shore, any shore. It was lucky the lagoon was calm. There was nothing for it but to sit up and paddle with his hands, he supposed. He began to do so. What did it matter which way? You couldn't go wrong here.

The only sound was the light, rapid slapping of wavelets under the trunk. It was a dark night. A firmament of stars, fierce and crackling, and no moon. He thought he could see the mainland because it ate a chunk out of the stars, a great black bite. But you couldn't really see it. And later the stars overhead had been eaten up too.

The water felt warm in his cupped fingers as he paddled. He sat with his knees pressed against either side to help steady him. More than anything, just then, he was relieved to be by himself, out of the vortex that trailed behind Jones and whoever his cohorts were. It was clear that they would bother with him no more, because they didn't need to. He was nothing, a Walter Mitty in the wrong place. And the wrong place had spat him out. It was a huge relief to be in the right place once more, where there was less money, much less, and less excitement and madness and drugs, but where he belonged.

A shooting star frothed past beneath his left hand. He stopped paddling. What was it? Probably a bonito, he thought. But it unnerved him. And he was tired. His shoulders ached as if he had been lifting weights. They felt abominably stiff. He would rest for a while. He lay back in the boat and waited, he wasn't sure what for. That didn't work, so he sat up and resumed paddling, keeping a lookout for any more waterborne shooting stars. The ache in his right shoulder got worse. He must have hurt it in the scuffle with the shark. What shark? What scuffle? he wondered. He couldn't keep up the paddling. Every stroke made the hurt worse. A colossal sleepiness overcame him. He lay on his back and shut out the stars, hung in universal blackness.

Dreams thundered in his skull.

He awoke to universal ache. His body was so stiff he couldn't even lift his head. The whole world was grey. Grey and drab-looking like an English afternoon in February. He decided he'd lie still and wait for the sun to warm him. Luckily the boat had filled with only two or three inches of water. His back, and the backs of his legs, lay in the water, but the rest of him was dry. In the night he had lodged his head on what was left of the rope. He thought he could feel it still there.

The happy feeling quickly woke up too and flooded him so thoroughly that he couldn't move at all now. Why so happy? He had saved the worm. He remembered, and felt doubly happy that he did remember. And now he was some-where he loved. And the girl. Paulina. Nikiri. He loved her. It hardly mattered if he saw her now; it was good just to feel this love. How did he know he loved her? Who knew? Who cared? The world was simple. It consisted of palm trees and islands and salty water in between, and a big mountainous mainland nearby where big trees grew and there were people on the islands who kept them clean. The people travelled between the islands in boats made of tree trunks that grew on the main-land and intended to love their islands and one another. Nikiri loved him and he her. He didn't have to think of her, her brown eyes and bronze face and tobacco limbs, because she was already quietly living in him. Once he lay still and the ache quieted he could feel her all through him.

And the worm was still alive: he could see it gratefully bur-rowing back into the earth, where it belonged.

Daybreak was pleasant. Gentle light, gentle sea, gentle islands like smudges of paint. The mainland was invisible today, lost in cloud. He would see these things as the canoe rose and fell. Everything had gone quiet: other than the tinkling of the ripples against the hull there wasn't a sound in the world. The whole of Darien had gone quiet. Quiet as a picture. Even he too had become silent. What was this sensation? It was like turning down the sound on the TV. Except here it happened to you too. When a little wave slapped, it slapped inside him.

The sun dislodged itself from the cement horizon, rising like a great old bloom. But quickly it shed its old petals and became too bright to look at. Rogers could move now. He propped his head on the side of the boat to get a look at what was going on.

Throughout the day the sun embraced you, kissing you right on the forehead. It heated up your flesh and warmed your wounds. He found he could rock from side to side. He thought he would need to move in order to bail and fish, but the leak seemed to have stopped itself, and he wasn't hungry. He'd fish once he was hungry. The fresher the better, if they were to be eaten raw. And anyway, he'd be picked up soon. Once he got back to terra firma he would tell everyone about the scam they were trying to pull on the Cunas. He wouldn't let it happen.

The sun was a hole and it drilled a hole just like itself in you. It made you its son: the sun's son. You joined the sun in its strange life. The sun was an eye. It looked at you, wheeling slowly round you, looking at you all the while, and you looked back at it. It created a new eye for you to look at it with.

When dusk came he couldn't remember how many evenings had arrived like this. Was this the second? the first? had there been many? Did he always live like this? And what did "live" mean? What was the darkness, and what was the light? What did "day" mean? It meant: "lie still and wait."

Morning came again and the sea was much rougher today. But the world was quieter. The reef had finally slipped away and gone where it wanted. The canoe was tipping right up, wriggling around, then tipping back. There was more water in it. He cupped one hand and found he could bail without moving. All he had to do was lift and drop the hand, tipping water over the side. Brown water, rust-coloured. Great heavy handfuls left the boat. He could feel the lovely weight of water like stones in his hand.

He manoeuvred himself on to his side, looked out, and came face to face with a blue rippled brow, which sank before his eyes, rushing under him, all in a rush and bustle, then the faint line of horizon swung into view. But only for a moment, until another mountainside of blue came hurrying in like a big housewife with all her shopping and her five children, hurrying down the high street. It made him dizzy to watch.

He tried the other side of the boat and saw the housewives heaving away from him, opening up gullies that yawned under the boat. His head swam. He caught another glimpse of open horizon. He looked past his feet, waiting to be lifted up high to get the view. The islands had all travelled away, leaving him alone.

That seemed right. It was right that he be here on his own. He only wished that the endless moving might stop. He closed his eyes and let his head sink. The bottom of the boat had become a sponge. Your belly gurgled and danced. Sometimes it slammed into your throat. Which hurt to begin with but he was used to it now. It was like having a thunderstorm within you. The thunder cracked and up came the lightning, into your mouth.

The sun nailed him to the board. Which was still again, a sheet of plywood that someone had painted green. Tap, tap,

tap, went the sun, fixing you to the board so you couldn't move anymore. This was fine. Never to move again. Only the silky rustle of your breaths like dark hills rising and falling, rising and falling. They were still permitted to move. But soon night would come and they too would be still. Then the whole world would be silent, transfixed by its own stillness, and darkness would whisper the last farewell to the last thing that moved.

Rogers was in the water. Silver water, with a shimmery blue-silver surface of mercury somewhere below him, or above. An animal, a grey creature, came up and nudged him in the side. A dolphin, he thought. Now he had broken out into a great bright cave. A dark triangle whistled past him, then came back traveling more slowly, quietly, then speeded up suddenly and shot past him close by.

Just a dog, a sea dog: a shark. It had gone. Then there was its blunt grey nose again, drifting up to sniff him, asking to be stroked, its head a lump of gristle. He jabbed at it. The body flicked and spun away. Part of it, the tail perhaps, caught him. He felt the knock on his arm. Then a moment later it was back again attempting to nuzzle him. He grabbed hold of it, got his arms right round and gripped tight, clutching his wrist in his fingers. He squeezed as tight as he could. The beast wriggled but he didn't let go. It hurried on in stilted spurts, carrying him with it. He felt it trying to thrash harder but he wouldn't release his grip. He could feel a panic wanting to rise in his lungs but getting waylaid. Who did it think it was, swimming up to him like that? He squeezed tighter, hoping to suffocate it, or at least hurt it. Then it dived. He clung on. His ears creaked and screamed and he let go. Some part of the beast knocked his calf as it vanished into the deep.

Then it was back and again he lunged at it, grabbed hold of it, and this time it pulled him streaking across the surface, riding the slippery mercury, then they were out in the broad bright cave again, knocking against a wall, the two of them, banging and banging against a sheet of iron. And now hooks had been sent down and were grappling with his arms, someone had hooked the damn fish with a great cable of a line, and dark big hands were reaching down for it, and for him, a boat hook was under his shoulder, digging in his armpit, pulling him up out of the water, hoisting him into brightness. Something was knocking rhythmically: ba-doom, ba-doom. Then it was a man's voice, saying, "Pull him, pull him," over and over. There was a hissing and roaring of water, and the silence had been broken now for good.

A NOTE ABOUT THE AUTHOR

Henry Shukman has worked as a trombonist, a trawlerman, and a travel writer. He has been a finalist for the O. Henry Prize, and his short stories have won an Arts Council Award in England. His first book of fiction, *Darien Dogs*, was published in the United Kingdom to great acclaim. His first poetry collection, *In Dr. No's Garden*, a Book of the Year in the London *Times* and *Guardian*, won the Aldeburgh First Collection Prize and was shortlisted for the Forward Prize. He sometimes writes for *The New York Times* and *Condé Nast Traveler*, and lives in New Mexico.

A NOTE ON THE TYPE

The text of this book was set in Electra, a typeface designed by
W. A. Dwiggins (1880–1956). This face cannot be classified as
either modern or old style. It is not based on any historical
model, nor does it echo any particular period or style. It
avoids the extreme contrasts between thick and thin elements
that mark most modern faces, and it attempts to give a feeling
of fluidity, power, and speed.

Composed by Stratford Publishing Services,
Brattleboro, Vermont
Printed and bound by R.R. Donnelley & Sons,
Crawfordsville, Indiana
Designed by Robert C. Olsson